D0065200

Mussels

Mussels

A NOVEL

Phillip Quinn Morris

RANDOM HOUSE
NEW YORK

Library of Congress Cataloging-in-Publication Data
Morris, Phillip Quinn.
Mussels.
I. Title.
PS3563.0874465M87   1989   813'.54   88-26555
ISBN 0-394-57527-X

Manufactured in the United States of America
Typography and binding design by Fritz Metsch

2 3 4 5 6 7 8 9

First Edition

To Penne J. Laubenthal

I would like to give special thanks to Emily J. Reynolds for all her help with this novel. Besides the parrot and all the laughs, thanks for unselfishly sharing this editorial talent you have. May you have good roads forever.

Mussels

One

ALVIN LEE FUQUA STOOD on the edge of the porch
thinking about all the years he had spent running trotlines before
mussel diving came along.

Alvin's daddy had been a commercial fisherman and made wildcat whiskey. Alvin's granddaddy had been a commercial fisherman
and made wildcat whiskey. Alvin's great-granddaddy had probably
just made wildcat. By the time Alvin got old enough to do any serious
whiskey running, moonshine had already seen its better days.

He had given up commercial fishing for diving for almost three
years now, but it seemed like all his life. As the thought of having
to go back to running trotlines and its lousy money occurred to him,
he took a deep breath, sucking both the smell and taste of the warm,
moist backwaters air into his mouth and nostrils.

He sighed, then took a long swig of Johnny Ray's aged wildcat.
He was drinking from a tall glass filled with ice, it all mixed with a
little splash of grapefruit juice.

Alvin swallowed the mouthful of whiskey. He didn't expect it
to push the thought of running trotlines from his mind; he expected
it to keep having to commercial-fish for a living from reoccurring.

Alvin took two more deliberate breaths of the air, tasting it, letting Beaulah Swamp know he knew where he was and where he was from. Then he took another drink as he contemplated his lost pursuit of the Mr. America title; he could feel the desire to compete again creeping back up on him.

In high school Alvin had started lifting weights as if it were the answer to all the world's problems, especially his own. After working out for a year, he determined that he was going to be Mr. America. He won Mr. Alabama in 1974, when barely twenty-three years old.

He worked out harder and got more muscular and veinier. Certain he was ready to walk up on the stage and take the Mr. America title, he entered Mr. Gulf Coast and got seventh place. Then he entered Mr. East Coast but didn't make the top ten. He couldn't understand it. He failed even to qualify for Mr. America. A national promoter, who called himself a trainer, told Alvin it was something about the structure of his hips. There wasn't anything Alvin could do about it, the trainer had said.

Alvin figured if he could win Mr. America, he could make movies with Burt Reynolds about hauling wildcat whiskey. But to make a movie with Burt Reynolds, and use all his knowledge of fast cars, fast boats, sawed-off shotguns, and whiskey running, he figured he'd have to be on Johnny Carson first. And he didn't know any way to get on Johnny Carson other than by being Mr. America.

He had had that dream when he was sixteen. At twenty-three it seemed at the end of his fingertips. But now here it was the summer of 1979, and at age twenty-eight not only did Alvin Lee's goal seem untouchable, but he almost felt an embarrassment for having ever dreamed it.

Right now he was dwelling on this so strongly he felt his thoughts could be heard. He snapped out of it and looked at Johnny Ray, who was half sitting on the two-by-four porch railing and half standing up, one foot on the porch decking and the other dangling. "I seen you hooked up that extra line to you compressor," Alvin said. He felt as if he had broken some kind of silence between them although he'd just walked out and stood for a few seconds. "So'd you go on down 'at slope in the channel we's talking about yesterday?"

"Yeah," Johnny Ray said. He took a pack of Marlboros out of his front pocket, took one out, and lit it up with a wooden match.

The match momentarily illuminated him. Johnny Ray's face was sun- and wind-weathered. His hair was bleached out to a dirty blond by the sun but, after the match went out, looked black in the shadowy darkness of the front porch. His forearms and neck, which were what Alvin was staring at, were more muscular than Alvin's. Alvin asked, "How'd you do?"

He grinned at Alvin Lee and said, "I made four hundred eighty dollars today."

"Damn. You run into a bed of washboards?"

"Yeah. Not only that . . ."

"What?" asked Alvin, moving closer to Johnny Ray. The music from the party inside was making it hard for them to hear each other.

"I think I run into an old riverboat," Johnny Ray said, and grinned wide enough to show the gold of his teeth.

"Naw."

"Purty sure. I don't want to talk about it now. We'll talk about it when we by ourselves and it's quiet. I got it sighted out. I know how to get back on top of it."

Alvin smiled at him and let it slide. He wasn't going to push what Johnny Ray didn't want to talk about.

All of a sudden the blare of the Charlie Daniels album was turned down, and the front porch stopped vibrating. Eddie came out and let the screen door slam.

"Johnny Ray, it Donna. She wanna know when it is you coming home."

"Tell her I be home when I git there."

Eddie went back in and let the screen door slam again.

Alvin Lee started to bring up the subject of Mr. America. "I don't know what I'm gonna do, Johnny Ray—"

Just then Freddy came charging out of the house with a baseball bat in one hand and six smashed beer cans in the other. He almost knocked Alvin off the porch as he passed. He ran into the front yard and, one by one, as fast as he could, batted the balled-up aluminum.

In his senior year Freddy had been the best baseball player at South Side High School, and in all of the county, for that matter. Better than Boots Jacobs even. Now, fourteen years later, ever since Boots had been lead-off batter for the Cincinnati Reds for the last eight months, Freddy had taken to doing reckless things with ball bats.

Though the sky was starlit, the yard was dark. Alvin and Johnny Ray could hear Freddy's bat hit the cans, then could actually see the smashed aluminum sail up into the air, over the divers' trucks and boats on trailers, over Alvin's and Johnny Ray's boats, which were at the dock in front of the house, on over Mud Creek, and clear the line of trees which formed the edge of Beaulah Swamp.

Eddie came back out on the front porch and said to Johnny Ray, "Johnny Ray. Donna says she wants you to come home. That you don't never spend no time with her."

"Tell 'er she want to see me, she can come out chere to Alvin Lee's. I'm out chere talkin' to Alvin Lee. We got some thangs we need to talk about. I'm out here having a beer with Alvin Lee." Johnny Ray took a long suck out of his glass of wildcat whiskey. "When you git done telling her that real mean, be real nice, tell 'er I ain't going diving tomorrow. That there's a low pressure coming in. I don't want to be trying to pull mussels out of the damn mud the way they bury theirselves up when it come a low pressure. Then tell her that I'll spend all day with her tomorrow. We go out, I buy her a bunch a clothes and shit. Then we do us some married kind of lovin'. But tell her quit calling out here ever thirty minutes. That the boys has to turn the record player down when somebody calls and that pisses 'em off 'cause they want to crank it up and party."

"Aw right! I hear ye, Johnny Ray," Eddie said.

Freddy walked out of the darkness up onto the front porch. He said to Eddie, "See there? Johnny Ray ain't pussy-whipped like some-body I know."

Eddie said, "I ain't pussy-whipped. I tell you one thang. I wadn't a married man, I'd be gittin' me some different pussy ever night. I guaran-damn-tee ye that!"

"I git my pussy. You don't be worrin' about me, you skinny son of a bitch."

Eddie and Freddy walked back into the house, poking at each other and letting the screen door slam.

Johnny Ray turned to Alvin Lee and said, "See that? What the matter with Freddy? Hittin' shit with his bat. He ought to be doing some real batting. And taking that old dope. I think I'll tie him up, give him a ass whuppin'. Don't nothing else seem to be working on his hard head."

He took another swig of whiskey, then laid his fruit jar on the railing. He unzipped his pants and started peeing off the porch.

"I can't ever compete again, Johnny Ray. My hip structure. If I can't ever be Mr. America with the hip structure, no use me ever bein' in intensive training."

"Aw shit. Fuck a bunch of hip structure."

"The number one trainer in the country told me that to my face."

"Fuck him," Johnny Ray said, and threw his cigarette out into the darkness. "That feller they's talking to in that magazine you had, he used to be Mr. Universe. And he said when he was judgin', he never took bone structure into consideration. That nobody could do nothing about their bone structure."

"I didn't even place in the top ten. Must be something to it."

"Shit. I told you not to listen to nobody's bullshit when you started liftin'. You let one shit-ass come along and put some idea about bone structure in you head."

"Hell, he ought to know."

"Shit, Alvin. He was scared of ye. Scared you'd beat one of his boys he had been sponsoring. Shit."

"I don't know."

"Shit."

They both were quiet for a moment.

"One thang's for damn shore," Alvin finally said. "Mussel diving's an ass saver. I's gittin' tired a scrambling around, making a hundred dollars a week running trotlines, hauling a little whiskey."

"It do make life easier."

The stereo was turned up to where they couldn't hear each other talk. Then the needle was shoved across the record, making a nerve-piercing sound.

They heard Freddy holler, "That's right, Eddie. Fuck it up! Alvin's stereo and my record album. Go ahead and fuck it up!"

A pair of headlights shone on the cars and trucks out front and then arc-scanned across the creek. It was Freddy's Camaro. Cliff got out of the car with two girls, who looked to be fairly young. Freddy had probably called and invited them to come. Cliff was just picking them up.

Alvin Lee and Johnny Ray watched them all walk in.

Johnny Ray said, "I better go in here, git me something else to drank," and did just that.

Alvin felt tense, like his body needed a workout. He could feel his muscles, his arms wanting light, slow repetitions. It was funny, he thought. Only after he had quit competing, after he had lost twenty pounds and two inches off his arms, after he had quit the training that had lasted eight years, was he able to feel his muscles and what they needed.

He still worked out lightly, mostly to maintain a physique and to get the high that he had gotten used to from the pump, surging a certain muscle group with blood.

Standing there on the front porch, Alvin slowly tensed and relaxed all his different arm muscles. He then drank the last of his whiskey and set the empty glass on the porch railing. Still thirsty, Alvin entered the living room. The two girls were sitting on the couch, sipping drinks and giggling at something Freddy was telling them.

Alvin nodded to them and walked on back to the kitchen. He reached into the refrigerator, got some grape juice, and took a long swig. There was a number two washtub of iced-down beer in the corner. He stepped over and got himself a Budweiser tall boy. But he didn't open it.

Instead, he walked out the back door of the kitchen and back around the house toward Mud Creek, to a little shack that was in the corner of the yard. He pulled a whittled wooden stop out of the latch, opened the wooden door, and turned on the light.

He walked to the bench press rack, where there was an Olympic-size bar with forty-five-pound weight plates on each side. He put his hand on top of the ones that were on the near side of the barbell and spun the plates the way he had seen Johnny Ray spin the wheel of fortune at an illegal casino in Phenix City, Alabama.

When the plates stopped and then moved back the other way a few inches, Alvin looked up. He saw himself in the mirror behind the squat rack, took off his shirt, and put it on a long shelf by the door.

He picked up a small bottle of ammonia, opened it, and put his hand around the neck. Then he stuck it under his nose and inhaled deeply, expanding his lungs. It made his eyes water, and he shook his head as he put the cap back on.

On the shelf by the door was an old turntable with side three of the Rolling Stones' *Hot Rocks* album on the spindle. He turned it on. The sound came from two speakers near the ceiling on opposite sides of the room.

Alvin got a pair of twenty-five-pound dumbbells, sat on the incline bench, and started curling very slowly. He looked at his arms in the mirror in front of him. He could see and feel them swelling up. They were probably only eighteen inches in circumference now; they had been over twenty a couple of years ago, but now they looked bigger and more cut up than ever. Somehow his twenty-pound bulk loss over the last couple of years, along with his deeper tan, made his muscles magically stand out in a higher relief. He went to a set of forty-pounders and did fifteen slow, alternate reps.

Alvin did two more sets of dumbbell curls, then went straight over to his pulley machine and did some close-grip push-downs for his triceps. He did them slowly and evenly. After three sets of those, he stood in front of the mirror. His arms were tight as ticks. He looked at the veins coming across the front of his shoulders, going down his biceps to his elbows. His arms looked more than half his width, even though he still had a fifty-inch chest.

Alvin went over and got the beer, which was still cold, and slugged it down. He got a quick rush off it. Then he went back and stood in front of the mirror, looking at his upper body and listening to the Stones. He felt euphoric.

He hollered aloud, "Not but a few people in the world . . ."

He started to say something else but then just stared at his dark, unruly hair and his dark blue eyes.

He thought about getting back up to the house. He didn't want Eddie and the others to stumble down to his weight room to "lift something" or ask him "to see if he could lift that."

Alvin put his shirt back on. It was one of the custom shirts that Ginger had designed for him. He had pumped up his biceps and triceps until the upper arms of the long-sleeve cotton shirt were tight on him.

He closed up the weight room and faded away from it. Alvin looked down to the creek and his musseling rig tied up at his dock. There was a cool breeze tonight. It was enough to make him want to steal away for a ride on the Tennessee River.

But Alvin turned back around and walked toward the house.

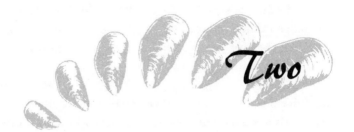

Two

ALVIN CROSSED the front yard back toward this home that his granddaddy had built. But it didn't so much look old as of a piece with the rest of Beaulah Swamp. A shinglelike siding, in the pattern of brown brick, covered the outside walls. The porch ran the length of the house, the tin roof forming its overhang.

After Alvin's grandfather had died, Freddy moved in with him. They lived in the house together until Cliff came up from South America to look up Freddy. When Cliff decided to stay, he and Freddy rented a cabin on down the river. But Freddy still stayed at Alvin's a good bit. The big bedroom was where he brought his girls, mostly. He said Cliff drank too much JW Black and sometimes talked too much, in too much detail.

Alvin was about to step up on the back porch when Johnny Ray walked out the kitchen door. He had a tall beer can in each hand. He tilted his head in the direction of the dock, meaning for Alvin to walk down there with him. Alvin did.

When Johnny Ray got to the dock, he sat down and started taking off his boots. Alvin walked up beside him. Dr. Dick was lying on the end of the dock. Alvin heard his tail give a couple of thumps. Then Dr. Dick made a god-awful yawn and went back to sleep.

Johnny Ray said, "Let's go out to the channels. I want to take you somewhere."

"I been wanting to get out on the river, too," Alvin said. He sat down and started pulling his boots and socks off.

Johnny Ray pushed one of the tall beers over to Alvin. Alvin pulled the tab, took a slug, then rolled his blue jeans up to mid-calf. He stepped down into the bow of Johnny Ray's musseling rig. The bottom of the boat was cold and damp but felt good to his bare feet.

Johnny Ray stepped down into the stern and cranked the Merc, as Alvin picked up a paddle and the spotlight, which he turned on the water ahead. As Johnny Ray slowly cruised the boat down Mud Creek, Alvin scanned the water, occasionally pushing a piece of driftwood out of the path of the boat.

Johnny Ray opened up on the throttle as the creek got wider and emptied into the backwaters. It was a dark night. Alvin spotlighted the waters, but Johnny Ray might have been able to steer the boat blind. He knew every tree, stump, or bar that impeded this route to the channel of the Tennessee River.

When they were up the river and across the channel, Johnny Ray cut the engine. As the boat glided to a stop, Alvin cut the spotlight and set it down.

He turned, putting both feet down in the bottom of the boat, facing Johnny Ray. The boat drifted slowly with the current. They were at a section of the river in which few lights could be seen—the factories on down the river a ways, the river town upriver around a bend. There were night noises of the woods and from the backwaters, but they were low and seemed far away.

Johnny Ray took out a cigarette and Alvin saw the flash of his face in the light of the struck match. Alvin picked up his Bud and sipped on it. It felt good. His arms were still tight and pumped.

Johnny Ray said, "She's right under here nearabouts."

"The riverboat?" Alvin asked, but he seemed more preoccupied with the sensation of his body, with the sensation of being out on the river at night.

"Yeuh."

Almost every day of his life Alvin had been in the channel of the Tennessee, yet he never knew exactly how deep it was. Maybe over a hundred feet. Alvin had a certain feeling when he was in this area, one he could not remember ever not having. He felt as though the river were bottomless.

"I found somethin' but lost it tryin' to git off the wreck," Johnny Ray said.

It wasn't like Johnny Ray to lose something. "What was it?"

"I don't even wanna figure out loud on it right this minute. Might be bad luck."

Alvin could see Johnny Ray grinning. He knew he would find out in time, so he let it alone. And he didn't mention to Johnny Ray that he was sounding like Alma by saying "bad luck."

Alvin did say, "Why you come off it?" What Alvin was really trying to get at was why Johnny Ray wasn't down on it right now. Since it was pitch-dark down there even during high noon, its being night didn't have anything to do with it. Except maybe once you came off the site, you'd have to have daylight to get your coordinates from the banks again.

"Compressor run outta gas fer one thang," Johnny Ray explained.

"You can get down on it tomorrow," Alvin commented.

"*We.* Day after tomorrow."

"Oh yeah. You taking Donna shopping tomorrow?" Alvin said, but knew diving a wreck wouldn't be put back a day for taking Donna shopping.

"Yeah. I got to go buy a new second-stage regulator. Mine was fuckin' up today. All my other ones need new diaphragms. Fuck 'em. I'll just toss 'em, git me a couple new ones."

"Yeah, I need a new one, too."

Johnny Ray flipped his cigarette butt overboard. "It was like a ghostie was after me. I was down deep. Almost a hunnert feet. Regulator wadn't feedin' right. Then run outta air. Kept suckin' on my mouthpiece, tryin' to git air, then figured there wadn't no pressure in my compressor. Had to come up. Damn, I's tired."

"You think you'll be able to find it again?"

Johnny Ray grunted in a little laugh. He took a pull of beer and then lit up another cigarette. "I tell ye, Alv. I won't be able to *not* find it agin. Right now it's suckin' me down to it. No way I can't not find that thang agin. Why you thank I'm out here just floatin' around in the channel?"

"Yeah," Alvin replied. He did know what Johnny Ray meant. It was like weight training. He used to be constantly asked: How could he do it? How could he be that dedicated? How could he train day in, day out? Didn't it get tiring? Alvin never could explain it; he just took the compliment. The truth was, he couldn't *not* lift weights. He would be lying in bed aching, his whole body throbbing, all the time unable to wait for tomorrow so he could do another muscle group.

"I wanna go down right now. Not day after tomorrow. But 'at's got to be the way it is," Johnny Ray said. Then he offered the scenario. "Tomorrow we git new regulators, gas up the compressors, the outboards. Git everthang ready. Day after tomorrow we set out 'fore daylight. Hook our boats together. I go down, you tend compressor. We'll use a utility line so who's divin' don't have to brang nothin' up, can keep workin' the wreck. I git tared, you go down. My compressor fucks up, we got yours."

"That's the way to do it," Alvin agreed, took the last slug of beer, and tossed the can into the water, imagining it sinking endlessly.

"Then," Johnny Ray said, "we go by my house. I got some mussels I got day 'fore yesterday in a fifty-five-gallon drum of water. We put the mussels in the bottom of our boats. Take 'em in, sell 'em, just like we been musselin'. We don't tell no damn body about this wreck. No damn body!"

Alvin nodded, figuring Johnny Ray could see him in the darkness. Alvin pondered the way Johnny Ray looked. There was no artificial light, just stars shining bright and close and whole clusters of galaxies visible. But in the dimness, Alvin could tell Johnny Ray looked different. As if there had been a change. Johnny Ray was always laid-back, but he still looked calmer.

The last time Alvin had seen Johnny Ray look like this was when Alvin's grandfather had died, before they began mussel diving. Both Alvin and Johnny Ray were running trotlines. And they were making and selling whiskey. Johnny Ray had taken over Alvin's grandfather's task of cooking the whiskey. They were hauling it down the river in boats and up into Tennessee in cars.

But things were getting slim. There had been several rough months in a row, in both businesses. The price of catfish was lousy as more of them were grown in ponds. As for moonshining, demand was down, the price of corn and sugar sky-high. Bizarre methods were being used by moonshiners to make the mash cheaper and ferment faster.

One day Alvin had come up to Hatchett Island in his boat to load up with wildcat to make a haul to Muscle Shoals. Johnny Ray had just gotten through bottling and boxing up a batch and was in another of his silent rages. All Johnny Ray said was: "You can damn near buy bonded whiskey as cheap as we can sell this wildcat. Hardly any use to do it."

When Alvin left the island with the boat full of rotgut, he had the feeling it was his last haul. Three nights later he was supposed to meet Johnny Ray on the island to pick up another load, but two days later he found a message at his house to meet Johnny Ray on the island that afternoon. Something was up, Alvin knew.

Alvin anxiously went to Hatchett Island. Johnny Ray met him. Johnny Ray had a grin on his face. Alvin couldn't think of anything to grin about. Even though times were tough, it wasn't Johnny Ray's way to give up. But all Alvin could imagine Johnny Ray saying was: "Fuck it, I don't give a shit anymore. They can raise catfish cheaper than we can catch them. They can make and tax legal whiskey cheaper than we can make illegal whiskey. To hell with it all. I quit. That's why I'm grinning."

That is all that Alvin could possibly figure Johnny Ray was

grinning about. Alvin just grinned back, almost nervously, and followed him into the heart of the island. There Alvin saw what Johnny Ray had been working on. A new copper cooker, new vats. A store shed full of corn and bales of sugar. It was set up the way Alvin had remembered it when he was very very small. "Back when they made whiskey right," Johnny Ray later called it.

All Alvin could figure happening was Johnny Ray saying, "I'm gone make one more batch. Make it right. Then blow the whole damn thang up."

But Johnny Ray didn't say that. He didn't say anything near that. What he did say was: "Know Old Man Howard out from Muscle Shoals?"

"Sure," Alvin said. He was an old man who restored Model A Fords. He preferred wildcat to bonded whiskey. They sold to him regularly. Two years ago a famous recording star, who was recording at Muscle Shoals, had come into his shop and bought the Model A he was restoring for about double what Old Man Howard usually got. Shortly Old Man Howard had an elite clientele of Nashville and Muscle Shoals recording stars.

"Know Old Man McGuire?" Johnny Ray asked.

"Sure," Alvin said. He had a small machine shop back this side of Muscle Shoals. He did the block work on the Smith brothers stock-car engines.

Johnny Ray continued. "I been doin' me some serious *re*search. And I found they's a whole clientele out there. Alv, I'm talkin' a clientele that'll pay more for a bottle of wildcat than for Chevy Regal."

Soon they made five times the profits at half the work. Johnny Ray and Alvin ran the trotlines only when the fish were biting. Alvin didn't get rich, but he managed to scratch out a living from the backwaters. Then, as the popularity of the moonshine cult began to wane, along came mussel diving.

Now, sitting in Johnny Ray's boat, drifting, Alvin felt as if a big change were coming again. It was almost as though Johnny Ray had foreseen musseling fading out so he was moving into treasure diving. Mussel diving did have a terrible liability that none of the divers seemed to heed. At a moment's notice the shell company could stop buying mussel shells, for whatever and a variety of reasons: It was moving to Texas to a more profitable market; Japan was flooded with mussel shells and would not be buying any more for a year. Almost anything one could think of could be a possible reason that the mussel divers' prosperity could end overnight.

Alvin knew Johnny Ray could always survive this. Whatever the backwaters tried to dish out to him, he was always a step ahead. Alvin felt he was living on borrowed time as far as the backwaters went, that he was supposed to have left years ago. That the backwaters had given him every opportunity in the world to leave and now he would be swallowed whole. No mercy. Alma had even had the sense, the strength to leave.

Alvin seldom craved alcohol, but now he did. The channel under him no longer seemed just deep and endless but threatening.

Johnny Ray cranked the engine and headed the boat back into the backwaters.

Mr. America, Alvin was thinking.

The boat glided to the dock. Johnny Ray cut the engine. Alvin moored the bow to a piling, then looked back to Johnny Ray.

Johnny Ray grinned. "To hell with mussels and pearls. We goin' after the gold."

It made Alvin's spine tingle.

Three

Johnny Ray carried his boots and went up to the house barefoot. Alvin watched him and sat on the dock, putting his socks and boots back on. He finally walked back up to the back porch, entered the kitchen, and found Bart standing at the refrigerator.

"Hey, Alvin," Bart said. "Ain't seen you in a few days. You been gittin' any pussy on the side?"

"They done changed where it was since I got some?"

"Shit," he said, and grinned. Bart liked to grin and say "shit," and every time he said it, Alvin thought he was going to squat down and do it. Bart was about five-four and weighed about 180. He had short arms and bow legs. Squatting down and shitting seemed a natural thing Bart was built to do.

It reminded Alvin not to pee accidentally on himself. Mussel divers spent several hours a day with their wet suits on underwater, so they just peed in them while they went on musseling. Alvin had had to work on being able to pee on himself when he first got into musseling, but now he was so good and automatic at it he feared being at a party, drinking, then just letting go.

"You been diving?" Alvin asked Bart. "I hadn't seen you on the river or at the shell place."

"Yeuh," Bart said. "I been working a flat, back toward the bridge. Some washboards, but a lot of maple leaf shells. I talk at you later, Alv." He headed for the bathroom.

Freddy almost ran into Bart. He was coming out of Alvin's bedroom, carrying an armload of albums. Alvin and Freddy kept the ones they didn't listen to much back in Alvin's bedroom.

Freddy sidled up to Alvin and pointed to an album cover of Kris Kristofferson. "Hey, Alvin, you think we put a Smith and Wesson to him, he'd take a drink a whiskey?"

"I don't know. Maybe if we pulled the hammer back, let him know we meant business. . . . Hey, Freddy?"

"Whut?" Freddy grinned.

Alvin thumbed through the record albums and pointed to a girl on the cover of one. "You thank she's ever sucked a dick?" It was a routine they went through together when they were out buying albums.

"Aw hell," Freddy said, and walked off into the living room.

Eddie came to the refrigerator and said, "Alvin. You sister from Birmingham is on the telephone, long distance."

"All right," Alvin said.

Eddie reached into the refrigerator. "She funny. She ought to be a comedian."

"She *is* a comedienne," Alvin replied.

He reached around into the crowded living room, got the phone, and pulled it as far as it would go, near the back door. He sat the phone base on the floor next to the stove and then stepped on out the back door with the receiver. He closed the door so that he could hear. He paused before he brought the receiver up. Alvin had been talking to Johnny Ray, talking in a manner similar to his own. Alma, however, had coached and coached Alvin since he was in his teens to speak distinctly and properly, as if it were his ticket out of the swamp and into the world. When he had decided to become Mr. America, he had readily adopted Alma's theory, not wanting to sound unlearned.

19

But when he was alone with Johnny Ray, he felt a traitor to Johnny Ray if he stepped out of his own dialect; occasionally he felt he was making fun of Johnny Ray when he was talking to him. He had confided this to Freddy once, and Freddy had said, "Aw, hell, Alv. Just be natural." But the trouble now was, Alvin didn't know what was "natural."

Alvin said into the phone, "Alma?"

"Alvin. Are you all right? I got this feeling that something was wrong. I felt something was trying to tell me something. Is everything all right?"

"Yeah. Everything is fine."

"Alvin, I'm scared. Last night I was doing my act, and right at the front table there was this f-a-t woman. I mean really f-a-t. I told Sam never again to let anyone that is f-a-t sit up close to the stage. You don't think I'll get f-a-t, do you?"

"No," Alvin responded quickly, a little peeved.

"Say I won't get f-a-t seventeen times."

Alvin sighed.

"Say it, Alvin. So it won't be bad luck."

Alvin knew not to argue. He said, "You won't get f-a-t, you won't get f-a-t," seventeen times in a row, as fast as he could, counting with his fingers the number of times he said it.

"Thanks." She paused. "Sam cut my act down to ten minutes. But he gave me a raise. Seventy-three dollars a week now. He tried to pay me sixty-eight. Can you believe it? Boy, I told him really fast that sixty-eight was bad luck. I made him say it three times. Sam gets all fidgety if you make him say anything over three times. So isn't that great? And I don't have to perform at any certain time. That's great, in case I'm something else. Last week I was a doorknob for three days. I'm beginning to explore my inner self as an actress, Alvin." Alma spoke very rapidly.

Alvin thought in despair how she had gone to nonliving things now. Two months ago she had been a tree for five days. After he couldn't reach her by phone, he had gone and found her in her large, sparse apartment, standing with her arms held out like branches, in a trance. She said she had *been* a tree and hadn't needed to eat because the sunlight had changed her chloroplast into energy.

She went on. "Maybe I should go to New York and study now? What do you think, Alvin?"

"I don't know, Alma. It's what you think that counts," Alvin said, handling her question by quoting Johnny Ray.

Alvin was careful to pronounce words properly with Alma so he didn't catch any shit. She had a conniption fit hemorrhage whenever Alvin would say "thank" instead of "think" or "you" instead of "your"—any of that. It was tough living on Mud Creek and talking to Johnny Ray and Eddie all the time and then being expected to talk right by Alma.

One time Alvin, Freddy, and Eddie were at the Twilight Café eating breakfast. Eddie was reading the paper and then said a word he had just read, "bicultural." He looked up all excited and said, "That's what *we* are! We're bicultural. We got our own ways; then when we go into Muscle Shoals or to Huntsville, we have to talk more proper and all that shit."

Freddy looked at Eddie with disgust. "Eddie, you not bicultural. You not even monocultural. You uncultural. You got swamp water for blood, swamp water for piss, river mud for shit, and mussel guts for brains. When we go to them clubs in Huntsville, them city girls take one look at you tell they girlfriends, 'I wouldn't fuck him with your pussy.' "

Alma's voice drifted back into Alvin's ear once again. "Alvin, I know I need to go there," she said, speaking of New York. "But I was watching this movie on TV the other night, and it was set in New York. And I saw some very f-a-t people walking along the sidewalks. And the sidewalks were so crowded, I just don't know how I could keep from bumping into one. Maybe all the f-a-t people will leave New York, and then I can go there."

"Yeah, maybe."

"Alvin, do you think I should be mad at Sam? The club is doing great. He said he wants me to perform more times, but not as long an act. I mean, I have like ten minutes. It takes me ten minutes before I get into my good stuff."

Alvin knew why Sam cut her to ten minutes. Her good stuff didn't make any sense to anybody.

Alvin noticed a tub of iced-down beer at his feet. He pulled one out, opened it, and started drinking.

"Do you think I should be mad at him for it?"

"Naw. Naw," Alvin said, getting by with saying "naw" instead of a crisp "no."

"Alvin, I'm worried about my stomach. I went to the bathroom in the middle of the night last night, and I thought I saw it pouching out."

"Naw," he said quickly. "It wasn't pouching out. You have the skinniest stomach of anybody I have ever seen. You are *so* skinny. Everybody tells me that, after you have been home and gone back to Birmingham. They tell me you are the skinniest person they have ever seen."

"Really, Alvin? Oh, I love you."

He had to tell her she was skinny thirty-seven times.

"Alvin, tonight I finally figured it out. I did two hundred and forty-seven sit-ups. That is the perfect number."

He slugged down his beer while she was talking. It was only his third beer of the night, but after the whiskey he had drunk on the front porch with Johnny Ray, he was really starting to feel it.

Alma told him she loved him nineteen times. Then she said good-bye.

"Bye," Alvin said.

Neither hung up the phone.

Alma said, "You hang up first."

"No, you hang up first."

Alma instructed, "When I count seven, we will hang up at the same time."

"OK," he agreed.

When she counted to seven, Alvin hung up. After he did, he

figured Alma had held on to the receiver and listened to his click. Only when she got another dial tone would she hang up.

He stood there in the darkness, holding the receiver with its button held down in his left hand, and a cold beer in his right, thinking how for the last couple of years he had thought of Alma as his kid sister, though at thirty-one, she was older.

Maybe it had to do with her appearance. Alma looked younger than Alvin. Sometimes she looked like a little girl, he thought. Sometimes she looked like a taller version of the seven-year-old Alma who had stood jumping up and down on the pier, trying to fly.

It was one of Alvin's earliest, though spotted, memories. He could remember his mother, herself slim, telling Alma she should eat all her food on her plate; otherwise, the wind was going to sweep her off the pier, blow her down Mud Creek and across the river. After the meal Alma would take Alvin, then four, out to the pier, instructing him to wait for a gust of wind. Then she would jump up and down, in great expectations of being able to fly. But little Alvin would try to make himself heavier because the thought of flying out wildly down the river was frightening.

Four

CLIFF WAS STANDING at the table, pouring himself a straight scotch, when Alvin walked back into the kitchen and replaced the phone receiver. "How in the hell you drink that stuff straight?"

"You guys get me," Cliff said, in his New York accent. "You can drink that kerosene you call corn liquor and won't even partake of this fine sipping scotch."

"But, Cliff, that 'shine hits ya stomach like thunder, hits your head like lightning. That's part of the fun of it. You don't go around pretending it tastes good. You sip on *that* shit like it's liquid candy."

Cliff barely listened. "I know drinking isn't everything. I know drinking is really nothing. I won't always drink. Someday something is going to come along that is going to be worth giving up drinking for. But until that day I'm going to keep on drinking."

Alvin patted Cliff on the back. He wanted to get back with Johnny Ray, to continue their earlier conversation about Mr. America. If Alvin could just get to talking to him about it, maybe he could come to some kind of conclusions.

Eddie walked up to the table to get another drink. He said to Cliff, trying to imitate him, "Jesus Christ, Cliff. You are consuming all of the alcoholic beverage. Jesus Christ." Alvin chuckled. He also thought it was funny how Yankees used "Jesus Christ" for a curse word. Eddie's intrusion gave Alvin an out to break away gracefully.

Just as he walked into the living room, the music stopped. One of the girls was standing by the turntable. She was flipping through some albums she had in her arm. She wore turquoise-colored tight jeans with her left hip jutted out, and had on high heels.

She turned her head around quickly, flinging her hair. "What do you want to listen to, Johnny Ray?"

Johnny Ray was sitting near the front door on a wooden stool, looking old enough to be the girl's father. His boot heels were hooked over the bottom crosspiece of the stool. He was moving his drink slowly up and down his left forearm, as if trying to scratch his arm with the glass.

"Don't matter to me, honey. Just something that makes noise."

"All of them make noise, handsome. What kind of music is it you like to listen to?" She jutted out her hip a little more, the move somehow making her look taller. She cocked her head down and looked up intently to Johnny Ray, as if she'd had on an imaginary pair of reading glasses and were peering over the frames.

"I like music that makes me want to drive down the left side of the road with the lights out, throwing hundred-dollar bills out the winda," Johnny Ray said.

Everybody hollered, and the girl put on some Steppenwolf. Then she turned around and grabbed Bart. They started dancing. Bart was grinning and having a good time, his dancing looking like a piston going up and down in time to the music.

The other girl, the younger one, had Freddy out in the middle of the floor dancing. She twirled around, and it made her flouncy skirt go up. Alvin could see her pantied ass for a second.

Alvin kept staring at the girl, clamping his teeth down hard together as if he were doing his last repetition of a killer set of curls. She made something churn in Alvin's mind. Then it hit him. All of a sudden he recognized the girl who was dancing with Freddy.

About six months ago Alvin had gotten up in the middle of the night and gone to the kitchen to get a drink of water. When he opened his bedroom door, he found the kitchen light shining. He walked on in and found this girl sitting at the table, clad only in a black T-shirt of Freddy's, her bare ass on the wooden chair. Her arms were dangling at her sides, and her head was down resting in a pizza.

Alvin had bunched her hair up into a ponytail. He raised her head to look at her; pepperoni and strings of cheese stuck to the side of her face. She made no response to Alvin's action, so Alvin let her face back down into the pizza.

He went about getting his glass of water. He was about to go back toward his bedroom, but he turned and stared at the girl. He thought it was strange he hadn't heard a sigh or seen one motion from her. He walked over and put his hand under her left breast, feeling for a heartbeat. She began moaning as if in sexual ecstasy. She took his hand and moved it up onto her breast. She sat up straight, arched her back, turned her head. She took one look at Alvin and threw up onto the pizza and then laid her head back down in it, passed out the same way he had found her.

I didn't thank I was that bad, Alvin said to himself.

Alvin walked to the big bedroom door and knocked.

Freddy moaned, "What?"

"Hey, man, I think you got a casualty out here."

Freddy jerked the bedroom door open and ran to the kitchen. He looked at the girl, Alvin standing beside him. Freddy said to Alvin, "What is it with women? They give you a little pussy, then think they own you clothes."

Freddy reached over and pulled his T-shirt off the limp body, trying not to get puke on it. He threw the T-shirt next to the washing machine. Then he picked up the naked girl and carried her to the bathroom. Freddy got her down on the floor, hugging the commode, throwing up. Alvin stood in the doorway, drinking his water, watching.

"Where'd you run into her?" Alvin asked him.

"Up at that strip joint on the state line."

"Hell, Freddy. She's too good-looking for that place. She's a little doll! I bet she's not eighteen years old."

"Yeah, she's nice." Freddy explained, "I'm rehabilitating her. Getting her out of that sleaze joint."

"Yeah. Brother Freddy, saving another young soul," Alvin said. He was completely awake now, no immediate desire to go back to bed.

"Goddamn, Alvin. I didn't fuck her. I's just kiddin' about her giving me some pussy. She's just a kid!" Freddy said. He picked her up and set her over into the tub.

"She looks full-grown to me. A little doll. But in pretty rough shape right now," Alvin said.

"I told Benton if I come up to his club, see something like this in there again, they'd be scraping his brains off the walls."

Freddy started running water into the tub. The girl started stirring around. Freddy said to Alvin, "Go put on some coffee. Something's wrong with her."

Alvin looked at her. "Holy shit, Freddy! Her face is ice blue."

Freddy looked up at her face. "Fuck!" He put his hand on her chest. He quickly dug her out of the tub, stretched her out on the bathroom floor, and gave her mouth-to-mouth.

In a few minutes she was screaming at the top of her lungs.

The next day Freddy had gotten word that Benton didn't like people coming in and stealing his dancers away or threatening his life. Johnny Ray had gotten word of *that* and gone up to Benton's place and sat down at the bar. Benton came running over. "Harold, get Johnny Ray a beer. Johnny Ray, listen. I didn't know she was that young and innocent. I tell my men to run girls like that off. I don't need trouble. I don't need a bad reputation. Tell Freddy no hard feelings. . . ." Johnny Ray just stared at Benton, then got up and left, never saying a word.

Now, Alvin looked at Johnny Ray, and remembered something Cliff once said about him: "He has presence." Eddie and Tony were standing around Johnny Ray, talking and laughing. Alvin couldn't hear anything over the music and noise of the party. Johnny Ray made a motion with his drink-free hand of an airplane going into a dive. Eddie and Tony were laughing and slowly getting drunker.

Alvin then looked over at Cliff on the couch. He was drinking his scotch and reading the back of an album cover. Alvin took a big gulp of beer and then went over and plopped down beside him.

Alvin, almost hollering to be heard, said to Cliff, "What is it with you, Cliff?"

"Reading this album," Cliff said, never looking up but taking another sip of scotch.

"Naw. I mean what are you doing? You always kind of on the outside of everthang. Like you just observing. Just quiet and silent. Just a-hanging out. What in the hell's on your mind anyway?"

Cliff looked over at Alvin with glassy, alcohol-hazed eyes. "Just like you said, man. Just hanging out. On the outside looking in. Maybe I might be on the inside looking out. Someday I might even be on the outside looking out."

Cliff looked back down to the album cover. Alvin figured he was far gone. About this time nothing he said ever made any sense. Alvin stood up and realized he himself was a cunt hair away from being drunk. He slugged out the rest of his tall beer and then made his way to the back porch.

He closed the kitchen door behind him. He stood alone by the washtub, bent down, got another beer, stood back up. As he was pulling the tab off, something swiped his elbow. He swatted at it, thinking it was a bug or something, but he hit an arm. He turned around to see the girl. She had touched his elbow to get his attention.

Alvin said, "Oh, hi. Excuse me. I didn't mean to be swatting at you."

"Hi. My cousin and I are about to leave. I just wanted to thank you for inviting us to your party."

"We were the ones that ought to thank you for coming. And this was just one of those parties that kind of just happened."

"Sometimes those are the best."

"Yeah. But I'm afraid you can't give me the credit for inviting you. Freddy must have done that. But that's the smartest thing he's done all month." Alvin tried not to slur his words and was doing a good job at it.

She smiled at his compliment and then asked, "You remember me, don't you?"

"I sure do. You are looking very lovely," Alvin said. He was looking down at her. She was short, probably not even five feet, but she was petite and built so that she did not look short. She had on a black dress that came to right above her knees and snugged her body in an elegant manner. Her neckline was a low V, and Alvin could see the inside of her breasts, which he had six months ago seen and touched. They now looked inviting but guarded.

"You saved my life that night. I want to thank you for that. I got a little messed up. I don't do that crap anymore."

"Well, it's Freddy that you can thank. If it hadn't been for him, I would have just left you to die in the pizza. Yeah, old Freddy's all right. But hadn't got a lick of sense."

"No?" she questioned in defense of Freddy.

"Naw. If he had any sense he'd been on to you, taking you around, trying to get you to marry him," Alvin said, but then felt stupid for it. He knew what he said must have sounded dumb to her. It made him feel so different. He got the feeling she thought he was a redneck and over the hill at almost thirty. An old burnt-out, over-the-hill, has-been Mr. Alabama, Alvin was thinking. Alvin couldn't help remembering when she had looked at him and thrown up.

She just smiled, admiring him even, but he couldn't help feeling uncomfortable standing there. She was so dainty, almost perfect. Through the beer, through the alcoholic haze, through the Beaulah Swamp air, he could smell her. It was nice. Eddie was right the time he had said, "Women smell different," and now Alvin knew what Eddie was trying to say. The girl made him feel inadequate, something that wouldn't be happening if he were Mr. America.

"I'm starting back at Florence State this fall," she said.

"Oh, good," Alvin said. With that information Alvin tried to invent a background for her. Her speech had a Yankeeish sound. She was probably from up North or was the kid of Yankee parents who worked at NASA in Huntsville. She was sent to her cousin's, who sounded very southern, if not country, to attend college. She had gotten all fucked up on dope and ended up dancing at the state line.

"I'm sorry for being what I was like that night. I can't believe I ended up in that type of shape," she said, and laughed.

Alvin stood there wondering how Freddy knew to run up and grab her off the stage and bring her to his house. How did Freddy know she didn't belong there? Alvin knew he never would have been able to know that, and if he had known it, his rescue attempt would have ended with his either being shot or getting arrested for kidnapping a minor.

"Yeah, sometimes we can find ourselves in strange predicaments," Alvin said.

A taxi came driving up to the house. Her cousin, with a drink in hand, and Freddy at her side, headed to the cab. The cousin yelled, "Becky!"

She reached up and kissed Alvin at the corner of his mouth, said, "Thank you," then ran to the cab.

Alvin wondered how she had reached the corner of his mouth to kiss him. She had seemed too short. Now, standing on the porch, he could still smell her, the feminine fragrance wedged into the Beaulah Swamp air. It made him think of Ginger.

Alvin took a good pull of his fresh beer and walked back into the house, feeling not really drunk but wild and reckless and arrogant.

He heard Johnny Ray in the living room. Alvin walked in and saw him over next to the television, laughing. Suddenly he stopped laughing and stared at Alvin. Then his eyes seemed to fog over.

Johnny Ray gulped and dropped his glass. He continued to stare at Alvin.

"Shit, Johnny Ray," Alvin said, grinning. "That 'shine too strong for you." He hollered, "Bart, go get some coal oil rags to put in Johnny Ray's britches so the pissants won't eat his candy ass."

Johnny Ray fell to his knees and held out his hands to Alvin. His neck muscles were contracting. He spoke as best as he could, but

Alvin could only see Johnny Ray's mouth move. He couldn't hear him over the screech of Charlie Daniels's fiddle. He hollered what he thought Johnny Ray wanted to Eddie, who was in the kitchen, "Johnny Ray wants some gin and ice in a tall glass."

Eddie brought the order and handed it to Johnny Ray. In a spasm Johnny Ray slung the drink against the wall, fell to the floor, and curled up against the wall.

Alvin laughed and hollered, "Aw! You doing Eddie. You doing Eddie when he got hit in the nuts with the baseball last week. Hey, Freddy! Come look at Johnny Ray doing Eddie."

But Freddy, who was holding himself up in the doorway, had seen it all. He said, "Shit, Johnny Ray is good. I don't know what he doing here fur. He ought to be making movie pictures with Burt Reynolds."

Alvin lost his grin and swallowed hard. He wondered if Freddy knew what his plan used to be, about winning Mr. America.

Alvin said, "Freddy, where you got the moonshine stashed? I'm tired this beer."

Five

ALVIN LEE FUQUA OPENED his eyes and saw a big foot beside his head. The toenails were rust-stained from the mud bottom of the Tennessee River, the way all mussel divers' toenails were.

Alvin raised up on his elbows then plopped back down. Although he didn't feel he needed to put a Black and Decker to his head and drill a couple of holes to let the pain out, he did have that cotton mouth, spinning feeling that he got in the morning after putting away more than a six-pack of beer and a half-pint of liquor on an empty stomach.

He smacked his mouth and said, "I think a dog done shit in my mouth. Dr. Dick, you sneak in here last night, shit in my mouth?"

He pushed Bart's foot away from his face and then put his own foot down on the floor to stop the bed from spinning. He stood up and did a double biceps pose, then closed his eyes and thought about Ginger Carpenter. He liked to think about her nice, tight, Dixieland ass and soft, firm body. But it didn't do Ginger justice to envision her with the cloudy mind he had right now.

He headed for the bathroom and found the door busted and

hanging on one hinge. Freddy liked to get handy with his feet when he got drunk. Or it could have been Eddie. Probably Freddy. Ever since Boot Jacobs had been lead-off batter for Cincinnati, Freddy could get a little wild. Alvin suddenly remembered him hitting the beer cans.

Alvin could also remember pumping his arms, going out to the channels with Johnny Ray, talking to Alma, and, like a hazy dream, the girl he'd once found passed out in the pizza. After that he didn't know. He figured, right before midnight, spacemen had come down, kidnapped him, taken him off, brought him back, and shot him with some drug to make him forget.

He pulled a beer bottle out of the toilet bowl and threw it in the trash can. Then he peed. When he got through, he opened up the medicine cabinet and got out some B complexes and vitamin C's to help him with his temporary ailment.

The kitchen looked as though Freddy had been doing batting practice on beer bottles. And where there wasn't broken glass, there were dirty glasses or empty cans. He poured himself a glass of orange juice to help himself decide when he would start cleaning up the mess.

Alvin walked to the doorway of the living room and looked in. More batting practice. There was enough aluminum lying around to reroof the house. Most of the cans were squashed top to bottom, the way Freddy, Bart, and Tony liked to do.

Some albums were laid out and hadn't been put back in their covers. But he didn't get mad. He had probably done it himself. Right before the spacemen got him.

Tony was on the couch asleep. Cliff was on the beanbag snoring.

Then Alvin saw Johnny Ray, and there was no question in Alvin's mind about Johnny Ray's state of health.

There wasn't any running over to take his pulse or check his throat, no feeling the chest, as he had done with the girl in the pizza.

Alvin didn't know much about dead people or had looked at many, other than if they were lying in state. Lying in a dead state, in a casket.

Johnny Ray was unmistakably dead.

He was all twisted up with his head against the wall and his eyes open. His tint was bad, and his body was rigid and stonelike, as though he were an ugly carved statue on its side. Alvin didn't know why, but he somehow felt there was no emergency about his best friend's being dead. And since he wasn't wondering *if* he was dead or not, Alvin wondered what had happened to him. Last night was a blank, which was unusual. He wasn't given to lapses of memory, and he hadn't drunk that much alcohol. But since he'd had more than usual, he figured maybe his brain cells' resistance was down, and the alcohol had killed off a bunch of them and numbed out most of the rest.

The first thing he thought of was Freddy. If Freddy had gone to the trouble of knocking the bathroom door in and having batting practice with all the beer bottles, maybe he had gone to the trouble of breaking Johnny Ray's neck.

But everybody knew you could throw Johnny Ray out of an airplane and all it would do was make him mad.

Alvin imagined him dying of some kind of seizure thing while they were all wild drunk. He could imagine them hollering, jumping around and hitting each other, with the Charlie Daniels Band about to blow the front windowpanes out, while Johnny Ray lay there dead.

Alvin looked around and saw the bottom of a broken glass over in the corner. He thought about the wildcat. But if it had been bad moonshine, all of them would be dead except Johnny Ray and Cliff.

Johnny Ray hadn't been shot. There would be a big hole in him, and blood would be all over the floor. Then a fear came over Alvin; maybe he had killed him. Sometimes folks killed members of their family, and then it all went dark. Something like that could have happened, he thought.

Alvin stood there wondering and figuring. He could have hit Johnny Ray over the head with a two-foot length of three-quarter-inch pipe or seen somebody else kill him, if that was possible, and now he had a mental block about the whole thing. Alvin knew things like that happened. He also knew that wondering and thirty-five cents got a cup of coffee at the Twilight Café.

After he had gone over and looked at Johnny Ray for a while really close up, Alvin punched Tony and Cliff awake and went and got Freddy and Eddie up. When they came into the living room, Tony and Cliff were staring at Johnny Ray the same way Alvin had earlier.

Freddy walked in, hollering, trying to sound cheerful over his hangover. "Goddamn, Eddie, you shit in here last night! Damn, it stinks." But one look at Johnny Ray, and he became very silent.

Eddie rubbed his head as if he were going to be able to rub out some of the alcoholic damage. Then he noticed Johnny Ray and said, "Shit!"

Tony walked over to Johnny Ray, bent over and looked at him, and said, "God, he's dead." Then he went over and sat in the La-Z-Boy recliner and stared at the gray screen of the Sony color TV.

"Goddammit!" Tony finally said. "I'm going to kill that son of a bitch that sold us that moonshine."

"That white lightning was some of Johnny Ray's batch," Alvin said.

"What about those two girls that were here?" Eddie asked.

"A taxi came to take them back to their car," Cliff answered.

"I's just wonderin' maybe one of 'em shot him."

Tony said, "There's no blood."

"Maybe they poisoned him?" Eddie suggested.

"Eddie, those girls didn't have anything to do with it," Freddy said.

"You couldn't kill Johnny Ray," Alvin said. "You shoot him, the bullets just bounce off of him."

They all looked at each other, and then Freddy said, "You reckon one of us killed him?"

"Couldn't but two people able to kill Johnny Ray," Alvin said.

"Who's 'at?" Eddie asked.

"Johnny Ray hisself or God."

"Musta been God," Tony decided.

"You reckon we gone die?" Eddie wondered.

"What do you mean?" Alvin asked, looking over to Eddie.

"Well, you know how Johnny Ray was into everthang first. Bodybuilding before anybody ever heard of it. Over to Vietnam and back before anybody else ever heard of the place. Took dope and quit before anybody around here seen any. And he was the first one of us to start diving," Eddie explained, proposing the idea that Johnny Ray had just started a trend of dropping dead.

Everybody was thinking about what Eddie had just said.

Then they all, except Freddy, stared at Johnny Ray. But nobody touched him or undertook to examine him closer.

Freddy just looked down. "I guess we better call the police, or sheriff, or ambulance, or whoever it is you supposed to call," he said. "We better git over and tell Donna."

Everybody but Alvin nodded in agreement.

"Yeah, I reckon," Tony said.

They all kept staring at Johnny Ray.

Alvin knew he should be the one to tell Donna, but he didn't especially want to. He didn't especially want to watch her go crazy.

Six

ABOUT TWENTY MILES east of Alvin's house, along the river, was Huntsville, and it was there that Johnny Ray's body had been taken for an autopsy. The doctor who performed the autopsy was in a hospital conference room, giving a briefing to the divers.

"The bends," the doctor said.

"Jesus Christ," Cliff said. "I didn't know he was diving that deep."

"Johnny Ray was obviously in deep water for an extended period," the doctor went on. "He failed to decompress properly, and it created nitrogen bubbles in his fatty tissue and then back out into his bloodstream. One lodged in his brain."

"Johnny Ray didn't have no fatty tissue," Eddie said. "He's all muscle. Musta went straight to his bloodstream."

The doctor started to say something about fatty tissue but paused and let it slide.

Eddie said, "I don't know anything much about the bends. Just if ye stay under very deep, you supposed to come up slow. Just come up slower than you air bubbles. That's the rules. Breathe out when you coming up so it don't bust ye lungs. That's about it. All of us at one time or another been down at least forty feet and the air supply go out. You drop you weight belt and float to the top, just keep exhaling on the way up so ye lungs don't bust. But this nitrogen bubbles. I don't know shit about that. We usually don't go down deep enough to worry about that."

"Forty feet is about as deep as you want to go in the Tennessee River," Cliff said. "It's not at all like clear-water diving."

"What are you diving for?" the doctor asked.

"Mussels," Eddie said. "This company, Dixie Shell, buys from us and sells 'em to Japan. The bottom of the Tennessee River is covered 'em. They started buying mussels for thirty-two and a half cents a pound, live weight. Divers that already knew about musseling came in from Oklahoma and Texas and started diving until they heard of somewheres else there was more mussels. Then a lot of us that was commercial fishermen got into musseling. See, we can make a hell of a lot more money musseling. Johnny Ray was the first one of us to git into it."

He had been excited telling the doctor about their profession until he mentioned Johnny Ray. He got a little sad and shut up. Freddy stretched around and then relaxed back in the comfortable blue-gray couch he and Eddie were sitting on.

"What happens if somebody comes in here to this hospital with the bends?" Freddy asked. "They just die or something?"

"No," the doctor said. "We race them over to the decompression chamber at the NASA base here."

The doctor's mentioning of fancy equipment brought Alvin to the brink of a rage. The shit-ass at the dive shop had said, "Your life depends on your equipment." But the thing was, at any time their equipment could fuck up and all they had to do was release their weight belt and float to the top. Mussel diving, all you had to remember to be safe was: Don't panic. Hell, Johnny Ray hadn't panicked. Six hours after he had been out of the water, he'd been kicking back and looking good. Maybe what Daddy used to say about "everthang that glitters ain't gold" is true, Alvin concluded.

His daddy had died at the beginning of Alvin Lee's bodybuilding competing career. Sitting there now, he worried that his decision to renew his career had made Johnny Ray drop dead on the spot.

"Ah shit," Alvin said, and only realized he had said it out loud when everybody looked over to him.

Cliff was sitting closest to Alvin. Alvin smiled at him and said, "Big Cliff." It put everybody's attention back on the doctor, except for Cliff's. Cliff thought: Johnny Ray died of the bends and I'm dying of the Channels.

When he had left New York to go to the Army, he had not wanted to go. Just having to leave against his will seemed of the magnitude of a holocaust. But when he got to California, back from the war, he found he didn't have a home to go back to. Southern California not exactly being a place for a New Yorker Vietnam veteran to be in the late sixties, Cliff headed across the border.

A few years later he had written his Army buddy Freddy and gotten a letter back pleading for him to come to Alabama; Freddy wrote him about the mussel diving, the whiskey that was flowing, and the women that all of a sudden were around.

And now, Cliff remembered something that happened just before he took up Freddy's offer and left Ecuador. One of the expatriates was about to go back to the States but became deathly ill. One of the English guys had said, "Ah, he's just got a bad case of the Channels." Cliff asked him what he meant, and it was explained as an old English sailors' term, that when their ships had been to sea for a long time, all of the crew would want to get home, but once they arrived in the English Channel, many of them would start puking and shitting, unable to enjoy the place they had longed for.

Man, race me off to that decompression chamber, Cliff now thought. I got a wild strain of the Channels.

And with the Channels, just the way Johnny Ray had been with the bends, Cliff knew he had been down too long.

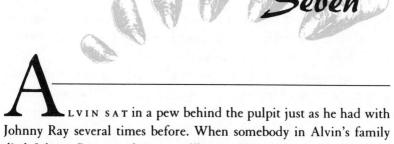

Seven

LVIN SAT in a pew behind the pulpit just as he had with Johnny Ray several times before. When somebody in Alvin's family died, Johnny Ray was always a pallbearer. When somebody in Johnny Ray's family died, Alvin was always a pallbearer. And when somebody else died, they were pallbearers together. But today Johnny Ray wasn't sitting next to Alvin in the pew behind the pulpit, being a pallbearer. He was lying up in the casket, being the dead person. And Alvin thought how from two years before Mr. Alabama till now everybody decided to drop dead.

The preacher walked up to the pulpit, and suddenly Alvin got bored. The preacher started talking about Johnny Ray, how good he was, and then he said, "Let us ask the question 'Will a man be saved from the fires of hell by his good works alone?'"

It pissed Alvin off, but he didn't jump up and beat the shit out of him because of Donna, who was over in the immediate family section, screaming her lungs out. Instead, he looked out over the congregation.

The church was packed, and it was beginning to get hot. The place was supposed to be air-conditioned, but he could see all the ladies out there trying to pump air on themselves with the little cardboard Baptist fans that were stuck behind each pew along with the hymnals.

Freddy was at Alvin's right, and to the left were Cliff, Bart, Tony, Eddie, a seventy-year-old commercial fisherman, Colter McFarland, and a cousin of Johnny Ray's, Rufus D. Since they also were pallbearers, they were seated up on the stage behind the pulpit, facing the congregation.

In the first pew Alma, skinny as a rail, sat next to Ginger. Alma was waving at Alvin. She had just come in from Birmingham for the funeral and hadn't gotten to say hello to him yet.

Alvin waved back. She threw him a kiss, and he threw her one back.

Freddy leaned forward and pulled a pint bottle wrapped in a paper bag out of his hip pocket. He took a good pull out and passed it on to Alvin, who himself took a fair taste. He passed it on to Cliff.

Cliff asked, "What is it?"

"Gin or vodka, one," Alvin replied. "It hadn't hit me good enough yet for me to tell." Cliff declined and passed it on down the line. Instead, he pulled a silver flask of scotch out from under his coat and took a strong nip.

Alvin began ignoring the preacher and started to whisper. "I remember Johnny Ray told me one time, 'I got religious feelings like this before, but I didn't know what to do about it, so I would end up going to church. I'd have all these ideas about things that had just come to me, and I would be sittin' there all excited and the preacher would stand up and tell me how I was goin' to hell and there awadn't nuthin' to do but get Jesus to get you in heaven after a life of strife and hanging out in nursing homes, and shit like that. And it would piss me off real big, so I would forget about all the religious stuff and just git drunk.' "

"Yeah. Johnny Ray could get to deep thinking sometime," Freddy agreed. "That's about the way I feel about it."

"I can't git over Johnny Ray dying," Alvin said.

"Me neither."

Alvin pulled a hundred-dollar bill out of his pocket and rolled it up into a little tube. He chewed up the corner of a piece of paper he had in his pocket and shot it through the tube. It hit Johnny Ray's corpse hand, down in the casket, in front of the congregation.

But Johnny Ray didn't stir, so Alvin put the bill back in his pocket and gave up on it.

Alvin sat there and wondered what the real truth was. Johnny Ray didn't just fuck up and drop dead. He must have got down in that sunken riverboat, and there must have been something down there that pulled at Johnny Ray.

He wouldn't have ever just dropped dead for his own personal benefit and left everybody.

The preacher could scream all he wanted to about death slipping in like a stranger in the night, but the truth of it was that if a stranger in the night broke in on Johnny Ray, Donna, and them, Johnny Ray would have just politely beat the hell out of him; wouldn't have been any tragedy, or stress, or nothing to it at all.

Alvin said, "Ol' Thomas McHarrington shot Johnny Ray in the head with a thirty-two one time. Johnny Ray took that revolver away and beat the shit out of him."

"Yeah," Freddy said. "I remember that."

"The bullet hit him on the forehead and scooted around under the skin to the side of his head. He come home. Donna cut it out for him. Never did go to the doctor. And now a damn bubble kills him."

"It's crazy, I tell ye," Freddy said.

"Only God in heaven knows when death will come like a stranger in the night!" the preacher hollered for about the tenth time. "Johnny Ray, a healthy man. Only forty years old."

"He was forty-two," Eddie hollered up at the preacher. "If ye gone be telling how old he was, at least git it right. Shit!"

The funeral director came rushing up the aisle, around the stage, and up to Freddy. He was of medium height, roundish, and looked as if his muscles were soft and toneless.

He scolded Freddy. "You must refrain from talking! And put those bottles away. This is a house of the Lord! A man has deceased."

"Fuck you, man," Freddy said. "And the horse you rode in on."

Eddie hollered down to Freddy, "He just pissed off Johnny Ray gone be buried at Hatchett Cemetery. Didn't git to sell Donna a plot. I done told him he sell Donna a expensive casket, I whup his ass."

Tony hollered down to the man, "Yeah, go sell somebody another hole in the ground. Shit. What some people got to do to make 'em a damn livin'."

"I shook his hand yesterday," Eddie said. "He got little soft hands. I bet he got a little pink worm dick. He goes back in the back of his funeral home, lays in a casket, whiffs some formaldyhide, and beats his little pink worm meat with his little soft hand." Eddie made a little jacking-off motion.

The funeral director stood at the edge of the stage, frozen, puffing, steaming, sweat pouring off his bloated face.

Alvin laughed at what Eddie had said. Then he turned to the funeral director. "Man, you thank we give a shit? My best friend's widow is down yonder screaming her lungs out. Deward and Jenny are scared shitless 'cause they mama's crying and hollering and their daddy's gone. My sister's out yonder fixing to do gyrations 'cause she's three pews over from a fat woman. And we damn near run out of whiskey."

The preacher was screaming over them, something about had you ever burnt your finger on the stove eye, and how would you like to burn all over your body that way for eternity.

Freddy looked hard at the funeral director. "Git you ass away from here, before you have to be goin' up to Robertson's shoe shop to git my ten and half boot outta you asshole."

As the man started walking away, Eddie stood up and hollered, "Hey, you in charge here or something? Tell that son of a bitch to quit preaching."

Freddy screamed down the row, "Send that gin back down this way."

Rufus D. had the bottle, about a third of a pint, and turned it up, swigging. Rufus D. killed it.

"I thought you wife made you quit dranking, Rufus D.?" Eddie grunted.

"He ain't pussy-whipped like you are, Eddie," Freddy said. "He don't take no shit off no woman."

"I ain't pussy-whipped. I git my pussy. You don't be worrying about me."

Tony said, "Damn, Rufus D. You all right. We gone have to teach you how to mussel-dive."

Rufus D. wiped his mouth and threw the empty bottle up between the preacher's legs to the back of the pulpit, as if there were a garbage can there.

He said, "Hell, naw. Ya'll ain't gone git me in one of them rubber suits, hook pipes up to me, weight me down, drop me in no damn river. Naw, sir. I'm crazy as hell, but I ain't that fucked up yet."

The preacher didn't flinch. He just thought it was lightning bolts coming out of his own head.

The preacher reared back, straightened up, then turned and yelled, "Do you know how long eternity is?"

" 'Bout as long as my dick!" Freddy hollered back up to him.

And Donna kept screaming.

Eight

CLIFF DIDN'T DRINK beer. He didn't drink Coca-Cola. He didn't drink fruit juices. He didn't drink Johnnie Walker Red. All Cliff drank was Johnnie Walker Black Label. He'd drink it four different ways: straight; with ice; with water; or with water and ice.

That afternoon, after the graveside service, Cliff was drinking JW Black and water on the rocks with Alvin, Ginger, Freddy, Alma, and Donna on the front porch of the Twilight Café on Plato Jones Street in Beaulah Town.

It was a dry county, but that didn't count for shit in Beaulah Town, or on Plato Jones Street, or on the front porch of the Twilight Café, or especially with Cliff, Alvin, and Freddy.

Ginger took a sip of her drink and then looked around. She whispered to Alvin, "Are you sure it's all right to drink here? Are you sure it's all right to *be* here?"

Alvin killed the last of his orange juice and vodka and said, "It's all right."

He hoped Ginger wouldn't start acting stupid. Alvin didn't think anybody who lived in a hundred-thousand-dollar house on Elk River and had her own business was entitled to act stupid.

When Alvin was at her house, or at the Dixie Lee Café uptown, or over in Muscle Shoals with her, he thought Ginger had to be one of the smartest people in the world. But when she got within three miles of Mud Creek, she could come down with the damnedest case of the dumb ass.

Alvin glanced over at Jenny and Deward, who were over sitting at the small table at the edge of the porch, eating chocolate ice cream. They looked as if they were hurrying to finish, as if Johnny Ray were coming to take them somewhere.

Alma took a little bitty sip of her Tab and vodka. "You don't mind that I have to go back to Birmingham this afternoon?" she said to Alvin. "I have a spot to do. Do you promise you don't mind?"

"I promise," Alvin said for about the fifth time, and hoping he wouldn't have to say it seventeen times in a row or some bullshit.

"Say, 'I don't mind,' seven times," Alma said.

"I don't mind," Alvin said seven times, very fast but not very loud.

"Oh, good," Alma said.

Then Alvin looked at Cliff. He had on a tailored suit he had gotten in South America. Cliff looked different in a suit. Alvin wouldn't even have imagined him owning a suit as Cliff didn't seem to own a lot. He didn't have a car, because he didn't want one. He had always just ridden with Freddy, Johnny Ray, or Alvin, hitchhiked or got a ride with Coins Collier of the Collier Cab Company, which was next door to the Twilight Café. Every once in a while he would drive Freddy's Camaro.

Ginger said to Cliff, "You're from New York. The city?"

"Yeah. The Bronx," Cliff said.

It was warm but pleasant, considering the time of day and the time of year. Above the table a ceiling fan made an airflow. The front porch of the Twilight felt like a cool watering hole after a day in the smothering church and the hot sun at the grave site.

Cliff undid his collar button, then pulled his tie off and put it in one of his coat pockets. He realized he still had his coat on, so he leaned forward a bit and took it off, too.

He said, "Yeah. The Bronx. I'm *from* the city."

Alvin thought Ginger was going to fuck up the quiet numbness of the group. Even Alma wasn't saying much. But Ginger's quizzing seemed to fit into the rhythm of the afternoon, and Cliff was acting gentlemanly about the questions, as he always did with the ladies.

Cliff got up and went inside the café. Alma got up and followed him.

Ginger asked, "Was it OK to ask him that?" as if she had thought she had run him off.

Nobody answered her. Nobody gave a shit.

After a while Alvin got bored. He didn't want to have to sit there and say something interesting; he didn't know what to say to Donna right now. The quiet made him nervous. Sometimes after funerals people would start talking about the deceased and how good they had been and how everything was going to work out for the best. It was probably like Ginger to start saying something like that about now.

Alvin said, "I'm gone go in here a minute. I'll be right back directly."

Alvin walked past the counter to the far side of the room. There were two pinball machines side by side. Alma and Cliff were standing close together, playing one. Alvin stepped up to the other, put in a nickel, and started playing.

He was ready for the day to be over. He wished they would all of a sudden go back to where they were supposed to be. All Alvin wanted to do right now was go to his house and be alone or maybe just sit there with Dr. Dick and Freddy. Put an album on and be on the front porch, drinking iced tea.

But the main thing Alvin wanted to do before that was put on some *real* clothes. Here he had just buried his best friend, and the main thing that bothered him right this minute was he still had on his suit pants, a dress shirt, and his dress Florsheim boots. Alvin liked dressing up in a suit, but it was like a costume to him. After an hour he was ready to get out of it and back into his jeans and athletic shoes.

Before pulling the lever back on the machine, Alvin looked down to try to wipe some mud off his pants. He gave up on it though after scraping at it with his finger; he was going to have to take his suit to the cleaners anyway. As a pallbearer Alvin never figured he was going to have to help dig Johnny Ray's grave out. But that had been what had happened.

Colter, Johnny Ray's uncle by marriage, who was the lead pallbearer and who at seventy still ran trotlines all year, had been fairly quiet the entire day. They brought the casket out of the hearse and set it on the straps over the grave. The preacher had them all bow their heads in prayer. About that time Colter hollered, "They hadn't finished digging the hole yet!" The funeral director, the one who probably had a little pink worm dick, came scuffling over quickly, to the vaultless grave.

He was taking it all in stride, obviously having given up on making everything come off smoothly and properly. After the church service, as they were about to leave for the grave site in procession, Eddie came up to him and said, "Hey, look, feller, no hard feelings. If I put a bad taste in ye mouth, wash it out with this," and handed him a bottle of Jack Daniel's. The funeral director graciously accepted. Eddie went back and got in the car that was loaded down with four of the pallbearers. He said, "See, I told ya'll he'd take him a drink. That's all he's pissed off about. He's just wantin' him a taste. He probably wants him some pussy, too. Them little soft hands, that formaldyhyde-smelling pompadour he's got, and his little pink worm dick, he probably don't git him much pussy. But I can't help him out there."

The funeral director had come over to Colter. Colter pointed down to the hole, told him it hadn't been finished. The funeral director explained to Colter that graves were only dug four and a half feet these days.

Colter said, "Aw shit, naw! A grave's supposed to be six foot deep. Four and a half foot, shit. What's thangs coming to nowdays? Damn near can't git a pure-D hunnert pur-cent cotton shirt. Got to go uptown, suck somebody's dick to git a decent shirt. Now ye tell me graves ain't six foot no more. Naw, naw. God wants graves to be six foot. Four n half, why, the casket might pop up outta the ground, piss off all the haints hanging around the graveyard."

Without any kind of direction or instruction, while Colter was carrying on, the seven remaining pallbearers picked up the casket and set it over in the grass out of the way. Then they took the lowering device out of the way. Two shovels were over on the other side of the mound of fresh dirt. Colter grabbed one, jumped down in the grave and started digging. He dug until it was finished. Colter, besides being a fisherman, was a damn good carpenter, always with his tape measure clasped on his belt even when he was out running lines. Colter would dig awhile, pull his tape from under his suit jacket, and measure the progress, making sure the grave was going to be exactly six feet deep.

Though Colter ended up doing three quarters of the work, one by one the other pallbearers pitched in.

Alvin's last turn down in the grave, he imagined himself down at the bottom of the Tennessee River digging for mussels, his suit a wet suit. Then his mind had begun to wander. What Colter had said about the casket popping out of the grave made him imagine the Hatchett Cemetery at midnight during a full moon. He imagined Johnny Ray's casket popping out of the ground. Johnny Ray was sitting up in the casket as if it were a dragster. As the casket popped out, the dirt would fall away, and there would be Johnny Ray with wild eyes, screaming a rebel yell. He would have the neck of a bottle of whiskey in one hand. And the other hand would be on the steering wheel of the casket. The casket would fly. Johnny Ray would be hollering and drinking, carefree but expertly, flying the casket, the way he had driven boats and cars, even flew crop dusters. He would land the casket on the river, and it would skim along the channel of the Tennessee River like a hydroplane. Then he would pull back on the steering wheel, flying back up into the air, yelling and drinking.

They finished the hole, brought the casket back over the grave, and the preacher gave a final prayer.

The immediate family waited in the air conditioning of the cars as the pallbearers filled the grave. Alvin thought it was going to take forever. Again Colter worked from start to end. The other pallbearers took turns with the other shovel.

When they finished, Colter patted the mound down with the back of the shovel. Then Colter had said something too simple, too direct to the heart, almost too true. Only the pallbearers had heard it, but as far as Alvin was concerned, it should have been the totality of the service, other than actually getting Johnny Ray's corpse buried.

"He was a good man," Colter said as he dropped the shovel handle and walked away.

Alvin noticed he was bouncing the metal ball between one of the flippers and a bumper. It was bouncing rapidly back and forth almost like one of those paddles and balls on a rubber band. As soon as Alvin took note of what he was doing, it threw him off. The ball shot down straight between the flippers. The machine was making a god-awful noise tallying up the points. Alma was on one side of the machine, cheering, and Cliff was on the other side. Alvin didn't know how long they had been standing there or how long he had been running up the score.

Alma kissed Alvin on the cheek. "Oh, Alvie, that's so good!" She and Cliff stepped back over to their machine and continued playing.

Alma had on a light-colored loose summer-looking dress. It had long sleeves and a high collar. She had on a broad-brimmed hat that was cocked over to one side. She looked as if she were dressed for a summer garden party, in spite of the long sleeves. The dress made her look very feminine, but like almost all her clothes, it hid her figure.

They stood together, Cliff operating the left flipper, Alma the right. She brushed against Cliff with her hip a few times, touched his right arm gently with her left hand several times, then put her left arm around his waist. They stood there pressed against each other lightly.

Alvin imagined how it must have felt to Cliff. He was not jealous but almost envious. Alma never flirted, not that Alvin had seen. She seldom had a boyfriend, didn't date that much for all Alvin knew. Neither did Cliff. In the year or so that Cliff had been living in Alabama, Cliff had not, to Alvin's knowledge, had a love affair going or picked up a girl. Sometimes one of Freddy's girlfriends would have a girlfriend, and Freddy would get Cliff to come along somewhere and escort the other girl. Cliff would dress up and be mannerly for his date. Whether Cliff ever broke down and fucked one of them, Alvin didn't know.

During high school Alma had dated one of her classmates regularly for a couple of years. During college Alma had seriously gone with a guy for two years. As he neared graduation, he planned to go back to Mississippi to live. Alvin thought they would have gotten married, but they didn't. He moved back to Mississippi. Alma had never spoken harshly of him. Alvin figured they got to the point they were going to get married or not get married and had decided on the latter.

Alvin had liked both of these guys. But after that Alma's love life seemed to be fucked up, and she had a tendency to go out with assholes. The last boyfriend he had known was about four years ago. Alma seldom spoke of her love life to Alvin, but with this guy, Alma would call Alvin on the phone about once a week, all in a dilemma. She just couldn't make up her mind. Just as Alvin thought Alma was going to get rid of him, she'd say, "Oh, he's so sweet, Alv. I think I'm in love with him."

Finally, after about five months of this, Alvin met him. Alvin and Freddy drove down to Birmingham and went out to a club with Alma and this Steve. He was several years older than Alma and worked in a brokerage house; his great joy in the world was hitting happy hour every day after work with some of his co-workers. He was "interested in Alma's career," was going to be her agent/manager, knew a lot of entertainment people. He spouted their names off as if Alvin were supposed to know them, but Alvin wouldn't have known the most famous stage producer in the world. Alvin just nodded and told him it was nice he knew all these people.

Alvin found him just a little less repulsive than the funeral director. Alma excused herself to the rest room. Freddy made some statement about a passing girl. Alvin didn't really catch it, but it sounded like something he would say to Eddie concerning women.

After Freddy went bird-dogging the girl, Steve punched his own right fist into his own left open hand, saying, "Yeah, sometimes you got to show a woman who's boss," thinking he was being one of the boys.

That was all Alvin needed. He grabbed Steve by the knot of his tie with his left hand. He hit him in the face with his right fist, more of a jab, not following through or shattering his face bones. Steve swung back at Alvin.

Alvin let go of his tie and caught his fist and squeezed until he heard the guy's knuckles popping. Then he got him down in the booth a little more and jabbed him about ten quick times in the face.

Alvin said to him, "I see why you like beatin' up women. You can't fight a man."

Having struck out with his prospect, Freddy walked back to the booth.

Alvin was getting off the man. Alvin said to Freddy, "He hits women."

Freddy, sitting down, said, "Nah. He's too much of a pussy to hit women. Probably just hits kids and kicks cats. Hell, Alma could beat him up."

Alvin said, "If *she* can't, *I* can."

Alvin straightened up the tie of the man, who was sitting there in terror. Then he pushed his drink back up to him. Alvin told him, "I was just playing. There's plenty more where that came from."

After Alvin came back home, a couple of days later, Alma called him and told him, "I finally ran Steve off. For good this time."

Alvin just said, "Yeah, I doubt old Steve'll be back," wondering how Alma could get so mixed up with a shit-ass like him. He wondered if she had actually liked him, or had just been lonely for *someone*, or had been duped by his "entertainment connection" bullshit.

In the last couple of years, when he was down in Birmingham,

Alvin had met a couple of Alma's male friends on different occasions. Alvin would comment, "Now he's very nice." But both times Alma had said, "Alvin, we're just good friends."

Alvin pulled the lever back and shot the third ball of his game.

He heard Cliff telling Alma, "So I came here to see Freddy, and I liked it. See, I'm a real southerner. I'm living here because I want to be living here."

They both chuckled. Alvin didn't hear the context of what they were talking about. He never thought Cliff was here because he wanted to be here. He had always thought Cliff was here more or less out of process of elimination. As though Beaulah Swamp were the farthest place he could get from anywhere.

Cliff and Alma kept talking back and forth as they played, but it all sounded like a mumble under the dinging of the two pinball machines. Alvin finished his fifth ball. He looked up at his score but had no idea whether it was high or low, knowing only he'd got about three fourths of his total points on that first ball.

He walked back out to the porch and sat down. Alvin gazed at Donna, whose eyes looked as if they weren't seeing. She wasn't screaming or crying, nor did she appear to be about to scream or cry; more as if she had just come off a five-day drunk and had promised God she would never drink again.

She finished her bourbon and water and rattled her ice, then sat the glass down.

Jenny came over and hung on to her and said, "Mama, I wanna go home."

"I do too, baby," Donna answered.

"If Alma will take me back to my car at the church, I can take you to your house now, if you want," Ginger said. "I need to go into town pretty soon."

"I think that would be good," Donna said.

Jenny got Deward, and they went and got in Alma's Volkswagen. Donna kissed Alvin on the mouth and said, "I'll call. Thanks for everything," and went and got in the passenger's seat to Alma's lemon yellow Bug.

Just as Alvin was about to go in and tell Alma that Donna and the kids were ready to leave, Alma came back out hurriedly. She was stepping in place as though she needed to take a piss.

She got Alvin by the arm and said, "Walk me to my car. We have to go now."

On the way to the car he was tempted to ask her why she always stepped in place like that when she had to leave. But he didn't want to hear a bunch of crap about getting f-a-t or bad luck. Instead, he diplomatically asked, "You've lost some weight, haven't you?"

"Oh, Alvin. I love you. You don't think my stomach is pouching out?" Alma asked, standing by the car door. She was pulling her loose dress tight around the stomach of her bony body.

"Naw. That's the skinniest waist I ever seen."

The sun was hitting her wavy salt-and-pepper shoulder-length hair to make it look grayer than it was. She looked as skinny as she ever did. It was as if her body couldn't get much skinnier or she'd need to go to the hospital. It was her face that seemed to show a little more weight loss.

Alma put her arms around Alvin and kissed him on the mouth. "I have to go," she said, and jumped into the car. "I'll call you when I get back to Birmingham."

She cranked the VW and then made a U-turn in Plato Jones Street.

Alvin stood and watched the car speeding off down the narrow road. Alma's thin arm stuck out the window and waved between gear shifts.

When he couldn't hear the Bug anymore, he went back to the porch of the café.

About two thirds of the people at the funeral had been from Beaulah Town, the black community where they were now, which was near Beaulah Swamp, the area where Johnny Ray, Alvin, Freddy, Tony, and Bart had been raised. The rest of the people at the funeral had mostly been divers' families, swampers, and close friends to Johnny Ray and Donna.

Out of respect for Donna, no one had come around the tables

for the last hour. Out of respect for the Twilight Café, Alvin and Freddy moved over to the little table where Jenny and Deward had been sitting so somebody else could sit around the big table.

But nobody came around. The day was kind of slow and deserted. To Alvin, it had an empty sort of feeling to it.

But then a late-model Chevrolet pulled up and parked across the road from the Twilight Café, in front of the pool hall. It had a strangeness to it, as though it didn't belong to whoever was driving it. Not as if it were a stolen, though.

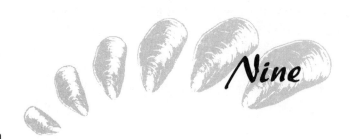

Nine

C OP CAR,'' Alvin said to Freddy.

"Or rented. Look like one of them rented cars."

Alvin didn't know anything about rented cars, but Freddy had lived for three months in California with Cliff while they were getting out of the Army, after being over in Vietnam. He figured Freddy knew what a rented car looked like.

Alvin said, "I bet it's a cop from the Alcoholic Beverage Control Board. Wantin' to throw somebody's ass in jail."

A man got out of the car. He was over six feet tall and weighed a slim 230 with just a little fat around the midsection. He had on dress pants and a knit shirt. His hair was neatly kept. He looked over at the Twilight and then walked over.

Nobody ate or drank at the Twilight except folks from Beaulah Town or swampers. But by the time the man walked up on the porch and sat at a small table on the other side, he wasn't interesting to Freddy and Alvin anymore.

Ida walked out with a couple more drinks for Freddy and Alvin. Freddy asked, "Is Cliff all right in there?"

Ida got their empty glasses and said, "He in dere. I doan know if he all right. Playin' ne pinball. But he ain't hittin' ne flippahs. He shootin' ne balls, but he won hit de flippahs. I tol' him, 'Shit, hit de flippahs.' He sade he wanna let de flippahs be."

Ida walked over to the man and then went inside. She came back out with a six-ounce bottle of Coca-Cola. It had a napkin wrapped around the base; ice and sweat were dripping down the side.

The man nodded at Ida as she set it down.

Ida walked back over to Alvin and looked him in the eye.

She said, "You sistah. She ain' eatin' agin, is she? You done got her out ah de horsepital wunst. She doan start eatin' she gone dry up, blow away. I doan know whut make her wants to git down pore to skin and bone. She the skinniest little thing. I tol' her that when she in ne back while ago with Cliff. I tol' her, 'Alma honey, you show is de skinniest little dang I evah seen.' She lit up, said, 'Thank ya, Ida.'"

Ida walked back in.

Cliff walked back out. He had a fresh glass of JW Black and ice. He leaned between Alvin and Freddy and pulled the string to the fan above the table. The fan slowly started turning and swaying. A coat hanger was holding it to the ceiling.

Alvin said, "Shit, is that gone fall?"

Freddy looked up at the fan and then back down and said, "Naw, not today."

Alvin was looking at the man. The man was catching glances at Cliff.

Cliff threw his leg over the back of a chair and, straddling it, sat down. "You got to live right to do right."

That didn't make any sense to Alvin, but it made sense for Cliff to say something like that.

Alvin was keeping an eye on the man. The man finished the Coca-Cola, put down some change by the empty bottle, caught another glance at Cliff, and left.

Soon Cliff discovered that he was out of Johnnie Walker Black.

Singing, "If I die on the Russian front, bury my dick in a Russian cunt," he got up and went back into the café to get him some more whiskey and pull the lever on the pinball machine.

Alvin looked Freddy in the eye. They had known each other all their lives, but in the last four years they had gotten to be really good buddies and friends. Freddy was just a few years older than Alvin.

Freddy said, "You main man done gone on," and then looked back down at the drink between his cupped hands.

"Yeah."

"Life's crazy. Death's crazier."

"That's true."

Freddy perked up a little. He said, "Man, what did you think about mussel diving at the beginning? Did you really believe it?"

Alvin answered instantly, "I didn't even place in the top ten in the Mr. East Coast. That national trainer said, 'Look, Alvin, you work out hard for a couple of years, place in the top five at Mr. Gulf Coast, you'll get an invitation to the Mr. America, and you might just take the Most Muscular trophy.' Then he told me about my hip structure. Fuck a Most Muscular trophy. I couldn't help but hate the man. He didn't care. It didn't bother him at all that my hip structure didn't make Mr. America hips. Just so there was a Mr. America is all he seemed to care about—a Mr. America that he could take credit for.

"I come back to Mud Creek all depressed. My granddaddy been dead for a couple of years. I found out Alma was in the Birmingham hospital laid up, dying. I went down there. The doctor told me she had something called anorexia nervosa. I said, 'Hell, she starving herself to death.' I got her out of the hospital. Then you moved in with me. All I knowed to do to make a living was trotlines.

"It was tough making ends meet then. I tore the foot off my outboard on a stump. The fuse box on the house kept blowing fuses. Needed rewiring. That's when Johnny Ray put five hundred dollars in my hand and told me pay him back when I could. I know he went uptown and took out every penny of his and Donna's savings account. She told me later, after it didn't matter none.

"Then right after that Johnny Ray started selling wildcat to those recording folks. Between that and running trotlines on the side, thangs eased up. One day I was running the lines. The surface of the water give way, and that's when I grappled that big cat into the boat. I took that channel catfish to the Twilight Café to weigh. Seventy-three pounds, the same weight Alma was when I took her out of the hospital. I knew it was a sign.

"Next day, when Johnny Ray come to me, he had found out all about the musseling." Alvin started smiling. "We got set up. Johnny Ray showed me how to do it. We only dove four hours that day. When I sold my shells, I got paid seventy-three dollars. Another sign. I couldn't believe it. It was legal. Heavy-duty! After that we been making a hundred to two hundred fifty dollars ever day we decide we gone go out diving.

"It was a dream, Freddy. I never expected on making any money more than just getting by. Unless I won Mr. America and cashed in on it."

Alvin took another drink of whiskey. He had just finished answering Freddy's question about what he thought when musseling began.

Usually he and Freddy just bullshitted, but once every couple of weeks they would get down with some confessing and gut spilling.

Alvin continued. "That was the first dream. The second one was about six months later. The second dream was Ginger Carpenter."

Freddy wiped some whiskey off his lips and said, "Yeuh. A firm-feeling woman do mess up you mind."

Alvin started in on the story he'd told Freddy at least five times: "I saw one of those highfalutin eighteen-foot inboard-outboard walk-through windshield runabouts drifting in the mouth of Elk River. I pull up, see if I could help 'em out. They had the engine cover flipped up. And there stood Ginger. I felt like thunder was shaking me and lightning was striking me. She look like what I wanted a girlfriend to look like ever since I was twelve and a half years old.

"I never seen this girl in my life, and first thang that comes outta her mouth is: 'You're Alvin Fuqua, aren't you?' I damn near dropped a load in my wet suit pants, right then and there."

Alvin laughed.

He said, "Instead of being real cool, you know, and saying, 'Yes, and your name?' Instead of saying something like that, I real quick say back, 'How'd you know?' She knew who I was because of me being in the papers on 'count of Mr. Alabama awhile back."

Alvin paused. They sat there drinking their whiskey slowly.

Then Alvin said, "Two big dreams come into my life. One right after another, but it seems they two dreams I'm gone have to wake up from. It seems like I'm having to wake up right now. Johnny Ray's dead. How much longer is musselin' going to hold out? What then? What about Ginger? I don't even know what going on with her."

"So what is it?" Freddy asked, with a half-full mouth of whiskey he was letting age in his mouth for several more seconds before he swallowed it.

"Seem like Mr. America is trying to look me in the face."

"If that the case, ain't but one thang to do, I reckon," Freddy said.

Cliff walked back out and sat down. His eyes looked wild, as though they had fire coming out of them. He looked at Alvin and said, "Your sister asked me if I saw many f-a-t people when I lived in New York. Why won't she say the word 'fat'?"

"She thinks it's bad luck," Alvin replied.

Cliff didn't react a bit as if that were strange. He just said, "We all should drive down one night and see her act again."

Alvin and Freddy just nodded in reply.

Ten

WHEN CLIFF CAME from South America, he had a hyacinth macaw with him named Santiago. When Freddy and Cliff moved into their own cabin, Cliff ended up leaving Santiago with Alvin.

There were some chickens that lived on a farm about a mile back up the old dirt road from Alvin's, and Santiago got into the habit of flying up there and fucking the hens. One day, though, Santiago was missing. Alvin searched for him. The farmer said he had been there that day, fucked his hens, then flew back toward Alvin's.

Alvin figured some shit-ass had shot him, and that was the end of Santiago. He lived alone until a dog took up there. He was more or less basset hound-shaped. One of his ears was about a third larger than the other. One of his little, short, stubby front legs bowed out. He had different sized eyes. Alvin named him Dr. Dick.

Even though Alvin lived there alone with Dr. Dick, there often was one of the guys putting up there, usually Freddy. Dr. Dick and Freddy got along just fine. Dick didn't like pot, and Freddy didn't like Liv-A-Snaps, so neither one got into the other's stash.

Right now Freddy was sitting on the porch, leaning back against one of the two-by-four posts that held the roof up. Dr. Dick was lying down at the edge of the porch.

Freddy threw the ball over Dr. Dick's head. Dr. Dick raised his head up off his paws, looked at the ball, and considered it. Then he got up, jumped off the front porch, and went over. After he sniffed the ball, he came back to the porch and went to sleep.

Freddy said, "Goddamn. I spend twenty-two cents on a fucking rubber ball for him, and he won't even pick it up. Hell, if he can't eat it or fuck it, he won't have nothing to do with it."

"Just like somebody else I know," Alvin remarked, leaning back against the wall in a ladder-back chair. He was slowly nursing some vodka.

Freddy pulled a bag of dope out of the pocket of his cutoff jeans. He asked, "You go by Donna's after you sold you shells today?"

"Yeah."

"How she doing?"

Alvin shook his head and said, "Hell, OK. But sometimes she seems to be doing all right. Then sometimes she don't."

"I guess it'll take time," Freddy said, trying to be comforting. "Me. All time does for me is fuck me up more. How was the kids?"

"Ah right. I reckon. They just sit around and watch TV. They don't seem to want to do much of anything. Not like them."

Freddy sighed. "I don't reckon. If I's a youngun, my daddy just died, I wouldn't be myself neither. You just wouldn't expect to lose you daddy that young. A lot of things you don't expect to lose that young. From eighteen to, say, twenty-two is four years, but nobody ever let you know it's four years, and it gits used up. When you seventeen, you think till you in the middle of you twenties is the rest of ye life. You think you reflexes get put on hold or something."

Since he was beginning to talk about reflexes, Alvin Lee thought Freddy would go get the ball bat and start hitting stuff because he was over thirty and never had made it to the major leagues.

Alvin was looking at Freddy. He thought how Freddy and he would have had a similar build, had Alvin never lifted weights. They were the same height, same length arms, same shoe size, same bone size, same skin tone. Thick chest, muscular arms, a natural V shape, slim waist, a no-ass, and slender legs.

Freddy had a wide smile, white, straight teeth that people in big cities paid thousands of dollars trying to get. He had windblown brown hair. Sometimes it looked dark, and sometimes it almost looked blond. When he smiled, crow's-feet formed from his eyes, but it didn't make him look any older than he was.

For a mussel diver, Freddy looked all right. If he had been a major-league baseball player and made a hundred thousand dollars a year, he would have been called handsome.

Alvin was taken out of his contemplation of Freddy's looks by Freddy's voice.

Freddy said, "How old was Johnny Ray anyhow? Forty-one?"

"Forty-two."

"Donna's about thirty-eight, idn't she? She don't look it, though. I told Cliff she was thirty-eight, and he couldn't believe it."

"Yeah. She's thirty-eight. Where in the hell's Cliff anyhow? I hadn't seen him out diving in three days."

"He had him some sinus. Said when he got three feet under the water, it felt like somebody was under his cheekbones trying to cut their way out with a bowie knife."

"That might tend to keep ye out of the water for a few days," Alvin observed.

"Yeah, it will," Freddy agreed. He strangled on a toke and did a lung cancer cough.

"Roll another one, goddammit," Alvin said, and then remembered how Johnny Ray had put down Freddy's dope smoking the night he had died. Alvin didn't know what he could do to keep Freddy from doing dope. Johnny Ray had said he was going to tie him up and give him an ass whipping. Alvin didn't think he could go that far. It wouldn't do any good anyway.

"Maybe she'll marry up some nice rich fucker. It'd be good for her . . . and the kids, too, prob'ly."

"Probably," Alvin said absently.

He knew Freddy was talking about Donna now. Alvin wasn't paying much attention to the conversation anymore. He was staring at nothing, thinking about Donna, and wondering what he ought to do. He didn't know how to help anybody. He didn't keep his best friend from dying from a little bubble. And now he didn't know any way to keep this friend from burning out his brain, to get him back to training so he could try out at some baseball camp.

Freddy asked, "Going over to Ginger's tonight?"

He knew the answer because Alvin had taken a shower and put on a clean pair of jeans and his best boots. But he didn't have a shirt on. He always waited right before he left to put his shirt on so he wouldn't get it sweaty.

"Yeah," Alvin admitted. He just stared out into the swamp.

Freddy said, "Gail has a shift break startin' tonight. I'm gone go over there and fuck her good for three days. You need to git *you* more cooter."

Freddy claimed a good fucking would cure about anything. Freddy would tell Alvin he just sensed he wasn't throwing it to Ginger enough.

Fucking usually got people into trouble, but it seemed as if fucking kept Freddy *out* of trouble. Freddy's most notable incident of this was his Atlanta trip. He had been reading up on something called aquaculture. He looked into growing some pond-fed catfish commercially, so made arrangements to meet with a representative of a company that sold aeration equipment in Atlanta.

Alvin took Freddy over to Huntsville and dropped him off at the airport. While Freddy was waiting for his flight, he struck up a conversation with a girl in the lounge and ended up at her apartment to commence on a close forty-eight-hour physical relationship.

Near nightfall Freddy called Alvin to inform him fate had postponed his business endeavors. Freddy was expecting Alvin to give him a ration of shit, but Alvin was dumbfounded.

Freddy said, "What's the manner, Alv? Huh? Speak up, man."

Alvin said slowly, "Man, they just broke into *The Andy Griffith*

Show. One with Barney in it. Your flight just crashed outside Atlanta, killed everbody on it."

The next day, when Alvin had gone over to Huntsville to pick Freddy up, all the way home Freddy had said, "See what I been trying to tell ye? Pussy's good for ye. Keep ye out of trouble. It just saved my life."

Sitting there on the porch, Alvin said, "Speaking of cooter. Why don't you start datin' that Becky girl? She is a little doll. Fucking Gail idn't gittin' you anywhere. You need you a girlfriend. You talk about me. If you don't call Becky up, go out with her, you crazy."

"Hell, Alvin. You worse than Eddie. Ya'll think we all eighteen years old in high school or some shit. That age don't have nothing to do with nothing. Shit, that girl isn't eighteen years old yet. I'm thirty-fucking-three. I'm twict her age. We not teenagers, Alv! You think I'd be sittin' on this porch if I's a teenager?"

Freddy's statement about Alvin thinking they were eighteen years old couldn't have been further from the truth. But Alvin didn't contest it.

Alvin just said, "She's a nice girl."

Freddy changed the subject quickly. "It was good Johnny Ray got that insurance before he died. Plus the stash I reckon he musta have had, being as much money as he made musselin'. I don't reckon she'll have to worry for a while."

"I don't guess," Alvin said.

"Unless inflation gets it all."

"Inflation? *Inflation*! The longer you play it, the more things cost," Alvin said in an advertisement voice.

Freddy announced, "That exciting new game every one is playing!"

"It'll outsell Monopoly," Alvin claimed. "You figured any more on it?"

"Inflation. Buy it today before it goes up," Freddy replied.

"Hey, that's good." He leaned back and stared into the swamp.

Then, reaching down to get the bottle by his chair, he poured some more vodka into his glass.

Soon he stood up and leaned against a two-by-four stud.

Freddy looked up at Alvin's bronzed upper body. He looked a lot different from even just a month ago. After he quit competing, he had quit his heavy intensive training. But when Ginger took an interest in him, he started doing a short but intense workout three times a week. Alvin had lost some weight around the waist, and when he breathed, Freddy noticed the ripples of his abdominals.

"You know, Alv, you looking pretty good."

"Yeah?"

The statement pulled Alvin's attention from the nothingness of the swamp.

"You ought to enter some contests."

Alvin took a slug of his drink. He smiled. "That's what Ginger told me." He looked at Freddy as if he were counting things in his head and said, "I might spend some more time training and enter one in another year or two. Just for grins. Start spending some time posing."

"Shit! Year or two. You oughtta enter now. Hell, you could win some trophies. You hadn't got a ounce of fat on you."

"Thanks."

"What you weigh now?"

"One ninety-eight," Alvin said. He had just weighed himself this morning on the scales in the back room of the Twilight Café. Then he had come home and measured himself. A thirty-three-inch waist, forty-nine-inch chest, and eighteen-inch arms cold, not even pumped up from exercise.

Alvin wondered if it was just coincidence that Freddy had also been thinking about his competing again. He sat back down in the chair, careful not to knock over the vodka bottle sitting down by a back chair leg. Looking out to the swamp, he saw himself back up on the stage again, this time with his muscles more highly defined, in total control of every sinew.

Freddy pulled a roach clip out of his pocket, clamped it on the joint, and took a couple of more tokes. "Yeah. That's what you oughtta do." He took his lighter, set the roach on fire, and sucked the smoke into his mouth. "And you need to start getting more cooter."

Alvin thought about the hip structure stuff some. "I should have took that offer in high school. That scholarship offer, from that junior college in Florida, to throw the discus." He was thinking had he pursued that course, he could have made it to the Olympics. A gold medal would have served him as well as a Mr. America title for getting him on Johnny Carson.

Freddy hollered, "Aw hell, Alvin! It would have just interfered with what it was you was going for. You went down there, you'da got a college education and quit training for Mr. America. If you'd got a college education, you'd be off somewheres selling insurance or something. Remember Rusty Williams? He went off on a baseball grant-in-aid, and you know what he's doin' now? Teaching junior high school in south Alabama. Goddamn! Don't you go to thinkin' if I done this, if I done that. Don't be poking at no dead possums."

Alvin thought how Boots Jacobs had just gone to some tryouts somewhere and got on a professional farm league team. But he didn't dare say that right now. Freddy might come undone.

He poured the rest of the vodka from the quart bottle, which he had drunk about the last fourth of at this sitting, into his glass and killed it.

Alvin leaned to the side, pulled his Seiko diver's watch out of his pocket, and put it on his wrist, then got up. He took his clean, ironed shirt from where he had it lying on the porch railing and put it on.

"See ya," he said to Freddy as he stepped off the porch.

"Take it easy. See ya in a couple of days."

Alvin crawled into his five-year-old Datsun 240Z, which he had bought last year. He whipped around in the yard and drove down the narrow road-causeway that went through the swamp to the paved county road.

It seemed as if the vodka had suddenly hit his head and brought a numbness over his body.

He reached under his legs on the floorboard. There were a couple fingers of wildcat in a Red Dagger wine bottle up against the seat.

Not wanting to take both hands off the wheel, he put the cap in his teeth and twisted the bottle open with his other hand. He spit the cap out, killed the wildcat, and then threw the bottle out the window, off into the water between some locust trees.

Alvin howled.

Then he cackled, "Ginger, I'll be there in a New York minute."

Eleven

ALVIN SAT on the patio deck of Ginger's house and looked out onto the Elk River. With his ankles crossed and propped up on the table, he gazed at the high bluffs on the other side of the smooth river, a tributary of the Tennessee River, and took the last swallow out of the glass of gin and tonic that Ginger had fixed for him.

He got up and went through the double French doors to the kitchen.

Ginger said, "This was the first day you've dove in a while, isn't it?"

Alvin knew she had said that just to be saying something. It seemed as if sometimes Ginger couldn't let silence alone.

He said, "Yeah." He pulled the gin over to him and started pouring some more. "I haven't been out in a few days."

"Have a good day?"

"All right. Nothing to jack off to about."

Ginger now stood sideways to him, and he enjoyed looking at her. Alvin thought how Ginger was the best-looking woman in the world. In the same sense as trying to say if Charlie Daniels, Doug Kershaw, or Jean-Luc Ponty was the best fiddle player in the world.

Alvin poured a splash of tonic water on top of his gin.

Ginger said, "If you drink a couple more of those, you're going to get drunk."

"Ain't no gittin' to it."

"Well, don't get too drunk because I've got to talk to you about something tonight."

"Heavy-duty. Just talk away anytime you get the notion."

"Let's go outside and eat. This is the most wonderful part of the day. I love the sunset."

They took two paper plates of sandwiches and potato chips out onto the patio. Ginger kept talking about the sunset, and Alvin was fading away from her.

The barbecue sandwich was all right, but he didn't have that much interest in eating right now. He had started drinking, and he wanted to do a good job of it.

"Are you getting back into the routine of things now?" Ginger asked sweetly before she took a new bite of the sandwich.

Alvin wished she would shut the fuck up. Everything she asked sounded stupid. She was sitting there looking like a goddess but making about as much sense as tits on a bullfrog.

Alvin said, "Yeah. Everything's goin' all right."

"That's good. Ahhh! Look at that view! This is my most favorite view in the world. I love to just sit out here this time of day. I feel so lucky to live here."

The view Alvin was looking at wasn't the sunset. It was Ginger.

He was looking at her tan face and her Cherokee cheekbones and her long brown hair. Ginger took her index finger and ran it along the hairline of her forehead and then flicked her hair out of her face. Alvin liked to see her do that.

"Oh, Alvin. I was thinking about you today. About the time we first met in the mouth of the Elk. I remember you stepping over into my boat. You were wearing that wet suit. I couldn't keep my eyes off you. I'd never met anyone like you."

She smiled at Alvin and took another bite. When she got it all in her mouth, she licked the mayonnaise off her lips. Alvin was thinking of the first time something else had happened.

Ginger kept talking after she had swallowed that mouthful. "Then I remember the day you walked into my shop, when you invited me to coffee. And all the customers and employees stopped to look at you. It was so strange. Just that minute before you had come in I was thinking about you."

"Heavy-duty," Alvin said.

It had been the same thing he had said that day when she told him she'd love to go have coffee with him.

He started to tell her to stop poking a dead possum, but he said, "Do you want something to drink? I'm going inside."

"Oh, stay out here, Alvin. It's so beautiful. September is so beautiful on the Elk."

"It's September already?" Alvin asked, confused.

"Yes."

"Oh. I'll be back."

"OK. But don't drink so fast, Alvin. Pace yourself."

Alvin started to say, "Pace yourself? Fuck pacing. I got two speeds, and if you don't like this one, I know goddamn good and well you won't like the other one. Where the fuck did ye come up with that pacing shit? Anything worth doing is worth doing fast no matter how long it takes. Stupid cunt."

He started to say all that, but he didn't, and decided to give her a break. He just said, "I'll be right back."

Alvin went inside and poured himself a good shot of gin and killed it. Then he fixed a gin and tonic. He went to the bathroom, peed, and then went back outside with his drink.

Ginger looked at him and smiled. She smacked her lips out at him.

For the first time ever Alvin felt there was something about Ginger that made him not want her. All the times there was something that had gotten on his nerves about Ginger, there was always something that made it all more than worthwhile.

But all of a sudden all the worthwhile things, whatever they were or had been, vanished. For the first time Alvin felt uncomfortable around her.

He sat down and said, "Yeah, it's a nice view all right."

A dog from up at the next house around the slough came up, and Alvin started feeding him his sandwich.

Ginger said, "You're not saying very much."

"I don't have much to say lately," Alvin said, then added, lying, "I haven't been diving in a few days, and it just made me tired today."

She asked, "Tired from *not* diving?"

"You know, like exercise. If you haven't worked out in a few days, that first workout is rough on you. And I think my ear canals are swelled a little."

"There's some alcohol in there."

"Thanks. But that's all right. I put some peroxide in my ears after I took a shower."

"Saving all the alcohol for the inside, huh?" Ginger said, trying to make a joke.

After ten minutes of silence, dark started setting in. They came back in. Alvin fixed them both a drink. They sat on the sectional furniture that was in front of the empty fireplace.

Alvin started kissing on her neck.

Ginger pulled her head away from him and said, "Don't, Alvin. We've got to talk."

She put her drink on the coffee table in front of them, then took Alvin's drink out of his hand and set it beside hers.

As soon as she did that, Alvin leaned on top of her. Though she was under him now, Ginger totally disregarded his maneuver.

"I've been seeing this other guy. Eric," she said.

That wasn't news to Alvin. Ginger had never pretended she was not seeing someone else. Alvin pulled the tail of Ginger's blouse out of her pants.

Alvin knew anything else Ginger had to say didn't matter. As far as he was concerned, everything had already been said. Now he knew it was some pipsqueak named Eric, and he probably lived in

Muscle Shoals, and it wouldn't surprise him if he sold insurance or was a doctor.

But none of that mattered. That was just obvious. Girls like Ginger limited themselves to one Alvin Lee Fuqua a lifetime. Alvin knew girls like Ginger didn't quit seeing Alvin Lee Fuquas for some other Alvin Lee Fuqua. You quit seeing an Alvin Lee Fuqua for an Eric. Alvin didn't need to ponder that any.

Ginger took his head and pushed it back so that he would have to look at her.

"Listen, Alvin," she said, "we've got to talk. I can't be lovers with you. I started seeing Eric long before I did you, and it's just come to a point where I've got to give us, Eric and me, a chance for our relationship to work out. If it is going to work out. That doesn't mean I love Eric more than you, Alvin. Maybe in different ways. But I've just got to give our relationship a chance."

Alvin forgot about Ginger for a moment and thought how he had once figured he was going to be Mr. America and be on talk shows, so he started studying etiquette. Alma would act like his date or the waiter and make him go over and over the situation until he got it right.

"Just the house red," Alvin mumbled. "We're just trying to give our relationship a chance. If we ever decide to really make it work, I'll git the good shit."

He moved his hands along Ginger's sides under her blouse.

Alvin thought: Lover? Relationship? What you talking about is fucking. That's why I got drunk, so I wouldn't have to talk to Ginger sweet and civilized about fucking, sport fucking, and fucking for keeps.

Ginger said, "Talk to me, Alvin. Goddammit."

But Alvin didn't talk to her.

Alvin moved his hands up to her breasts.

Ginger pushed lightly on the crooks of his arms.

She said, "Alvin, we can still lunch together. We can still see each other. I just can't be your lover right now."

Alvin said, "You got a nice set of tits."

He pulled his hands out from under her blouse. "Don't ever let nobody make you thank you ain't got a nice set of tits, Ginger. Might take you out the graveyard. Them tits make some them men dig theyselves out of they grave."

Ginger pushed more on Alvin's arms, and he slid on down her. He started to undo her pants; but she shifted, and it caused Alvin to roll off onto the floor. Ginger tugged at him, but he stiffened to resist her.

Ginger said, "Alvin, get up."

"Uh-uh."

"Alvin, get up and go upstairs and sleep."

"Aw, eat shit, Ginger."

"Get up and at least lay on the sofa," Ginger said.

She was now standing over him.

Alvin said, "Go out to the Hatchett Point Cemetery, and show you tits and see if it raises Johnny Ray up."

"Alvin, you're so drunk you don't even know where you are."

Alvin looked up at Ginger. He suddenly lost the stiff resistance in his body.

He felt as if he were on Mud Creek, the Tennessee, and the Elk River all at the same time.

"I know exactly where I am. For the first time I know exactly where I am."

"Where's that, Alvin?"

"Up shit creek."

Twelve

ALVIN WOKE UP and looked at his watch. It was about a quarter to midnight. Moonlight was coming through the huge paned windows that lined the front of the house on both sides of the fireplace. He stared at the beams of the ceiling and the railing of the upstairs hallway.

Then he sat up, looked around the room some more and then back at his watch. He felt like he had been sleeping for days, but he knew it couldn't have been two hours at the most. He was sober, but he felt strange. He felt a lot had happened in a short time although everything seemed to be moving slowly.

He walked to the double doors and looked out at the Elk. There seemed to be a fog settled around the banks. He walked back into the kitchen and splashed his face off in the sink, then got a glass of water and sat at the kitchen bar on a stool. There was a notepad sitting over to the side, and it reminded him he should leave something for Ginger so she wouldn't think he was mad at her. He pulled the notepad over and positioned it in a splotch of light.

Dear Ginger,

Thanks for supper. I woke up and felt like getting on back home. Even though I laid heavy on the gin I remember every-thing you told me. I think you are all right and want you to go the way that makes you happy.

Love,
Alvin

Reading it over, he couldn't tell exactly how it would sound to her. He wanted it to sound straightforward and not contain something for her to read between the lines. At first he thought it sounded a little too formal, but he decided he wouldn't sit there figuring on it, so he tore it off the pad, laid it on the middle of the bar, and sat a spoon on it so Ginger would find it in the morning.

The corner of his eye caught his watch. It had been only five minutes since he woke up, but he felt he had spent half an hour just writing the note. He needed to get out of there and get to bed at his house as fast as he could.

Alvin left silently and got in his car. He started it and drove up the steep gravel road that was Ginger's driveway. Then it leveled out, and he sped away.

He came to the gravel county road, where there was a clearing in the woods.

Everything got lighter, it seemed. He stuck his head out of the window and looked up. There was a full moon, and clouds traveled across it and obscured it.

Alvin accelerated and drove down into a hollow faster than he normally would. When he bottomed out and was coming back up, he kept it floorboarded. Soon he had to downshift. It was so steep that Alvin felt the car might flip back on him. When he topped the hill, he gained speed.

A rabbit crossed in front of him. Alvin braked. The car skidded on the gravel. Just as he was about to sideswipe a barbed-wire fence at the shoulder, he straightened the car out and regained control. A couple of rocks hit the underside of the car so sharply that he thought they were going to come through the floor pan.

At the highway he took a left. There were no other cars on the wide four lanes. A double yellow line separated the westbound lanes from the east, where Alvin was headed.

The road looked purple. And it felt as if it were cushioned.

Suddenly he felt uneasy, bordering on fear. He was scared he would see a figure up ahead, beside the road. As he got closer, he'd see it was a hitchhiker. He then couldn't help thinking that when he pulled even with the figure, it would look directly at him and it would be Johnny Ray.

Alvin sped around a curve and headed into about a mile-long straightaway. The speedometer read ninety-five. But he still felt as if he were moving slow as molasses.

He was sure there was going to be a figure along the road somewhere. Now he feared that when the figure looked at him, it would be himself.

He raced down into a hollow, across a bridge, and then up a hill. He slowed, but his tires still squealed as he took a right onto a narrow paved road. This was the road that would take him the ten miles to his driveway.

Here it was a little hilly, and there was an overgrowth of grass and trees on both shoulders. If a car came in the other direction, he would have to pull to the shoulder, and his car would hit the tall Johnson grass that lay over into the road.

Soon the road was flat but still winding. There was always the danger of a cow in the road. Alvin kept an eye out but kept going about eighty.

He wasn't so much scared he would run into a cow as that there would be one in the road which would force him to stop. Then the figure would approach the car.

Alvin Lee Fuqua didn't feel safe at all.

He wished he could sit down and have a talk with Johnny Ray, his granddaddy, his daddy, and his mother and try to make sense of things. Driving along, he felt they were trying to talk to him, but he just couldn't hear what they were saying.

Alvin felt as if he were supposed to be doing something he wasn't doing.

He was in the marshland now. Not three miles from his house. The road was raised, and there was swamp on both sides of it. Alvin was going seventy, though it seemed to be taking hours to get home. He slowed to make a curve and saw a little white figure shining along the roadside in the distance. At first he thought it was a possum, but then Alvin realized: Dr. Dick!

He slowed down and then stopped beside the dog. Leaning over, he opened the door and pushed it wide.

As he did, the fear came back on him and he was scared to look. He wondered if it was really Dr. Dick or if the figure of himself would be standing there. Or Johnny Ray.

It seemed as if this night was going to last forever. It seemed already like days since he had woken up on the floor at Ginger's. He wondered why this night was so strange.

When the door opened, Alvin looked down at Dr. Dick, sitting on his haunches. He stared at Alvin through his different-sized eyes.

Alvin said, "Ark! Hey ya, Dr. Dick! What you doing out here?"

Dick jumped up into the passenger seat. Alvin leaned over, closed the door, and stepped on the accelerator. He patted Dr. Dick while he drove, wondering about him. Dr. Dick had shown up soon after his grandfather had died. Alvin wondered if he had sent him. He wondered if Dr. Dick knew about it.

After a short distance he took a right and drove down the narrow dirt causeway back into the swamp. When he got to his yard, he parked the car and got out.

Dick jumped over into the driver's seat, off onto the ground, and ran up to the front door to wait for Alvin.

Freddy wasn't there. Alvin wished he were, especially tonight. Even though he often had a woman with him when he stayed there, and they kept to themselves in the big bedroom, Alvin felt good knowing Freddy was there.

And Alvin liked Dr. Dick being there.

The house glowed softly in the moonlight. He made a double biceps pose and said, "This old shack here is a *real* house."

He walked up on the front porch and opened the screen door. Freddy had padlocked the front door. Alvin fumbled around in his pocket and found the key. He unlocked the padlock, took it off, and hung it there, then pushed the door open.

Dr. Dick ran in.

Alvin turned the living room light on. He stepped on in, the screen door slamming shut.

Dr. Dick was in the kitchen, sniffing around on the floor. He trotted back into the living room and headed for the La-Z-Boy recliner.

But Dr. Dick stopped abruptly short and sat on his haunches, staring into the chair. Then he looked at Alvin and stared back at the chair.

Alvin felt pressure all around him. "Oh shit," he whispered, wondering what, or who, was sitting in the chair. He thought about running out of the house but knew very well that whatever was sitting there could be sitting in the passenger seat of his Datsun, too.

Alvin took two large quick steps over toward Dr. Dick, so "it" wouldn't have a chance to whirl around on him.

He looked in the chair and froze.

Cliff opened his eyes and gazed at Alvin glassily.

Alvin stared at Cliff. Cliff looked dangerous. Sometimes he could look almost fragile and feminine. Often, timid and peaceful. Sometimes his straight black hair would sweep across his forehead in such a way as to point down to one side of his cheekbone and jawline. Several times it had caught Alvin's eye. It reminded him of the faces of female models in the high-fashion magazines that lay on the coffee table at Ginger's house. It didn't match Cliff's having been in a war or having recently returned from the jungles of South America.

Cliff mumbled, "Hey, man, what's shaking?" Then he pulled a bottle from between his legs and took a long pull of JW Black.

Alvin blurted out, "I'm going to be Mr. America. Right this

minute I'm going into intensive training. I don't care if it kills me. I'm gone train so intense I don't care how long it takes me. I'm tired of putting up with all this shit."

He stood there stunned, partly from the sight of Cliff, but mostly from what he himself had just said. He hadn't planned on saying it, but he knew it was the dead truth.

"I hear you, man. I'm not going to wish you luck. I saw all those fuckers wishing each other luck. But I *knew* I was coming back. The only thing was, I didn't know I didn't have a home to come back to. So in the end, in the final analysis, the joke was on me."

Cliff took another pull. Alvin stood there gazing at him, waiting for him to continue after he set the bottle back between his legs, but he didn't say anything.

"There ain't no free tickets to paradise," commented Alvin.

"And I ain't no goddamn wizard," Cliff added to finish out one of Johnny Ray's seldom-said quotes.

Then Cliff sighed, and it looked to Alvin that some of the harshness and dangerousness dissipated from him. Cliff said, "I belong here."

Alvin didn't know exactly what Cliff meant. If he had said it a couple of minutes earlier, before his sigh he might have meant, "I belong sitting in this chair this minute." Had he been a little more gone, a little drunker, he might have meant, "I belong on this planet, I belong in this civilization," something very cosmic.

After pondering this a moment, Alvin figured he meant that he belonged on the Tennessee River with Freddy and everybody.

But since Cliff never made any statements like this, Alvin asked, "What do you mean?"

"I was pulled here, man. I was drifting down the Napo River, and man, I started getting the thought I need to go find Freddy. Where he is, is where I'm supposed to be. I belong here. When I got back into a town, I wrote him a letter."

All Alvin replied was: "Yeah."

Alvin walked into the kitchen, got a Liv-A-Snap, and tossed it to Dr. Dick. Then he continued on back to the bathroom. "I just take me a pee in Purple Commode."

Johnny Ray had come over just after Alvin had redone his bathroom. He returned from the bathroom to say, "That's the first time I ever shit in a purple commode. I mean that thang is purple, not no damn near purple." From then after it was Purple Commode.

After they had begun musseling, a lot of Alvin's buddies started hanging out at his house more often because with their new incomes, they didn't have to work as many hours. Alvin's house almost became their pivot point, other than the shell place and the Twilight Café.

All his buddies were invited to come over at any time whether he was there or not. Under the far end of the porch was a key to the padlock, on a nail. The back bedroom window was also unsecured. Sometimes Alvin wondered why he ever bothered to lock up when he left. No one had ever attempted to break, or had broken, into his house. If someone had wanted to break in, he could have just chopped the door down with an ax, for there were no close neighbors in sight.

Sometimes Alvin would come home to find Johnny Ray in the living room reading a magazine. Freddy and Eddie might be in the kitchen playing dominoes. But everything quiet. Johnny Ray just wanting to be away from his house for a while, not having to do anything. Eddie just wanting a little break from his wife.

Last February it was so cold that Freddy and Cliff had moved back in with Alvin until the weather broke. Johnny Ray had hung out there, too, and brought in groceries. It was so cold that month, they hired somebody from Beaulah Town to come by, bring firewood in, and keep the wood heater going. They just drank and played dominoes and backgammon all month.

Alvin bought groceries, but only occasionally and not much quantity. Freddy, Eddie, Johnny Ray, and Cliff were always bringing beer, sodas, garden vegetables over. Since Johnny Ray had died, Alvin had bought groceries more frequently. He figured maybe Johnny Ray's death had killed the flophouse status of his place. All the guys had come by since the death, but mostly just for a few minutes. But almost none of the visits were like it used to be, where they would just walk in with a case of beer, wondering why women had to rearrange the furniture all the time, or Alvin would come home to find one of the guys there, propped up, watching a movie, eating popcorn.

Other than Freddy, Cliff was the first person that Alvin had found lounging around in his house since the death. He wondered if Freddy had brought him over there and locked him in the house before he went over to Gail's or if Cliff had gotten a taxi and had crawled through the bedroom window.

Alvin flushed Purple Commode.

Alvin turned around, stuck his finger down his throat, and threw up in Purple Sink. He knew he had to get the poison out. Opening the medicine cabinet, he grabbed a lot of vitamins, realizing he might not feel like having an intensive training workout tomorrow. Not that he couldn't drive himself to. But this time he would listen to his muscles more. They could tell him when they needed light weight, heavy weight, or no weight. Or two-a-day workouts.

Tomorrow he would straighten up his weight room, reorganize it. He could get a notebook and start writing up routines.

He walked in the living room, around the La-Z-Boy recliner, and started to say something.

But Cliff was gone.

Maybe he was in the big bedroom, asleep. Alvin didn't check. It was all in keeping with the strangeness of this night. To him, it seemed, Cliff had vanished into thin air.

Thirteen

THE SUN WASN'T high enough yet to get over the water oaks, so the dock was still shaded. Alvin stepped off the front porch and walked down to it. He had on a pair of river-stained Hanes underwear. On his left arm was his wet suit, and in his right hand was a white plastic Alabama Crimson Tide cup, full of orange juice.

He threw the wet suit down on the dock and sipped on the orange juice while looking at Freddy's short, wide, beat-up, old wooden, flat-bottom, half-ass boat that they had had to pull from the river bottom on more than one occasion.

He said, "I don't know why the hell Freddy don't take the time to drive into Muscle Shoals and git him a new aluminum boat. Shit."

Then he took a Prestone antifreeze container full of gasoline and filled up his compressor engine. When he put the cap back on the engine tank, he noticed the new fifty-foot air line rolled up in the bottom of the boat near the bow.

That was the extra fifty feet of line Alvin had been going to put on so he and Johnny Ray could go down deeper to get more mussels. But on his last morning Johnny Ray had already put his hose on by the time Alvin got down to the dock. Alvin hadn't felt like going to the trouble of unscrewing his regulator, putting the other hose onto his old hose, screwing the regulator back on, taping another fifty feet of rope on, taping it on the line every six inches, then fixing it to the weight belt. He had told Johnny Ray, "I'll wait till tomorrow to go on down."

Dr. Dick sauntered down to the dock, found a splotch where the sun was shining, and lay down in it.

Alvin said, "Take a rest, Dr. Dick. You been working too hard."

Bending down, he strapped a diver's knife to his leg. He stood back up straight too fast and felt as if he were going to throw up and faint, so he started taking some deep breaths and drank some more of his orange juice.

Just then Sheriff Jennings's car came down the causeway and parked by Alvin's Z.

Why does that son of a bitch have to show up now, Alvin thought. I feel like shit. He felt a little bad thinking that, because Carlton Jennings was actually a pretty good guy. But to Alvin, any sheriff was still a sheriff. It took a lot of energy to deal with sheriffs, and he had rather not deal with one on a hangover.

Twelve years ago Alvin and his daddy had just come in from running trotlines and had a mess of big catfish. Carlton Jennings, who had just taken his first term as sheriff, came to the dock. Alvin had thought he was there with a warrant to look for moonshine, but he was just asking about some Yankees that had escaped from the county jail. He had told them how he was planning a fish fry for all the inmates and ended up buying the whole mess of cats.

Each year Sheriff Jennings gave a fish fry, and every year he bought the fish from Alvin.

Dick stood up and started barking. Alvin said to him, "Good boy. You can be quiet now." Dick lay down and went back to sleep.

The sheriff got out of his patrol car, adjusted his belt, and waved down at Alvin.

"Fixin' to go out musselin', I see, Alvin."

"Yes sir."

They shook hands.

The sheriff started looking down at the stuff in his boat. Alvin didn't like sheriffs looking around at his stuff.

"Well, that's whut I see in those diver's boats when I go across the river," the sheriff said. "An air compressor. I reckon you use that to fill up ye air bottles."

Alvin thought what a dip shit he was to think they used scuba. And if they did, they sure as hell wouldn't call them air bottles. But Alvin said, "We don't use air bottles. We just breathe straight from the compressor."

"Ain't that handy? Yeuh. I see the air line now. What's that two-inch water pipe thang?"

"Homemade air filter. See, the air comes out the compressor tank, then through the air filter. There's busted-up charcoal in there with a Kotex stuffed in each end to keep the charcoal from getting out in the air line."

"Kotex?" the sheriff asked with a snort, as if Alvin had done something taboo, like showing him a picture of a naked girl.

The sheriff giggled.

"Yeah. And there's mineral oil instead of crankcase oil in the base of the compressor motor to help the air being purer." Alvin pointed down to the different parts of his apparatus. "Then a fifty-foot air hose comes out the filter. I got a rope taped to the line so I can let myself in and out of the boat without pulling the fittings out of the air line. Then there's the second-stage regulator that I breathe from at the end of the line."

Alvin stopped there, not because he didn't have any more to say but because he didn't feel like giving a seminar.

The sheriff nodded his head as if he understood exactly how everything worked. He paused, then said, "I heard yaw lost one of you divers."

"Yes sir. He was the best."

"I hated to hear that. I understand he had a wife and two kids."

"Yes sir."

"They doin' OK, aren't they, Alvin? I mean, they don't need any kind of help from the state, or anything, do they?"

He didn't like the sheriff calling him Alvin as if they were close personal friends. But he answered politely anyway. "They seem to be doing all right," he said. "I saw Donna just yesterday—" He stopped talking abruptly. He had almost let it slip out about the insurance policy, and that was none of the sheriff's business.

Johnny Ray had been drunk about a year ago, when a young insurance salesman came to his door. Johnny Ray bought a life insurance policy because he felt sorry for the kid, plus he was drunk, and he had just gotten through making $376 that day. It was a $50,000 policy, straight life with double indemnity.

Donna bought a Corvette three days ago.

"They'll make it OK," Alvin said.

"That's good," the sheriff replied. "Maybe she'll meet her another fine man."

"Maybe."

"You be careful out there now, Alvin. That divin's dangers."

"Maybe, I reckon. But not as dangerous as sheriffing."

Alvin had noticed when he went to town and people found out what he did for a living, some hated his guts for it. Word had been out how much cash the divers earned.

He decided they were jealous. These people couldn't stand the idea of somebody, without the use of a formal education, doing something with no set hours or boss to deal with and making more money than they did.

And it just hit him that the sheriff had a hidden hatred, too. But he realized that he was jealous because Alvin had a more dangerous and exciting job than he did.

Alvin wondered if he was making a mistake by making the sheriff less jealous of him.

The sheriff was trying to hide a smile because Alvin had "admitted" his job wasn't as dangerous as sheriffing. He said, "You just be careful out there. It seems like a innerstin, honest way to make a living."

"Well, it idn't all that interesting after a while," Alvin said. "You just do more or less the same thing ever day. But sheriffing, I bet no two days are ever the same."

He pictured the sheriff getting up every morning at 6:30, going to the jail at 7:30, to the courthouse at 8:15 to do some paper work, drinking coffee at the Dixie Lee Café from 10:00 to 10:45, riding around until noon, going home for lunch, riding around until 3:30, going to the jail to watch *Andy Griffith* reruns, then walking around the square from 4:00 to 5:30, trying to act like Andy Griffith. He'd ride around from 5:30 to 7:00 stopping crime, and then do whatever he did at night.

Sheriff Jennings laughed and was prouder of his job after Alvin had glorified it a little.

The sheriff said, "No two days alike in the sheriff business all right." He pulled out a small Swisher Sweet, and lit it. "Think the Tide'll win their opener?"

Alvin figured that since the Tide had won about every game they ever played, it was safe to say, "Yeah, I think they'll win."

The sheriff took a draw on the cigar, nodding his head as though that statement alone showed that Alvin knew everything there was to know about football.

"I'm going to give the fish fry this weekend," he informed Alvin. "I just dropped by to see if you could git me the catfish."

"Yes, I can run some lines."

"It won't interfere with ye musselin', will it, Alvin?"

"Naw sir," Alvin lied.

Sheriff Jennings pulled out his billfold. "Heuh. Let me give you something on them thangs, Alvin."

Alvin held up his hand to signal stop. "No sir. I'm not taking anything. I want it to be my contribution to the county. I didn't give anything to the Cancer Society this year. And I know it's a good cause to give the inmates a fish fry on Bear Bryant's season opener."

He figured he had stored up a couple of favors from the sheriff that he could use someday, the kind of favors only a sheriff could deliver. Other than that, Alvin would receive a Christmas card with

Sheriff Jennings's slobby-looking family picture on it, like every other registered voter in the county.

"Well, thank ye, Alvin," the sheriff said.

He put his billfold back in the hip pocket of his khaki pants and buttoned the flap down. Then he added, "You can be rest assured everbody up the courthouse and jailhouse know where the catfish come from. You a good sort, Alvin. All you divers, ya'll the time willing to help out. Last blood drive, I think, all you divers come up and give a pint of blood. . . . Who is that comical feller?"

"Freddy?"

"I think so. Used to be a big baseball player around these heuh parts."

"That's him."

"He tried to give a quart," the sheriff said, and then chuckled. He spit out a leaf of tobacco that had gotten hung between his teeth from the cigar.

What the sheriff didn't know was that Freddy lost a two-hundred-dollar bet with Eddie that he could get them to take a quart of blood from his arm.

Alvin didn't want the sheriff to talk anymore about blood drives. He had never donated blood and didn't intend to, ever. He figured it might make his arms shrivel up. Alma used to donate blood to lose weight, until she got down so low in body weight that the blood bank wouldn't take it anymore.

"All the divers think you a good sheriff, too," Alvin said. He didn't want to encourage him to start hanging around the river. He might start snooping around, trying to make his job a little more exciting.

A faint flash went through Alvin's head. It was faint from the liquor, and his body was sweating from having the wet suit on. But it felt good to Alvin because it was sweating the bad out from a past he wasn't going back to.

Alvin said, "Well, Sheriff, I'll start running those lines three days before you need the fish." Alvin didn't dare let on he didn't know the exact date of the Alabama Crimson Tide season opener. "That way, if I don't have a good run, I'll have a couple more chances at it. If I do have a good run, they'll stay on ice just fine and fresh for three days."

"Sounds good, Alvin."

"I got to go musseling now," Alvin said, half to the sheriff and half thinking out loud to himself.

Fourteen

ALVIN MANEUVERED slowly down Mud Creek.

The creek in front of his house was only about twenty feet wide, but even in the winter, when the TVA let the water level down, it was still deep enough to get his boat from the dock to the river because his daddy had dynamited out all the shallow places years ago. If a bar started forming, Alvin would drop a couple of sticks in and blow it back out.

He eased through the islands, stumps, and trees of the back-waters. His movement made the sun flash through the treetops like Freddy's strobe light.

When he was out of the stumps and snags and into water he knew was at least five feet deep, he turned the forty-horse Mercury that was on his sixteen-foot superwide green aluminum flat-bottom boat wide open.

Only being careful not to hit driftwood, Alvin circled around to the other side of Hatchett Island, and he slowed down. He turned on his depth finder. It registered five feet. He knew he was on the flat so he eased the boat on out toward the channel.

The Tennessee River was at least three miles wide here, and it looked as if he were halfway between either bank. Alvin looked up and down the river. He saw only two other divers, and they were way down the river. Alvin liked that.

As he was puttering along, he put his diver's flag up and put his gloves on. When the depth finder hit fifteen feet, he cut his outboard off.

Washboards grew to be the biggest of the varieties of mussels in the Tennessee River. They were usually about ten inches long and weighed about three pounds. And were ridged like an old-time washboard. Alvin would start working the sand bottom here and work toward the channel. At about twenty-five feet deep the sand bottom would turn to mud, and in that spot, for about three or four feet toward the channel, would be some huge washboards.

Alvin cranked his compressor engine, put the ladder over the side of the boat, put his weight belt on, leaned over the side and spit into his mask and rinsed it out, hung a tow sack around his neck, put his regulator mouthpiece in his mouth, and crawled over the gunnel of the boat.

He held on to the gunnel, pulling himself to the bow, then held to the air hose, which went over the bow from the compressor. He let himself slowly down toward the bottom.

Although the water was clear at the surface, the visibility got dingier and dingier until, as he touched bottom, there was barely enough light to see the yellow silhouette of his glove when he brought his hand up to his face.

He squeezed the nose of his U.S. Divers Pacifica mask while he swallowed, clearing his ears. Getting down on all fours, he cleared his ears again. The tow sack was positioned to the side of him. He readjusted the mouthpiece and lay out on the bottom. Only the toes of his aged Adidas and his hands touched the sand.

His hands made sweeping motions as his fingers raked the sand. He hit a shell. As soon as he felt it, he knew it was too small since his forefinger and thumb could touch when he put his hand around it. It was a three knot. Alvin could feel the knots, even though he couldn't see them.

But he put it in his sack anyway. His daddy had always kept the first fish he caught every day, whether it was a game fish or not, because it was good luck. So Alvin always sacked his first shell of the day, no matter how small or bad it was.

On the next sweep of his hands he hit a big washboard buried halfway down in the sand with its lips pointed up. The cash register went off in his head, as Johnny Ray would say. No matter how many shells Alvin found in a day, every time he hit a big washboard, there was an excitement about it that didn't diminish with each one he found.

He put the big washboard in his sack.

The mussel divers referred to deep water as anything over thirty feet. Alvin didn't like to stay in deep water if he wasn't finding shells. There was no light at all, and he always thought there was a huge catfish waiting to attack him.

Of all the catfish, of all the other assorted species of fish he had caught on his trotline hooks, Alvin, in deep water, would get to imagining there was some two-hundred-pound channel catfish monster lying in wait to get him back for all his brothers, sisters, children, and cousins that Alvin had taken from the river.

There was also a tendency to believe a river monster lurked down there. He had found out the other divers thought the same thing. Donna had said, "Johnny Ray says he gets paranoid if he's in deep water and not finding any shells." But Donna had just learned the word "paranoid," and she liked to use new words every chance she got. Alvin figured she had probably heard the word from Cliff.

Alvin felt light-headed, more than just weightlessness. He knelt and tried to shake the feeling off.

He threw up in his regulator.

He stuck his tongue in the mouthpiece hole and pushed the button on the regulator, shooting air to clear all the puke out. Taking a hit of air, he removed the mouthpiece to rinse his mouth out in the river water. Then he reinserted the regulator and resumed feeling for mussels.

He started pulling big mussels out of the sand, putting them into his sack as automatically as he could so he could have most of his attention on thinking.

He thought, as if he were talking to Johnny Ray: In January I'm gone enter Mr. Gulf Coast. But not to win. Uh-uh. Just so I can qualify to enter Mr. America. Just place in the top five. Then I'm goin' to enter Mr. America next September. Now that's the son of a bitch I'm gonna win. I'm gonna lay low till Mr. America. After I win and I'm on the Johnny Carson show, I'm gone start being in movies with Burt Reynolds. Where I belong. I'm gonna be a whiskey runner. See, I won't need any acting lessons or anything, because I already know all about whiskey hauling. But the main thing I gotta do right now is lay low so nobody'll try to figure out what I'm up to and git jealous. I don't want anybody to give a shit about what I'm doing.

That's what I got to do mainly right now. Is lay low.

Alvin had worked himself into deep water. He had a sackful of shells, so he reached behind him at his weight belt, got hold of his air line, and started pulling on it. When it was taut, he stood up.

The boat was right above him. He began his ascent. The blackness gave way to murkiness, and he could hear the humming of the compressor above. Reaching the lighter strata, he looked up and watched as globs of air bubbles soared toward the surface.

When he was about five feet from the top, he looked out through the dingy but clearer water.

There, about fifteen feet away, was Johnny Ray. He had on his clothes and was treading under the surface of the water. He was breathing, and when he exhaled, the bubbles floated next to his face and through his flowing, long sandy hair, which was swaying and waving with the current.

Johnny Ray had no particular expression on his face. He was just looking at Alvin.

Alvin just looked at him.

Johnny Ray's mouth moved as if he were trying to tell Alvin something, but all Alvin could hear was the exhaling of his own air bubbles. He figured that what Johnny Ray was saying had to do with Mr. America.

After a few more seconds Johnny Ray began backwatering farther out into the dinginess until Alvin was not even sure he could still see an outline of his figure or if he had swum on away.

Alvin imagined that Johnny Ray had his casket floating up, moored on to his own boat. He imagined Johnny Ray pulling himself out of the water and up into the casket, somehow magically drying off. Then he would crank up, probably the jet propulsion engine he had in the thing, and skim off down the river.

Next, Johnny Ray would pull out a bottle of whiskey and take a long pull. With the neck of the bottle in his nonsteering hand, he would press a converter button and a bubble would come up over the cockpit of the casket. He would skim back near Alvin's boat, put his casket into a submarine dive. He would speed by Alvin in his submarine casket, drinking and hollering.

Alvin hung there on to the air line, waiting for a couple of minutes, but Johnny Ray didn't show back up, with or without his submarine casket.

It looked as if there weren't any turning back from Mr. America now. He might be able to lay low from everybody else, but Alvin surfaced, knowing he would never be able to lay low from Johnny Ray.

Fifteen

Out by the back porch Alvin peeled off his wet suit. Then he hosed it down and laid it on the railing to dry. He took his socks off, hosed them and the Adidas, and laid them up to dry, too.

He walked inside, to the bathroom. He turned the shower on, stepped into the stall, and stuck his head under the stream of water, pulling his underwear off while he watched the color of the water draining down go from dark to muddy brown to almost clear. He stayed in there scrubbing until all the warm water had been used up. Then he toweled off and flushed his ear canals with Swim-EAR, which aided against infection and swelling.

Now that his face was clean, he could shave. He stood before the mirror. There was the red imprint from the dive mask along his cheekbones and around to a line above his forehead. After a day of diving, sometimes this imprint lasted into the night. It was that way with all the divers. Sometimes, when a gang of them would go into a restaurant together in Muscle Shoals, people would look at them as if they were of a different species.

After shaving, Alvin dug the mud from under his finger- and toenails. Then he splashed himself about with rubbing alcohol, followed by body talc. He towel-dried his hair a bit more, then fluffed it out with his fingers.

He was finished with cleaning up. Sometimes, when someone would tell them that mussel diving was a bizarre, tough way to make a living, Freddy would just say, "Hell, the toughest part's cleanin' up."

The day's dive and the shower had cured his hangover. Now the idea of a workout excited him. All his muscles felt as if they could use it.

So Alvin put on some tight bikini underwear, which he preferred to a jockstrap, sweat pants, white athletic knee socks, and some new leather Adidas shoes. Then he put on an old gray sweat shirt, with the sleeves cut to three-quarter length and the neckband cut out.

A little protein drink, he thought. My muscles could use some protein sitting there for them to suck up.

He put a scoop of ice cream, skim milk, banana, and a portion of dried protein powder in the blender and let it stir for about half a minute.

As he poured it off into a glass, he thought how he hated these sons of bitches. How it fucked up a perfectly good milk shake, stretched your stomach out. Weighted you down like a tow sack full of mussels. Made you burp until you wanted to throw up, made you fart gunpowder farts, and made you shit until your ass was raw. He wondered how he could do some of the dumb-assedest things.

Alvin poured the shake into the sink, then turned the water on to rinse out the blender, glass, and sink itself.

Another album came on in the living room. Alvin realized music had been playing ever since he got out of the shower, but only now did it dawn on him that there was someone else in the house.

He stepped into the living room. There sat Cliff in the big chair, nursing a bottle of JW Black. Alvin thought: Maybe he spent the night here last night? Damn, he might have even stayed in the chair all night. When Alvin was gone, maybe Cliff just went out on the porch to take himself a leak. Who the hell knew?

Cliff didn't really seem to be drinking the whiskey. He would run his tongue around the mouth of the bottle, turn it up, and let it wet his lips, then lick his lips, put the bottle up to his nostril, and take a good whiff. He was drinking at it, more than he was drinking, almost just tasting it really good.

Alvin wondered if Cliff took a drink *every* day. If he did, he was the only person he knew of that did. Even Freddy would go two or three days without having a beer. Johnny Ray hadn't drunk every day. Eddie's wife braked down on Eddie's drinking.

Every damn day? Alvin wondered. I can't see how nobody would want to drink ever damn day.

Cliff asked, "Hey. You go out today?"

"Yeah. Just got cleaned up. You?"

"Yeah," Cliff said. He looked mellow. "Are you going out again tomorrow?"

Alvin didn't know why Cliff was asking all these seemingly useless questions. Then he remembered that Freddy had gone off tomcatting. He wondered if Cliff was lonesome; he always spent the most time with Alvin when Freddy was away. For some reason Alvin was thinking that maybe Cliff even disliked being alone.

Alvin leaned back against the doorway, wondering what he could drink in place of his protein shake. He thought perhaps orange juice, wishing orange juice were loaded up with protein. He considered putting the protein powder in the orange juice but then realized that would just fuck up some perfectly good orange juice.

Then Alvin remembered Cliff had asked him a legitimate question. He popped out of it and said, "Naw. I'm gone run trotlines tomorrow."

"For catfish? Like you guys used to do?" Cliff asked. He perked up and put the cap back on his bottle of JW Black.

"Yeah." Having done it all his life, Alvin couldn't imagine someone not knowing what it was or how to do it.

"May I go?" Cliff asked, almost begging.

Alvin was a little bit stunned. He had never seen Cliff this excited. He was like a city kid who was going to be taken out in a boat fishing. Sometimes Cliff would get to hollering and laughing, telling jokes, when he was drinking heavily. But as far as his being actually interested in anything, Alvin never saw him like this.

The only other time Alvin had seen him look really interested in something was when he and Alma were playing pinball that time.

"Sure, you can go run the lines with me. You can even help me do it," Alvin said, and then stepped back into the kitchen. He got a glass, reached into the refrigerator, and poured himself some orange juice. He hollered back into the living room, "You want to work out with me?"

"No thanks. I'll just sit here and listen to the music if you don't mind."

"You know I don't."

Alvin walked down to his weight room. He put the Rolling Stones on the turntable and turned it up. He took a good whiff of ammonia.

He picked up a pair of twenty-five-pound dumbbells to warm up with. He curled them to his shoulders and then extended them from his body, slowly letting them down to his sides.

Next, he picked up a pair of forty-five-pounders. He resisted the weight as he lowered them to his sides.

Negative repetitions! His muscles liked them. They would carve out the fat from between his muscle tissue. They would "cut him up," define his muscles. He did more and more of them, feeling them burn.

He took his sweat shirt off and stood before the mirror, doing more sets of the stiff-armed exercises for the shoulders. It was going to be so easy this time because his muscles knew what to do. He had never listened to his muscles before.

His tanned body reddened with the flush of blood. A network of blue veins stood out on his chest and the front of his shoulders.

He had only begun to work out!

He had not been training at all in months, and right now he looked even better than when he had taken Mr. Alabama.

His muscles wanted more negative laterals. He didn't have to jump to another exercise. More of this exercise. Burn them. Burn them. Burn the fat. Make the muscle tissue hot, his muscles were telling him.

After ten excruciating repetitions of the tenth set, Alvin dropped the forty-pound set of dumbbells onto the bare wooden floor.

He looked at himself in the mirror, at his whole body. His head was light, but he felt as if he were in control of his total life.

Sixteen

EARLY THE NEXT MORNING Alvin Lee lay back against
a piling of his dock. It seemed cool because he wasn't used to being
out this early in the fall. He was barefoot and had on a pair of faded
blue jeans and an old black T-shirt Freddy had probably left over
there.

Since Alvin had a washer and dryer, Freddy and Cliff did their
laundry over there. Even though Alvin was all built up, he and Freddy
wore the same size underwear, T-shirts, and some knit shirts; even
some of their jeans were the same size. All of Cliff's clothes were
smaller, but Freddy and Alvin, except for their shirts, ended up with
each other's clothes a lot.

Alvin wiggled around in the T-shirt. When he realized it was
a bit tight, he knew it must be Freddy's. Probably the same one the
girl Becky had been wearing that night.

But the tightness of the shirt felt good. As if it were massaging
his upper body. He was enjoying the muscle ache in his deltoids and
calves from the workout of last night.

Dr. Dick was asleep with his head on Alvin's leg.

Alvin hadn't wanted to unrig his mussel boat to run trotlines, so he had taken his daddy's old fishing boat, which he kept out of the water under a lean-to behind the shed. He had taken Freddy's eighteen-horse Johnson off Freddy's boat and put it on his daddy's. He wound the trotlines in the bottom of the fishing rig, just as his daddy had done on so many mornings.

From Freddy and Cliff's cabin, it was ten minutes by boat and fifteen by car. As Alvin expected, he heard Johnny Ray's boat coming up Mud Creek. He and Dr. Dick got up.

As Cliff pulled up to the dock, he said, "Thanks for letting me come with you. I have never seen trotlines run," as if Alvin were doing him this big favor.

"Ain't no seeing to it. You gone be helping me."

As they got into the fishing boat with Dr. Dick, Alvin gestured toward Johnny Ray's old boat and said, "How do you like your new rig?"

"Unbelievable! I'm so glad that Donna sold it to me. Much more efficient than borrowing that old V hull of Freddy's. I'm making more money. You know, having your own proper equipment makes something more interesting. I should have known that."

"Yeah, it do," Alvin said, then, "good, good," on Cliff's improved musseling business. But he wondered if Cliff would go out diving again for another four or five days. One hundred and fifty dollars could buy a good bit of JW Black, if that in fact was what Cliff's life revolved around.

Alvin took the cord and wrapped it around the top of the outboard crank. He gave the gas tank bulb a couple of pumps, pulled out the choke, and then gave the cord a yank. It started. A cloud of blue smoke came up from the foot of the motor.

He adjusted the engine to run a little leaner, then engaged the engine forward. They cruised slowly down Mud Creek toward the Tennessee.

As he steered out of the mouth of the creek into the backwaters, he realized that the muscle soreness he had today was the kind he had got when he trained for Mr. Alabama.

He'd like to pretend that those past eleven years hadn't happened, that he didn't know what failure and confusion were. He wanted to believe that opportunity was something that could come his way anytime he wished.

He spotted his empty Clorox bottle float out from Cowford Point. It seemed no time until he came to it and cut his motor.

He said to Cliff, who was in the bow, "Just start pulling the line in. I'll wind the empty line onto these racks. When you git a cat, I'll show ye how to take him off."

Cliff started pulling the line in slowly. "You know there's something peaceful about being out on this river alone."

"Yeah."

"But, Alvin, do you ever sense some strangeness out here? Anticipate the bizarre?"

"Yeah, even just running trotlines out here. There was nobody on the river when I used to do it. I was sure Mrs. Higgins would find some way to haunt me.

"See, I quit throwing the discus for the track team in high school. I was training for Mr. Alabama. No way I's going to stop doing that. For the sake of time and sleep and my Mr. Alabama training, I quit the track team.

"I had this civics teacher, Old Lady Higgins. She'd been teaching since the Stone Age. Johnny Ray had said she wadn't from shit. He didn't like her neither.

"When she found out I quit, she said, 'You could have gone to the state meet. You're throwing away the chance to get a college education and participate in one of the oldest and purest sports of Western civilization.'

"This old lady hated my guts. For some reason, she hated all the swampers. Ask Freddy. Anyway, she hated me extra because I wouldn't memorize the Preamble to the Constitution. She'd throw that up to me ever chance she got.

"Ever damn class started out, 'Alvin Lee Fuqua, where's your text, young man?'" Alvin said, mocking her voice again. "I always told her I forgot or lost it. That fucking book was heavy. My muscles were all the time sore from working out. I didn't need the extra load.

And ever fucking time I told her that, she'd squawk back at me, 'You'd lose your head if it weren't connected to your shoulders.'

"Two days after she told me I's making a big mistake by quitting the track team, she was stupid enough to pull out in front of a Greene Construction dump truck at the Muscle Shoals bridge and get her head cut off. It went into the channel of Shoals Creek. The rescue squad spent three days diving and dragging for it but never found it.

"At school during break, I said, 'That old woman'd lose her head if it wadn't tied onto her shoulders.' Loggins, the principal, overheard it. He didn't think it was funny. Me and Johnny Ray . . . see, Loggins was a classmate of Johnny Ray's back in the eighth grade. Right when Johnny Ray had gotten himself 'graduated' by whipping the shit out of Loggins. They expelled him, so Johnny Ray never went back to school. He claimed his diploma was at the end of his right hand."

Alvin held his hand up in a fist to demonstrate what Johnny Ray had meant.

"Anyhow, me and Johnny Ray had already decided Loggins wadn't from shit. Loggins brought me into his office. He was gone give me a speech on respect, give me some licks, and then make me run laps around the track field until I dropped. I wadn't 'bout to run no fucking laps and fuck up my training. I told him I'd been having a hard time finding crawfish lately. Loggins asked me, 'What?' I told him I been wantin' an excuse to break his fucking neck and cut his shit-ass up for catfish bait. I stared at him and walked out.

"I got expelled for that. Next day Johnny Ray went up there, busted Loggins's office door in, and beat the living shit out of the son of a bitch. He told Loggins I's two months away from a high school diploma, something that had been denied him some years ago for beating him up. Johnny Ray told him wadn't it funny how things sometimes come 'round in circles. Then he told him if I wadn't back in class the next day, he was gone kill him.

"The next day I's back in class."

"Johnny Ray was all right," Cliff said. He stopped pulling the line long enough to look at Alvin. Then he went back to pulling the line in.

Alvin continued, "What all this leads up to is what we was talking about gittin' spooked out here and shit.

"I figured one morning, about daylight, I'd be at the bow of this boat working trotlines, and there would be something heavy on one of the hooks. I'd pull it with some effort, and then Old Lady Higgins's head would bust through the surface of the water. It would be all fucked up, with slime and silt, and the head would say, 'It's unpatriotic not to memorize the Preamble to the Constitution of the United States of America.'

"When I was out here, I be scared of that, but once I got back to the dock, cleaning the fish, I would think about it and hope if it happened, I'd have the cool to say, 'All kind of shit gits hung up in these trotlines,' cut the line, and throw the head into the channel."

Cliff pulled the line in a few more feet, and the surface of the water erupted.

He screamed, let go of the line, and jumped backwards, almost into Alvin's lap.

"It's all right. It's all right, Cliff," Alvin said reassuringly. "Just a big cat."

He could feel Cliff shaking and could see the chill bumps pop out on him.

Alvin knew he didn't mean to be telling no goddamn ghost story, but Cliff sure was spooked.

Alvin got up and put a cushion on the stern thwart and patted it. "You sit here, and just wind the line into the tray. Put the hooks like I was doing."

After showing Cliff exactly where to hang the hooks after taking off any old bait, Alvin got up in the bow. Luckily a hook had caught on the gunnel, so not all the line had been pulled back into the water.

He started pulling the line back in.

Cliff reached in his hind pocket and pulled out a small, thin metal flask and took a sip of whiskey.

The surface erupted again. Alvin pulled a big channel catfish over into the bottom of the boat. It must have weighed fifteen pounds. He showed Cliff how to hold it and take the hook out.

"Then you just put it here in the live well box," he said, tossing the fish into it.

The fish made a noise for a while and then settled down.

Every few feet Alvin would pull in a two- or three-pound catfish. Cliff was getting them off the line and into the live well with no trouble after the first couple of ones he did.

They continued working the trotline in silence for a while.

Finally Cliff said, "I got a book the other day in Muscle Shoals. A dive book, with decompression charts in it. In a section concerning the bends, it stated that it seldom affected divers at less than a hundred feet. Would you say Johnny Ray probably only went down to eighty feet all day?"

"I don't know. He only had a hundred feet of air line. To be down ninety feet, he'd a had to been damn near straight under the boat. Probably he down seventy, eighty feet. I don't know."

"I don't know why I brought that up," Cliff said, almost apologizing.

Alvin shrugged, but it reminded him of something. "That time they put Alma in the hospital and she had all them needles and tubes stuck in her, she made me lay my hands on the IV bottle and make all the fat and calories go out of the liquid. Then I had to say it would make her f-a-t seven hundred and seventy-three times. When I come back home, I went to that bookstore in Muscle Shoals and got a book on anorexia nervosa. It said that it most often occurred with girls in their teens or early twenties who were from upper-middle-class families.

"Shit. Alma was damn near thirty then. And she shore as hell wadn't from no upper-middle-class family. It wadn't the kind of book that would help me answer my questions. I wish they'd divide the books in the bookstores into two sections: The ones that's full of shit in one place, and the ones that aren't in another. Hell, when I first started musselin', I bought a book on diving, and it said the first rule of diving was never dive alone."

Alvin pulled in a catfish. "Shit," he went on. "I reckon river diving ain't like clear-water diving."

Cliff didn't say anything. Alvin looked back at him. Cliff was a little behind at keeping the line and hooks racked up. He was sitting there sucking on his flask.

Alvin wondered if he was actually drinking the whiskey or just tasting around on it, as he had done yesterday. That'd be funny, Alvin thought, if Cliff just liked the taste of whiskey. That he didn't really give a shit about gittin' drunk. Wasn't trying to escape life or his problems or whatever it was that somebody was supposed to git drunk about.

For a while Alvin had worked out at a gym uptown. There was a guy that came in and would work out like mad. Alvin approached him one time, trying to show him more properly how to handle the weights, giving him a more efficient workout program.

Finally, when no one else was around, the guy had looked around, making sure no one could hear him. He got up close to Alvin and said, "I'm not bodybuilding."

Alvin had said, "Oh, you workin' out for strength. Well, you cut down the repetitions, it'll build strength."

The guy said, "Naw, I don't work out for strength neither."

Alvin looked at the guy, trying to figure what else there was besides strength or bodybuilding. Health or maybe rehab an injury. Alvin asked, "Well, what is it you work out for?"

The guy got up real close to Alvin and said real low, "Man, I work out for the pain." Alvin thought he meant the "no pain, no gain" stuff he'd seen on TV and nodded.

But later this fellow explained his theory: He figured that to survive, he had to experience so much pain. And he figured he was going to put in his quota in a weight room. So far it seemed to be working; his old lady didn't give him damn near as much shit, and his boss had given him a raise.

He went on to tell Alvin that he was about 99 percent sure his theory was correct and that Alvin should invest in weight equipment because once he released his theory to the world, everybody would be working out for pain.

Soon afterward the guy Alvin remembered as Randy pulled out in front of a speeding locomotive. Alvin went around for a couple of days saying, "No pain, no train," but it wasn't so funny because he had kind of liked the guy.

Now Alvin looked at Cliff. He imagined asking him, "Why is it you drink Johnnie Walker Black all the time?" and Cliff answering, "I just like the taste. But the gitting drunk part is hell. I wish they made it in a nonalcoholic form."

Alvin was smiling, almost laughing now.

Cliff caught Alvin's expression. He smiled back and said, "What?"

"You funny, Cliff."

Cliff just grinned and got back to winding up the empty trotline. Then he looked back up at Alvin, and like a boy asking for some ice cream, he suddenly pleaded, "Alvin, let's go pretty soon to that club in Birmingham and watch Alma's act."

"All right, Cliff. We'll do that pretty soon. Only trouble is, I don't know when she's goin' to go onstage. I don't think she or anybody else does either."

Seventeen

ALVIN PACKED the catfish down with ice in a number two washtub. He threw all the heads across Mud Creek, into the swamp. Then he washed the dock down with the hose.

The patrol car came around the house. Dick barked, and Alvin told him it was OK. Dick went back to sleep in the boat.

The sheriff got out of the car and looked around for a couple of seconds, adjusting his belt, as if he were about to investigate an armed robbery. But then he smiled and waved at Alvin.

Sheriff Jennings had two trustees with him, and they followed him down to the dock.

The sheriff looked at the catfish and said, "Mighty fine cats, Alvin." Then he said to the trustees, "Take 'em on, boys."

The trustees took the washtub to the patrol car and put it in the trunk. There were a couple of gloves and a baseball in the car, and they got them out and started pitching in the yard while the sheriff talked to Alvin.

"You sure you won't take any money for all that work?"

"No sir," Alvin said.

He didn't really want to have messed with the catfish for free, but he thought that if he took money for it, he would be more connected with the sheriff. Then he began to wonder if maybe the opposite was true.

"That's real honorable of you, Alvin. The folks at the jail shore do appreciate it."

Alvin watched the trustees. The lanky sandy-haired one turned his head and spit a stream of Red Man tobacco. Then he adjusted his greasy Shell cap, stood up straight, and got a grip on the ball with both hands, near his chest. He looked over his left shoulder at the runner on first. He was at the Riverfront Stadium. Alvin could tell. He could pick up on things like that. Freddy used to do it.

The sheriff drawled, "Yeah. You a mighty fine feller, Alvin. I wisht there was more folks in the county like you. Not that there ain't a fine crop of folk here."

"Thank you, Sheriff."

The sheriff took the cellophane off a pack of Swisher Sweets cigarillos and crumbled up the cellophane and stuffed it in his pocket. Alvin could tell he wasn't the put-it-in-your-pocket kind. He was more the throw-it-on-the-ground type. Alvin could pick up on things like that, too.

When the sheriff got the cigarillo well lit, he paused, then said, "Alvin, I need you help on somethin', and you might be the only feller that can help me."

Might? Alvin thought. Mites grow on a chicken's ass. But he didn't say anything.

Sheriff Jennings leaned on one of the two-by-fours and sighed. He looked down at the floor of the porch, then up at Alvin and said, "It's about you deceased buddy's widow wife. Johnny Ray, I believe, was his name. Her name's Donna."

Alvin stiffened up.

The sheriff continued, "I thought maybe if you could help me out a little, I wouldn't have to carry out any kind of legal actions."

"What do you mean?" Alvin asked. He was thinking about how he wasn't Johnny Ray. Johnny Ray could handle anything.

"Well, it seems the welfare department has made an investigation into the case."

"Donna doesn't need any kind of handout from the government," Alvin said angrily. "She'll get by fine."

Sheriff Jennings relit his gone-out cigar and then shook his head, saying, "That ain't it, Alvin. Her kids hadn't been goin' to school. And the school sent the truant officer out there to see what was goin' on, and it seemed Donna had went off somewheres and left her little younguns by theirselves."

"Like I said, Sheriff, I'm sure it's just a passing thing. Donna's just getting readjusted to thangs without Johnny Ray."

The sheriff took a long draw off his Swisher and shook his head. "I tell you exactly the way it is, Alvin. I got some papers in that glove compartment over there." He pointed to the patrol car.

Alvin looked at it and noticed the sandy-haired trusty was at shortstop now.

"Those papers order me to go over to Donna's house and get those younguns and take them up to the welfare office, and they goin' to put 'em in foster homes until Donna can prove herself fit as a mother." The sheriff said the last with emphasis, as if he hated to say it, but it was the naked truth of the matter.

Shocked and ashamed that he hadn't been keeping a better check on the kids, Alvin looked up at the sheriff. If Johnny Ray hadn't gotten himself killed, he wouldn't have to be bothered with all this, and he could put all his attention on becoming Mr. America.

"What's the welfare hauling off and doing a thing like that for?"

"I'm telling you, Alvin, them younguns ain't gettin' took care of. Younguns can go downhill fast if they ain't looked after. I know. I have to see it all the time."

Alvin sat down in the chair on the porch and, putting his elbows on his knees, just stared at the floor.

Sheriff Jennings went on solemnly. "I have to take younguns out of unfit homes all the time for the welfare department. It has to be done. But I don't like to take a child away from its natural mother.

And I know Donna is a fit mother. I know she's just having a hard time now with her emotions and life and all."

"Yeah. Maybe she's having a rough time of it," Alvin agreed.

"Like I said, I don't want to take no child from its natural mother if it's any way possible. That's why I wanted to talk to you about it first, Alvin. Before I took any actions. Do you know any way I could get around having to go get those kids? Do they have any kinfolk they could stay with for a while? The welfare people said they didn't have no granddaddies or grandmamas or anything."

"Nah. I don't think Donna has any folks around these parts."

Funny, he'd been thinking about that, kinfolks. It never dawned on him before. It seemed as if the backwaters were cleaning everybody over forty out. Or as far as his and Johnny Ray's family went. Then he thought about Donna, Goddamn Donna. Why did Johnny Ray have to go drop dead? The only one around here with any damn sense. . . .

"I tell you what, Sheriff," Alvin finally said. "If you hold off on that paper or warrant, whatever it is, if you don't take those kids, I'll see that they get to school and are proper fed and clothed."

Sheriff Jennings put his hand on Alvin's shoulder. His sore shoulder.

"Alvin, you a blessing. I'm not saying this is going to keep those kids out of a foster home, but it shore won't hurt. See, legal-wise, I've been ordered to go out and get those younguns into the custody of the state."

"I understand."

"But like I say, it's my job as sheriff to serve the people as best I can, and sometimes I just don't think a body can do that by acting strict by the book."

Alvin looked out at the trusty in left field. He was back against the wall. He spit and adjusted his cap. He looked up, and his hands dangled at his sides. Half of his left hand was out of the glove. He flipped his left hand up just in time to keep the ball from hitting him in the face. He spit and threw the ball. No runs. No hits. No errors. No men left on base.

"I reckon that's right," Alvin responded. "You a good man, Sheriff Jennings." He didn't mean to say that, but it made the sheriff leave proudly.

As the sound of the sheriff's car going out the causeway faded, he could hear the humming of Freddy's old eighteen-horse Johnson coming up Mud Creek.

Eighteen

F
REDDY HOLLERED, "You quit musselin'?"

"Naw. I'm going out tomorrow. Cliff go out today?"

"Yeah. He back at the house gittin' all drunked up."

Freddy cut the motor, and his boat coasted until the bow hit a piling of the dock.

Alvin said, "Wouldn't a thought he'd a went out two days in a row."

"Me neither. Made a hundred and ten dollars today. Before he got so far gone on the alcohol, he started talking about the Civil War and shit. Asking if they had paddle wheels that were armed on the Tennessee River. Bunch of shit like that."

"Yeah," Alvin said. "He was talking about that a little bit today when we come in. I told him how the TVA backed the water up. How in the War Between the States the Tennessee River wadn't no wider than what the channel is now. Not too much wider."

"He was all excited," Freddy said, and pulled his boat around next to the bank.

Alvin never told anybody about him and Johnny Ray going out that night that he died. It was as if Johnny Ray had wanted it to be a secret, so Alvin had kept it a secret even though it probably didn't make a rat's ass anymore. Alvin wondered for a minute what was going on with Cliff getting into paddle wheels but then disregarded it. When you came out of the backwaters and were coming toward the channel, could see up and down the river, it was almost as if you expected to see a paddle wheel.

Alvin looked down to Freddy's boat. There must have been four hundred pounds of washboards in it.

"Damn," Alvin said. "I'm surprised you didn't sink the boat. Where'd you git all those?"

"Out from Hatchett."

They used a multicolored '63 Chevy pickup to carry their mussels to Dixie Shell. Alvin backed the truck up to the dock, but near the bank to one side where Freddy's boat was.

Freddy started shoveling the mussels into the bed. Alvin acted as though he were helping but was careful not to overwork his muscles. He needed all his energy for working out and muscle recuperation.

Freddy stopped shoveling, opened his Gott cooler, and got out a can of Dr Pepper. He held it up toward Alvin and said, "Want one?"

Alvin looked at it, at the little chunks and flakes of ice falling off it. He almost said, "Hell yeah," but then he thought of the sugar and empty calories. He thought of his abdominals.

He said, "No thanks. I'm not thirsty."

Freddy popped the top and took a slug, then bent down and fumbled through the mussels he hadn't shoveled yet. He found a few with deformed ridges and lips, and he threw them up on the wooden table on the dock to inspect for pearls. He set down the Dr Pepper on the end of the dock plank after giving it a good pull and shoveled some more.

Alvin said, "You weren't out for four hours, were you? I used you outboard this morning to run those lines." He hadn't seen Freddy leave but knew he hadn't gotten that outboard back on his boat until right before noon.

"Hell, I checked up on my crop before I musseled. Those plants on the other side of the bridge are about eight foot tall. And I ran into Bart over at Cowford Landing, and I been bullshittin' with him the last hour."

"You got a lot of musselin' done in a short amount of time. Hell."

"Aw shit, Alvin, you wouldn't believe it. It's been a crazy fuckin' day. This mornin' me and Bart went uptown. We ridin' around, figured it about time we redone our air filters and change the mineral oil in the compressors. We went in this store, bought a couple boxes of Kotex and several pints of mineral oil. This snooty ol' girl that gone check us out, she say real shitty, 'What yaw gone use all this far?' I says, 'We like doin slimy shits on women that's on the rag.' "

Alvin started laughing.

"Man, I thought Bart gone drop a load right then and there." Freddy laughed.

"He do give that impression sometime."

Freddy continued telling his day. "She just stood there paralyzed. We had to git somebody else to check us out. Then me and Bart at the landing bullshittin'. Turpin Adams come in. He was all fucked up. He got caught down deep in a snagline."

"Shit. Did he have his knife on him?"

"Yeah. He'd a been caught down there dead if he hadn't. His compressor engine run out of gas before he could get back topside. He didn't have his wet suit top on. Just a T-shirt. He's in black water, got tangled up in that thang before he knowed it. Man, he was all cut up. His upper body was. Bloody. He was going home, clean up and wash down in alcohol."

"Goddamn," Alvin commented.

"If that wadn't enough. Damn, it must be a full moon. Eddie and Tony come in. Together. They had put two lines on Tony's compressor."

"Broke the first rule of mussel diving," Alvin said.

"Always dive alone," they both said in unison.

"The second rule . . ." Alvin began.

"You don't make any money sitting up in the boat," Freddy

said. Johnny Ray had made up that rule, but it stuck because of how true it was.

"So what happened to them?" Alvin asked.

"So, one of 'em supposed to go one way, the other the other way."

"No way to keep directions in pitch-black water."

"Yep," Freddy agreed. "Tony accidentally grabbed Eddie's leg. Eddie come around scared and stabbed Tony. Got him in the leg."

"Shit. He fucked up?"

"Not too bad, don't reckon. Looks real shitty. Eddie was gone take him to the doctor, sew it up."

"Eddie's all right. He can come up with some of the dumb-assedest shit sometime, though," Alvin said. He was looking through the mussels in the pickup, checking for one that might have pearls that Freddy missed.

A thought occurred to Freddy, and he giggled. "Mickey Mouse was in divorce court, see. So the judge says, 'I understand you claim Minnie Mouse's crazy and you want to git a divorce from her.' Mickey says, 'No, Your Honor. I was misquoted. What I said was, "Minnie's fucking Goofy." ' "

Freddy laughed. Alvin laughed along with him, although he didn't get the joke.

He asked, "Shit. One of Bart's?"

"Yeah," Freddy said. He stopped shoveling and reached down to put the top back on the cooler. "Johnny Ray woulda liked that one."

"Too bad he ain't here."

"I know." He pulled out a piece of bologna and shook it at Dick on the dock, saying, "Dick, wanna jump?"

Dr. Dick jumped up in the air to what seemed an impossible height for his stubby little legs. Freddy threw him the bologna.

Alvin said, "Some morning you gonna wake up and go into the kitchen and there's going to be Dick, and he's going to be eight feet tall and he's goin' to say, 'Freddy wanna jump?' "

Freddy laughed. "Shit!" He sucked down about half of the Dr Pepper.

Alvin took his knife and worked it between the lips of a mussel. Sliding it toward the hinge, he cut the muscle that held it closed tight. He opened it wide and ran his fingers around the meat, checking around the inside of the lip, but nothing was there.

He threw the mussel over into the truck and said, "We need to try to work out some more on Inflation."

Although he didn't need the Inflation game now because he was going to become Mr. America, he tried to keep it alive because he thought maybe Freddy needed it.

Freddy said, "I hadn't thought nothing else out."

Alvin laughed.

"What's the matter?" Freddy asked. He had picked up the shovel again and was slinging shells into the truck. It sounded as if he were throwing rocks.

Alvin answered, "When they come out with Inflation, they'll be two guys like us buy it. And they'll go home and be laying it out, and on the inside cover on the instructions'll be our picture and a story of how we come about to invent it. And one of 'em'll laugh and point to you picture and ask the other guy, 'Hey, you think he'd smoke a joint?' "

Freddy laughed and said, "Shit!"

Alvin kept opening the culled-out shells, but all he found was a dark brown pearl the size of a BB. It was what the mussel divers called a dead pearl. It was worthless.

Freddy sat down on the dock and rolled a joint.

Alvin said, "Damn. You smoke that shit all the time."

"I smoke marijuana ever day, and I don't think it's habit-forming."

Alvin threw another opened shell into the truck. It made a wood-sounding hit against the other shells.

"Have you happened to 'ave seen Donna lately?" Freddy asked.

"Naw. Why?"

"Bart said she'd gone crazier'n a shithouse rat in a hailstorm."

"What'd he mean?"

"Said she'd started fuckin' like a mink. Goin' over to Huntsville and Muscle Shoals all time, gittin' picked up. Fucked some recording star. Stay gone off three 'n' four days at a time."

"How'd Bart know?"

"Guess he'd been over to Huntsville and seen it. Said he saw her hisself over at the Hour Glass, out on the dance floor French kissin' somebody. Then they left, with her just hanging on to that man like a leech. I just hope she don't come around here wantin' to fuck. Johnny Ray's dead and she's good-lookin', but I still wouldn't want to be faced with the situation."

Alvin said, "I know what you mean."

"She put that ol' cooter in my face, I might just have to nail it. Johnny Ray or no Johnny Ray."

"I know what you mean."

Freddy pulled his wet suit off and, picking his joint back up, leaned back against a piling and took a toke.

He said, "Ol' Cliff. Yeah, he done a lot of musselin' in the last couple of days. Seem like something put a little high life up his ass."

"Huh, yeah. You know, sometimes I think that cop-looking man, that day of the funeral at the Twilight, had his eye on Cliff. Ya know?"

Freddy gave a grunt. He said, "What was it with Johnny Ray? I bet he made a thousand dollars a month on pearls."

"At least," Alvin agreed.

"It was like them mussels would make a pearl just so Johnny Ray could find it. Sometimes I thank he was from somewhere else."

"I think he was."

"Makes me depressed to know somebody like him can die."

Alvin slid the knife into a washboard and opened it. The river water spilled out of it with all the slimy mucus trailing. He held it away from him to avoid the stench. Suddenly, and for the first time, it seemed so sickening to him.

He pulled a pearl out of the thin meat near the lip and threw the open mussel into the truck. It hit the metal behind the cab and sounded like a rock.

"Find one?" Freddy asked.

"Yeah. But it's dead."

Nineteen

FREDDY PULLED the pickup onto the narrow unloading area of the far side of the old barn-looking cotton gin. It was the same area where, until a few years ago, farmers had pulled the huge metal trailers full of machine-picked cotton. Years before that, wooden wagons had carried the handpicked cotton.

The abandoned gin was perfect for Dixie Shell to transform into a buying station. There was a place for the mussel divers to pull up and unload. The huge building that once held the ginning equipment was now the space used for sacking shells and piling them up for the trucks that would come for them.

Freddy said to Alvin, "Now don't you hurt yourself helping me unload these thangs."

Alvin grinned and said, "I done cleaned up and everthing, Freddy," trying to justify his apparent laziness.

Freddy shoveled the last of the shells into a large metal container, the bottom of which was about five feet from the ground. Alvin tapped the counterweight of the scales back and forth a bit, until he had the indicator on the zero line.

He called, "Five hundred and three pounds!"

"Goddamn!" Freddy sang.

Emma came waddling around the corner of the gin. She was smiling and had a receipt book in her hand.

She said, "Oh. Hello, Alvin. I don't see you for several days, and now twice in the same day."

Emma was tall and stout and looked to be a strong country woman. She and her husband, Charlie, were from Oklahoma. They came to Alabama when Dixie Shell began buying the mussels out of the Tennessee River. They were at what might be called retirement age, but as country folk never really did retire, all the mussel divers referred to them as old folks, and treated them with the utmost respect.

Alvin responded to her greeting. "I just come along to keep Freddy straight."

"He needs it," she joked.

All the mussel divers were crazy about her, and not just because she was the one who dished out the hundred-dollar bills.

"Five hundred and three pounds!" Freddy screamed.

"My," Emma said, writing the amount down in her book. She started multiplying rapidly. "All my boys did well today." She called all the divers "my boys." "One hundred eighty-eight dollars and sixty-three cents," she announced to Freddy.

"All right!" he shouted.

"I'll be around at the trailer, getting your cash ready for you," she said, and walked back around the building.

Freddy tripped the lever to the five-foot heavy metal cube that held the mussel shells. They fell through a trapdoor onto a three-foot-wide conveyor belt. Alvin threw the switch, over on the wall, that started the belt slowly moving. As the shells fell out onto the belt, they were carried up a thirty-degree incline for some ten feet, then fell off into a rotating cylinder. The cylinder, which had three-inch holes in it, was a couple of feet in diameter and was set up at a thirty-degree decline. As the mussel shells slowly tumbled down the cylinder, any shell too small for the buyer's needs fell through one of the holes, being culled. The unculled shells were deposited out the end of the cylinder into a huge metal vat that was partially filled with water. Underneath were gas burners.

In the morning the burners would be started. The mussels would open; the meat would fall away from the shells. The vat would be drained; the mussel shells, shoveled into another rotating cylinder. The meat would fall into another vat. The shells would be deposited in an enormous pile inside the large main room. Workers would shove the shells in gunnysacks, ready for shipment to Japan, where small fragments of the mother-of-pearl would be used for oyster seeding. Farmers would show up to get the mussel meat to feed their hogs.

When Freddy and Alvin drove around the trailer, Emma's husband Charlie, Bart, Eddie, Tony, and Turpin Adams were sitting nearby at a picnic table, drinking beer.

Turpin's huge upper body was a mummy-looking mess of gauze. Tony was wearing a pair of cutoff jeans. His lower left leg was all bandaged up.

They all hollered at Freddy and Alvin.

Charlie softly said hello to them and went back to drinking his beer.

Eddie tossed them both beers. Freddy opened his and started drinking. Alvin tossed his back.

As they sat down, Freddy said, "Is it safe to sit down, or are you going to stab somebody else today, Eddie?"

"Aw, you go straight to hell, you McMenafee-looking thang, you," Eddie came back with.

"Us McMenafees hold our own. And I don't see none of you Jacksons winnin' no beauty contests." Freddy shook his bottle, spewed some of his beer on Eddie, and sat down. "I might look like a McMenafee, but I git my pussy anyway."

"I git my pussy," Eddie defended. "You don't be worrying about me." He turned to Alvin and said, "Speakin' of pussy, I hadn't seen that highfalutin girlfriend of yours around, Alvin. How she doing?"

"Damned if I know," Alvin mumbled. He turned to Tony. "How are you doing?"

"All right." He smiled. "Emma cleaned me up, and ol' Charlie here sewed me up. Didn't even have to go uptown to the doctor."

He slapped Charlie on the back, and Charlie smiled, even though it had interfered with a sip of beer.

Turpin pulled a bottle out from under the table and took a slug, then passed it around.

Turpin said, "Charlie had to sew up a place on me, too. I didn't feel a thang."

He thunder-laughed, as though getting fucked up in a snagline and then his being so drunk he couldn't feel being sewed up were the funniest thing that ever happened to him.

Freddy said, "What's wrong with you, Bart? You over there beatin' your meat?"

Bart was at the edge of the picnic table, hunkered over as if he were taking a shit. He was unusually quiet. He looked over at Freddy. "What's it to ye? At least I don't have no stump-broke heifer tied up in my backyard."

There was a calf from a nearby farm that hung out in Freddy's yard at the cabin, and Bart liked to make as though Freddy were fucking it.

Freddy grinned. "That heifer's better than that ol' Ulrich girl-friend of yours I used to fuck on the side."

Bart looked back down at what he had been fooling with.

Freddy asked, "You playin' with yourself, or what?"

"Yeah. I'm fondling my jewels. What's it to ye?" Bart whipped around and held out three pearls, the size of marbles, toward Freddy.

Bart said, "Best day for pearls I ever had."

Two of the pearls were virgin white. One was white but streaked with a rainbow of color.

"Shit." Freddy sighed and almost dropped his beer. He reached for the pearls and said to Bart, "You tryin' to be like Johnny Ray or something?"

Eddie looked at Alvin and asked, "How's Donna and the kids doing?"

Alvin all of a sudden felt different, as if he didn't have as much in common with the rest of the divers anymore. And he hadn't liked being reminded of Ginger. Now Eddie asking him about Donna, as if he were supposed to be responsible for her.

"What you askin' me for?" Alvin snapped. "Goddammit, Eddie. No wonder Freddy picks on you so much. You can ask the dumb-assedest questions. You want to know about Donna and them, you go over there and find out youself. I'm not her husband and they daddy. Do I look like Johnny Ray? I'm not Johnny Ray."

Alvin went back to the truck.

Emma walked out of the trailer with Freddy's money. Freddy got up, took it, gave a hand motion of bye to everybody, and then followed Alvin away.

Twenty

ALVIN PULLED IN at Stinnett's American Station, in Beaulah Town. He sat in his car while it was being filled with gas. He noticed Troy and Buck sitting on a barbershop bench between the station and the Twilight Café. Alvin didn't want them to see him, but Troy spotted him and waved, so Alvin went over and sat down.

"You put ethyl in that little skitter?" Buck asked.

"Yeah. I like high octane."

"I hear ya."

"Bad about Johnny Ray," Troy said.

"Yeah," Alvin said.

"You still doin' dat deep-sea divin' in ne river?"

"Yeah."

"I reckon 'at's a good way to go if de Lawd calls," Buck said. He pulled the ring on a can of Possum sardines. It opened a quarter of the way back; then the ring broke off.

Alvin took it, pulled the top off with his fingers, and handed it back to Buck.

Buck said, "I liked dem nother kin' ne best. Dese kin' teah up."

Troy said, "Yas suh. I reckon id's a good way to go. Mae Ida's boy—what dat muthafucka's name?"

"Clayton?" offered Alvin.

"Yeah. He mought neah drownt. Shit, yeuh foe last. He sade everthang tuwned blue and he saw his whole life. Claimed he lived it plumb over, for dey pull him out and give'm dat respiration."

Alvin almost said, "Johnny Ray didn't drown!" but he didn't want to get into any talk. He wouldn't have even walked over if it weren't for all the wildcat he had hauled to Troy and all the cooking Buck had done with his daddy.

Buck said, "Main come by wid one dem moe-sheens up in ne boat." He was lining sardines side by side on top of a double Zesta cracker. "I ax, 'What dat moe-sheen for?' Dat main, he sade, 'Id pump ahh down to me.' I sade, 'You stay on top de water you wone need no ahh be pumpin' down to you.'"

He stuck the whole double cracker in his mouth and chomped a couple of times. Then he put an RC Cola bottle to his mouth and, turning it up, slid the bottle down until half the neck was in his mouth. His Adam's apple jumped up and down, and pieces of crackers floated to the top of the RC. He let the bottle down, got it out of his mouth, burped, and began lining up some more sardines while he went on. "Folks ain't got no damn sense no moe, "Buck said. "Doan even know how to fix de top of a sahdeen cane so's you kin git 'em open. I wisht you daddy wus still livin'. Hadn't had no good wildcat in ten yeuhs. I jest drank Foe Rose nowdays. Ax Troy. 'At's all I drank." He paused for a moment and looked thoughtful all at once. "Show wus bad 'bout Johnny Ray drownin'. Mae Ida's boy drownt. Sade everthang tawned blue. Whole life went foe his eyes."

"Shit, Buck," Troy said. "Mae Ida's boy didn't drown. He still alive."

"That lyin' muthafuckah. He tol' me he drownt."

Buck jammed the new cracker in his mouth and chomped, then stuck the bottle down his throat again. Alvin watched the bubbles in the RC. Buck brought the bottle down and burped cracker globs on Alvin's left pant leg.

Two little girls were holding on to one of the metal poles that supported the front overhang of the building. They started giggling.

One of them said, "Wanda say you one dem musclemen."

Before Alvin could say anything, the other girl said, "You is, too. You name's Alvin. Show huh you muscle. You done showed it to me an' Melvin one day down at Troy's."

Alvin had on a long-sleeve shirt. He flexed his right bicep in the basic show-me-your-muscle pose.

Wanda walked up, felt his bicep, grinned, and said, "See deah, Michelle."

Michelle walked up slowly, reached up her light brown arm, and felt Alvin's bicep with her left hand. Then she stood back and gawked at him with her blue eyes, as if Alvin had already won Mr. America.

Alvin didn't want the little girl to do that. He didn't want her to look at him as if he were Johnny Ray or something. He wasn't Johnny Ray. Alvin thought: I'm sorry, little girl. You lookin' at the wrong person.

Michelle asked, "You on de TV?"

"Uh-uh," Alvin answered. He thought: Don't do this to me.

"Wus you on *Hiwaya Five-O* las' night?"

"Uh-uh."

Wanda pulled at Michelle's arm. "Come on. We gotta git home."

Michelle followed Wanda sideways, looking back at Alvin, until they turned the corner of the building.

Alvin said, "I gotta go."

Troy said, "Yas suh. I got to git back to de house. Bidness be pickin' up."

"See ya'll later," Alvin said as he was walking away.

Alvin was impatient to get to Donna's. He went back to pay for the gas and got in his car. Before he cranked it up, a Ford Mustang with mag wheels pulled up on the other side of the pump, facing the opposite direction.

"Hey, Alvin. What's happening, man?"

"Hi, Ralph."

"Hey, you burn white gas in ya Z, man?"

"Yeah."

Ralph stared at him with the same look that had been on the little girls' faces. Alvin didn't want Ralph to look at him as if he were Johnny Ray. He didn't want him to look at him as if he were supposed to be able to do something. As if he had just made a movie with Burt Reynolds. Alvin wanted to be left alone.

"Hey, man," Ralph said. "All right! Lookin' good! Pumpin' that iron? I hear ya, man. All right!"

"How's it going?" Alvin asked. He wanted to get the hell out of there.

"Hey, man. Sorry to hear about Johnny Ray passing." Ralph took a sip of Colt 45 malt liquor that had been sitting between his legs on the car seat. "That dude"—he shook his head and smiled—"he was all right."

Alvin cranked his Z and said, "I know, Ralph. Look, you take it easy," figuring he'd reply, "I'll take it any way I can." But Ralph just gave him a thumbs-up sign for a good-bye.

Pushing the clutch in, Alvin slipped it in gear and let out on the clutch, screeching off.

He drove through Beaulah Town and out to Donna's house. Pulling into the driveway, he parked behind Donna's Corvette. He looked around. It looked as though a dog had strewn garbage over the front yard and it had been rained on several times. The glass in the front storm door was broken.

He got out and walked through the empty Coca-Cola bottles in the carport, then rang the bell at the kitchen door.

The place didn't look the same as it did when Johnny Ray lived there.

Twenty-one

ALVIN RANG the bell twice, knocked on the door, and Jenny came to let him in. She said, "Hey, Alv," as if she could have given a rat's ass who it was, and ran back into the living room to watch TV with Deward.

All the doors to the kitchen cabinets were open, and most of them had crayon markings on them. There were about fifteen different brands of cereal on the counter. Tarzan, a big yellow cat, lay asleep between the Cap'n Crunch and the Cocoa Puffs.

Alvin leaned against the kitchen counter and looked in at the living room. It looked as if the same people that had been in the kitchen had been living in there. He heard a door open and, looking down the hall, saw Donna walking toward him.

She hugged him and kissed him on the mouth. "Alvie, honey. What a terrific surprise!"

"Hey, Donna. Thought I would come over."

"Glad you did."

Donna pushed some coloring books back on the table and set down the bottle of fingernail polish she had in her hand. She threw some clothes off the chair and told Alvin, "Sit down. Want a drink?"

"No," he said firmly.

He watched her fix herself a vodka and orange juice. She had on a pair of Calvin Kleins that he figured must have taken her the better part of a quarter hour to get into. She wore a black Lynyrd Skynyrd T-shirt, and under it was a set of boobs that looked like a pair of first-pick Valencia oranges with wadcutter .38 slugs sticking out of them.

He thought how, in that same kitchen, about fifteen years ago, he would spend thirty minutes scheming just so Donna would bump into him and then touch him. He'd had a bad crush on her but had never known how to handle the way he had felt.

Looking down at the table in front of him, he saw a Walt Disney coloring book. On the front cover was a picture of a dog with the name "Goofy" written under it.

Suddenly he understood the joke that Freddy had told him earlier in the day. He laughed, saying, "She's fucking Goofy! Aw, me."

"Who's crazy?" Donna asked.

"Naw. Mickey Mouse is in court, and he wants a divorce from Minnie Mouse, and the judge says, 'I hear you claim Minnie's crazy.' And Mickey says, 'Naw, Your Honor. What I said was: "She's fuckin Goofy." ' "

"Well?" Donna waited. She sat down. "Did they get the divorce?"

She set the drink down, pulled the nail polish in front of her, and opened it. She shook her hair back out of her face. It was a naturally streaked blond; some of the strands were light brown, but others were platinum.

"Yeah. I think so," Alvin said, just to give a reply.

Her fingernails were already painted to a deep red, but she started putting another coat on them. "I've got to leave in thirty minutes."

"Are you going to leave those kids by theirselves?"

"Sure," Donna replied. "All they do is sit in front of that damn TV all the time. I got a date with a recording star in Muscle Shoals."

"Donna, why haven't you been sending those kids to school?"

"What do you mean?"

"The truant officer said the kids haven't been showing up at the school."

"The shit-ass that came out here? His main trouble is I wouldn't give him any pussy. And I'm not spreading my legs for any shit-ass bastard. I don't give a rat's ass who he is."

If there was one thing in the world Alvin hated, it was a shit-ass. He admired Donna's ability to recognize shit-asses. And more, he respected her nature not to cooperate or render any sexual services to them.

Alvin wondered if this was some recording star that she had known before Johnny Ray had died. Johnny Ray had gotten hooked up with some of the Muscle Shoals recording people when they were selling the high-grade wildcat to Old Man Howard. For some reason Alvin wanted to ask Donna, "Did you ever fuck anybody else while you were married to Johnny Ray?" but he didn't want to sound like Eddie, whom he had just gotten pissed at for asking something kind of similar.

Alvin said, "Well, the kids need to get to school, on time and all. Especially tomorrow."

"They can't go to school tomorrow!"

"Why not?"

"We're going grocery shopping tomorrow. Hell, I haven't been home in four days. I want to spend some time with my children."

"Shit, Donna. That's what the welfare department gets all pissed off about. You leaving the kids."

"They can stay fine without me. Jenny's almost thirteen."

"She's eleven."

"I spend quality time with Jenny and Deward. Some folks don't even talk to their kids. Let the welfare department raise hell to *them*. And I don't whip them or be hollering for them what to do."

Alvin wondered where the hell she got the idea of quality time. It almost sounded as though she had been hanging around Ginger or somebody. Quality time sure seemed to suit her needs right now.

Donna continued. "Anyway, tomorrow they have to help me shop. See, on TV they see all these foods they want to eat." She pointed around the counter with a half-painted nail. "And see, most parents don't give a shit what they kids want to eat."

"God, Donna! You got to cook for those younguns. They can't live off that cereal shit. I'm a bodybuilder. I know about these things. You got to eat the right stuff. Especially those little ones."

Donna reached over to the far side of the table and got an open box of Frosted Flakes. She slid it over to Alvin, making sure not to mess up her nails.

She said, "Read the shit in that stuff. Vitamins A to Z. Them little mothers are just bustin' out with vitamins and minerals and all kinds of shit."

Alvin pushed the cereal box out of his face and said, "Look, if those kids don't start showing up for school and it don't look like they proper cared for, the state's going to take you children away from you and put them in foster homes."

Donna wasn't shocked by the statement, nor was she curious to know how Alvin had found out about what the welfare department had confronted her with on several occasions, when it was able to find her at home.

She finished painting her little fingernail, looked at Alvin, and shook her nailbrush at him as she talked. "I'm not letting the government tell me how to raise my children. And I'll tell you something else. If that shit-ass shows up here one more time trying to raise hell, I'm going to shoot him right between the eyes with Johnny Ray's three-fifty-seven Magnum."

Alvin just looked at her as she put another coat of polish on her nails.

He said, "Do it for me, Donna. Get those younguns in school in the morning."

Donna kept painting her nails. Tarzan came up and breathed in Alvin's face. The kids came running into the kitchen. It was a commercial break. They jerked the refrigerator door open and stood there looking in, kind of hopping in place as though they were fixing to jump into the refrigerator.

Donna turned to them and said, "If ya'll are going to spend the night with Alvin, go get yaw's stuff together and get loaded up."

They started screaming, "We goin' to Alvin's. We goin' to Alvin's," and they ran back to their rooms in the back of the house.

"I didn't—I—" Alvin protested.

"The bus comes by about seven-thirty," Donna said.

The kids ran right back by him and out the side kitchen door, dragging duffel bags.

Donna put the brush back in the nail polish bottle and tightened it. She reached over and grabbed Alvin's face, careful not to swipe her nails, and gave him a kiss on the mouth.

Then she walked back down the hall, into her room, and closed the door.

Twenty-two

THE KIDS HADN'T EATEN supper, so Alvin went through town to get a barrel of Kentucky Fried Chicken. All the while he was driving, the kids were jumping up and down in their seats, hollering.

Alvin cursed silently and realized he'd made two mistakes: He'd tried to tell Donna what to do, and he'd told her to do it for him.

When they got to Mud Creek, the children stormed into the house and flicked on the TV. Alvin relaxed back in the La-Z-Boy, feeling his muscles just aching.

He thought how before his muscles got used to any one routine, he would change it. This time he was going to listen to his muscles. He knew his muscles were kind of like Donna: They were going to do what they wanted to anyhow.

He looked at Jenny and Deward, who were in the middle of the living room, on the floor, watching TV and eating the fried chicken.

"Don't ya'll have any homework to get?"

"I don't know," Jenny said. "We haven't been to school this week."

"Well, did you bring you schoolbooks?" Alvin asked. He figured they must be in the duffel bags they brought with them.

Deward looked up at Alvin as though he were bothering him from watching the TV. He said, "We don't have any schoolbooks."

"Why not?"

"They got lost somewhere. And if I knew where they were, they wouldn't be lost. And if I knew where I last had them, I'd know where they was."

"You be glad you don't have Old Lady Higgins for a teacher," Alvin said. "You be glad she went and got her head cut off."

Deward was back looking at the television, not paying any attention to Alvin.

There was a rumble, and headlights flashed through the windows. Alvin knew it was Freddy's Camaro.

The door opened, and Freddy walked in with a tan blond debutante. He looked stunned that Johnny Ray's children were lying around in the middle of the floor, but that lasted only an instant.

He announced, "Alvin, this is Judy. Judy, Alvin."

Judy said, with a forced smile, "Hi, Alvin."

Alvin looked at her. She had on a miniskirt. It looked like a waitress or barmaid's outfit.

"Hi, Judy," he said. He tried to imitate her smile but didn't do too good of a job at it.

"This is Jenny and Deward," Freddy said.

Judy said hello to them.

Deward, Jenny, and Dr. Dick just stared at her for about fifteen seconds and then turned back to the TV.

Judy said to Freddy, kind of sweetlike, "What a funny-looking little dog."

Without looking away from the TV, Deward said, "He ain't funny-looking. You the one that's funny-looking."

Judy just smiled. She put her hands on the back of her thighs, slid them up over her small, tight ass, and rested them on top of her hips, with her grapefruit-size tits sticking out and her back arched.

"This is so pretty," she said, surveying the living room, and followed Freddy into the kitchen.

In a moment the couple passed back through with Freddy carrying a three-quarter-full bottle of Southern Comfort and Judy sashaying behind him with a couple of glasses. They went into the big bedroom and closed the door.

"Go turn up the TV, Deward," Jenny said.

Deward got up and turned it up almost full blast.

"It's loud enough already. Shit," Alvin yelled.

Jenny hollered, "That girl'll probably start screaming."

"What you talking about?" Alvin was yelling now.

Jenny turned the television down a bit and said to Alvin, "When they start fucking, she'll probably start moaning and screaming."

"When did you start saying that word?" he asked.

"Which one?"

"Fucking."

"Oh, about two weeks ago."

A commercial came on. Deward started feeding Dr. Dick the chicken legs. Jenny went and got herself a Coca-Cola, came back, and planted herself in front of the screen again.

Alvin stared at them. He didn't know what to say to them, and there didn't seem to be anything they wanted to hear except that TV. So he went back to his small bedroom and closed the door. Johnny Ray would have whipped her ass, but he wasn't Johnny Ray.

He took off his clothes, put on his posing trunks, and stood in front of the full-length mirror. He stood sideways and did some stomach vacuums, trying to touch his backbone with his navel.

He thought: It's coming along. It's been long coming. But this time it's gittin' there.

He faced the mirror and stood relaxed, with his arms at his sides. His blood vessels stuck out everywhere, from his head, to his chest, to his upper arms. He had never seen blood vessels with the flow and continuity of his, and he was proud of them.

He flexed his abs, and the ripples jumped out.

There's not going to be a bit of fat, he thought. My fat intake is gone to go to zero. When they talk about cut-up Mr. Americas, they, by God, gone to talk about Alvin Lee Fuqua.

Sticking his right big toe out, he placed it on the floor and pressed down. His right thigh erupted into three entwined sections of muscle.

When he examined his legs, then his chest, there was something about them that didn't seem right. Then it hit him.

He went to the bathroom. He got his double-edged razor and shaving cream and sat on the edge of Purple Bathtub, with his feet in it. He rubbed shaving cream all over his legs and began shaving from the top of his thighs down.

Judy burst into the bathroom, stared at Alvin, and said, "I'm sorry. The door was open."

She froze in front of Purple Sink, watching him shave his legs.

Alvin kept shaving. "That's okay," he said, looking up to smile at her. One of his own smiles this time.

Jenny ran in, went over to the commode, pulled her pants and panties down, and started to pee. "You don't have on your black stockings anymore," she said to Judy abruptly.

Judy started backing out of the bathroom, then turned and ran.

Jenny finished, got her pants back up, and ran off to the living room.

When Alvin finished shaving his legs, he shaved his chest, stomach, and then under his arms. He took off his posing trunks and showered off.

He went back to his room and posed a little bit again with his newly shaved body. He felt cleaner, sleeker, less inhibited. He was sure he could now slide from one pose to the next more effortlessly. As he looked into the mirror, he knew he was going to start hitting negative resistance repetitions harder than Cooter Brown hit wildcat whiskey. Then he wondered, If he got some steroids, maybe he wouldn't have to eat as much.

Alvin put his clothes back on and then dragged a mattress from the back porch to the living room. The kids didn't even look up from the TV. Deward was still handing Dick pieces of chicken out of the big barrel, never taking his eyes off the screen. Dr. Dick would go over in the corner and eat the chicken, then walk back over and Deward would hand him another piece.

Alvin was about to ask the kids if they wanted to put bed sheets on their mattress now when he noticed Dr. Dick go over and puke by the stereo. He looked around. There were little blobs of puke all over the living room. He went over and yanked the barrel out of Deward's little hands. There was just one piece left in there.

"Shit, this was supposed to last a couple more days," Alvin said loudly. Deward didn't seem to care, and Alvin got to thinking that he shouldn't eat that crap anymore. There was too much fat in it. It was a sign: Deward fed that shit to Dr. Dick, and Dr. Dick puked. Somebody was trying to tell him something. Maybe Johnny Ray.

Alvin was on his knees, wiping up the puke, when he felt pressure on his head. Then he felt it inside his head so painfully that he wished he could drill a hole in it to let some of the pressure off. He had a hard time holding his body up. Every time he swept his hand across the floor he felt himself hitting and pulling out a big washboard, stuck down in the carpet.

I'm getting the Mussels! he thought. He never knew if this strange disorientation ever affected any of the other divers. He had the feeling this sensation had happened to him several times before. But he couldn't remember the first time. He would have even thought this was the first time, it was so strange, but since he seemed to know what it was and had even gone to the trouble of naming it, it must have happened before.

The pain eased up. It became hard to finish the cleanup because he felt as if he were floating around the room, feeling along the floor, pulling up mussels in the same kind of way he floated almost weight-less at the bottom of the river.

After finishing the carpet, Alvin got sheets and pillows and fixed up the mattress on the floor. Then he told Jenny and Deward good night.

He went into his bedroom, pulled off his clothes, and got into bed. He felt as though he were drifting around. He couldn't keep his balance. It was as if he were standing up, even though he was down flat. His head hurt so badly he started to moan. He could hear himself moaning but couldn't feel himself doing it.

Then Ginger appeared.

She was kneeling beside him on the bed. He reached up to grab her hand; but it was a mussel, and he pulled it out of what felt like mud. Then Alvin's sense of balance went, and he found himself on his stomach, facedown in his pillow.

He turned over on his side, and there she was. It was real, just like Ginger, but he knew it couldn't be. He knew that he had the Mussels and that his senses couldn't be trusted. That's all he knew for real.

He started to kiss Ginger, but there was a mussel at her mouth. The lips of the mussel were in the same place as her lips should have been. He pulled the mussel out but wasn't sure if it had been there for a mouth or if it had just been stuck in her face.

Then he put his hand between her legs and found a mussel there. He pulled it out but didn't know if it was her vagina or had been stuck between her legs, up in her torso.

Alvin rolled over on his other side. As his eyes were open, he could see the room get lighter, the way it would if someone had opened his bedroom door. He turned and looked toward the door.

It was Donna.

He didn't know if it was real or not.

Donna said, "Hi," and stared at him, grinning.

Alvin said, "Hi," because he always spoke when spoken to, even when he had the Mussels. That was the way Johnny Ray would have handled it. He didn't see any use in lying there trying to figure out if it was real or not.

Donna walked over to the bed and sat down beside him, the same way Ginger had a little earlier. Alvin couldn't tell how much earlier or how long Donna had been staring at him. With the Mussels, he couldn't trust his sense of time.

Donna stared at him with glassy-looking eyes. She had a demonic grin on her face. Alvin thought about his father. He didn't know for sure if his father was really dead or if he himself was a mussel diver and training for Mr. America. He couldn't remember what age he was. Time had been thrown all out of whack. For a moment he wondered if Donna was his mother and he was three years old. Then he thought about his father again.

His father had said, "Now, boy, you git around somebody that's a stranger or that just ain't right, you watch out for they eyes. Them funny people can hypmotize ye. Everthang might seem fine and smooth and dandy, but everthang that glitters ain't gold, boy."

But Alvin looked Donna right in the eyes, and her face seemed to get clearer and brighter. There were no shades on the windows, and the light from the outside gave a little light to the room; but it still seemed the room lightened up a little more.

Donna said, "Oh, Alvin, I've got it all figured out."

It didn't matter to him whether Donna was really there or not. "What you got all figured out, Donna?"

"I can't make love with you."

"No?"

"No," Donna said, as if that one decision had solved all her problems and made all life grand. "But you're going to be my number one person. I want to know all about you and know all your pains and all your joys and share them with you. Oh, Alvin, you're too good to ever let go. Hold me. Hold me!"

Alvin got up, put his arms around her, and held her. She squeezed so hard he could barely breathe. He was trying to figure out what she meant about all his pains and joys.

"Oh, Alvin, I've loved you for a long time. I've been making love to you for a long time."

"What do you mean, making love to me for a long time?" he asked quickly.

"Oh, maybe not making love to you with your body. But I've been making love to you for a long time."

"How long?"

"Oh, ever since you were fifteen."

Alvin thought how that was about when he had the crush on her. Somewhere in there. He was thinking if what you thought had anything to do with what happened to you later, he was in big trouble.

Donna continued. "Even long before then, I've been making love to you almost without stopping." She eased up on hugging him some. She jerked him closely again and said, "Hold me! Hold me! Oh, Alvin, I want to know all about you."

"You know everything about me."

"Sure. I know who your folks were. I watched you grow up. I know how old you are. But I want to know *you*. Everything."

She leaned back from him and looked into his eyes. She shook her head back and forth in short, slow motions, as if she were trying to see all there was to see about his face. She was grinning. Then, all of a sudden, she jerked him to her and held him tight.

"Oh, Alvin, you're just too good. I'm not going to let you get away that easily. Hold me!"

Donna broke away from him, slid her hands around his face, and held it cupped in her hands. She shook her head, gazing at him. Then she shook it harder, to mean no, and said, "I want to, but I can't make love to you until I know you."

She jumped up and took off her T-shirt and shoes. Then she peeled off her jeans. She wasn't wearing anything else. She got back on the bed, lay on her back beside Alvin, and pulled him on top of her. "I want to make love so badly, but I just can't."

Donna rubbed his face with both hands, then ran her fingers through his hair and around his ears. Sliding her fingertips to the top of his head, she pushed him down her body until her arms were extended. The same way Johnny Ray had pushed his head under water so many times when he was small and Johnny Ray would be horsing around with him in the water.

Donna grabbed the edge of the bed.

Suddenly she threw her head back in an arch and screamed, "Right there. Oh God! Right there! Don't stop!"

Twenty-three

THE NEXT MORNING Alvin woke up clearheaded and alone. The Mussels were gone. He looked around but could see no evidence of Donna. It didn't matter.

He slipped on his pants and went to the door. When he opened it, he could smell sausage. He walked on into the kitchen. Deward and Jenny had cooked breakfast. There was a plate of cold sausage and eggs, covered in grease, that had been left for him.

He almost puked at the thought of eating it. A note beside the plate said, "We went to school. Here is your breakfast. Signed, Deward and Jenny."

Dick pawed at the back door. Alvin went over and let him in. Dick started licking up a broken egg on the floor. Alvin set his plate of food down on the floor for him.

After stirring up three raw eggs in some skim milk he wandered into the living room, drinking it. The room was a shambles. He was wondering how they could leave their things strewn around this way but realized it was all his stuff. All their things and their duffel bags were gone.

He walked on past the mess and out the door, down to the dock.

He pulled his T-shirt and jeans off and lay down on the dock in just his posing trunks, to sun. He was about to nod off when he realized his muscles were letting him know that they were under repair and that he shouldn't work out for the next couple of days.

He decided no matter how loud the weights called him, he had to lay off for two days. Then it would be time for an excruciating workout.

Alvin went to sleep in the sun, awakening a short while later to a thumping on the dock. He looked up and saw it was Cliff in his boat, the bow bumping a piling.

"Hey, Cliff," Alvin said, and propped himself up on his right elbow.

"Did you go out today?" Cliff asked.

"Naw. I'm not goin' out."

"Neither is Freddy. Mind if I take the pickup to haul my shells?"

"You know I don't," Alvin replied.

"Alvin, what about tonight?"

"Tonight it's gone be dark."

Cliff smiled. "No, I mean, do you want to go down and watch Alma's act in Birmingham?"

Alvin decided suddenly that that was the perfect thing to do.

"Yeah, let's go," Alvin said, and then grinned. He would get to see Alma, make Cliff happy, and be physically unavailable to his weight room, so that his weights could not pull him, lure him, to lift them while his muscles were telling him to lay off.

Cliff smiled again.

Birmingham was about a two-hour drive from Alvin's house. Alvin got ready and left around two-thirty to head over to Freddy and Cliff's. He played a few rounds of dominoes with Freddy while Cliff went off to Dixie Shell to sell his day's dive.

Alvin opened the next game with a double five. As he laid it faceup in the middle of Freddy's small, rickety kitchen table, he said, "We didn't knock you out of any pussy last night, did we?"

"Naw, shit naw. I git my cooter. You start knocking me out of any of my cooter, you know about it," Freddy stated.

Shortly Cliff came back and got cleaned up. He walked into the kitchen, where Alvin and Freddy were still playing dominoes. He was wearing some jeans Alvin knew cost three times as much as a pair of Levi's, loafers, a dress shirt, and a corduroy blazer. He put on his diver's watch and then kind of pressed it down on his wrist. He cracked his knuckles.

Cliff announced, "Well, I'm ready."

Freddy looked over and said, "Hot damn, Cliff baby. You gone have to beat them city women off with a two-by-four."

Cliff grinned and then asked, "Freddy, you sure you don't want to go?"

Just as Cliff asked, Judy drove up to the front of the cabin in her Toyota and got out, answering Cliff's question.

Alvin and Cliff drove out of the way a bit to go to a dive shop across the river to get some new regulators. Then they continued on, having to stop once halfway down for Cliff to take a shit.

As they were entering the city, they stopped and had supper. They had plenty of time to kill.

It was nine o'clock when Alvin pulled in and parked at the far end of Morris Avenue. They got out of the car and started walking down the old street, which was once the commerce center of the town.

Alvin asked, "Do you mind walking a short ways?"

"No," Cliff said.

"The clubs are down on the opposite end, but it's a nice walk. I like Birmingham. Especially the old part like this. They've redone all this. Renovated it back to the way it was original. I hadn't spent all that much time here, but I feel familiar with it. You know what I mean?"

"Sure do."

Alvin continued, "This street here and Market Street. Used to be a lot going on here. When I was little, I would come with Johnny Ray, hauling wildcat whiskey for my daddy. It's a big city. There were lots of Greeks and Italians here, but I always felt real comfortable."

Alvin paused.

"This was the town I took Mr. Alabama in."

Cliff lit up a cigarette and said, "I hear you, man."

Alvin was looking around at all the lights, the neon signs.

Alvin said, "Yeah. It's fun talking about this stuff. It's stuff I forget till I come back here. I remember one time I was six years old. Daddy had this old '47 Chevy delivery van. The stills were on Hatchett Island, and we took the whiskey from the island to Hatchett Point in a wooden barge. We loaded the van up with a hundred cases of moonshine. Just me and Johnny Ray in the van. I was sitting on an upside-down Pet milk case. There wasn't a passenger seat in the van. Just this milk case bolted down where a passenger seat would have been. Anyway, I'm sittin' up straight and stern like I was a big shit, you know."

Alvin laughed a little. They stopped walking to look into a shopwindow, but Cliff was still listening wholeheartedly to what Alvin was saying.

Alvin continued. "We hauled that truckload to a bootlegger Daddy sold to regularly in the produce district. We brought it to this warehouse here off Morris Avenue, and after we unloaded, Frankie, he was my age, that was the bootlegger's son, he started playing around in the back of the van. Frankie keeps tuggin' on my shoulder, sayin', 'Come on, Alvie. Let's wrestle. Let's play back in here.'

"I didn't want to be acting like a six-year-old kid in front of Johnny Ray." Alvin smiled. "I told Frankie, 'I don't play. I quit school because they had recess.' I had heard Johnny Ray tell a man that one time down by the old cotton docks at Beaulah Town, and it sounded the appropriate thing for me to say.

"He kept tugging on me. I told him if he didn't quit, I's gone hit 'im. He tugged agin. I stood up, turned around, and hit him in the nose with my fist. He stumbled back to the middle of the van and dropped to his knees. His eyes rolled back, and wine-colored blood started flowing out of both of his nostrils. He fell on down and lay on his face.

"I knew there wadn't anything I could do about it. I knew I couldn't take the punch back. I just watched the blood flow onto the bed of the van.

"I knew I had killed him and that I was headed for the electric chair. But Johnny Ray came back, and Frankie got up and held his nose and said, 'I'm all right.'

"Then I figured I was saved from the electric chair but would be sent to the Birmingham Industrial School for Boys. There was Frankie, the evidence. A lot of shit went through my head then, seeing myself working there and then getting transferred to Drake State Penitentiary to work in the cotton fields. Then being released and standing on a deserted road, holding my thumb out, trying to get home to a place I didn't know was still there or not."

"I know the feeling all too well," Cliff commented. "Such things do happen."

Alvin said, "I was feeling like shit for hitting him. Then his daddy walked up while Johnny Ray was tending to him, and his daddy asked, 'What's the matter?' And Frankie said, 'Nothing. We was just playing.'

"I couldn't believe it. That hurt, man. Then on top of that, when he went to leave, he said, 'Bye, Alvie,' and damned if I couldn't even remember his name. I just had to say, 'Bye.' The whole thing made me feel lower than mussel shit."

"I know exactly what you're talking about," Cliff said, and they walked on down the avenue.

Twenty-four

THEY SETTLED themselves into a small back corner table of Downtown Sam's Cosmic Café. Alvin saw Sam behind the bar, talking to someone.

Sam had always liked Alvin, giving him free drinks anytime he came in. Alvin wanted to be sociable and not come into his place without saying hello. But on the other hand, it had been well over a year since they had seen each other, and he was afraid Sam wouldn't remember him. Alvin didn't want to walk up to Sam as if Sam were supposed to know who Alvin was, embarrassing both of them. Alvin just let it slide.

There was a quartet up onstage, playing something that sounded like an odd mixture of country, jazz, and the blues. They called themselves Red Sammy and the Blue Ribbon Boys.

Cliff was looking around at the people in the club. Alvin started listening to the band.

The singer was singing, "Unplug the support system and pump me full of lead, don't want to be anybody's favorite vegetable, don't want to be your favorite cabbage head. . . ."

A girl walked up to the table and said singsongy to Alvin and Freddy, "Hello. What could I get for ya'll to drink?"

Alvin turned around to answer, and at first he thought it was that girl Judy. She had on an outfit similar to the one Judy had been wearing last night. He thought she and Freddy had gotten in a quick one, and then she had gotten in her car and rushed to work.

Alvin looked around quickly for Freddy. Then he noticed her more closely and realized it was only a resemblance.

Cliff said, "A double Johnnie Walker Black on ice, please."

"A glass of water," Alvin said.

"You't some of that Perrier water everbody's been drinking, or you just want some tap water?"

"Just some tap water."

When the waitress came back with the drinks, Cliff asked her, "Is Alma Fuqua going to perform tonight?"

"I don't know," she snapped. "You another one of those Yankees?"

"I'm her brother," Alvin broke in. He didn't know why she got upset about the question, but he didn't want to hear her bitching about Cliff being a Yankee.

"Aw, you that one that's a muscleman," she said, and smiled. "I just got aggravated. See that tableful of folks up near the stage?" She pointed to them.

"Yeah," Alvin and Cliff said.

"Anyway, they come down here every night this week, asking me when Alma Fuqua's going to be on."

"There's nothing wrong with that," Alvin responded.

"Yeah. But a couple weeks ago there was this group from up at Harvard. They were doing some paper for college about the South. I don't know what the hell they have to come down here for. Come study the South. Shit. So, now there's another bunch of Yankees up there. Sittin' at the same damn table. All they drink is wine and want me to run back and forth getting them free popcorn. The trouble is neither bunch knew how to tip."

Cliff assured her all Yankees weren't like that.

"I reckon they just fucked up," she concluded.

"So you reckon Alma will be here tonight?" Alvin asked.

"I don't know. The last I saw her was four nights ago. She and Sam were backstage fighting. She was hollering, 'There's a f-a-t woman out there! Get her out! Get her out!' She wouldn't go on because there was a fat woman sitting beside the stage and Sam was trying to tell her he couldn't tell the woman to leave."

That answered Alvin's wondering if Alma ever put that f-a-t crap off on anybody else. "Did he fire her or something?" Alvin asked.

"Hell, naw. He's not going to fire her. She can get away with anything," she replied, and walked away.

Cliff said, "If she doesn't show up, maybe we better go see if she's okay."

"Aw yeah. We'll go by her place all right. I doubt she'll go on soon. She usually hangs out for a good while before she goes on."

The waitress came right back, put their orders down on the table, and quickly left. The speed with which they got it and the lack of a tab were indications to Alvin that they were getting special treatment.

Cliff took a long sip of his JW Black, looked around, and then said, "I like this. I'm glad we came."

"Yeah, me, too." Alvin looked around and then back to Cliff. "Hey, Cliff, why you so interested in coming down here, seeing Alma perform?"

"I used to be a comedian," Cliff stated.

Alvin looked over, noticing Cliff very closely.

"I didn't know you were a comedian."

"Used to be," Cliff corrected. He slugged down the rest of his drink. "The last time I went up on a stage, three hundred people just stared at me for five minutes. That was in California after I got back from overseas."

Alvin had never thought of Cliff as a comedian. He never carried on the way say, Freddy and Eddie did. He never *tried* to act funny. But sometimes he just *was* funny.

Funny in ways that seemed different. Like the time he was going back up to New York for a visit. They were sitting around, and after Cliff got off the telephone with the airline company, Eddie asked him, "Well, are you on the plane?" meaning did he get the reservation settled. Cliff just looked over seriously and said, "Not right now." There was something about it that was hilarious to them all, except Cliff. Alvin didn't know if it was the timing, tone of voice, or what he had actually said.

Although he had never suspected Cliff of being a comedian, something about it made a lot of sense to Alvin now. It was simple to imagine Cliff up on a stage, playing to a packed house, having each person in the palm of his hand, not letting up on them, then just as they were recovering from a bout of laughter, Cliff hitting them again.

What made that so easy to imagine was this sense Alvin had about Cliff. He had always felt that Cliff was holding back in some way. There was something that Cliff knew, something he could do, something he was very professional at, that someday he would cut loose to master.

And it was simple imagining Cliff coming back to the river, hanging out, and again being unassuming. But all the while he was unassuming, something deep within him building up, ripening. Just as Cliff had said that Johnny Ray had a presence to him, so did Cliff have a presence to him; a presence, Alvin thought, of potential, of mastery, of professionalism.

It had been the same way with Alvin's bodybuilding, but only for the first time did Alvin realize this. Backstage he was never the loud, visible bodybuilder. He quietly warmed up, then went out, and after the first pose he owned the audience.

"I never even considered the judges!" Alvin mumbled. Only after the trainer had told him that shit about his hip structure did Alvin ever worry. He realized that was where he had gone wrong. It had nothing to do with getting into the realm of higher competition. Before, he had just gone out and done his job. He got out on that stage and took each one of the audience on a ride they couldn't get anywhere else. Only a ride Alvin Lee Fuqua could give!

Just then, without their having ordered, the waitress came over with two more drinks. She said, "It's starting to get crowded in here."

She put another scotch and water down in front of Cliff. She put a drink in front of Alvin and said, "Here, big boy, try this Wimp Water with a twist of lime. It's the latest craze."

Alvin spied down on it and said, "OK. What is it?"

"Perrier with a twist."

Cliff took a sip of his drink and said, "Thank you."

Before she walked away hurriedly, she said, "Oh! Alma's fixing to go on in just a few minutes."

Alvin said, "All right!"

But Cliff didn't say anything. He was staring at the stage. Alvin saw beads of sweat break out on his forehead, and in the light of Downtown Sam's Cosmic Café, he seemed to be a strange color.

Twenty-five

THEN THERE's the librarian fuck," Alma said. She held her hands close to her chest like a little rabbit and said very curtly, "Fuck."

Downtown Sam's Cosmic Café roared with laughter. There must have been close to three hundred people packed into the place now. Standing room only, literally, for about 10 percent of those there.

Alvin had to lean just right to get a good view of her. Every time he put his attention on the glass of water he was drinking, he noticed Cliff. He was taking in every word and move of Alma's. Laughing like everyone else, yet not missing a thing.

Alma took the microphone from the stand and paced the stage a bit.

She stopped, turned to the audience and said, "I also call it the Sunday school fuck. It is said very snooty with no particular emphasis. The *F* has a peculiar pronunciation with the 'librarian fuck.' The word could easily be misunderstood to sound like 'cluck.' "

Half of the audience was still chuckling.

"Now. I've gone over fuck, FFFFFuck, fucKKKKK. The thing is these are only said by women. Yes, badly as I hate to say it, the world is not equal. In an age when it's hip to have men equal women equal men, it's not true. Women aren't men. Men aren't women. Especially in the way they say 'fuck.' Women emphasize the consonants. Whether it be the 'librarian fuck,' the 'career woman fuck,' the 'good ol' girl fuck,' whatever, the emphasis is on the consonants. Now, the way men say 'fuck,' they emphasize, that's right, the vowel."

Alma seemed to turn on energy. Energy seemed to come out of her. Even when she wasn't moving, she seemed hyper. This was the way she was now.

She imitated a woman, in a voice other than her own: "Darling, I'm pregnant."

Alma flipped over to being a man: "Fuuuuuuuuuck!"

"No dip shit, we've already done that. Now you've got to Wuuuuuuuurk. OOOOOOOOvertime. Lot's of woooooooorking ooooovertime. The goddamn hospital wants nine hundred fuuuuuuucking dollars up front," Alma said in the woman's voice.

The whole place cried with laughter again. Even the waitresses and bartenders had stopped to listen to her. She was hot.

As the applause died, Alma continued, "Now the only exception to this vowel/consonant rule in regards to the male/female is what I call the Southern Belle."

Alma now did an exaggerated Southern Belle accent: "Fuuck. Why caan't we go to New Awluns now, honey? You know my puussy just itches to be in New Awluns this time ah yeuh. Oh, honey, if you take me to New Awluns this week, I'll give you one of those repulsive blow jobs you love such every day while we auh theuh. Oh, my goodness, what a decent girl has to go through nowadays just to live a tolerable life. Fuuck."

It was all that was needed to get the crowd roaring again. Alvin thought: You own them now, Alma, just like after I give my front lat pose. Take 'em home now, baby. Take 'em home and give 'em dessert.

Alma said, "What is it to most men? The attainment of pussy is the ultimate?"

She said in a hippie, druggy voice: "Like I must unrelentingly use my dick up until nothing is left but a pussy."

Alma said in a Bart voice: "Shit. Look what you did, dip shit. That ain't chlorine. You accidentally dumped highly toxic lethal chemicals into the water supply of the town."

"Hey, you don't be worrying about me. I git my pussy," Alma said quickly in an Eddie voice.

Then the voice of a high-minded judge: "This man is found not guilty. He gits his pussy."

Alma zapped off the last lines rapid fire. She stood, hands on her hips while the crowd whooped and hollered.

When it was quiet, she asked, "You know what it is men can't stand that women do?"

There was some rumbling in the audience, guys hollering, "Spending money." Soon several people were screaming, "What?" up to Alma.

She waited until the whole place was absolutely quiet. Then she brought the microphone close to her mouth and whispered, "Masturbate."

The crowd cracked up.

"That's right." Then she said in a Bart voice: "Aw man. Shit. I would have done it for her. Shit. That pussy going to waste."

Alma got hyper again. She began working very fast, but it was very effective in her delivery. "And you think the fact that women masturbate drives men crazy, I tell you something they can't . . . that makes them go insane: two good-looking lesbians."

In a Bart voice: "Two pussies going to waste. Oh man. It's a crying shame. Shit."

Now she was Alma again: "See, if it's two bull dykes, it's OK. Just two ugly women out of harm's way. Two princesses, they can't stand it. Two good-looking pussies going to waste. What's a good-looking pussy anyway? Men can't stand to see a pussy go to waste."

Then in a new voice Alma joked: "She was home watching TV? Hell, she could have been fucking me. Pussy going to waste."

Alma paused and let the audience chuckle. Then she said, "See,

I was born and raised in a place in the swamp way out from Muscle Shoals."

Over to the right side of the stage, at two tables pulled together sat a large group of guys. When Alma mentioned Muscle Shoals they applauded and cheered.

Alma walked over to the guys' side of the stage and looked at them. "What, you guys from Muscle Shoals?"

One of the guys said back to Alma, "We're recording there now. Playing backup."

"Yeah. For whom?"

After a few seconds' lag none of the guys gave up a name.

Alma stepped over toward middle stage and said out to the audience, pointing back to the musicians, "OK. Some famous musician in the middle of this gang here. Always action at Downtown Sam's Cosmic Café."

The audience laughed but knew there probably was some famous musician over in that dark corner.

Alma walked back over to the group. "Sorry, sorry. But I was feeling mean. I did some studio work at Muscle Shoals for a couple of weeks one summer when I got out of high school."

One of the guys asked interestedly, "Yeah?"

"Yeah. Played French horn. Backup. For this guy Lanny Lange. I was supposed to get two cents a record or some shit. But Lanny decided to prove he was a *real* musician. Shot some speed, got drunk, and drove his car off the Shoals Creek Bridge. No, I didn't get pissed about that or nothing."

The audience contentedly listened to Alma talk to the musicians. She continued talking. "Then I got a scholarship, majored in music at the University of Alabama."

The crowd started hollering and yelling, "Roll Tide."

Alma looked out at the audience in such a way as to make the whole place get very quiet. "Hey, this isn't a goddamn pep rally," she abruptly screamed. "I'm trying to talk to these gentlemen over here. Fellow musicians. Now shut the fuck up!"

Alma turned to the musicians. "Yeah, after I got my degree, I got out, found out I couldn't play anymore."

The musicians laughed. Alma threw them a kiss and said, "Good luck with your recording."

She stepped downstage and looked out into the darkness. She focused on a bunch of eight sitting together. "Oh my God!" she said. "Yankees? Right?"

"Right," one of them answered. The rest giggled.

Alma asked them, "What's the greatest football team in the history of creation?"

One of them said, "The Alabama Crimson Tide."

The crowd yelled and clapped, hollering, "Roll Tide!"

Alma hollered, "Shut up!" but knew the question was calculated to make the audience yell. She told the Yankees, "You pass."

One of the Yankees said to Alma, "We're med students at the University of Alabama in Birmingham."

"Oh, thank God. We had some Harvard Yankees in here for a while. They were doing a thesis on, can you believe it, Southern humor. I mean, Harvard! War, famine in the world, pussy going to waste, and these fuckers were doing intensive study on Southern humor. They would come in here not to just listen to me but to study me. I mean, in a way it was flattering, but I think they were wasting their time. I'm not saying I'm a nothing, but the United States Research Institute did hire me to go out in the forest and see if a tree makes a noise when it falls."

The crowd began laughing, roaring, then clapping. The laughing stopped, but the applause built. Alma nodded to the audience and said, "Thank you," softly several times.

As the applause died out, Alma got very hyper again. Alvin almost swore he could see sparks coming off her.

"Hey, I don't take drugs," she said. "I shoot heroin in my temple, drive down the left side of the road a hundred miles an hour with the lights out, throwing hundred-dollar bills out the window. Just getting high off life."

The audience screamed louder than ever. Alvin was caught up.

"You've done it," he yelled at his sister. "They want to take you home with them. You have *arrived*." He imagined himself in front of the crowd sliding into his side chest pose.

Alma paced. The audience slowly quietened. Without looking toward the crowd, she said, "Hey, look. The world's full of apathy, but I don't give a shit."

Alma strutted silently. Then she exclaimed, "You know, I tell you something else about men."

There was laughter because they knew it was coming.

"They don't have fantasies. A man's idea of a fantasy is this . . ." Alma switched over to a different voice: "Wull, it's this hot, good-looking fifteen-year-old girl with a Corvette. And aw, man, we do it on top of the Corvette, in a houseboat, everwhurs."

She continued as herself. "That's not a goddamn fantasy! That's just a streak of good luck or more trouble than you can get out of, whichever way you wish to look at it. Now a woman, her idea of a fantasy is . . ." Alma went into a calm, dreamy voice: "Well, it's this guy from the Planet Madreperla, and if we need to go somewhere, we just transport there instantaneously. Oh, and he is so handsome. We are married. He can be a man, a woman, a child, anything he wants to be, and oh we go about being so gay and carefree. There's this thing we can do for sensation that is infinitely superior to sex.

"Now that's a goddamn fantasy! I tell you something else. Sometimes you get this fantasy during sex bullshit. The guy says, 'Well, I have something to confess. When we were making love, I kept fantasizing you were my eighth-grade girlfriend and we were doing it under the bleachers. I just wanted to tell you that.'

"That's not a goddamn fantasy! You were just confused, dip shit. You didn't know where the hell you were or who the fuck you were with. I just wanted to tell you *that*. And I have something to confess. When we were making love, I kept fantasizing I was having an orgasm. But don't worry, I'll handle it later tonight by myself to the sounds of the lesbians downstairs making out as their screams of ecstasy drift out into the hot summer night. I just wanted to tell *you* that."

The audience exploded with laughter, whistling and applauding.

Cliff was clapping and looking admiringly up toward Alma. Alvin hollered, "You own them, Alma. Run, run. Take it and run. Get the fuck out."

Alma continued as soon as she could. "OK, OK. So, I've been giving the swinging dicks a hard time. And you say, 'Well, Alma, in this cold world what type of man do you like, what type of man are you looking for?' "

Alma looked up to the ceiling as if contemplating the man of her dreams. Then she said, "In this cold world I'm looking for a man who's just looking for a warm place to come."

The crowd took a couple of seconds to get it. Then, one by one, everyone began laughing hysterically.

Alma waved to the audience. She bowed. "Thank you. Thank you very much. You've been kind. Very kind. Thank you for coming to Downtown Sam's Cosmic Café, a *cool* place to come."

The volume of the applause rose. Alma put the microphone back in its stand. She threw kisses. As she made a gracious bow, the Muscle Shoals backup musicians stood up and applauded.

Alvin thought, The Vulcan. That's the way it was when I gave 'em the Vulcan.

By the time she finished bowing Alma faced a standing ovation. She held up her right arm. Her left arm was by her side and her wrist cocked back.

Alvin said, "I taught her how to do that. In her living room-studio I taught her the Vulcan." He was proud.

As Alma quickly ran offstage, Alvin thought he saw the outline of a skeleton under her floppy, loose-fitting clothes. It rattled him. He tried to recall her appearance on the stage. Her material had distracted him from her physical image. But now he realized she did look very skinny, her face slim, her eyes big.

Alvin kept rolling it over and over in his mind. That while she was performing, she was able to *be* something else, somebody else, masking her body. She did practice and practice, for days even, being a tree, being a doorknob.

He concluded maybe she did look fine. Everything looked a distorted blue in the lighting of the Cosmic Café.

Cliff was clapping madly. He yelled, "Bravo! Bravo!" He stopped clapping and turned to Alvin, shouting to be heard. "Alvin, I knew there was something about Alma the first time I met her. What a routine! What energy. How poignant. Merciless delivery. I knew Alma was a genius!"

Alvin sat back down, thinking Cliff was coming out of his cage. He never hung around the riverbanks saying "bravo" and "poignant." Not only was he a comedian, but he was also a critic.

The audience was still cheering, but Alvin knew she wasn't coming back out for an encore or curtain call. He imagined Alma running down the back alley of the Cosmic Café, turning the corner, and running through the seedy section of Birmingham. He imagined her slipping into a small café. She would order a diet soda. A lady, perhaps in her mid-thirties, would approach Alma. She would have on big loop earrings and would be wearing a cape. She would be tall, stunning even, but a little worn. She might be one of Alma's actress friends and also be an artist. She would be a little shy of talent but trying to prove her artistic ability by all her promiscuous, passionate love affairs. Almost the same way that Alma tried to prove her comic talent by acting as crazy as a shithouse rat.

The lady would sit by Alma and tell her that she had just seen her perform and that Alma had a unique look, something regional yet cosmopolitan, and that she wanted to do her in oil. And to prove what an artist she was, that she was worthy of doing her in oil, she would move closer to Alma and start moving her hand along her thigh.

Alvin jumped back up, standing with the rest of the customers of the Cosmic Café.

"Come on, Cliff. We got to find Alma."

Twenty-six

CLIFF HAD NOT HEARD Alvin's call to go find Alma. And Alvin did not run to find her. He just stood there clapping along with Cliff and the rest of the patrons of Downtown Sam's Cosmic Café.

Perhaps his worry had been unfounded. She couldn't have been a skeleton in baggy clothes because Cliff would have noticed this, too. She was probably backstage, and if she were running down back alleys and into the other café, she could take care of herself. She had lived in Birmingham alone for several years now. She knew how to handle herself. So what if the crazed-out artist was telling her she wanted to do Alma in oil?

The emcee came to the microphone. He put his mouth very close to it and said in mock-serious tones, "Alma Fuqua has left the building. I repeat, Alma Fuqua has left the building," in the way announcers at rock concerts do.

The crowd chuckled, but came to life again when the emcee declared, "Wow! Isn't she adorable?"

There were scattered yeahs.

"We all know she's funny, but isn't she just adorable?" the emcee repeated. "A pleasure to watch perform. And speaking of performing, we have Red Sammy and the Blue Ribbon Boys coming back up in about ten minutes. In the meantime, order up another round of drinks. We've got raw oysters fresh from the Gulf, and we'll have you some more fine entertainment in just ten or fifteen minutes."

As the emcee was walking off the stage, Cliff turned to Alvin and asked, "You want to order a dozen oysters?"

"Yeah, I could go for some oysters," Alvin said. "I'm gone go back here and see Alma."

Alvin meandered to the side of the stage. He ran into the emcee. Alvin said, "I'd like to see Alma."

The emcee said, "Oh, I wasn't kidding. She's gone. As soon as she came off, she went running out the back door." He noticed some girls sitting at a table. "Hey, babes," he hollered, and went over to sit with them.

Alvin came back and sat with Cliff. "She's gone already. We can go over to her apartment in a little while and see her."

They sat and ate the oysters, listening to Red Sammy. Cliff had another drink. After paying their tab, they sauntered out and back down Morris Avenue to Alvin's car.

Birmingham was a big, industrial mining town situated on mountainous terrain. As they were driving up one of the mountainsides toward Alma's apartment, Alvin pointed out to Cliff the statue of "Vulcan," the symbol of Birmingham. It was a huge monument on a nearby mountain, the god proudly holding a torch. When there were no deaths caused by car crashes or other violence, the torch lit up green. When there were, it burned red.

The torch of the "Vulcan" burned green.

Alvin was explaining all this about the "Vulcan" to Cliff as they found Alma's yellow Volkswagen parked under a streetlight in front of her apartment.

"She lives on the top floor," Alvin said, pointing to a dark window of the old two-story house turned apartment building.

He parked the Z behind Alma's car, and they got out, facing the front porch on the ground floor. There Alvin noticed two ladies sitting in a swing, eating something out of a cup with a spoon.

They were giggling between bites. One of the girls looked to be in her late teens; the other, her mid-twenties. The younger girl had her left leg over the other's right leg with their ankles crossed, their locked legs slowly rocking. They were slim and very attractive.

They were obviously the lesbians Alma had spoken about. It wasn't something she had just made up. And Alma was right. The thought of two beautiful girls being lesbians was upsetting, almost an affront, to him.

But for all Alvin knew they might not be lesbians. They might have just been inspiration for Alma's material. Two girls locking ankles did not necessarily constitute anything. Alvin was thinking how women could get away with a lot more than men. Girls could kiss, walk with arms locked, sleep in the same bed together and get away with it. A guy could watch another guy pose and get accused of being a faggot.

Alvin and Cliff walked along the side of the house. As they passed, Alvin said hi to the girls.

The girls giggled and waved.

They walked up the wooden stairs that went along the outside of the house to the back, up between two doorways upstairs. Alvin knocked on the door to the right.

No answer. No noise inside.

Cliff said, "It's dark. She must not be here."

"Her car's outside, but that don't mean anything." Alvin tried the doorknob for the hell of it, but it was locked. He knocked again anyway.

He was thinking she must have gotten a ride to the club. And that she had in fact run to the little café, where the crazed-out lady had approached her. Alvin knew he should have gone with his intuition.

"Would she be somewhere else?" Cliff asked.

"Here. The club. This place they have acting classes several blocks from here. But it's too late for that," Alvin answered, stepping away.

Cliff stepped up to the door and shook the doorknob.

Alvin thought perhaps she *was* at that café. But by now that crazed-out lady had lured Alma to her studio, to do her in oil. He imagined her having Alma take off all her clothes and greasing down, the way a bodybuilder does when he poses at a contest. And the crazed-out artist saying, "Here, Alma, honey, let me help you," moving over closer and rubbing oil sensuously, saying, "Oh, Alma, you have the Look. Regional yet cosmopolitan. What a rare creature you are!"

Alvin said, "She leaves the front windows open. Sometimes they're up, if it's not too cool. I didn't notice when we drove up."

Cliff led the way back down the wooden stairs to the sidewalk in front. They looked up at the old house.

The girls had gone in. The cool autumn night was beginning to get breezy. Alvin noticed what must have been the girls' bedroom window downstairs. It was raised halfway. He imagined screams of ecstasy, as Alma had called it, coming from within.

The two windows above the porch roof went to Alma's living room and bedroom. Cliff and Alvin walked over to the other side and climbed up some latticework to the roof.

There were no lights on at all in her apartment.

Cliff heaved on the first window, and it raised up about six inches. Alvin got alongside him, and they lifted together. The window gave up, and they crawled in.

Alvin turned on the light. The large room had a look of emptiness to it. The double bed had no headboard and was unmade, with the covers tossed about.

They walked into the kitchen and living room.

On the kitchen table was an empty box that had held a dozen doughnuts. A couple of empty pint ice-cream containers. A Twinkies wrapper. Four empty soda cans.

Hell, she's binged, Alvin thought. For some reason he couldn't get the crazed-out woman who presented herself as an artist out of his mind. He imagined the woman showing up at this apartment after Alma had binged. Alma crying to her. The woman pulling Alma to her breast, telling her, "Come to my studio, Alma, my pumpkin. I can get all the fat, all the sugar, all the calories out of you. Oh, my studio is oh so magical."

Cliff came up behind. "Looks like she had some guests for snacks," he said, motioning to the remnants of Alma's binge.

All Alvin responded was, "Nah," and he walked on into the living room.

It was bigger than the bedroom by a bit and was separated from the kitchen area by a breakfast bar. The living room looked more like a studio. On the opposite end of the room were a microphone stand and a series of full-length mirrors.

"Where she practices her act," Alvin commented.

Cliff wandered off to the bathroom and announced she wasn't in there either. They converged back in the bedroom and settled themselves into the two director's chairs that were near the closet door. Alvin noticed that besides the chairs and the bed, the only other furniture in the bedroom was an old chest of drawers.

"Well, we can just crash here," Alvin suggested. "If she comes back tonight, she'll probably notice my car."

"Or leave a note on the door that we're inside," Cliff offered.

"I wonder where she could be?" Alvin wondered aloud, but also meaning, I wonder where that artist's studio is.

They heard a little squeak: "Here I be."

Alvin started to laugh. He knew where she was now. One time he and Alma had gone with Johnny Ray to get Buck's wife on a cold night, when he was going to be cooking whiskey all night long. They had gone into the house, and there was no fire in the wood heater. Johnny Ray had said, "I wonder where she could be." They had heard a little squeak: "Here I be." They found her between the mattresses of the bed, trying to keep warm.

Cliff and Alvin looked at the bed.

Alma stuck her head out from under the covers. She was so thin, she had been hidden under the wrinkles. She leaned her head over a waste can beside the bed. Sticking her finger down her throat, she gagged, but nothing came out.

Alvin went over and sat on the bed. "Alma. Alma."

She looked up at him. She was emaciated. There were dark circles around her eyes. The smile on his face went away.

It was hard for him to believe this was the same person that just a couple of hours earlier had been on the stage, sounding like thunder and moving like lightning.

"Oh, Alvin. What are you doing here?" she said weakly.

"We came to watch your act. You were great," he answered. Alma didn't notice the "we." She hadn't noticed Cliff.

"Oh, I can't go on again, Alvin. There's a f-a-t woman out in the audience."

"Alma, what's the matter?"

"I binged! I binged! I ate some doughnuts at a café down from Downtown Sam's. Then I stopped on the way home and got some doughnuts and ice cream. I ate them. I'm trying to get it all out. Tell me I won't get f-a-t three hundred and twenty-seven times. I have to go back to sleep now. Promise me you'll say it three hundred and twenty-seven times. Promise."

"I promise," Alvin said. He looked at Cliff. "We've got to get her to a hospital."

"No, Alvin. If we take her to a hospital, they might fuck her up. Where is that medical center we passed?"

"Three blocks back down the mountain. We gonna take her there?"

"No," Cliff said. "You stay here. If she wakes up, get her to drink a little water. I'm going to get some things."

"What you gonna do?"

"Just watch her. I'll be back in a little while." He went to the door, unlocked it, and disappeared into the night.

Alma had run down to the little café. Alvin was sure it was the same one he was thinking of, yet he didn't even know the name of the place. He imagined how she ran down the alley, back up to the other street, and into the café. Eating the doughnut and wanting to binge but knowing she couldn't binge there. He could imagine her paying her tab and running back down the street and alley to where she had her car parked behind Downtown Sam's Cosmic Café. She driving toward her apartment, stopping at the convenience store. Then coming home, sitting at the kitchen table and woofing up the sweets and sodas, going to the bathroom and throwing it all up.

As they had been eating the raw oysters, Alma was stuffing that first doughnut into her mouth. The time sequences all fit in for Alvin. Then they came to her apartment.

It all fit in, except for one thing. Alvin was sure the crazed-out artist had been involved. But there was no time slot for her. Maybe Alma had sat eating the doughnut in the café, slowly, trying to restrain herself, taking pleasure in planning her binge, her little private misdemeanor.

Alvin could imagine the crazed-out artist in her avant-garde garb approaching Alma, sitting beside her. Telling her she looked regional yet cosmopolitan. And her humor, regional yet cosmopolitan, even universal. That she wanted to capture it all in oil. Alma, having been oblivious to the woman, contemplating her private sin she was about to commit. Thinking of the throwing up she would have to do, the sit-ups she would have to do in penance, the nonstop dance in front of her mirrors to burn up all the calories. And in celebration of her conclusion that it was going to be worth it, Alma sticking her finger down her throat, spraying the crazed-out lady with her puke. Alma never even noticing that she was there.

Alvin was satisfied with his solution.

He pulled the director's chair up to the unmade bed. He got a pen out of his pants pocket and found an old paper bag lying by the bed.

He started saying, "You won't get f-a-t, you won't get f-a-t, you won't get f-a-t." He made a mark on the paper bag every time he said it.

Twenty-seven

WHEN ALMA WOKE up the next morning, she looked at the IV in her arm and the bottle hanging beside her bed.

Alvin watched her blue eyes. They seemed bigger than usual because her face was all bony from not eating.

Alma saw Alvin and said, "This won't make me f-a-t, will it?"

"No. No."

"What's in it, Alvie?"

"Food and vitamins. No calories or f-a-t at all, though." He remembered Cliff saying something about its being glucose and a vitamin solution.

"Vitamins!" Alma screamed. "Vitamins make me hungry."

"These won't make you hungry. These are special vitamins."

Alvin wondered how Cliff had gotten the equipment—if they just sold you stuff like that over the counter, or what. For some reason, as Alvin was trying to figure out how Cliff had gotten the IV, he imagined how Freddy and Eddie would do it: slipping into the hospital, making a lot of noise, and stealing one from a patient in a coma. Then, on the way out, Freddy holding things up by trying to make out with a nurse. And when Eddie tried to prompt him on out, Freddy saying, "Hey, just because you don't git your pussy, don't be trying to knock me out of mine." And then Eddie saying, "I git my pussy. You don't be worrying about me."

Thinking about it, he almost laughed out loud, but he didn't want to have to explain it to Alma. Besides, he smelled breakfast cooking. Cliff was out in the small kitchen, making it. It was late morning, and Alvin was about to starve. Cliff had gone out to get some food because there was none in Alma's apartment, except for 173 boxes of Jell-O.

The smell brought him out of his thoughts. When he realized he was staring at his sister with an IV in her arm, the smile came off his face.

She was saying, "Take all the calories out, take all the fat out, Alvie."

"I already did."

"Do it one more time. I got the vibes that you should do it one more time."

Alvin stood up by the IV stand and laid his hands on the bottle, as if he were going to heal it of brain cancer. Then he gave an ear-piercing scream and jerked his hands off the bottle.

"Oh, Alvie. Thank you. Thank you. Thank you. Thank you. Thank you. Thank you. Thank you. Now say I won't get f-a-t seven times."

"You won't get f-a-t. You won't get f-a-t. . . ." Alvin continued seven times. Then Alma nodded off to sleep. Alvin went into the kitchen and sat down with Cliff.

"She's going to be all right," Cliff said. "You go on back if you want. I'll look out for Alma. I'll take her off the IV tomorrow and get her to eating food."

"Good luck."

"I can do it."

"OK. I think I'll go around downtown a few places today and then go back up home tomorrow."

"All right."

"How are you going to get back?"

"I can take the bus," Cliff said.

Alvin walked over to the front window of the living room. He leaned against the frame, sipped his coffee, and looked down to the sidewalk. The two girls were sauntering around, holding hands, talking.

They were both dressed cozily. The young one had on wool shorts, knee socks, and a heavy turquoise-colored sweat shirt. The other wore snug, pressed jeans, and a waist-length rabbit coat. They were obviously eager to wear their winter clothes. What they had on was fine for early morning or night, but the fall days were still warm.

He watched them hold hands, walk down the sidewalk a ways, turn, then walk arm in arm back. Then they stopped and embraced each other. They stood there French kissing for about a full minute. Each one's long blond hair falling all over the other. When they broke, the young one ran back into the apartment. The other walked across the street, got into a Volvo, and drove away.

It blew to hell Alvin's theory that they were reunited sisters.

He turned back and faced Cliff. "So how is it you figure you can get Alma to start eating?"

"I'm not exactly sure. When I was overseas, I was a prisoner and was starved down to about a hundred pounds."

"Damn," Alvin said. The fact that Cliff had been a prisoner of war was not as interesting right now to Alvin, though, as the fact that Cliff seldom spoke of Vietnam and when he did he often referred to it just as "overseas."

Cliff said, "Oddly enough, I was a medic, especially trained in recuperating emaciated victims."

"Goddamn," Alvin remarked. "You a medic. A comedian. A critic. What else you do?" It seemed he was only now finding out about Cliff.

"After a while it was strange," Cliff explained. "I felt like the joke was on them. I didn't need food. If my body could just waste on away, I could fly. I would be free. After a while to me food was poison. It was waste. It was fetters."

Sometimes trying to understand Cliff was worse than trying to understand Alma. "But, Cliff, I don't think getting drug off to war in some foreign jungle and locked up and starved to death is the same as throwing up doughnuts because some f-a-t woman was hexing your act by her very presence at Downtown Cosmic Sam's." Alvin, after he said that, realized for the first time he was finally fed up with Alma's f-a-t bullshit.

Cliff crossed his legs and said, "That's right. When I was broken out of prison, I still didn't want to eat."

Alvin let it slide. He didn't know what to say. Alma's conduct was beginning to remind him of Buck's brother Tommy in Beaulah Town, the one who refused to change his clocks to daylight savings time. For six months out of the year he showed up to work an hour late and left an hour late. Nobody after the first few days gave a shit at the city's motor pool. He did his job; they left him to solve all the bullshit problems of the day that everybody had been trying to pawn off on everybody else, and he was left to cut off all the compressors and lock up. It had its attributes. Alma's conduct didn't.

Then it hit Alvin. This was the first time he had seen Cliff participate in anything. Cliff was always there, carried his weight, fit in with the swampers, wasn't a fuck-up, was downright likable. But there was something about Cliff. He didn't participate. He kind of stood back. Alvin had a lot of confidence in Cliff. For some reason he knew he was going to get Alma to quit starving herself.

Cliff said, "I think a lot about that first time I met you, Alma, and Johnny Ray. We all sat around eating popcorn and watching that movie on TV."

Alvin smiled. "Aw, yeah. That one where that guy escaped prison and he goes back to his home island on that little sail canoe? Yeah. He hadn't had any water for three days, and he sees that shark circling down below, dives down in the water with his knife. Wrestles the shark, stabs it to death with all them other sharks circling around. Drug that shark back up on his little canoe and started eatin' it raw."

Cliff chuckled and said, "Yeah. Johnny Ray kept saying, 'Now he's tough. That's one mean son of a bitch.'"

"Yeah, yeah. What was the name of that movie?"

"*Hurricane.*"

"Yeah! Freddy kept bitching about the name. Said the name of the movie should have been *Typhoon* because it was in the Pacific. That hurricanes were in the Atlantic."

"Yeah." Cliff laughed.

Alvin had never had exactly this kind of rapport with Cliff before. He said, "You know, Freddy knows all kind of shit like that. He knows all the presidents, all the capitals of the states, all the states."

"Sometimes he comes out with some remarkable information," Cliff agreed. "You know, that was a very enjoyable evening. But there was something kind of haunting about it."

"What was that?"

"Alma."

"Alma?"

"Yeah. She looks just like Dorothy Lamour. Haven't you ever noticed?" Cliff asked.

"Who's Dorothy Lamour? I mean, I heard of her. She the one that flew across the Atlantic, wasn't she?"

"No. That was Amelia Earhart. Dorothy Lamour was the leading lady in *Hurricane*."

"Aw," Alvin said, but he couldn't remember what she looked like. All the leading lady film stars of the thirties and forties pretty much looked the same to him. All wore dark lipstick. And looked worried sick about their men and what they were going to wear that night to a party. Alvin personally never knew any women that worried themselves sick over their men or what they were going to wear. As far as *Hurricane*, he couldn't remember exactly how anybody looked in it. All he could remember was that fellow jumping down and stabbing that shark.

"Yeah, so it's like I'm watching this movie," Cliff said. He leaned up a bit, was almost laughing as he talked, hyper, a bit like Alma doing her comedy act. The hand that wasn't holding his coffee cup was flying around in gesticulations. "There's this thirties movie star on the television. I look at the screen. Then I look over the same fucking person sitting over on the couch. Different hairstyle, different makeup. But to me looks like the same goddamn person. Nineteen thirties, TV. Nineteen seventies, couch—same person. I couldn't figure it out. I look around. Nobody else seems to notice it. I think what the fuck is this? Am I in the twilight zone? Am I supposed to fucking jump up and holler, 'They look the same'? Is everybody just got poker faces wondering when the fuck this New Yorker will notice that the leading lady of the thirties movie is fucking sitting on the goddamn couch beside me? As the movie went on, was Johnny Ray going to be in it? I didn't know what the fuck was coming down!"

Cliff sat there laughing, took a sip of coffee. "I've wanted to say that for a long time."

Alvin smiled at Cliff, glad Cliff was enjoying himself. "And now here we are over a year later in *her* living room," Alvin said.

"Yeah, isn't that fucking wicked?!"

Out of the blue Alvin asked Cliff, "What do you want to be?"

"What?" Cliff came back quickly, as if he had been caught off guard.

"What do you want to be? I don't mean, be happy, be rich, be content. I mean, what do you want to be?"

"I don't know. It's funny, the only thing I can remember wanting to be was a comedian. I never became one. I went off to war, then strayed around South America all these years. Now I'm here. Way back then when I wanted to be a comedian is the last time I can remember actually wanting to be something."

"So why don't you be a comedian?" Alvin said, and took a sip of coffee.

"I don't know anything funny."

Alvin strangled on the coffee he was swallowing. He spit out coffee, gasped, laughed. He went down to his knees, now laughing, coughing out what he was strangled on. Alvin was lying on the floor. High-pitched, between uncontrollable laughter and gasps for breath, he was saying, "So why don't you be a fisherman? . . . I don't have any bait. . . . Oh, God, Cliff . . . you're funnier than Alma."

Twenty-eight

AFTER BREAKFAST Alvin drove downtown, parked, then started walking, just looking at the city and the mountains; the sights were so different from back home.

Unlike many swampers, he felt he could survive anywhere: the country, the city, the swamp, the streets, New York, California. But he had never lived anywhere but where he had lived.

The streets he was walking felt familiar.

He soon found himself in the back alley that went behind Jefferson Hall, the old theater where he had taken Mr. Alabama. He walked up to the stage door and tested it. It was unlocked, and he went in. Backstage was down a short hallway. He stood looking at all the ropes and counterweights. The curtain was up.

Alvin walked to center stage. The place was deserted. He stomped his boot heel firmly on the wooden stage floor, then looked up at the balcony.

His muscles let him know they wanted to pose—right now, on the stage of Jefferson Hall. He took his shirt off and tossed it out of the way. Twisting around, he gave a left bicep pose, then a side chest pose that accentuated his pectorals and right tricep.

Relaxing all his muscles, he looked out into the audience. He put his hands up and out above his head, then brought them down in an arch, extending his latissimus dorsi, ending in a front lat pose.

It was his most magnificent pose. Alvin knew there was no man alive that had a front lat pose as grand as his. Nobody. Alvin felt it alone was enough to fill the thirty-five hundred seats out in front of him. It alone could make life appear in each one of those seats.

He brought his arms out, relaxed the latissimus dorsi, clasped his hands together, and flexed his trapezius muscles, which went from his shoulders to his neck; it was the pose known as the Crab.

The Crab had caused him to win the Most Muscular trophy at his last, but failed, contest. Alvin's Crab was impressive and gained applause, but it was not one of his favorites.

Then Alvin did the pose he was most noted for.

He did the Vulcan.

At the Mr. Alabama contest, on this very stage, he had thought to end off with a front lat pose. A standing room only theater was resonating with applause. Alvin had not wanted just to bow and walk away. He came out of the front lat pose and held his closed right hand up high in the air. The audience recognized the Vulcan, the god that looked over their city night and day. He was giving them a tribute.

He held the fist of his hanging left arm out a bit, as though holding the handle of the blacksmith's hammer. It brought the audience to their feet. The medley of screams seemed to fuse into a rhythmic, rolling cadence.

Alvin stood there in the pose, motionless. No jerk, twitch, breath, or any movement could be seen from his body. For minutes he stood there as they cheered. They were giving him a tribute, but he was giving them back the admiration they were showing.

At the first wavering of applause, Alvin stepped back, brought his arm down and bowed, and then rushed off the stage.

It was just as well he had been the last in a three-man pose-off. No one or nothing could have followed it. He couldn't even return to the stage; it would have destroyed the effect. He'd thrown on his warm-up outfit and slipped out the backstage door.

Alvin looked out at the empty auditorium. He put his shirt on. He went out among the seats, climbed to the balcony, and sat looking down at the stage.

"Next time," he said. "I'll do the same with the audience at Mr. America."

He got up, went upstairs into another wing of Jefferson Hall. He was just wandering around. Down a corridor he saw a door with a sign on it: CHAPEL.

He went in.

It was a small room, two sets of pews, about fifteen rows. There was a small stage at the front. He walked down the aisle and took the one step up onto it. He got behind the lectern and grasped the edges, the way Cliff held on to the pinball machine at the Twilight Café.

Bone structure. One's own muscles, listening to them. That's what he could tell them about.

He opened his mouth to begin orating, but as he looked over to the right, he saw an old man sitting on a stool on the other side of the piano, right next to the American flag. The man had on a work uniform.

"You the janitor?" Alvin asked.

"Naw. I'm the custodian."

"You fuckin' off?"

"Naw suh. I'm takin' a break. I be fuckin' off in 'bout ten minutes."

"Aw," Alvin said.

The man stared at him, then took a paper sack from his hip pocket. It contained a pint bottle. He took a slug and handed it out to Alvin.

Alvin's muscles told him it was all right to take one. He looked at the bottle a couple of seconds, then walked over and accepted it. He turned the bottle up and took a modest slug.

"I don't give a damn for a Most Muscular trophy," Alvin stated.

"Nuh suh. Don't mean shit," the old man said.

"It's the big one or nothing," Alvin said.

"The big one. 'At's the one 'at counts."

"Unless it was something else you were going for in the first place."

"Aw shore. If it was the one in the fust place you wus goin' fer."

Alvin said, "Ten years ago hip structure didn't matter much."

"Didn't mean shit."

Alvin went back to the lectern and looked out to the pews. He said, "But today it's a different story."

"Time shore do change thangs. Somepin don't mean shit one day. Then that all folk give a fuck about the next."

Turning to the old man, Alvin asked, "You come in here a lot?"

"On my breaks."

"But not to fuck off?"

"Naw suh. I fuck off somewheres else."

Twenty-nine

ALVIN DROVE away from Birmingham alone, leaving Cliff to return on the bus. He drove straight to the county seat, a small town five miles north of Beaulah Town. The swampers never called the county seat by name, just referred to it as uptown.

As he pulled in, he said out loud, "Let Cliff handle Alma. Let them be crazy together. Maybe they'll get married, and none of it will interfere with my training anymore."

He knew Alma's acting crazy had never messed up his work, but the threat was always there that he would be right in the middle of some intensive training and Alma would pull something as she just had.

Now there was Cliff, thank God, Alvin was thinking. Let Cliff take care of all that f-a-t shit now.

Around the corner from Ginger's dress shop, and about a half block down the street in an old building, was the North Alabama Power Lifting Gym. It wasn't a spa or a business gym, but a working-out place for the North Alabama Power Lifting Club.

Alvin had trained there some when he was preparing for the Mr. Alabama contest, even though the other guys there weren't into bodybuilding much. They were into strength. They came to the gym to get away from their wives and to get ready for the Alabama Power Lifting Meet and the Gulf Coast Open Bench Press Contest.

Alvin parked down by the gym. Before he got out, he inspected the streets to see if they were safe from Ginger.

Sure enough, she came strutting down from the courthouse square, as if she were doing a panty hose commercial. She bounced across the railroad tracks, then turned down the sidewalk that led to her dress shop.

He sat there thinking what she had said when he had seen her last: "Alvin, I may not always be your lover, but I will always be your friend."

Sitting there now, he said to himself, She must've heard that in the movies.

He had heard somebody else talking when she had said that. He could catch on to things like that. Every once in a while he caught himself saying things that sounded like somebody else talking, and when he did, it made him mad.

Alvin had settled things with Ginger. He had called her and told her he was glad she was going to give herself and that Eric guy a chance to see what would happen. He had gotten Ginger off his back without having to "still be good friends," whatever that meant. Alvin just didn't want to be running into her uptown, having to listen to her polite bullshit.

When the streets were safe, Alvin got out and walked to the power lifting gym. He pulled open the heavy wood and glass door, stepped in, and looked around.

There were two guys that Alvin hadn't ever seen before, working out on the bench press. He thought everybody in north Alabama who lifted weights knew who he was, but they didn't seem to recognize him. Not that he gave a shit. It just seemed unusual.

They looked at him and nodded, but they didn't pay him any attention because they were getting ready for their three-repetition set, and they had a lot of concentrating to do.

Alvin thought, In about a year ya'll will look like the rest of the slobs that's been hanging out here for ages.

He didn't understand them, the power lifters who frequented this gym. They had all looked the same and talked about the same things for the last ten years. Every once in a while a new energetic young lifter would be admitted to the circle, and it was no time until he seemed to look, act, and talk like the others. His progress would slow down to the rate of the others.

Something about it reminded Alvin of his old man's attitude about weight training. He didn't see any point in lifting anything that you were going to set back down in the same place.

Alvin waded through the heavy black Olympic weight plates lying around and dodged the edges of Olympic barbells that were on racks and benches everywhere.

He walked across the dead lift platform and headed back toward the office. That's when he saw Roger.

Roger had always liked him, been kind to him, he knew. But there was something about Roger that was repulsive. He didn't know if it was because Roger walked around as though he owned the world with his 270 pounds or because he thought he was King Shit because he could bench-press 500 pounds.

Since Alvin had been Mr. Alabama, and Roger held the Alabama state bench press record in the superheavyweight class, maybe Roger felt they were kin.

He came over and shook Alvin's hand, and said, "Big Al!" as if they were great buddies.

Alvin was about to puke, having to look at his tight, huge gut. He thought, Why don't the son of a bitch put a shirt on and cover up that flab? The big dumb fucker. He thinks I like him or something and just want to come around.

Alvin felt guilty about bullshitting when he didn't want to bullshit, so he said, "Roger, I was wondering if I could get some Dianabol from you?"

"You gone start competin' agin? You lookin' good. But you sure dropped a lot of weight. Been cuttin' up?"

"I've lost some weight."

One of the things that irritated him about Roger and people in general, when he had to come uptown to get something or do something, was that they wouldn't answer his questions. Roger went off on a trail now, and it would take Alvin ten minutes to get him to answer what should have taken a second.

"I just want to tone up a little bit," Alvin said.

"Man, Big Al, you oughtta come up here and start trainin' with all the boys agin. They all still around. Chuck, Larry, Dan, Billy Ed, all of 'em. Man, they'd be tickled to have you back up here. All time somebody mentionin' you."

"Aw, Roger, I'd like to," Alvin lied. "But I'm set up at home, and I just wouldn't feel like driving in from the river all the time. You know?"

"You oughtta come an' do benches a couple times a week. Shit, man. Whatchew benchin' now?"

"I haven't done any heavy benches lately," Alvin replied.

"Hell, oughtta start doing some heavy benches. Git you in the one-ninety-eight-pound class. Or way you looking, we could git you in the one-eighty-one class. I got five-fifteen last week. And I just started back up eatin' 'em Dianabol two weeks ago."

"That's good."

"You still mussel divin'?"

Alvin thought, Give me the Dianabol, you tub-of-lard motherfucker, and let me git the hell out of here!

But Alvin just said, "Yeah."

"What do they do with them thangs anyway? They buy the whole thang or they just weigh up the shell?"

"They pay you live weight. They cook the meat out and give it away for people to feed their hogs. They ship the shells to Japan. They strip them up, seed oyster beds with them. Ever cultured pearl you see has a tiny piece of mussel shell in its center."

Alvin said all that as fast as he could, as though he were reading it off a card. He hated for people to ask him what mussel shells were used for. They already ought to know or not ask.

"I'll be dogged!" Roger exclaimed, as if it were the most fascinating thing he had ever heard. "How they git all them shells over to Jay-pan?"

"Truck to Mobile. Train to San Francisco. Ship to Japan."

"Any say they make pearls out of em?"

"Yeah."

"Well, do you ever find any pearls in them mussels?"

"Every once in a while."

"They worth much?"

Alvin didn't think he would be this big a pain in the ass.

But he just smiled and said, "Hey, Roger. I'm kind of in a hurry. Let me get those D's before I forget them."

"Sure. Come on over to my desk, Big Al."

Alvin thought, Finally! and was about to answer Roger's question when he realized Roger had already lost interest in whatever the answer might be.

Roger plopped his repulsive body behind his desk and was so stiff he could hardly bend around to search in his drawers for the pills. He pulled out a .44 Magnum revolver, acted as if he were aiming it at somebody, and then handed it to Alvin.

Roger said, "Look at 'at baby. Just got it last week. Man, don't you thank that wouldn't tear up somebody's ass. Blow a hole in 'em size of the bottom of a lard stand."

Alvin handled the gun as if he gave a shit. He said, "Yeah. That's nice, Roger. I wish I had one."

"Hey, I thank I can git you a good deal on one. Smith and Wesson."

"I better pass."

"Let me know. Shit. One them'll do some talkin'."

Roger finally put the revolver up and pulled out an empty box of kitchen matches that was full of steroid pills.

"How many you need, Big Al?"

Alvin was only going to get a couple hundred, but since he was having to go through so much bullshit and questions, having to look at Roger's fat, slick, tight gut and the blue stretch marks between his upper pecs and arms, he said, "Five hundred."

Roger poured a handful of the small blue pills into an empty Tampa Nugget cigar box and started counting them out, two and three at a time. When he got a pile counted out, he would pick them up with his fingertips and put them into an empty Skoal tobacco tin at the edge of the desk.

Alvin thought that was going to take Roger all day. By the time he got through, all the other slobs would be off work, in here, asking him a bunch of bullshit questions the way Roger did. As if they all wanted to be big buddies.

All at once, clapping and cheering could be heard coming from the gym. He figured somebody had lifted something. Then he heard plates clanging together.

Alvin picked up a power lifting magazine that lay on the desk and started looking through it.

Roger stopped counting and, looking up at Alvin, said, "You ought to come over tomorrow night and do benches with us. Then we'll go over to Huntsville for some beer and pizza."

Alvin's muscles cringled; they couldn't stand it. Alvin listened to his muscles.

"I'm already tied up this week," he said. "Maybe some other time."

He closed the magazine and put it on the desk, then noticed the back cover. There was a picture of a white bottle, and written on it was "Pure-Pro." The ad read: "100% assimilable liquid protein with all amino acids."

Alvin didn't have time to read about it. Sticking the magazine in front of Roger, he pointed to the bottle and asked, "What's this, Roger? What is it?"

"Pure-Pro."

"What's that?"

"Liquid protein. Somethin' new they come out with," Roger said.

"What's it do?"

"Shit, Alvin. Id's just like powder protein except it's liquid and it don't have no fat or carbohydrates or nothin. Just pure-D protein."

"They got it in Muscle Shoals, or you got to order it?"

"They got it in Muscle Shoals."

"How much is it?" Alvin asked, but he didn't care what it cost.

"'Bout ten clams a quart."

"You mean ten dollars?" Alvin wanted to be sure.

"Yeah."

"You use it?"

"Shit, Alvin. I'm a superheavy. I don't use none of that shit. The liquid protein I drink they call Bud. If you want to bench heavy, you gotta do heavy benches. Give me a handful of Dianabol, a six of Bud, and load de bar down. 'At's what I say. But now, if you bodybuildin' or tryin' to stay in a lower-weight class, that's a different game. All I know about is superheavy benches."

Alvin felt ashamed he had thought so badly about Roger. About his fat gut and stretch marks, his three-rep sets and .44 Magnum.

He still wanted Roger to hurry up, but now it was because he wanted to get over to Muscle Shoals to get a 240Z carload of liquid protein.

Thirty

THERE WASN'T any more worrying with mixing up protein shakes that tasted like mussel shit. There wasn't any more worrying about bloating his stomach with too much fat and carbs, trying to get enough protein. No more worrying whether even to drink the protein shakes. That was all over.

Alvin had been sipping on a bottle of liquid protein all the way back from Muscle Shoals. He took the last slug out of it as he pulled up next to the front of the house and parked.

He smiled and looked at the front porch that ran the length of his house, at the two front windows, the front door, and the six two-by-fours holding up the overhang. He gazed at the porch swing beside the left window and the two ladder-back chairs in front of the right window.

It was good to get down to see Alma. To know that she was in good hands now. It was good to get back down to Birmingham for a couple of days, and it was good to get away from Mud Creek. It was all good, but Alvin was glad to be back home where all his stuff was.

He put five of the steroid tablets in his mouth, let some saliva build up, then swallowed them. He got out of the car and took the first of seven cases of liquid protein out of the back.

As he set the box on the front porch, he heard Deputy Dawg say, "Hold on they-uh, Musky."

The front door was open. Alvin walked over, pulled open the screen, and looked in. Jenny and Deward lay in the beanbag, drinking Dr Pepper and watching the *Deputy Dawg* show.

He closed the door back, and looking at the yellow light bulb on the front porch overhang, he wondered, Are they supposed to be here? But he was too excited about the existence of liquid protein in the world to figure anything.

Suddenly Deward flew out. "Hey, Alv. Where the hell you been the last two days? You gittin' worse than Mama."

Alvin was startled. He said, "I went to Birmingham to see Alma," almost in defense.

"She doin' all right? She still a comedian?"

"Yeah. Yeah," Alvin said, as though he needed to answer both questions.

He unloaded the other cases onto the front porch. Deward started picking them up and carrying them into the kitchen. When Alvin followed the boy in, he saw five large carryall grocery sacks on the table. He pulled one of the sacks over and saw Froot Loops and Chips Ahoy!. Between two of the sacks, Tarzan, the cat, was sleeping.

For a moment he wondered if he had come to the right house or what the hell was going on. Then he heard the channels change on the TV. He went to the doorway of the living room. Jenny had a Dr Pepper in one hand and the remote control in the other.

Alvin asked, "What the hell's going on?"

Jenny got up and walked into the kitchen. She said, "Hi."

"How'd ya'll and all this stuff git here?"

"Oh. We've been shopping."

"Who? Who's been shopping?"

"Mama and us. She come got us out of school about one-thirty, and we went shopping and ate. Then we come out here. She went off somewhere, though."

"Goddammit! I fucking get ya'll in school and she gets you out. What's going on anyway? Ya'll living here now or something?"

Jenny looked at the floor. She opened and shut her mouth a couple of times, like a catfish out of water.

She had long, stringy, naturally streaked blond hair and clear emerald eyes. She was almost a miniature version of Donna, except for the tits and ass. Jenny's hair was messed up at the moment, and she pulled the strand that was in her face behind her ear and gold loop earring.

She told Alvin, "I don't know. Mama just brought us out here and told me to tell you she left some food, in case she don't get back."

Jenny looked as though she were going to cry.

"Look, I'm sorry. I'm not mad at you. I just want to know what you mother thinks she's up to and where she is."

"We're not going to have to leave, are we?" Jenny asked.

"No. No. You can stay as long as you want," Alvin reassured her.

He had said that mostly because of Johnny Ray. But then he looked down at Jenny, and he felt that she might be all right. He never had liked kids much, even when *he* was a kid. He had never understood the things they liked to do. But he thought it might be possible that Jenny, and even Deward, too, might be different.

Alvin stepped forward, put his arm around Jenny, and hugged her. He really didn't know how to do it because he had never hugged a child before. He had never even been hugged much as a child. Johnny Ray was probably the only grown person that had hugged him.

Jenny put her arm around Alvin a little bit. Alvin retreated, embarrassed and ashamed. He was ashamed he didn't know how to hug her, hold her, and make her feel comfortable about it. He knew this, because he could remember a few times his father had tried to hug him. But Alvin had felt his father's shame, and he had been embarrassed about it for his father.

Jenny went back and lay beside Deward in the beanbag. Alvin

looked in at them. Then he fixed himself a glass of ice water and went out onto the front porch.

He leaned up against a two-by-four and stared out through the swamp, as if there were something out there to look at.

He felt it was time for a workout. His muscles were wanting latissimus dorsi work.

He was looking at the swamp, feeling his muscles, thinking of nothing. Then he heard the theme song to *The Andy Griffith Show* playing in the living room. He knew where Sheriff Jennings was. But he didn't know where Donna was.

Thirty-one

ALVIN OPENED up the windows of the weight room. He turned on the window fan, and soon the fifteen-by-twenty-foot space was perfect for him: cool and airy but not air-conditioned.

After turning on the Rolling Stones album, he sipped on some iced-down orange juice. Then he stood at the mirror, flexing out his latissimus dorsi in a pose that Ginger had called his wings. Sometimes when he was walking around without a shirt on, she would say, "Do your wings." Alvin would give her a quick front lat pose, and every time she would gawk and say "Goddamn."

He took a strong sniff of ammonia, then jumped up on the chinning bar and knocked off some pull-ups just to warm up with.

There was an Olympic barbell, with a big black forty-five-pound plate on each end, sitting on the floor at the foot of a bench. It looked like a locomotive axle with wheels. That's what Freddy had a bent for calling the barbells, when Alvin had been training for Mr. Alabama. He would say, "You going to go down in the shed to pump them train wheels up and down?"

He got a wide grip on the barbell, bent over with his back parallel to the floor, and began rowing the bar to his chest.

After a quick set he loaded the bar down with twice the weight. He grunted and screamed as he rowed. Now it was intense. There was no flashing through his mind of what Ginger had called his poses or of what Freddy had called his barbells. It was just him, his weights, and his muscles.

Increasing the poundage each time, he did five more sets of rowers, followed by six sets of pull-ups, with weight plates dangling from a special harness for that exercise.

He went to the mirror and did a front lat pose. His latissimi dorsi were surging with blood. It seemed to him that the V of his body was about a third more broad than when he first walked into the weight room.

Time to switch to a pushing exercise, he thought. He should work on his chest muscles, the pectorals, next. That would encompass pushing movements. He wanted to do heavy bench presses, but to do them, he needed a spotter, someone to pull the weight off him if he became exhausted or unable to press the barbell on up into its rack.

He would have to substitute dumbbell bench presses. He grabbed a set of 120-pounders and then sat on the end of the bench. After pulling the bells to his shoulders, he lay back on the bench and popped off fifteen repetitions of presses before letting them drop to the wooden floor.

Quickly he hopped up and again stood in front of the mirror. Huge veins popped out everywhere—on his chest, shoulders, fore-arms, biceps. Alvin did a side chest pose. When he relaxed the pose, he noticed Deward in the mirror behind him, gawking.

Alvin thought, Shit, I don't need this. I'll have to run him out if he gits to buggin' me.

But Alvin didn't interrupt Deward from gawking at his body. When someone saw a bodybuilder's body, relaxed and unpumped, usually he'd think it was unbelievable when he saw that same body thirty minutes later in a workout, when muscles were pumped and veins were flaring.

Alvin turned to Deward.

The eleven-year-old boy said to him, "God, I wisht I had me a set of arms like that. I won't ever, though."

Alvin spoke through clenched teeth, "Start shittin' in one hand and wishin' in the other," as if he were having to talk through all the brick walls that people like Old Lady Higgins, with their false bullshit, tried to build around young people.

Alvin continued. "Start liftin' that iron. They'll grow."

Deward had said the same thing that Alvin said when he was fourteen and had stared at Johnny Ray's seventeen-inch arms. What he told Deward was the exact same thing Johnny Ray had told him in response.

Deward said expectantly, "I can start lifting?"

"Listen, Deward. What I'm doin' is very important. I can't be disturbed. I can't be interrupted. You want to ask me questions, you ask them when I'm not working out."

"I understand, Alv. You workin' out."

Alvin moved over to the far corner of the workout room, where there was a short bar that he used to do light high rep curls on. He threw a ten-pound weight on each end and called to Deward, "Come here."

Deward came over, smiling.

Alvin said, demonstrating at the same time, "Grab it like this. Flip it at your chest. That's called cleaning the bar. Then push it up. That's a military press. Do a bunch of those. If it's too light, add some weight. Then do some of these." Alvin demonstrated. "These are curls."

"All right! All right!" Deward hollered.

Alvin went back over to his dumbbells. He heard Deward's little bar start clinging.

When Alvin grabbed the dumbbells, his muscles told him he should do bench presses on the Olympic bar first. Some pure-D bench presses. Five sets of bench presses. He got up and loaded the bar down, then looked over at Deward.

"Deward, come here. You gone spot me."

"I'm gone what?" he asked.

He came over and looked up at Alvin as if he were ready for anything.

"You gone spot me. A person that looks after somebody while they liftin' weight is called a spotter."

"I'm gone look after you?" Deward knew something must have happened for him to be that important.

"Yeah. A spotter. If the lifter can't get the weight on up, the spotter lifts it on up for him."

Deward looked to the Olympic bar that held three huge black forty-five-pound weights on each end of it.

Deward said, "Alv, I don't reckon I'm stout enough to lift that off of you. I only done one set of them military presses so far."

"Naw, naw." Alvin shook his head. "You wouldn't have to lift the whole weight. On my last repetition, that's doing it one time. Like you lift something up and down ten times is ten repetitions—"

"I know."

"So on the last rep, I might be tired down, my muscles strained out. But if you lift, say, the equivalent of twenty pounds, it's enough that I can push, say, three hundred pounds on up."

"I'll be dogged," Deward remarked, all excited and smiling. "I can do that," he assured Alvin.

"And after I lay it in the rack, if the bar is wigglin', you just hold it in place in the rack till it settles down."

"All right."

Alvin took some deep breaths and then lay on the bench. He took the bar off and did seven repetitions of bench presses. On his last rep Deward, standing at the back of his head, helped guide the bar back onto its stand on the rack.

"Good. Good," Alvin praised. "You go git you a set now."

Deward ran over to the corner and started clanging his little bar up and down in the air.

Alvin stood in front of his favorite mirror. He clasped his hands and flexed his pecs. His bronze chest was now blue with veins. He let his arms down to his sides and let his upper body relax.

His muscles required more sets of bench presses. On the last set Deward had to pull up hard to help Alvin get the bar back on the rack.

Deward asked, "Did I do all right, Alv?"

"You did perfect, Deward."

Deward smiled really big and said, "I done all them military presses and curls. What I ought to do now?"

"That ought to be it for today. You don't want to work you muscles so they can't rest up for the next workout."

"All right," he agreed. "You need any more spottin', Alvin?"

"Naw, that's it. I'm just going to do some leg raises and stuff now."

"I'm gone git back up to the house," Deward said, heading for the door. "Maybe Mama's come back." When he was going out the door, he said, "I'm gone add more weight next workout."

Alvin hopped up on the chinning bar and hung. Stiff-leggedly, he began bringing his feet up to his hands, slowly and deliberately. His abdominal muscles were telling him they wanted all the fat burned off them.

Out of the corner of his eye he noticed his musseling dry suit hanging over in the corner behind the weight lifting equipment. It was in storage, along with a pair of long johns, waiting for the cold of winter.

Dropping down from the bar, he looked at his dry suit and smiled. He had an idea.

Thirty-two

FROM AROUND THE END of March until the middle of November all the divers used wet suits, made of neoprene. They allowed water to permeate them, while the body heat stayed trapped, creating a warm layer of water next to the skin.

But in the middle of winter the Tennessee River was too cold to make a wet suit practical. The mussel divers who chose to dive during the hard winter months switched over to the more expensive but much warmer dry suits, made out of a rubber that did not allow water passage. Properly fitted, especially around the hood, and worn with a pair of long underwear, the dry suit was often not just warm but hot. A dry suit didn't let water in and didn't let body heat out.

Alvin thought about this while he stared at his dry suit. It would be the perfect thing to put on to sweat off some fat. He went over and slipped on the long white underwear. Then he pulled himself into the dry suit, zipping it up, but leaving off the hood. He hopped back up on the chinning bar and started doing some more leg raises.

Then the idea occurred to him that it would be better working his abs underwater. He would be weightless. Maybe that would help. He wanted his abs smaller, not bigger.

He walked out to the dock. It was almost sunset.

He took his rig out to the flat off Hatchett Island. Because of the buoyancy of the dry suit, Alvin put on an extra-heavy weight belt. He cranked the compressor and let himself over the bow. Slowly he lowered himself down by the air line, to the bottom of the river. He was in about nine feet of water.

Alvin lay down and started doing leg raises. He experimented, trying to figure out how best to do them. He didn't have quite enough weight on. And he was in mucky bottom. Where he had intended to let down was supposed to be coarse sand. Maybe he had drifted off the flat.

Standing up, Alvin jumped toward the surface, expecting his head to break through so he could see which way was which. He didn't get that high, but he liked the feel of jumping, so he started bouncing up and down. Then he began pulling his knees up into his body, like leg raises, when he was going up in the water, pushing them out straight when he came back down.

Alvin got another idea.

He reached back and got his air line, which was fixed to the back of one of his weight belts. He slowly pulled himself back up to the bow, made his way to the port gunnel, and pulled himself in. He found another empty weight belt at the back of the transom. He put four five-pound weights on it.

He strapped it around and around his ankle. Then he took off the second weight belt at his waist, which also had four five-pound weights on it, and strapped that onto his other ankle.

He let himself back down to the bottom and began bouncing again. His muscles liked the new exercise.

It was the perfect abdominal workout. He squatted and then lunged up toward the surface, pulling his knees up to his chest, then straightened them out as he started sinking again. He swallowed to clear his ears each time the pressure changed.

After a hundred such bounces he pulled himself up to the surface on his air line. He had worked himself down into about thirty feet of water. He was hot; his thermal underwear was damp with sweat.

He held on to the ladder at the water's surface.

It was pitch-dark. There was a slight wind up, and the waves banged him against the boat. He let the regulator drop out of his mouth, took his mask off, and tossed it over the gunnel into the boat, pulling the hood of his dry suit back.

The coolness of the night felt good on his face, but it also made him realize how hot and tired he was. He tried to pull himself on up the ladder, but he couldn't because of all the weights.

When he stuck his head under to undo his weight belts, he forgot he had taken the regulator out of his mouth. He inhaled the river water and got strangled.

Quickly he emerged above the water, coughing and gasping until he could breathe again.

This time he held his breath as he stuck his head underwater. With his right hand holding tightly to the ladder, his left hand finally got the weight belt on his left ankle unwrapped. He slowly lifted it over the gunnel and pushed it into the boat.

He repeated the process, switching hands, and got the other weight belt off and into the boat.

Now he held on and rested. His shoulders were aching. It felt as though his legs and abs were about to cramp.

He tried to pull on up the ladder, but a wave swelled up and slammed him against the boat. When it receded, Alvin fell back into the water, only holding on with his right hand. He got a foothold back on the ladder and with a surge pulled himself over the gunnel and into the boat. He got to his knees and pulled the ladder in. Then he reached over and killed the compressor engine.

He lay down in silence, dark silence.

The boat tossed in the chop. He unzipped the dry suit. The cool air hit his body.

Stumbling back to the stern, Alvin looked around at the darkness. He lay back down, exhausted. His aching muscles felt good.

Thirty-three

WHEN ALVIN WOKE up, the room was light, and Donna was massaging his right leg. He looked over at the clock. It was one o'clock.

He felt stiff, as if he had set up in concrete. He remembered that it had taken him four hours to find his way back to Mud Creek last night.

Donna started massaging his other leg.

She wore a long-sleeve blouse that was unbuttoned, except for the bottom two buttons, and a pair of panties.

Alvin looked at her. She was staring intently down at the leg she was working on. He felt as though he had a mild case of the Mussels. Everything looked distorted, as if it were happening in another time.

He watched Donna get up and go to the phone, the long-corded one that could be taken almost anywhere in the house. She picked it up and punched the buttons.

He heard her say, "Ferris Edwards? . . . Yeah. This is Donna. Johnny Ray's widow wife. Lives down by the river . . . Yeah . . . Fine

. . . I want to board and batten my house. . . . No, the one on Mud Creek. . . . Yeah, that one . . . Take you three or four days with your whole crew? . . . OK, I'll see you soon."

She hung up, and he watched her change her blouse. Then he dozed back off into a sound sleep.

A couple of hours later he woke up, put on some clothes, went into the kitchen, and sat down at the wooden table his grandmother had stripped down with lye to paint, forty years ago. It was her last project before she died. It was down to bare wood, a large heavy table with lathed ornate legs, with some of the old green paint still down in the grain of the wood. But to Alvin it looked finished, as if it were supposed to look that way.

He pulled his spiral notebook from under Tarzan, the cat, and opened it. On the first page was a list of measurements for each of his body parts and a column for the goal of that body part.

Beside the waist entry was written, "25 inches."

Alvin flipped through several pages of workout routines. A page where he had written down in ink, "Exercises for the lats: bent-over rowers, dumbbell rowers, weighted pull-ups, wide-grip pull-downs on the pulley machine, pull-overs." The next page was written in pencil: "Five sets of rowers, three sets of pull-overs." Following was a list of leg exercises. Poundages were written and crossed out under each exercise.

Then he found a fresh page. He wrote: "January—Mr. Gulf Coast (fifth place). September—Mr. America. Waist, 23″.

The kids came through the front screen door and hollered, "We're home!" and let the screen door slam.

They had walked the half mile down the causeway from where the school bus had let them off on the country road.

Alvin turned around, looked at them, and said, "Oh, hi."

"I got something for you, Alv! Look here," Deward said, setting his books on the table and fumbling through his notebook.

Jenny picked up Tarzan, held him to her breast, and stroked him, singing, "Tarzan's so purty."

Deward got two sheets of lined side-punched paper out and handed the first one to Alvin, who took it and looked at the drawing Deward had made.

It was a muscleman in a front double biceps pose. His fists were half as big as his head. His biceps peaked up to ear level. His lats tapered out into a V, to a waist that was almost nothing. From the waist two legs forked. There was a smile on his face. Off to the side of the page was printed "Alvin," and there was an arrow that pointed from the word to the figure.

Alvin looked at Deward and said, "This is good. Real good."

Deward smiled and handed him the other sheet. He stared at it from Alvin's left side, while Jenny moved around so she could stare at it from the right.

It was a man with the same proportions as in the first drawing. He was standing at the bottom of a river. He had on a wet suit with a weight belt around his waist and a sheathed knife strapped to one of his calves. He was holding his arms to the side; a big mussel was in each hand. There was a catfish with a handlebar mustache swimming by. Again, the man was smiling, bubbles going to the surface from his mouth, and "Alvin" was printed on one side of the paper, with an arrow pointing to the man.

Alvin said, "This is real good. Both of 'em. Thanks, Deward. I think I'll tack these up in the weight room. Naw. I think I'll tape 'em up on the refrigerator." He had seen a movie where they had taped kids' drawings up on their refrigerator.

Deward was really excited. "You want *me* to do it? I'll get some tape."

"OK," Alvin said, handing him the pictures.

Deward ran off with them and soon returned with the tape.

Donna walked into the house, wearing a blue denim work shirt, tied in a knot above the waist. She had done all the shopping and housework since the kids had been staying there.

Ever since Alvin was big enough to half ass walk, he had had work to do. But for the first time, ever since the kids had been there, he hadn't done anything to "put food on the table."

When Donna walked in, the kids squealed and ran over to hug her.

Jenny said, "I have a note from the teacher you have to read and sign."

Deward hollered, "Me too, Mama. I have a note you have to read and sign."

"All right. All right. First let's have refreshments," Donna said, as if she were excited about all of life. She fixed the kids a Dr Pepper, herself an iced tea.

She asked Alvin, "You want anything, sweetheart?"

"I think I'll take a glass of ice water." He closed the notebook and pushed it across the table, next to the wall.

Donna fixed Alvin's ice water and set it in front of him.

He said, "Thank you."

She fixed the other drinks, and then she and the kids sat at the table with Alvin. Jenny gave her the note.

Donna read it aloud. "Jenny has been talking back to me." She flipped the note over to search for any further comments. "I guess that's all she had to say." She looked at Jenny and said, "That's so good, dear. You're doing so well at school."

Jenny smiled.

Donna reached over and got Alvin's pen. She flipped the note over and wrote, "Dear Mrs. Turner, Thank you for the note. Yes, Jenny usually speaks when spoken to. She is very good in this respect. Her late departed father, Johnny Ray, taught her this. Signed, Donna."

She handed the note back to Jenny.

Jenny said, "Thank you, Mama."

"Read mine, read mine!" Deward hollered.

Donna took the note and read it aloud, "I have caught Deward drawing several times while I was conducting class."

She looked at Deward and said, "That's so good, honey. You're doing so well at school."

Deward grinned.

Flipping this note over, Donna wrote, "Dear Mrs. McIntire, Thank you for the note. Yes, Deward likes to draw. I believe he gets his talent from his late departed father, Johnny Ray. Johnny Ray himself had strong artistic tendencies until death took his young life away. Signed, Donna."

She handed the note back to Deward.

Deward said, "Thank you, Mama."

The children ran off into the living room. Alvin could hear the television blast on. Donna walked back out the side kitchen door, leaving Alvin there alone. He finally got up and went to his room to do a little posing.

When he opened one of his drawers in search of some posing trunks, he found the pile of papers and belongings of Johnny Ray's that Donna had given him. There was a point, about a month after his death, that Donna got rid of a lot of Johnny Ray's things. Gave his clothes to charity. Sold Cliff the boat. And gave Alvin a pile of his things, which included some personal notes and maps.

On the top of the pile was a folded-up map of the section of the Tennessee River in which they dove, actually called Wheeler Lake by the TVA, but none of the divers or commercial fishermen ever thought of the Tennessee River as a series of dammed-up lakes. One could have gone up to an old commercial fisherman who was running trotlines on "Wheeler Lake," actually floating in it at the moment, and mentioned Wheeler Lake, and he would have just thought you were talking about some pond probably back near the Mississippi state line.

Alvin looked around his bedroom. There was a bare spot on one of the walls where the map would look good as a poster.

When he unfolded the map, a scrap of brown paper bag fell out of the folds. Alvin inspected it. There were pencil lines and scribbles marked on it, but he couldn't make out what any of it meant.

Only after he got the map up did he see that a point in the channel of the river had been marked in blue ink.

He found the torn-up paper bag and looked at it again. The same markings.

Alvin quickly formulated a scenario; Johnny Ray came off the sunken riverboat or whatever it was he had run into that day he had died. Up in the boat he found a paper bag, found a pencil, scribbled out some bearings. Went home, cleaned up. Got out the map, made markings on the map, folded up the map and sketchings, come back over to Alvin's.

Alvin's heart began to beat rapidly as he considered that it might be a treasure map he had just tacked up on his wall.

Even if it was, the place would be hard to get back down on. But then he remembered Johnny Ray's words: "I won't be able to *not* find it agin. Right now this minute it's pulling me down. Right now it's sucking me down to it. No way I can't not find that thang agin."

Alvin was thinking maybe that was what had killed Johnny Ray. Maybe that night it was pulling him down there so hard that it sucked Johnny Ray right out of his body, just leaving the body to rot there on the living room floor.

That made more sense to Alvin than a little nitrogen bubble killing him. That theory had some sense, had some logic to it.

But Alvin didn't ponder Johnny Ray's death long, or his last few words, or even sunken treasure. About then Alvin's muscles started calling him. They wanted to pose.

Thirty-four

ALL YOU EAT is itsy-bitsy pieces of steak and drink that damn red stuff," Jenny said to Alvin as she walked away from the supper table with her empty plate.

Everyone but Alvin was finished with supper. He had a small country-fried steak in his plate and a large glass of liquid protein before him. He had spent the entire suppertime slowly cutting up his steak into sixty-four pieces.

Donna went to the back bedroom. Jenny and Deward went to watch TV. Alvin sat quietly, not saying a word, eating his steak.

Thirty minutes later he finished supper. He walked to the doorway that separated the kitchen from the living room. The kids were still watching the television. Jenny sat in the La-Z-Boy, drinking a Dr Pepper from a heavy Twilight Café beer mug.

Alvin walked over, jerked the mug out of her hand, and threw it through the television screen.

He said, "All you do is watch that damn TV."

Deward got a coloring book and started coloring. Jenny got a book and started reading. Donna came into the living room, unplugged the set, and cleaned up all the glass, as if someone had dropped and broken a plate.

Alvin watched her, thinking about the five hundred dollars he was going to have to peel off for a television from his cash stash that his twenty-dollar-a-day liquid protein habit was eating at. Alvin was even getting mentally prepared to start having to hear a bunch of shit and having to get in his Z and drive all the way to Huntsville to one of those places that stayed open until 10:00 P.M. just to get another TV so Jenny and Deward would miss only about an hour of viewing.

Then he noticed nobody really gave a shit about the television.

Alvin sauntered on out to the front porch and sat down in a ladder-back chair to get his dose of just staring out into the swamp and smelling the musky odor of Mud Creek.

He heard a rumble coming down the causeway. Shortly Freddy's Camaro whipped around the house and pulled up to the front porch.

Freddy was alone. He smiled and said, "Hi." He had on his black river gambler's hat. He left the engine idling. It was purring. He must have just gotten it tuned, Alvin thought.

"Come on," Freddy called. "Let's go to the Twilight."

"I'm just a-sittin' here," Alvin said for a response, but Freddy couldn't tell if he meant he was busy sitting there or if he was bored and just happened to be sitting there.

"I see," Freddy said. He looked around, noticed Donna's Corvette. Then the kids could be heard hollering at each other. "Donna and the kids move in?"

"Man, you know, I don't even know. They been stayin' here. Got a bunch of their shit here."

Freddy asked, "She gone rent out her house or lock it up or what?"

"You know, I don't know that either. Never bothered to ask Donna about that," Alvin answered sincerely.

"When the hell is Cliff coming back. You heard from him?" Freddy asked.

"Aw, shit naw," Alvin said like he was complaining. He had forgotten about Cliff and Alma. The day he had come back and decided to let them take care of each other, he had more or less pushed them out of his mind, no longer feeling responsible. That had been maybe three weeks ago, but now at the mention of Cliff he was alarmed. He felt as though he had left them locked in Alma's apartment, and now they lay in there dead, having been left without food or water. Dead from lack of care. He couldn't believe he had forgotten them.

Then Alvin said, half lying, "I was going to ask you if you'd heard from him. He's still down there with Alma, I guess. I figured since I hadn't heard from them, everthang's going all right."

Alvin resisted the temptation to run into the house to call them, all the while feeling he should really phone the Birmingham rescue squad to have them go straight over and break into the apartment, see if they could revive them.

"Yeah, that's what I figured," Freddy said. "Thang is I got some insulation all cut, ready to put in the attic. I's needing him to hand it to me, so I wouldn't have to be up and down the damn ladder."

"Hell, I'll go help you do it," Alvin volunteered, in an effort to make up for having caused the death of Cliff and his sister.

"Aw, man, that fiberglass shit git on you skin, it itches. I'll just wait for Cliff."

"I don't give a rat's ass," Alvin said. "It'll help stretch my muscles out some. You just rinse off in cold water. You wait for Cliff you might be waiting a spell."

"You got that right."

"Let's give them a call. See what they up to," Alvin said, sounding phony. He knew he should have confessed he had forgotten them, left them trapped, to starve.

Freddy got out of the car, followed Alvin inside.

"Freddy!" Jenny and Deward hollered, but then went back to what they were doing.

Alvin grabbed the phone and walked on into the kitchen. He pointed at the refrigerator, sat down at the table, and punched off Alma's number.

Freddy reached in the refrigerator, got a beer, held it to Alvin, who shook his head no. Freddy sat across from Alvin and opened his beer, not knowing it had been one of his own he'd put there about two months ago.

Alvin said into the telephone, "Alma! How are you doing?"

Alma shrieked into the telephone, "Alvin! Oh me, we were just thinking of you!"

"Yeah? Freddy's over here. We thought we'd give ya'll a call. How ya'll doing?"

"Great. Hey, baby, we'll be up to see you in a week or two." Alma paused. "Oh. Cliff wants to speak to Freddy."

Alvin handed the phone to Freddy. Freddy said, "Hey boy . . . yeah . . . yeah." Freddy laughed at whatever Cliff was saying. "All right. See you then. Bye." Freddy hung up the phone.

Alvin sat there dumbfounded that Alma hadn't talked to him again. Alma seemed fine. Alvin was confused, wondering if it was really true that he and Cliff had walked into her apartment three weeks ago to find her at death's door. Or had it been a bad dream? The way Alma just sounded, the crispness of the whole conversation— it didn't seem to follow her lying there dying, making him say she wouldn't get f-a-t.

Freddy said to Alvin, "Well, I guess we'll see them in a week or two."

"Yeah. Come on, let's go put that insulation in."

They walked back outside to Freddy's car. Alvin got in the passenger's seat of Freddy's Camaro. Freddy backed up and then took off down the causeway.

Freddy said, "I just put a new three-fifty in this baby. Got high-performance fuelly heads."

Freddy accelerated, let up on the gas, then accelerated again.

"Responds real nice," Alvin commented.

"Yeah boy, she do. Been drivin' it a lot. Just got it broke in good yesterday."

Alvin liked the feel of being a passenger. For the last few weeks it seemed every time he went somewhere he drove himself. Right now he was just enjoying the feel of it, of clipping by the trees, of the car taking the curves, of the g's against his body in the bucket seat.

Soon Freddy pulled up to the little cabin that he and Cliff rented. It was a small clapboard green rectangular house sitting among some tall pines and oaks on the waterfront. At the front door was a cinder block for a step. There was no porch. Alvin wondered how he got by without one, even though the side of the house to the river was a screened-in Florida room that went the length of the house.

All the windows, even including the front and back doors, were jalousied. That and no insulation in the attic meant it was an icebox in the winter.

They got out and walked in; the door was unlocked.

Alvin stood in the small living room. The walls were varnished paneled pine; the ceiling was open two-by-ten joist beams. Both the beams and the bottom of the one-by-four decking of the attic were unpainted.

The bathroom had a door, but the two doorways to the small bedrooms only had curtains hanging there. Alvin thought maybe that was one more reason Freddy had wanted to bring his girls over to his house: for the privacy of a lockable bedroom door.

Alvin looked about. Dark curtains hung over the windows. A stuffed secondhand maroon velour armchair and couch sat in the living room. Looked the same as it had three weeks ago, but somehow darker.

He picked up a *Skin Diver* magazine that was lying on the coffee table and started thumbing through it.

Freddy asked, "Hey man, you't somethin' to drank?" as he opened up the old small refrigerator door.

"Some ice water."

Freddy fixed Alvin some water, himself some Pepsi on ice, and came back in the living room and plopped down on the sofa. Alvin sat in the armchair.

Freddy took a sip of Pepsi and then motioned over at the magazine Alvin was flipping through.

Freddy said, "Yeah, me and Cliff got this idea going. We already sent for some brochures down to the Florida Keys. This winter, when it gits real cold, we thinking about going down there and taking some scuba diving classes."

"Classes?" Alvin asked, unbelieving. "You spend six hours a day about two to three hundred days a year under the water, not up in the boat, but actually under the water, breathing through a regulator, and you gone let some little dip shit like that feller over at the dive shop teach ye how to dive? Shit!"

"Naw. You have to have a certification down there to get air. And there's a lot of women in them classes. Good-looking women."

Alvin could understand that. But he couldn't understand Freddy going to the trouble to get certified for something. He even seriously doubted if Freddy had a valid driver's license.

Alvin said, "Aw, man. If ya want air, you just toss the bonehead a five, tell him you left you dive card back up in Alabama."

"Shut up and just listen a minute, *Eddie*," Freddy said. "We want to learn all about this ocean diving. Come hard winter, we go down there for a couple months. See, Cliff and me thinking about gittin' into treasure diving. If we start gettin' into it now, maybe we be making some money off it by the time musselin' dies out. Who knows? And who knows how many more years musselin's gone hold out. You know?"

Alvin was thrown into a mystery, almost a confusion. He was wondering what Freddy knew. If Freddy knew more than he did. First of all, he was winterizing their cabin. He must somehow know and expect Donna and the kids to be living at Alvin's place for a while, meaning he and Cliff wouldn't be able to move back in with him as they had last February.

Then the treasure diving. Alvin wondered if he knew he had a treasure map hanging on his bedroom wall. He wondered if he knew Johnny Ray had planned to slide into treasure diving.

"Sounds like a good idea," Alvin commented.

"You want to git in with us on it?"

"I don't know yet," Alvin said, but knew this winter he would be in intensive training. January would be Mr. Gulf Coast.

"You can take Donna and the kids if you want."

"Yeah. I'll see when it gits closer to time," Alvin said.

On top of all the wonder was all this planning ahead Freddy was doing. It wasn't like him to insulate the attic until it was thirty degrees outside. It wasn't like Freddy to send off for brochures, to plan anything, to look ahead beyond mussel diving.

Alvin automatically invented a plot to explain Freddy's actions: After Johnny Ray's death, he and Cliff were probably at the cabin alone. Cliff was in the chair Alvin was now sitting in. He was drinking Johnnie Walker Black on ice. Freddy was pacing the floor, drinking a bottle of Miller beer. Freddy was saying, "Johnny Ray's dead. I can't believe it. Thangs have got to change. We got to start lookin' ahead, Cliff."

That was the only thing that Alvin could think would explain Freddy's new practice of planning ahead.

"Yeah, that all sounds fun," Alvin said as he got up. It was all kind of spooky to him. "You't me to be bringing the insulation in?"

Thirty-five

A WEEK LATER, exactly to the day that he helped Freddy with the insulation, Alvin again was sitting on the front porch when Freddy pulled up in his car.

Freddy asked, "You gone come to the fish fry tonight? Emma and Charlie's been askin' about ya."

Dr. Dick came and jumped up in Alvin's lap, but there wasn't enough room to lie up there comfortably, so he jumped back down, lay up against the house, and went to sleep.

"I don't know. I think I'll just lay around here."

"Goddammit. Everthang's fucked up. Cliff off at Birmingham. You laid up here. Ain't diving or nothing."

"I'm in intensive training and laying in the sun."

Freddy disregarded what Alvin had said. He had a bottle of Country Club malt liquor between his thighs.

Freddy continued complaining. "And Eddie's so pussy-whipped, his old lady damn near won't let him out of the house lately. He'll be lucky if he gits to bring her to the fish fry. Shit, everbody doing something else. Everthang been fucked up since Johnny Ray went and died." He took a long suck of beer in defiance to the world.

Jenny came out, holding Tarzan. Tarzan seemed to be as big as her upper body, but she held him as if it were no trouble at all. Deward was right beside her.

They both said, "Hey, Freddy!"

"Hey, Jenny. Deward."

Deward said, "Hey, Freddy, is your car fast as one them Burt Reynolds's cars that he hauls wildcat whiskey in?"

Jenny hollered, "Damn, Deward. Don't be stupid. No car nowhere as fast as a Burt Reynolds car. Don't be stupid."

Freddy was about to respond, but Donna walked out. She stood by the kids and said, "Oh, hello, Freddy."

"Hi, Donna."

"I saw you at the dock today. I was gone come down, say hey, but I was busy."

"That's all right."

Everything was quiet for a second. Freddy looked up at the four people and a cat staring at him and the dog asleep on the porch.

He said to Alvin, "Anyhow, the fish fry is at the shell place tonight."

Jenny held Tarzan with one arm and tugged at Alvin with the other. She cried, "Let's go!"

Deward said, "Yeah. Can we go?"

"Please, Alv," pleaded Jenny. "Let's all go. Purty please?"

At the same time Deward was hopping up and down, saying, "Let's go. Let's go. Let's go."

Alvin shouted, "All right, goddammit! After I take a hot bath."

The kids screamed with joy and ran into the house. It woke up Dr. Dick, who looked around and then went back to sleep.

Donna came over and kissed Alvin on the mouth. "Sweetheart, do you want me to boil some extra water for the tub, like last night?"

"Yeah. That would be good, Donna."

Freddy was taking this all in, especially the way Donna had kissed Alvin.

Donna turned to him and said, "See you at the fish fry."

He coughed and said, "Yeah, Donna. See ya there."

After Donna walked on in the house, Freddy said to Alvin, "Man, I didn't mean to start no damn world war. I didn't fuck you up, did I?"

"Naw. Don't worry about it."

"Listen, Alvin. We need to have us a long talk. And soon, too."

"Yeah. That would be good," Alvin said, and smiled.

Freddy smiled back and said, "One them long talks where we go out to the channel of the Tennessee River at night, and just drift-fish and look for flying saucers and do some git-down rock and roll bullshittin'."

"Yeah, Freddy. That would be good."

"Yeah, we 'bout overdue. If Judy hadn't come over last week after we got done with the insulation . . . but you know how it is."

"Got to git it while it's hot," Alvin said, quoting Freddy.

"Let me git outta here," Freddy said, cranking the engine. He waved at Alvin and cruised on back down the causeway.

Alvin walked into the house and on back to the bathroom. Purple Tub was plugged, and hot, steamy water was pouring into it. He took his clothes off and put his foot in the water. It was scalding. He stuck that foot on in, and then his other. He slowly sat down and then lay back.

Picking up a half-empty quart bottle of liquid protein that was lying by the tub, he read the label and then turned it around and read the ingredients. He smiled, took the cap off, and started sipping on it.

The tub was not quite full, but the hot water had turned luke-warm, so he cut it off. He lay back again and took some long sucks on the protein. His muscles told him they liked the hot bath, that it was good for them. Alvin was pleased.

When the bottle was empty, he put the cap back on and floated it in the water, pushing it down to his feet and pushing it back up with his toes.

He didn't want to go to the fish fry. He'd much rather sit out on the front porch when he got through with his hot bath. And if he wasn't going to sit out on the porch, he could think of plenty of things he'd rather do than go see all the divers and listen to their bullshit. It just all happened so suddenly that Alvin was into going to the fish fry before he knew what had hit him.

Deward came into the bathroom. He had a shirt on a hanger in each hand. Holding them up, he asked, "Which shirt do you think I art to wear, Alv?"

"It don't matter."

"Wull, which one?"

"The plaid one. If I's you, I'd wear the plaid-looking one."

"Yeah? That was the one I's cottoning to."

Alvin looked at Deward's unruly hair and broad chest and thought: The son of a bitch is built like Johnny Ray. Fucker's gonna be stout.

Last year the farm league baseball team Deward was on, the South Side Gators, was on *The Admiral Andy Show* in Muscle Shoals. When Admiral Andy knelt down and stuck the microphone up to Deward to ask him his name, Deward hit him three times in the face, bloodying his nose and making Deward a perennial hero at the South Side Elementary School.

Deward had explained to Johnny Ray how he had seen Admiral Andy putting the microphone up to the other kids, asking them their name. But that Admiral Andy kind of whirled around and all of a sudden stuck what he thought was a sawed-off shotgun in his face, and at the same time a stenched breath like that of the village drunk, Pone McGuire, hit him in the face.

Johnny Ray had told Deward that he had done good.

Deward stood looking down at Alvin with a funny sort of gleam in his eyes. Alvin wished he wouldn't look at him that way because he knew he couldn't do things for him the way Johnny Ray had.

Deward said, "You had a good workout, didn't you?"

"Yeah. Real good. You a good spotter."

"Did I pick up when I was supposed to?"

Alvin knew he just wanted to hear it again. "Sure did." And he had. Alvin was stunned at how naturally Deward had taken to assisting him on his sets of movements with the barbells.

"You reckon I'll ever be as good as you?"

"Better," Alvin said.

"Naw," Deward said, smiling.

He ran out as Donna walked in with a teakettle of hot, almost boiling water. Alvin spread his legs, and she poured the water slowly between his feet.

"Ahhh. That feels good."

Donna said, "There was some primitive tribe that dipped their balls into boiling water to kill the sperm. For birth control."

He said quickly, "I'm not trying to control any births," as if Donna might have a cup of boiling water for him to dip his balls down into. "I'm just trying to get my muscles good and warm."

She kissed him and walked out with the empty teakettle.

Alvin was just relaxing and getting adjusted to the new hot water when Deward came running back in. Jenny was right behind him. She had a comb and a hair clasp.

She pushed Deward aside and said, "Put this in my hair, Alv. See, I want my hair on this side to come behind my ear, but on this side, I'm going to have it over my ear." She pulled her hair back to show Alvin how it would look. "Like this. Or do you think I ought to let it come down over both ears?"

"I don't know," he said, hoping she wouldn't make a big deal out of a stupid fish fry.

Deward said, "Billy Joe at school said there was this man up at the Tennessee line that fucked this dog, and now the dog's gonna have puppies. And they don't know if it's going to be dog puppies or people puppies. Can we git one, Alv? I mean, if it's dog puppies?"

Alvin said seriously, "I don't know about that. It might grow up a little and then turn into a people."

"Like tadpoles?"

"Yeah," Alvin said, thinking how Deward caught on quickly to things.

Jenny sat on the tub with her back to Alvin while he clasped back her hair.

She said, "This is going to be fun."

"Well, we not going to stay long."

"Why come?" Jenny asked. She turned around and stared at him for the answer.

He tried to think of anything just to get out of the fish fry as soon as possible. "Well, I thought we'd eat right quick and go over to Muscle Shoals and see a movie."

Jenny shrilled and clapped.

Deward said, "Oh boy! What movie we gone see? Can we see one with Burt Reynolds in it?"

"If they's one on."

The kids ran from the bathroom, hollering, "Mama! Mama!"

After drying off and putting on a pair of underwear, Alvin walked into the bedroom. Donna was in front of the mirror, brushing her hair. She had on a khaki outfit.

Alvin thought: Not you, too? It's just a damn fish fry.

He asked, "Where you think we goin'?"

"Fish fry and the movies. The kids told me you said we were going to the movies. That's going to be so nice." She stuck her hairbrush down in her purse and said, "I'm going to go see if the kids are ready," and walked out.

Alvin stood in front of the mirror and did a stomach vacuum. His stomach appeared to go up inside his rib cage and his rib cage expanded out, showing the ribs up to his pecs. He relaxed and measured his waist with a tape measure. It was twenty-seven inches.

He thought: I need to git down to twenty-two.

He put on a pair of his not-too-faded Levi's, and they swallowed him. They had fit tightly two months ago. He thought: No damn wonder they thought my hip structure was fucked up. All that fat.

Looking around, he found a pair of Donna's Calvin Kleins and put them on. They were a little tight but better than his. He put on one of his dress shirts that Ginger had made for him. It was floppy-fitting.

The nights were getting cold, so he pulled a sweat shirt over his shirt. He looked in the mirror. It was one of his sweat shirts that had

"Mr. Alabama" across the front. He imagined how it would look with "Mr. America" on it.

Donna came back into the room and pulled Alvin's collar out. She whirled him halfway around and fixed the collar at the front. Then she hooked her hands over his shoulders and said, "Thanks, Alvin. You don't know how happy this is making the kids."

Alvin couldn't figure it out.

He said, "It's just an old fish fry. There's a big fish fry at least once a month somewhere." He wanted the kids to be happy. He wanted Donna to be happy. Still, he didn't feel good about it.

Donna got his denim jacket out of the closet and put it on him, then stood in front of him and smiled. He looked into her green eyes and was hoping he could find some of Johnny Ray's confidence and power in there. Maybe Johnny Ray had left some in there from looking into her eyes the way Alvin was now, but he didn't see any.

All he saw was somebody looking at him as though he had what Johnny Ray had. It made him feel he wanted to confess, but he couldn't, and he didn't want to have to pretend.

He knew he was going to have to be able to give, and if he didn't have it to give, he was going to have to get it. Alvin felt all of this as a single impression. He didn't think it in words. It wasn't like when he talked to himself or figured.

Donna said, "Hold me."

He held her, but he was having bad feelings about the fish fry. Now Alvin understood what Johnny Ray had meant when he'd say sometimes, "Thangs ain't right. Don't know whut it is yet, but thangs ain't right."

Thirty-six

ALVIN PULLED UP at Robert's Crossroads. It looked unusual for there to be lights coming from the Dixie Shell Company. Emma and Charlie closed around sundown every day.

Deward said, "Boy, sure is a lot o' cars here." He leaned up between Alvin and Donna. "How many cars you'd say's here, Alv?"

"Twenty-five. Thirty."

Pulling over into the acre and a half field by the old gin building, he parked by a brand-new four-wheel-drive Chevy pickup. As soon as he stepped out, Alvin could hear Bart hollering and Eddie laughing, over the noise of everybody else.

They all got out of the Datsun, but Donna and the kids waited for Alvin to make the first move toward the building. Alvin figured they thought he was the leader, so he headed for the fish fry with them walking slightly behind.

As they came up along Emma and Charlie's trailer, those two came out.

Emma stepped up to Alvin and hugged him, saying, "I've been asking about you but didn't get much news." She stepped back and looked him up and down a couple of times. "My, you've lost so much weight. Your face is so thin. What was the matter with you?"

"Nothing," Alvin said.

Donna and the kids were standing behind him, looking at Charlie. Charlie was standing behind Emma, looking at Donna and the kids.

"Did you have the flu?" Emma asked.

"No ma'am."

"Well, are you feeling better now?" Emma asked, as though Alvin had replied that he had just gotten over a case of malarial disease.

"I'm feeling OK now."

"Well, good," she sang. She patted him on the back and said, "Now get in there and get you a big old helping of catfish and hush puppies and get some meat back on those bones. I want to see one of my star divers back bringing those mussels in."

A tingle flashed up Alvin's spine. He didn't think anybody would expect him to eat anything just because he had come to the fish fry.

As Emma hurried off to make sure that everyone was fed, Alvin turned to Charlie. "How's those Sooners doing?" He asked to be nice because Charlie and Emma were from Oklahoma.

"I don't give a damn for football. I'm for the Reds. And I don't give a damn for the TV. Just want to hear it," Charlie said, in a soft and smooth way.

Alvin thought, Way to go, Charlie. Let 'em have the damn football and TV. Fuck 'em.

He said, "Know what you mean. Hang in there, Charlie." The divers called Emma and Charlie by their first names because they didn't know how to pronounce their last.

Alvin stood in line at the food table behind Deward. He had done well, he thought. He had made it past the people sitting on the hoods of pickups outside and in through the big opening in the side of the building. He thought he had done just fine to get by without anyone recognizing him.

If he hadn't tripped over the number three washtub full of iced-down Millers, when he looked around to see all the people eating catfish and sitting in lawn and ladder-back chairs, and gunnysacks full of mussel shells, he would have done perfectly.

Now, as a lady handed him a plate, he had the shakes, wanting to get back out as slyly as he got in. The smell of cooked-out mussel shells pierced through his sinuses and hung there. They smelled the way they always had, but now the smell nauseated him.

The lady serving asked, "Do you want more tartar sauce?"

Looking down, he saw his plate was filled with fried catfish, potato salad, baked beans, and a ton of hush puppies.

"Come on, honey! You't some more tartar sauce o' not?"

"Naw. No ma'am."

Alvin meandered quickly through the chairs and tubs of beer, with Donna and the kids following. Outside, just out from the overhang of the building, they found a tailgate on an old Ford step-side pickup, where they could eat. Just as they set their paper plates on the tailgate, Bart came running up.

Donna flinched.

Bart had a plate of catfish in one hand and a can of Miller in the other. He put his Miller arm around Alvin's neck. He was trying to say something, but all he was doing was spitting potato salad on Alvin's sweat shirt.

Finally, he said, coherently, "Yeah, if it ain't good to be seein' ye out, grits ain't groceries, eggs ain't poultry, and Mona Lisa was a man."

He took his arm from around Alvin so he could get a long slug of beer. He took note of Alvin's body.

Bart exclaimed, "Man, what happened?"

Then Bart noticed Donna and the kids standing there, and it was like Bart had been shook stone sober all of a sudden. He opened his mouth, but it froze.

To Alvin, it felt as if he had just hollered, "Johnny Ray!"

Bart closed his mouth, opened it, took a slug of Miller, and went drunk again. He waved his arm and said, "Shit, ya'll didn't git nothing to drink. Let me git yaw some beer or ice tea."

"Thanks," Donna said. "But I was just going back to get us some iced tea."

She and Jenny went back into the building, and Eddie and Tony walked up.

Eddie said, "I said to Tony, 'Who's 'at with Donner?' and Tony said, 'Shit, 'at's Alvin.' I said, 'Hell, 'at ain't Alvin.' Got to looking. Goddamn. You been sick?"

"Naw."

"What was matter with ye?" Eddie asked, wondering what it was that had sucked Alvin down in weight.

"Nothing," Alvin replied.

Eddie pulled out a pint of hip-pocket pass-around whiskey, took a slug, and handed it to Bart. While their attention was on the bottle, Alvin threw three of his hush puppies into the weeds.

Deward had been watching him, and he threw three of his into the weeds, too. Eddie only saw Deward do this, so he figured Deward didn't like hush puppies.

Bart handed the bottle to Alvin, who shook his head and said, "No thanks."

Eddie, Bart, and Tony stared at each other with catfish mouths. Alvin had always been a connoisseur of rotgut. And Alvin had always been sociable.

Bart asked, "Whut's wrong?"

Alvin wanted to tell him about how he was in intensive training, how alcohol wreaked havoc on one's body, and how he thought it sucked power out of one. But he didn't tell him that.

Instead, he said, "Yeah. I'd like a swalla. But I take one slug, I'd turn yaller, and that'd be the end of the world for me." The end of the world sounded more final than bodily death. Folks were dying all the time.

"Why's 'at?" Tony asked, as if he wanted to know where the Communist was that had told Alvin that, so he could beat the shit out of him and Alvin would be free to take a good pull.

"Can't have a drop of liquor for one year," Alvin explained. "I had hiptightus."

"Wull, shit in my mouth and say no more!" Bart hollered.

"We figured ye'd been sick," Eddie said. "But didn't figure in such a bad way."

Tony said, "I thought you looked a tad yeller. Hey, man, anything we kin do to help ye out?"

"Naw, thanks, Tony. I be all right now," Alvin said.

They all seemed to loosen up, relieved that Alvin hadn't gone strange on them. They all sighed, as if they could rest easy that Johnny Ray's protégé was still one of the gang, that he hadn't turned faggot or something.

Alvin looked around him. They were passing the bottle around, sucking on it. And they were staring at him, smiling. He took a bite of potato salad and swallowed it, but it was hard to get down.

"Where's Freddy?" he asked, trying to get them to quit staring at him. "I saw him awhile ago, said he was coming."

"Aw yeah. He was here," Eddie explained. "He brung that girl with them tits."

"They all got tits, ye dumb shit," Tony said.

"I'm talking about that one with the big tits that he goes out with. Judy. She was wearing a pair of white pants and spilt somepin all over 'em. So Linda said she had some pants that would fit her. So Freddy was gone run 'em by our house, let Judy get 'em on; then he was gone stop by Beaulah Town, git some more whiskey at the Twilight. He'll be back directly."

"How's Linda?" Alvin asked.

Linda was Eddie's wife, his good-looking wife. Alvin figured that if he questioned them, they wouldn't start asking him a bunch of dumb-ass questions.

"She's crazy. High-strung as ever. Just like a damn woman." Eddie smiled and took a pull of whiskey.

"She got you ass tied around her little finger," Tony commented when the bottle was passed to him.

"You don't be worrying about me. I git my pussy. You ought to be talking. Sandra Lynn's got you ass tightened down to you balls," Eddie said in defense.

"At least I got enough damn sense not to haul off out of the blue and git married on everbody," Tony snapped back.

Eddie stated, "We either fucking or fighting." Then he asked rhetorically, "What else you want out of life?"

Donna and Jenny came out of the gin through the two-ton-truck size opening, where trucks used to haul the baled cotton out.

Alvin watched them, hoping they would be able to save him from having to eat any more food.

He thought there wasn't any more room for anybody to stand around this tailgate. When Donna and Jenny come up, maybe they'll all leave.

A tall, wiry man cut in front of Donna and headed toward the tailgate, as though he had some business with somebody in particular.

He hollered at the four of them, "Any ya'll goin' out chonder to Texas? They found a lot of shells out yonder. Any ya'll goin' out yonder to mussel?"

Alvin didn't want to get asked any more questions, and he didn't want the tall, wiry man around him. He didn't want Eddie, Tony, and Bart standing around him drinking and trying to get him to eat. He wanted to get the hell out of there with Donna, Jenny, and Deward.

The tall, wiry man walked on up and said, "Any ya'll goin' out yonder to Texas?"

Alvin knew if that man didn't go on and leave him alone, he was going to have a conniption fit.

Thirty-seven

DONNA AND JENNY WERE SITTING near the opening of the building, on a couple of tow sacks full of mussel shells. Anyone walking by nodded hello to them but did not bother what appeared to be a privacy they were holding around the area they occupied.

Inside the building Bart and Eddie were hollering at each other. They could be heard over the entire fish fry.

Bart hollered, "It is, too, Eddie. It's different."

"It's all the same," Eddie shouted back.

"Tennessee beer is seven percent alcohol. Alabama beer is five percent, and Florida beer is three-point-two."

"Aw hell, Bart."

"You go up the edge of Tennessee, have a few, you git light-headed. Then go down to the Redneck Riviera, and you can drink beer all day long on the beach, not git drunk."

Alvin stood alone at the tailgate with Deward, but without the isolation of privacy that Donna and Jenny seemed to be able to hold. He kept looking back at them, wishing they would come back over to the tailgate. He was thinking about telling Deward to go over and get them.

Alvin heard some people hollering at Eddie and Bart for arguing, and they quieted down. He saw Eddie's wife walk out of the building. Alvin figured Freddy was back. Judy came out after Linda, and they both looked over at Donna and the few other women there.

It looked as if they were having a contest to see who could wear the tightest jeans. One thing was for sure, he thought: Mussel divers kept company with good-looking women. There wasn't a cull in the whole fish fry.

The Texas talker wedged in between Alvin and Deward. Alvin wished he would go away as he asked for the fifth time, "You goin' out yonder to Texas to mussel?"

"Uh-uh," Alvin said.

"I heard 'at out in Texas you could git half a ton 'em maple leaf shells a day out yonder."

Alvin put the piece of catfish he had in his fingers back on his paper plate. He felt that the couple of bites of potato salad, baked beans, and catfish he'd eaten had made him gain ten pounds. It made him feel sick and weak, and he was tired of pretending to eat.

He said, "That's a lot of mussels."

"Wull, how long you thank 'is musselin's gunner holt out here? You gunner mussel all winter long?"

Alvin slung his plate out into the weeds.

Alvin looked up at the Texas talker and said, "I don't give a fuck about mussels!" and walked out into the darkness.

The guy walked alongside him. He said, "I shore didn't mean no harm by askin' you 'at stuff. I's just wunderin' what all a other divers had on thur mines."

Alvin stopped but didn't look at the man. "I know," he said. "No harm taken. I'm just not in the mood to answer any questions."

When he walked on, he noticed Deward was a half step behind him. He stopped again, knelt down, and said to Deward, "I'm going to go out here and pee. You go back and find Mama and stay with her right now."

Deward ran on back to the gin, and Alvin went on out in the sage grass and peed. As soon as he finished and got his pants zipped up, he started taking quick, short breaths. Then he bent over, sticking his finger down his throat. All at once the food he had eaten ran out onto the ground.

He sighed and said, "God, that feels better." He smiled, then spit several times, trying to get his mouth cleaned out.

Walking back up to the edge of the building, he leaned up against a locust post that held up part of the overhang. He looked around for the kids and Donna but didn't see them. He didn't want to go inside to try to find them. He didn't want anybody else to talk to him. He would just wait for them to come out, and they could slip away quietly.

He thought he was hidden in the shadows, but Gifford McLowry walked up and shook his hand.

Alvin thought that Gifford wasn't too bad. He had known Gifford all his life. He was Johnny Ray's age, and Alvin had known him mostly through Johnny Ray. Gifford was like most of the mussel divers, occupational background-wise. He was a whiskey-running commercial fisherman turned mussel diver.

Gifford asked, "How's everthang?"

"All right. And with you?"

"Fine. Nice seein' ye."

"Nice seeing you, Gifford. Seem like I hadn't seen you around much since last winter."

It was true. He used to come by the house, drink whiskey, and play dominoes with all the boys. Alvin took a second look at him and seemed to remember him more. Gifford looked old to him. In fact, he was several years older than Johnny Ray. Gifford had fought in Korea. Now it all came back to Alvin.

"Aw shit, Alvin. I just been musselin', fightin' with my old lady. Just took her and my younguns down to the Redneck Riviera. Stayed down in Gulf Shores fer damn near two weeks. We went down in that new Jeep I just bought."

"That's nice, Gifford. I reckon I'll hold on to my old Datsun for a spell."

"Yeah. No matter how much money I manage to make musselin', me and the old lady manage to piss it away."

That made Alvin think. Looking out into the field at all the mussel divers' automobiles, he knew who was there; he could recognize their vehicles. He considered the thirty-some-odd divers at the fish fry and figured roughly that each one of them made anywhere from twenty to sixty thousand dollars a year. He figured that a group of lawyers or doctors would have to get together to claim a better income.

Alvin had thought all of that in a flash and didn't know what it had to do with anything, but nevertheless, that was what had hit him.

The sheriff's patrol car stopped at the crossroads and then turned onto a little worn path of a road that led up to the gin. It parked by Alvin's Datsun.

"What in the hell is that son of a bitch doing here for?" Alvin asked. He had forgotten about the sheriff.

There was an upside-down five-gallon can and a fifty-five-gallon drum next to Alvin. Gifford propped his foot up on the can and leaned over on the drum.

He said, "Emma and Charlie had some compressors stole from 'em the other night, and they had to git the sheriff out here to make up a report, so the insurance would pay for 'em. Emma said she told the sheriff to come by tonight and have some catfish for his supper if he was on patrol."

"Aw," Alvin said. He still didn't like it.

"You musta not been here yet. She told everbody that the sheriff might drop by tonight. He don't care none about the beer. He don't mind 'at. I reckon Emma thought some of us might be smokin' that ol' merrywanner and the sheriff might walk up on us. Emma's purty good about keepin thangs like 'at in mind."

"Yeah. Emma's all right," Alvin replied. His eyes followed the sheriff into the gin.

"He was all right!" Gifford blurted out.

Alvin thought he was talking about the sheriff. He asked, "What do you mean?"

"I mean Johnny Ray was an all right dude."

"Aw yeah. Johnny Ray. He was heavy-duty," Alvin confirmed.

"Remember 'at time me and Johnny Ray ran that wildcat whiskey up into Elk River and he let you go along with us? You wudn't seven or eight year old. And when we got to the Elk River Mills Bridge, them deputies poured gas on the water and lit it. And old Johnny Ray, man, he run right through it with them double fifty-five Mercs wide open. Remember 'at?" Gifford asked, grunt-laughing.

"Yeah," Alvin said. But he felt like saying, Naw, you dumb fuck. Why don't you go on and tell me about it! He was ready for Gifford to move on.

Neither Donna nor the kids had come out yet, so Alvin figured maybe they had gone to the toilet. That would be good, he thought. He could get them and leave and for sure miss Sheriff Jennings.

Gifford sighed and took a drink. For the first time since he had come over, Alvin realized he had a big Alabama Crimson Tide plastic cup full of whiskey.

Gifford offered, "You't a sip, Alvin?"

Alvin was looking at the lighted opening of the gin for Donna and the kids. "Naw. No thanks, Gifford."

Gifford set the cup on the fifty-five-gallon drum. Putting his hands on Alvin's shoulders and looking into his eyes, he said, "I've got to talk to you, Alvin."

Alvin didn't say anything in response because Gifford now had his back to him and was climbing up on the drum. He turned around and sat down with his knees up close to Alvin's side, then leaned over to bring his face up close to Alvin's.

What is it with this I've-got-to-talk-to-you shit? Ginger used to say that, and now Gifford, Alvin was thinking.

Gifford confessed, "That big blue bird you had. I shot him, Alvin. I didn't mean to. I was huntin' rabbits and he come out of a tree and it spooked me. Damn near shit on myself. I'd done shot him before I knowed whut had happened."

"OK," Alvin said, as if it didn't matter. He had cared about Santiago and had been distressed when he couldn't find him, but now it didn't seem to matter. Alvin thought about how Deward had hit Admiral Andy in the face. But Alvin didn't feel like telling Gifford he had done good. Santiago liked chewing the furniture up and shitting all over the place, but he wasn't an asshole like Admiral Andy was.

To Alvin, thinking about Santiago always reminded him of when he first met Cliff. Freddy had brought him in from the Huntsville airport. Cliff had four pieces of baggage, one a small suitcase-looking thing with small holes. Something inside started making a cluckinglike noise. Soon Cliff had opened it up, and there was a big brilliant blue macaw that commenced to squawking. Dr. Dick had come into the living room, sat on his haunches, and stared at him. After a while the bird, Santiago, had flopped down off the suitcase and waddled over to Dr. Dick. Nose to beak, Dr. Dick had started sniffing but moved away quickly when Santiago opened his beak to preen Dr. Dick's whiskers.

Freddy, using two-by-fours and heavy mess wire, had built a cage, a section of a room actually, in a corner of the back porch. Cliff also got him a big metal cage, so he could be brought into the house when it was cool.

Santiago took a liking to Alvin right away. He had instantly been able to handle Santiago, even better than Cliff.

It was when they began taking Santiago outside and putting him on the porch railing that he had begun flying about. It had bothered Alvin at first, but Cliff had convinced him it was all right. That Santiago should be free, on his own some, should not always be caged.

Gifford's voice shook Alvin out of his memory.

"You don't understand, Alvin. I killed that big, purty bird. Then I didn't come tell you. I just buried him and hid it from you. I'm sorry, man. It wadn't right. I couldn't help killing him. I didn't do it on purpose. But I didn't have to hide it from you. I've saved up the money. I'm gone buy you another one. You kin git 'em down in Birmingham."

"Look, it's all right, Gifford. I'm not upset about it. And you don't have to buy me another macaw. I forgive you. You just forget about it."

"Oh, God. Thank you, Alvin. You a good man. You don't know how many hours of sleep I lost over this." Gifford shook his head humbly. He was relieved. Looking up at Alvin, he said, "You a good man. Yessiree, you a good man. You one of God's own."

"Thanks, Gifford." He repeated, "It's all right now. Forget about it. It's not important anymore."

Gifford asked, "Do you know what it's like to kill somebody by your own hands?"

"Naw, man," Alvin said quickly. He was looking at Gifford now. He wished he would leave all that shit alone. He didn't want to hear about Korea.

"I hope you never do, Alvin. Really."

Alvin didn't know why this was happening to him. He held his face against the post and looked through the people who were stirring around outside the building opening, down along the other edge of the building, past Emma and Charlie's trailer, and up a little path to the shadowy silhouette of an outhouse.

Staring at the outhouse, he saw two figures come out, one twice as tall as the other. They got clearer as they walked closer to him and more in the direct light.

Gifford lit up a Marlboro, and Alvin moved his head away from the post so the red tip of the cigarette would not interfere with his line of vision.

When the figures got almost to the edge of the trailer, Alvin was relieved to see that it was Donna and Jenny. They were holding hands.

Now Alvin wondered where Deward was.

There were about five divers, whom Alvin knew personally, gathered around the tailgate where he had been eating earlier. The Texas talker was in the midst of them, and most of the other five divers' faces were turned to the Texas talker. He seemed to be raving about something. But also Alvin noticed something under the tailgate.

As the Texas talker moved, unblocking the light of the building, Alvin realized it was Deward squatted down like a frog under the end of the truck.

Through the general roar of the noise of the fish fry, the Texas talker could be heard to almost scream, "Look at him, he's sick. Polin' Johnny Ray's widow. Johnny Ray not even good and cold yet. He's sick in ne dick and sick in ne head!"

Alvin's attention focused on this fellow. He was staring at the Texas talker when the man's head bent back like a dog howling at the moon.

There was a piercing scream.

Gifford disregarded the sound and said, "You know what it's like to—" He stopped talking long enough to take a long sip of the whiskey.

The Texas talker turned around and swung at something, and Alvin saw Deward knocked back toward the opening of the building.

Alvin hopped around Gifford and the barrel and sprinted toward Deward, who was lying on the ground up next to the side of the building. Before he could reach him, Freddy ran between them.

Freddy was charging toward the Texas talker. He made a couple more strides, and then his feet came off the ground.

Sheriff Jennings was on the outside of the gin now.

Alvin was looking down at Deward, who was still holding his pocketknife in his hand.

The Texas talker looked toward Freddy and said, "He purt near hit me in the head with 'is feet!" He was holding his thigh, which was bleeding profusely.

Several divers were on top of Freddy, holding him down, and the sheriff was on top of the divers. They were holding him down so that he wouldn't go to jail. They didn't want Freddy hurting anybody that wasn't worth going to jail for.

The Texas talker stood up near the pile.

Donna came over quickly and started attending to Deward. Jenny was right behind her.

Alvin stood up and stared at the Texas talker, who turned around and saw him. Alvin charged and then brought his feet off the ground in the same way Freddy had just done. The heel of Alvin's boot hit the man a couple of inches to the right of his throat, snapping the collarbone, which tore through the skin. It snapped out just as though it had been cocked under the skin, ready to pop out with a tap of the trigger.

The man fell back several feet and lay on his back with his knees up and his arms spread out. His collarbone stuck out. He was hollering and crying.

Alvin hit the ground, rolled, and got back up on his feet. Then he fell down. Nobody was around him, but he fell.

All the way down, he tried to stay up.

All the way down, he didn't think about the man or about the few inches he had missed from hitting him where he meant to. All the way down, he seemed far away.

He was back looking at the blood coming out of the nostrils of the boy, that first time he had ever hit somebody. That first punch in Birmingham that had put the bootlegger's kid to his knees, semi-conscious. Someone who had no animosity for Alvin, a strong liking for actually. Fucked up, Alvin was thinking, but not of *now*, of that time.

Thirty-eight

WHEN HE FIRST OPENED his eyes, Alvin thought he was in the hospital staring at Alma in a bed with an IV in her arm. Then he realized that it was he who was in the bed staring at an IV bottle and that he had just come to.

Alvin's folks had not been doctor goers, so every time a member of his family had gone into the hospital, it was usually to die. Alvin had been in a hospital only to look at somebody. He had never been in to be looked at until now.

Only a couple of seconds had passed since Alvin had awakened. He moved his arm, and there was a tube attached to it. Sitting up quickly, he ripped the tape off his arm and pulled the needle out as if it were a tick. He slung it away from him. The IV bottle rocked.

He didn't know what had happened to him. The last he could remember, he was hitting the ground. He didn't know what to do now. He didn't know what to do about all the glucose that had been injected into his body. He knew he couldn't throw it up like food. It was already in his bloodstream. He could feel it forming a layer of fat under his skin.

Alvin thought, This is whut I git. Alma and IVs. Now me and

IVs. It come around to me. Maybe I's supposed to stayed down there with her, looking after her. Maybe I wadn't supposed to dump Cliff off on her. Aw man, it come around on me.

That was all he could figure why he ended up in this shape, but all Alvin knew for sure was that he had to get out.

He jumped over the bed rail. He was in a hospital gown that was about to rot off him from being washed too many times. Looking around, he found his clothes in a little closet by the bed and put them on, checking his pockets as he did. They were empty. He thought the hospital had taken his money and driver's license, but then remembered he had not put his stuff in the pockets when he put on Donna's pants last night.

Or was it last night? Shit, he thought. I might been in here a damn week. That would be a shitload of glucose built up. I got to git it out. Maybe I'm not beyond repair.

He knew he had to sneak the hell out. There was too much he didn't know. A big white drape hung down from a track on the ceiling, dividing the room. He tiptoed over and peeked at the other side. There lay Buck, trying to get the back open on a ten-transistor portable radio.

Alvin just froze there. It seemed like some kind of sign or something he needed to figure out.

Buck looked up and said, "Hey, boss man."

"What are you doing here?"

"Dey bring me up heah 'bout evah twenty yeahs to sobah me up. One dem twenty-yeah checkups. Sobah me up, see if I'm alive. Don't see whut diffunce it make. Mostly dey don't know shit round heah. You dade o live. Drunk o sobah."

"Oh," was all Alvin could say.

Buck looked at him with big, sad, glassy-looking eyes, and said, "Git me outta here, Alvin Lee. Git me home back to Beaulah Town."

Alvin said, "You need to stay here, Buck. They can make you well here. This is a hospital. That's what hospitals are here for. See all the stuff they got around here and the people around here they got to make people well with?"

But he was thinking, Don't do this to me, old man. Don't ask that of me, please. Don't look at me like I can give you your youth back. Don't look at me like I can do something about something.

Buck said, "This place is fer dying." Tears ran down his cheeks. "If they could make people well, dis place wouldn't be heuh." Buck didn't even bother to wipe the tears. They flowed. "I'm too old, Alvin Lee. Dey brang me heuh, I mought not make it back out."

Alvin wanted the tears to stop, just as he had wanted the blood to stop coming out of the nostrils of the little boy that he had hit years ago. He didn't like to see old folks cry. It hurt him. Just as children shouldn't have to bleed, so old people shouldn't have to cry.

But Alvin didn't know what to do about it. He wasn't God. He wasn't even Mr. America.

He looked back at the door, then moved around the curtain and up to Buck's side.

Alvin asked, "Do you know what I'm doing here for?"

Buck stopped tearing and smiled. "You been whuppin' ass. Man, you ought to not been passed out last night. That woman whut ride around in 'at blue spootnick, she run up down ne hall 'bout to whup ass. That man you whup, he laid up down ne hall. She about gone whup his ass agin. Po-lice running around. Man whut shot up de pool hall with 'at ma-chine gun 'at one time—"

Alvin interjected, "Freddy?"

"Yeah. He run 'round 'bout to put some dat Jap fightin' on everbody's head."

"What about this little boy, Buck? You know anything about the little boy?"

Buck slapped the radio against the bed railing, trying to get it working. He said, "Johnny Ray's boy?"

"Yeah."

"Dey sewed up his mouf. Mouf was busted."

"How come it to be busted?"

"Dat mane you whup hit 'im."

"Why come?"

"He stab 'im in ne laig."

"Why?"

"You doan know shit. Dat mane, he sade you pissin' on Johnny Ray's grave. Doan know why he sade dat. But dat boy stab de muthafuckah wid a Case Double X."

"What happened? Where all—what else happened?" Alvin asked.

"De poh-lease run evahbody out. You laid up in here. Folks runnin' in. Hollerin'. Poh-lease fixin to lock everbody up, so they all git de fuck out. Them horsepital folks runnin' 'round don' know to shit or wipe they ass, 'cause you don' got no idennyfication. About to have themselves a shit hemorrhage. They don' know fuh show who de fuck you is. Dey wantin' a inshowunce numbah. 'At woman wi' dat spootnick threw my radio at de nuss. Done fuck it all up."

"Why'd they put me in here?"

"De nuss. I ax de nuss. She sade you run out a nutrition. Dat's all lese muthafuckahs round here talk about. Tell me I ain't got no nutrition."

He leaned over and got a Hershey bar out of a drawer and peeled the wrapper off.

Buck asked, "You holdin' a Snickers bar?"

"Uh-uh," Alvin said.

Alvin started to walk back around the curtain, looking at the door. He was in the old wing of the hospital. He opened one side of the old window and swung it wide.

As he jumped, he heard Buck call, "Wish't I had some ah you daddy's good ol' wildcat."

Alvin fell the nine feet to the ground, rolled, and got up on his feet. He tore the hospital tag off his wrist and started running. Running not just from the hospital but running to the North Alabama Power Lifting Gym.

He needed Dianabol. He needed to get the glucose out. He knew he was going to burn it out with body heat, burn it out before it gelled.

The gym was two miles away, and he kept running.

Thirty-nine

THE RED LIGHTS on the railroad crossing signal started flashing, and the bell started clanging. Alvin pumped his hands up and down like pistons as he ran.

He said, "Lightning started flashing. Thunder started crashing." It was part of a whiskey song Johnny Ray used to sing and play on the guitar.

Alvin was a block away from the tracks. He didn't have time to wait on a 150-car freight train and stare at L&N boxcars clip by. He was already in a fast run, and he dropped down into a fast sprint.

He was afraid he was going to run into the train, but he felt he couldn't stop running, so he quit looking at the train and kept sprinting down the sidewalk. Just as he crossed the track, he could feel the force of the locomotive splitting the air, the same way he had felt the force of tugboats splitting the water.

He cut in front of a '63 maroon Chevy that was waiting at the crossing on the other side of the tracks and slowed into little, short pumping steps so he could pull to a stop at the door to the North Alabama Power Lifting Gym.

Alvin walked in.

Roger and the two guys he had seen last time were the only ones in the gym. Roger looked over at Alvin, waved his hand up to him, and then looked back to the floor.

Looking at Roger's outfit, Alvin noticed he had on a red T-shirt with a yellow muscleman shirt over it. A shiny black weight lifter's belt separated the top half from a pair of green sweat pants. On his feet were shiny black combat boots. Alvin thought he looked like a fucked-up Santa Claus.

Roger started breathing in and out deeply. He paced back and forth behind the bench, concentrating. He walked by a metal post and hit it with the bottom of his fist. Then he inhaled really big and tightened up his lifting belt.

The taller of the other two lifters said, "Come on, big boy. You got it. You got it."

Roger walked quickly to the bench, lay down, got a grip on the bar, and then nodded for the bar to be handed out to him.

After it was, Roger let it down to his chest and held it there a moment, motionless. The taller lifter clapped his hands loudly once. Roger pressed the bar back to arm's length. The other lifters guided the bar back onto the rack.

Roger jumped up, and all of them hollered.

The short guy hollered, "Wooo, baby! Five-thirty!"

After slapping Roger's back three times, the tall one asked, "You'ta take it back down for some reps?"

"Naw, I'm going over to the power rack and do some half benches. Some heavies."

Alvin walked over to Roger. Roger was pumping his arms in and out as if he were doing some bench presses.

"Big Al. How's it going?" Roger said.

"Okay. Listen, Roger. I need some more Dianabol."

"Shit, man. I hadn't got any."

"What?"

Roger walked over to the power rack, where they were loading the bar to do bench presses from a position where the bar was already several inches off the chest.

He slapped a couple more forty-five-pound weight plates on one side of the Olympic barbell. He said, "I hadn't got any more. I'm low myself. There's a bench contest in Rome, Georgia, next month and everbody's eatin the Bol like M&M's. I'm going to Birmingham next week to get some more."

The tall guy stood at the opposite end of the bar with a forty-five plate in his hand and asked, "What you want of the first set, Rog?"

"Six."

"Next week?" Alvin asked.

Roger slapped another forty-five on the bar, a thirty-five, a five, and a two and a half, then put the collar on and tightened it. The other guy did the same at the other end. Roger looked up at Alvin, finally taking note of him.

Roger asked, "You been sick?"

"Had a little cold," Alvin lied. "You think you could get me some Dianabol today?"

Roger started breathing in and out. He strutted back and forth behind the power rack. His gym shoes squeaked on the concrete when he made his snappy turnarounds. Alvin thought the shoes were crying for mercy.

"When I'm sick, I lay off the Dianabol," Roger said. "If you sick, you need to lay off the Bol. Take a lot of C. Them vitamin C."

"You reckon I could get some Bol from Billy Ed?"

"Billy Ed benched four, day before yesterday."

The other two lifters were loading their bar, a lighter bar at another rack. They hollered over the rumble of the train to Roger, "Holler when you ready."

"You reckon I could get some Bol from Billy Ed?" Alvin asked again.

Roger rubbed some chalk on his hands and said, "He's eatin' all the Bol he can git. Three-fifty to four hundred pounds in five weeks.

He cottons to that Dianabol now like stink on shit." He tightened his belt and hollered over at the other rack, "I don't need no spot on these. I'm gonna let some heavies down on my chest in a few minutes, though. After five sets of these."

When he lay down on the bench and got under the bar, Alvin said, "Save me some Dianabol next week."

"If they's any left, man."

Just as Alvin turned the doorknob to go out, it hit him what he hated about Roger. He looked back at the blob that was making the six-hundred-pound barbell go up in the air and then ping down against the two one-inch-thick pins in the power rack.

Alvin walked out. He looked at the boxcars clipping by, looking as though they were sliding along on Olympic barbells.

Alvin walked up to the railroad track. He was getting ready to run. As soon as the caboose passed, he was going to run.

He thought of Roger and said, "I hope his head falls through his asshole and breaks his neck."

To his left he could see the caboose. Cars started crossing the tracks again several blocks down. He lifted his right heel and put most of his weight on the ball of his foot.

He thought he could hear his name called but knew it wasn't possible over the noise of the train.

Then he felt a tug at his shoulder.

Forty

C OFFEE?'' Ginger asked, taking her hand off Alvin's shoulder.

Alvin hadn't heard anything she had said except that last word. Maybe that was all she had said. It seemed he had been standing there feeling the cold wind hit his face long enough for it to be numb.

He asked, "What about coffee?"

Ginger laughed and said, "Do you want some?"

"Oh yeah."

He followed her across the street into the Dixie Lee Café. She started to sit down near the front window, but Alvin kept walking. He sat in the back booth and faced the front door. Ginger went back and slid in opposite him.

The waitress came back and asked, "Whut ya'll want?"

"Coffee," Alvin said.

"Sugar?"

"Naw! Hell, naw!" Alvin almost hollered. "I don't want any more sugar ever."

"Aw right, honey. I won't put no sugar in it. Calm down. Want any cream?"

"No'm. Black. Hot. As hot as you got it." He needed to get his insides as hot as they could get. He knew he had to do that to get all the glucose out.

Ginger told the waitress, "I think I'll have a Sun-Drop Cola and a cinnamon roll."

"Thank agin, honey!" she said dramatically. They both looked at her, and she dropped back into her normal voice. "We ain't got no cinnamon rolls. Bread man shorted us on 'em this mornin'. Got honey buns."

"I'll take a honey bun," Ginger replied. Then to Alvin she said, "I have such a sweet tooth lately and have been so tired."

"Maybe ol' Eric done knocked you up."

"Alvin, please. Don't be so crude," she said, and then squirmed around in her seat a little, as if what Alvin had said had some credence.

"I heard that on the TV last night," the waitress said as she was writing on her pad.

"Excuse me?" Ginger asked, looking up at her.

"I said, 'Thank agin.' I heard that on the TV last night."

"That was real funny," Alvin said as she walked off. He had meant it literally, not trying to be smart.

He was glad he had come in. He hadn't thought about coffee helping him out. Now he thought it would help clean out his system. Do some burning. He knew he needed a plan for right now.

"How much?" asked Ginger.

"How much what?"

"Weight have you lost?"

"Oh, I don't know."

He figured the best way to get home was to head south on the railroad tracks, running. He would run five miles south to the trestle near Beaulah Bay. There he would head out into Beaulah Swamp.

The waitress brought the coffee, Sun-Drop, and honey bun, and set them down.

Alvin picked up his coffee and killed it.

"I never seen nobody do 'at before," the waitress said. "Y'awnt anythang else?"

"Another cup of coffee."

Alvin would crawl down the trestle into the knee-deep water grass and then wade, swim, run, and climb for a mile and a half, going west.

"Doesn't that burn?" Ginger asked.

"I hope so," Alvin said.

He would crawl up on the county road, stand up and take a deep breath, then run in a fast jog the mile to the Twilight Café.

The waitress brought another cup of coffee. Alvin killed it and ordered a third.

Ginger asked, "Are you all right?"

"That's one thing I am. I'm all right. You ask Johnny Ray."

At the Twilight Café he would buy a box of Ex-Lax on credit, because he didn't have any money on him. The Ex-Lax would help cleanse his system.

She took a bite of her honey bun and looked around to see if anybody was listening. Then she grinned and asked, "Are you on something?"

"Not nothing like I'm going to," Alvin said. "I'm going to own the Mr. America title."

"Are you sure you're all right?"

"I said I was all right. Johnny Ray said I was all right. Anybody that's ever been from shit said I was all right."

He would eat the Ex-Lax as he ran the county road from the Twilight Café to the causeway. He would lean his body at a forty-five-degree angle as he turned at his mailbox and went onto the causeway. From there to the front porch he would sprint.

The waitress brought the coffee, and he killed it, saying, "One more, please."

Ginger said, "God, Alvin. You're not coherent."

"Coherent . . . coherent," Alvin said. "I used to know what that meant." For a second he thought it meant to stick together. "Yeah. I hope that glucose don't coherent to me. I got to burn it off."

He would sling the front door open and walk as fast as he could to the kitchen to drink a quart of liquid protein.

The waitress brought the coffee, and Alvin downed it. He got up, looked at Ginger, and asked, "What you eatin' all that sugar stuff for?"

Then he walked out.

Ginger stood up and called, "Alvin?" as he went out the door.

He stepped between the tracks and stood on a crosstie. He just realized he had been with Ginger. He knew he had been with Ginger but couldn't remember what went with the face. He could remember her whining about relationships; he could see her face as plain as if she had been standing there in front of him. He had seen her often over the last couple of years and still he didn't know who she was or what she was about.

He stepped to the next crosstie, and the next, then he started landing only on every other one.

He was running.

Forty-one

ALVIN HAD a strong, hard jog going. Donna's Calvin Kleins were slick, mud-coated from the knees down; the water and mud had been warm, but now he was numb from the chill of the cold late-autumn breeze.

He turned and ran up on the wooden platform porch of the Twilight Café. Paying no mind to the mud oozing from his boots onto the floor, he was about to walk on in when he noticed Cliff sitting at the little table on the porch.

Cliff had a backgammon set in front of him. He pulled a bottle of scotch, half hidden by the table, from between his legs. He took a slug and replaced the bottle. The cap was on the table. Alvin knew he was doing some serious drinking if he didn't put the cap back on.

Alvin couldn't make any sense of Cliff. The last time he had seen Cliff, had had that talk with him in Alma's living room, Alvin thought he would never see Cliff drunk again. That life was exciting and adventuresome to Cliff. That with a little hard work and perseverance everything was going to be fine.

Alvin pulled out a chair beside Cliff, but the chair hit something. He looked down. It was a clothes bag and an army duffel bag.

Alvin said, "I thought you were in Birmingham."

Cliff answered, "I was. But I'm here now."

"What about Alma? How is she?"

"Oh, she's fine. I said she would be."

"Is she here?"

"No. She's down in Birmingham," Cliff answered.

Since the talk in Alma's living room, Alvin had expected to see Alma and Cliff always together. He didn't know what happened. Maybe Alma didn't like Cliff, but Alvin couldn't see that. Nor could he see Alma saying, "Oh, Cliff, we can't be lovers now. I've got to give my relationship with Downtown Sam's Cosmic Café a chance to work out, if it is going to work out." He couldn't see Cliff saying, "Oh, Alma, I'm just not ready for a commitment."

He couldn't see either one of them saying any of that whiny bullshit that Ginger was given to saying.

Alvin pushed the duffel bag over, pulled the chair out, and sat down. He decided not to ask any more about Alma. Instead, he asked, "Going somewhere?"

"New York. Going there. I don't know if I'm getting there. Going, getting—different things."

Cliff looked over at him. His eyes were glassy, and they didn't look to be seeing. Alvin figured he just pointed them his way to be polite.

Cliff looked back down at the board and shook the cup, then blew in it and rolled a die. "Lover's Leap," he said, in a voice that sounded sober. He moved one of the white pieces. Reaching out with both hands, he twisted the board around so the opposite side was closer to him now. He put two brown dice in the cup and started shaking it.

Alvin leaned up to him. "Could you git me some Dianabol up there? Ship them down to me?"

He sat waiting for an answer. Cliff was moving his mouth, but nothing was coming out. The porch knocked off the cold wind, and the late-afternoon sun was hitting Alvin directly, warming him.

Finally Cliff said, "Write it down, man. See, you've got to

write it down and spell it correctly. Print it. When you get into technical things, just a few letters could mean something else. You know?"

"Yeah. You got a pen?"

"M-I-A. P-O-W," Cliff mumbled, but it didn't make any sense to Alvin. Then he said plainly, "No, Alvin, man. I don't have a pen," and turned the board around.

"I'll be back. Don't go," Alvin said. He went inside and walked up to the counter.

Ida said, "Hey, baby."

If he had been somebody else, she would have told him he was going to catch cold running around wet, but Alvin was a swamper. She didn't pay any attention to the mud.

"Would you let me have a pen and a box of Ex-Lax on the tab?"

"Writin' pen, baby?"

"Yes'm."

She handed him a nineteen-cent black Bic ball-point pen and a box of Ex-Lax. She put it on the tab. The tab meant the joint account that Alvin, Freddy, Cliff, and Johnny Ray had there, now minus Johnny Ray. They never separated it; one or the other paid it off about every week or ten days.

When Alvin turned around, he noticed Freddy over in the corner at the table for two, next to the pinball machine. He didn't know why Freddy and Cliff were sitting apart.

The only other people in the café were four men from Beaulah Town, at the main table. They worked the day shift at the nuclear plant down the river. They had just gotten off work and were having the plate of the day for supper.

They looked at him, each nodding his head in a backward motion to Alvin, who nodded his head in a forward motion to them. The men returned their attention to their table, eating and talking.

Freddy had a pencil and was scribbling around on a number four torn-apart brown paper sack.

Alvin sat down across from him and said, "Thanks for last night."

"I didn't do anything," Freddy said, and looked up. Alvin could tell he was both stoned and drunk.

Alvin thought, What in the hell's the matter? First Cliff. Now Freddy's all fucked up. I thought the next time I saw him, he'd be studying some diving book or something. They musta shit-canned their planning-ahead campaign.

Alvin said, "Cliff said he was going to New York."

"You know 'at man in the rented car that day ah the funeral?"

"Yeah."

Freddy was looking down, drawing. "He was a private detective. Hired to find him and bring him back to New York," he said slowly through the drug and alcohol.

"Like on television?" Alvin asked.

"Yeah."

"Who hired him?"

Freddy was still drawing. He said, "His wife."

"What wife? I didn't know he 'as married."

"He ain't."

"How can you have a wife and not be married?" Alvin asked.

He took the top off his pen, reached over, and made circles on the edge of the paper sack until the pen started writing. Then he put the top back on and stared at Freddy.

Freddy said, "He was married before he went overseas. He was lost or some shit, and then a POW for three months. Somehow thangs . . . the information and stuff, got mixed up and his wife thought he had been missing in action for over a year. Anyways, she got married and has two kids by her new husband."

"Yeah? Shit!"

Freddy erased something and then brushed the erasings off with the back of his hand. He continued. "He didn't want me to tell anybody. Before now. The detective was just hired to find him for sure the first time. See, Cliff's folks knows where he is. His ex-wife has wanted him to come up and settle thangs several times. The last couple years I've put him on the plane several times to go up. But when he gits to Atlanta or New York, he gits a plane back. Don't want to see her."

"Why don't she come down here?"

"Hell if I know. That's between them."

"I reckon," Alvin stated. He started eating the Ex-Lax.

"Now she's hired the detective to bring him home to New York to talk to her. The private eye talked to me. I talked to Cliff. I told him to go on up, tell everbody to go to hell, then come back. No big deal. But he acts like he won't never be able to come back."

Alvin didn't say anything. He just ate the Ex-Lax.

"Me and nine other fuckers went up to North Vietnam and busted Cliff and three other fuckers outta prison."

Alvin sat stunned for a moment. Then he shook his head, as if to knock Freddy's words out of his mind.

Alvin said, "Come on. Let's go talk to Cliff."

"That detective's on his way to get him."

"Come on and sit with him till he comes."

Freddy put his pencil in his front pocket and started folding the paper up.

He said, "I can't. I just can't."

Alvin stood up and pushed the chair back under the little table. Freddy had finished folding up the paper. He was about to stick it in his pocket.

Alvin asked, "Could I have a scratch end off that paper?"

Freddy was putting the paper on in his pocket. Realizing what Alvin said, he slowly took the paper out and unfolded it. He pitched it out on the table, where it lay with one side up from having been folded.

"Take it all," he said. "It was plans. I was bustin' ye out in the morning. But I see ye already busted out."

He reached down to the floor by the wall, got a glass of tequila, and set it on the table, saying, "Sheriff Jennings found and cut down two hundred ten-foot-tall marijuana plants day before yesterday."

He put a newspaper, folded back to a quarter page, out on the table.

Alvin glanced at it. There was a picture of Sheriff Jennings standing in a boat full of marijuana plants.

Freddy said, "I checked. They were mine. But it don't matter. Johnny Ray was right. 'Dope don't go nowhere. It ain't from shit.'"

Alvin saw Ida coming with the plate of the day. He walked out without saying anything, went over, and sat by Cliff. Setting the paper down, he started printing out "Dianabol."

Cliff said, "I've got him in a back game." He had all the "opponent" pieces hemmed in. He started shaking the cup.

"How am I going to get it?" Alvin asked.

"What?"

"The Dianabols. How you gone send 'em?"

"What?" Cliff asked, as if he didn't know what Alvin was talking about, as though he must have been out of it when Alvin had asked him about it the first time.

He motioned for what Alvin had written down. Alvin handed him the paper.

Cliff said, "This is Dianabol."

"I know."

"You are going to take this for bodybuilding?" Cliff asked, sounding sober for a minute.

"Yeah."

"Man, you don't need this shit. This is the worst thing you could take. Dianabol is an anabolic steroid for old people. It has female hormones in it."

"Really?" Alvin asked. He instantly realized he had been fucked over for years because of Dianabol.

"Yeah, man. You don't need any steroids. And if you did take any, Dianabol is the last thing you need. Fuck that shit."

Cliff tossed the note back onto the table. He took a stout pull of Johnnie Walker Black.

Alvin figured no damn wonder he had that hip structure problem. He had been taking female hormones. And no wonder Roger was so fucked-up-looking. Poor guy. Roger was all right, just fucked up from all the Dianabol.

"Thanks, Cliff!" Alvin said.

Something must have changed. He must be living right, now. Roger had been out of the deadly Dianabol, Ginger had mystically been there to turn him on to coffee, and Cliff had been there to fill him in on the truth about Dianabol, Alma was all right, and Freddy had even acted as if he were going to quit dope.

Cliff started shaking the dice cup again.

Alvin thought, Liquid protein. Ab work in my dry suit. Body heat. That's what I need.

"Yesterday was my birthday," Cliff said.

His statement startled Alvin. Not knowing what else to do, he said, "Happy birthday."

"I was thirty-eight years old." Cliff put the cup down and started stirring the game pieces around with both hands, like stirring up dominoes.

Alvin said, "I don't know," but didn't know why he said it.

"You ever been to New York?"

"I told you before, Cliff. I never been nowhere." He looked back at Cliff, as if he had just thought of something. "How long is a New York minute?"

Cliff stopped stirring the pieces. Looking at Alvin, he said, "A New York minute is sixty New York seconds," and then looked back down and started stirring the men again.

A rented car pulled up in front of the Twilight. The detective got out.

Cliff reached down into his boot and pulled out a .22 Magnum Blackhawk revolver and pointed it at the front tire of the car. He pulled the hammer back.

Alvin said quickly, "Alma. What about Alma, Cliff?"

"She's going to be just fine."

Alvin took the revolver out of Cliff's hand. Alvin asked, "You like her, Cliff?"

"Oh, sure." He smiled.

"I mean for a girlfriend, you know?"

"I told you we fell in love. Didn't I? You know, when we were watching *Hurricane*."

"Maybe ya'll could start datin' or something," Alvin suggested.

"I'm a married man. Till death do up part. I'm not dead yet."

"Of course not," Alvin interjected.

"That could be a matter of opinion, I guess. I guess there's just so long somebody can just go on hoping. I guess some folks can go on hoping longer than others. Can't say which one's right, which one's wrong. I guess both could be right."

That was the first drunk philosophical thing Cliff had ever said that made any kind of sense to Alvin.

"Sounds good," Alvin said. Alvin realized he needed to know about Alma. What she was up to. How she was actually doing. If she still had her job. When she was coming up to see him. All those things. Even if Cliff were coming back soon.

But the detective had come up and stood back away from them. Alvin laid the revolver on the table, straightened up the backgammon set, and closed it.

Cliff said, "If I get there," but said nothing else.

"You'll git there, OK. When you get there, everything's gone be just fine."

Alvin got up and stepped back. The detective stepped forward, got the bag and duffel bag, then stepped back and nodded to Alvin.

Alvin nodded back and then looked at Cliff, who was still sitting, looking down at the table. He lifted the whiskey bottle and took another long pull. Then he put it on the table and screwed the cap back on.

He pulled the backgammon set up to his chest and looked as if he were about to stand up, the way one stands up and pushes out the chair with the back of the knees at the same time.

Alvin thought he should at least let the hammer down on the revolver but decided not to touch it. Cliff, the detective, Freddy, or Ida could worry with it. It wasn't his.

Alvin said to Cliff, "When you git back, we'll have a big birthday party for ye."

Cliff grunted.

Alvin said to the detective, "Yesterday was his birthday."

The detective nodded.

Alvin was about to turn around.

Cliff leaned forward a bit as if he were about to stand. Alvin stood still. Cliff turned his head toward Alvin, looked at him.

Cliff said, "No matter where you go, there you are."

Alvin turned around and started running. He didn't want to have to watch Cliff stand up.

Forty-two

DEWARD WAS SAYING, "I stuck it in and twisted it. But then he jumped back. I didn't git to twist it real good."

Deward poured the teakettle of scalding water into Purple Bathtub. Then he set the kettle down and demonstrated for Alvin how he had stabbed the man with his pocketknife.

Alvin smiled, said, "Awww!" in response to the temperature of the water, and took a pull on his liquid protein.

Jenny came into the bathroom with a stewer of dying-down boiling water. She asked, "You't me to pour it in?"

"Yeah," Alvin said.

She poured it in at the foot of the tub, and Alvin spread his feet so they wouldn't get scalded.

Deward bent over in Alvin's face and said, "See my stitches?"

"Yeah. Those are nice."

"We had fun last night, didn't we?" Deward smiled. The steam from the tub was making his face sweat and his hair curl.

"Lot of fun."

Jenny pushed Deward back and said, "We studied about reptiles today. Miz Stovall said there wadn't any alligators around here. And

I said it was, too. Then she read outta the cyclopedia. Then she said it was too cold here for alligators. And I said I didn't care what the cyclopedia said. There was alligators around where I lived 'cause my daddy caught one one time and brung it home for us to play with till it run off back into the swamp. There's alligators around, idn't it? Out there. Me and Deward's going out there and catch one."

Alvin slid down more in the tub and closed his eyes.

He said, "They might be a few out there. If you gone find one, you better do it in the next day or two. They hibernate like snakes. This far north, a alligator'll hibernate."

Tarzan padded into the bathroom, and Jenny put him on her shoulder, stroked him, and said, "Tarzan's so purty!"

Deward touched Alvin on the shoulder and asked, "Kin we use you boat to go look for alligators?"

Alvin took his hand and slashed at the water while he considered it. He thought: Burn. Burn. Burn out that glucose. And Dianabol.

He answered, "My musseling boat won't get up in the swamp. Take that wood skiff at the edge of the yard and pole in there."

"Aw, goody," Jenny said.

She and Deward ran out.

Alvin slid down until the water was up to his chin. He said, "Burn. Burn. Burn out that glucose and Dianabol." Then he drank the last of the protein and threw the bottle over into the metal waste can. There was a crashing sound.

It startled him. He thought it had been the plastic bottle hitting the metal, but then he heard it again.

It was coming from the living room. He got out of the tub, dried off his reddened body, and put on some clothes.

When he got to the living room, Donna had already torn the paneling off one wall. She was standing with her feet apart, leaning forward a bit. Her fists were on her hips, with a hammer in one fist and a crowbar in the other. She was staring at the wall.

She said, "This paneling has to go. What do you think would look good?"

"I don't know," he said, looking at the two-by-four studs and at the insulation hanging out. He thought the paneling had looked good. He had just remodeled the house a couple of years ago.

A car came around the house. Neither of them paid any attention to it, but soon there was a knock at the door. Alvin opened it, and there stood Sheriff Jennings.

Alvin said, "Hey," and pushed the screen door open.

The sheriff walked in and said, "Gittin' hog-killin' weather, ain't it? Supposed to git down to thirty-eight tonight."

I got to put the heater in, Alvin thought. I got to keep it hot so the glucose don't gel.

Alvin said, "I got to get that heater in here."

The sheriff said, "I'm sorry I got to do this, Alvin. I got a warrant here to arrest you for assault and battery. I got to take ye in."

Alvin took strong note of the sheriff and said, "We givin' you a lot of business lately, ain't we?"

Donna slammed the crowbar up against the wall and then stepped back. She said, "I think I'll get it Sheetrocked and wallpaper half of it and put barnwood on the bottom."

"You won't have to stay, Alvin," the sheriff explained. "You kin make you own bail. 'At feller's wife pressed charges. She'll cool off in a few days. I don't thank it'll come to nothing. I'd a done the same thang you done had I been in your shoes."

"I hadn't even cut any firewood this year," Alvin said. "Maybe I could get the kids to go around, collect driftwood while they lookin' for alligators. Till I can git some wood cut."

The phone rang, and Donna answered it.

The sheriff said, "Let's go on up there, Alvin, and git it done and over with."

"I got to get the heater in here first, Sheriff. I can't let them younguns freeze." Taking note of the sheriff again, Alvin said to him, "Hey, would you mind helping me load up the heater from the shed and set it up in here?"

"Well? . . . We need to . . . I don't want those younguns—"

Donna hollered, "Telephone!"

Alvin stepped over and got the phone. He said into the receiver, "I'm all right."

Donna asked the sheriff, "You think barnwood would look good in here?"

"Yes, ma'am."

"But just up to here. Then a chair rail. Then wallpaper up here." She pointed with the hammer to show him where it would all come to.

Alvin said into the phone, "Naw, don't come out here now. I'm busy now. Then I got to go somewhere."

The sheriff said, "That would look good."

"Come out in 'bout a year," Alvin said, and hung up the phone. Walking toward the front door, he told the sheriff, "Come on."

The Vulcan Deluxe II wood burner was in the corner of the weight room, where Alvin kept a bunch of things stored. He got the pickup truck and backed it up to the weight room door. Pushing the door open, he stepped in and headed over to the corner to clear a way for the wood burner to be taken out.

The sheriff walked in behind him, looked around, and gasped. "My doggies. Look at these iron bells! I never seen such."

Iron bells! Alvin thought. He had never heard that before.

The sheriff was wandering around the weights. Alvin carried a wooden two-by-four frame and some bricks out to the truck.

When Alvin walked back through, the sheriff said, "You lift these thangs? They look heavy."

"Yeah."

"How much can you put over you head?"

How much can I put over my head? Alvin thought. Goddamn. He hadn't heard that one in a long time. It was usually, How much could you bench-press?

"I don't know," Alvin replied. "I just kind of pump them up and down, don't try to see how much I can do."

"Aw," the sheriff exclaimed, as if Alvin had just explained everything he ever needed to know about weight training. "You used to be the Alabama weight lifting champion, didn't you? I heard that."

"Yeah," he answered, to keep it simple. He didn't want to have to stop and explain the difference in weight lifting, power lifting, and bodybuilding.

"That's some accomplishment."

"Thank you." Then he said what he thought the sheriff wanted to hear: "But it didn't pay a damn penny. Lot of work and not a penny for it."

"Well, that's ashamed. But it seems sometimes some of the most worthwhile thangs they is don't pay much."

That made Alvin sorry he had let the sheriff think he was a weight lifting champion. Sorry he let him stay ignorant of the different types of weight training.

Alvin said, "Three-fifteen."

"Whut?"

"Three-fifteen."

"Whut?"

"Three-fifteen. That's how much I've put over my head before. Clean and jerk. Bring it up to you chest like this, then jerk it up," Alvin said.

He paused to demonstrate.

"But that's weight lifting," Alvin explained. "That's one thing. Then there's power lifting. That's just strength. You don't do any jerking around. In power lifting, you squat with the weight, lay on a bench, and push it up—"

"Bench pressing," the sheriff said proudly.

"Right. And then you do a dead lift, just how much you can pick up. Then bodybuilding, that's what I was into." Alvin meant that was what he *is* into but didn't want to let on. "In that you just try to build up you muscles."

"Now, isn't that interesting," the sheriff said. "Now that goes to show you. If we hadn't took out the time to have this little talk, why, I would have thought all that stuff, all that strong man stuff, was all the same."

The sheriff shook his head as if he'd just tapped into some kind of philosophy of life.

They loaded the wood burner into the pickup, drove it to the house, and backed up to the front porch.

Inside, Alvin pulled the furniture away from the wall, out into the middle of the room, so he could put the square border on the floor near the chimney. After he got the border situated just right to satisfy him, he and the sheriff started making trips out to the truck, carrying bricks in so that Alvin could set them inside the frame, creating a hearth to set the heater on.

Donna was still staring at the wall. She asked, "You think something like boats and trees would be a good wallpaper? You know, some kind of picture. Like a scene."

As the sheriff was handing Alvin the bricks, he looked over at Donna and said, "Yeah, I thank a scene would be good. My wife put up some wallpaper in the kitchen that's just flowers, and I don't like it a-tall."

Alvin finished placing the bricks.

He and the sheriff struggled in with the Vulcan Deluxe II wood burner and set it on the hearth. Alvin stepped back a couple of times to judge it and adjusted one edge or the other, trying to get it straightened up to the wall.

Then he brought in an armful of stovepipes from the truck. The pipes had been cleaned well when they were taken down last spring, but just in case, he handled them carefully so as not to get any soot on the floor. He put up the stovepipes, connecting the heater to the chimney.

The sheriff lay back in the La-Z-Boy for a bit, catching his breath, then stood up and said, "Wull, I guess it's time now, Alvin." He started reading a Miranda card. "You have the right to . . ."

As he was reading the card, Alvin remembered Johnny Ray reading the instructions to hooking up a dryer at his house: "Step one. Insert the . . ." He had mumble-read for about two minutes and then said, "Aw, I see. The first thang you do is throw them damn directions away."

257

Alvin said, "The first thang you do is throw them damn directions away."

Sheriff Jennings looked up from the card and said, "Do whut?"

"You don't have to read that. I know how to put the pipes up."

The sounds in the room suddenly seemed far away to Alvin. A sound like gushing water shot through his head. He stared at Donna. She looked as if she were floating up and down, as if she were standing in a boat that was tossing about in whitecapping water. There was a fog between them.

The sheriff finished reading the card and waved his hand toward the door. He said, "It won't take long, Alvin."

Alvin walked to the door. He felt a weightlessness, as if he were walking at the bottom of the river.

Alvin knew he had the Mussels.

Forty-three

ALVIN SAT in the back of the patrol car. He still felt as if he were at the bottom of the river. He ran his hands along the cage that separated the back seat from the front, looking for mussels.

He felt a sharp stomach pain. Getting up on the back seat, he pulled his blue jeans down. He was thinking he was crawling up onto a riverbank on all fours and had pulled the pants to his wet suit down when it all cut loose.

A burning stream of shit shot through the cage, onto the front seat, and oozed off the edge onto the floorboards, as though somebody had spilled a Twilight Café chocolate milk shake.

The sheriff rolled down the window.

Alvin imagined the sheriff running around and finding the two trustees he had brought out with him to get the catfish. Alvin imagined him telling them, "He done shitted all in the patrol car. I don't like arrestin' them Fuquas. When I took office, I tol' myself I'm gone let them Fuquas be. I done went arrested one, and he done shitted all in the car. Drippin' off everthang."

Alvin said proudly, "I hadn't done one that good since I had dysentery."

The sheriff asked, "You sure you don't need to go back to the hospital, Alvin?"

"Hospitals give me the shits. That's what's wrong with me now."

"I ain't crazy about 'em neither. I had some kidney stones took out last year. But if you ill a-tall, it's a law. I'm supposed to git you medical attention while you in my care if you request it."

"I'm not requesting it."

"I thank it's a federal law."

"Laws are made to be broken," Alvin quoted Johnny Ray.

"'At's right," the sheriff agreed.

After trying to figure out whether it was a federal, state, or insurance law, he started back talking about how he had to take Alvin to the hospital if he requested it, and Alvin kept talking about how he wasn't requesting it.

Alvin found some dirty napkins on the back floorboards and started wiping his ass with them.

The sheriff said, "The hospital called up 'cause you run out. I tol' 'em I didn't have nothing to do with that. They thought maybe you's dangers. They's worried about ye. I said, 'Shoot, he'll pay his bill. Ever Fuqua I ever knowed was good for his debts.'"

"Yeah," Alvin commented.

"Why come you to drop off like you done?"

"Flu," Alvin responded without hesitation.

"Never seen flu make a body drop off like that."

"Mud Creek Flu." Alvin was tugging around and finally got his pants back on, buttoned, and zipped up.

"Never hearda 'at before."

"That's 'cause nobody but Tennessee River swamp folk git it. You can only get it once in you life. It's part hereditary. Part from living on Mud Creek."

"That what you sister got that made her drop off that time, too?" the sheriff asked quietly, as if he were being let in on a secret.

"Yeah. See, doctors can't cure it. No sense in going to a hospital. Not if you want to get rid of it. Going to a hospital could mean the end of the world," Alvin said quickly. "It almost got Alma."

This had all just come naturally to him. It sounded as if it made so much sense, Alvin felt as though he had made it come true just by saying it.

"Wull, what cures it?" asked the sheriff.

"Mussel soup. And you have to stay on Mud Creek. Breathe the swamp air there. Donna's gone cook up the soup for me."

"And that cured you sister?"

"Yes, sir. May sound strange. Don't be telling folks. My grand-pappy told me it was best not to be telling folks about it. It was our problem and to keep it to ourselves."

The sheriff lit a Swisher and blew smoke around, trying to kill off the shit smell some.

The sheriff said, "I'll be dogged! When I's a boy, I knowed of these folks at the edge of Tennessee. This family would git this rash, and just dewberry juice from 'at holler there would cure it. I'll be dogged. I knowed something was wrong."

He turned on the emergency light and pushed the accelerator down more.

"Listen, I'll git 'em to hurry up at the jailhouse and git you right back to Mud Creek."

"Be careful not to tell. Some don't understand. Not like you," Alvin said. He didn't like to ask people not to tell stuff, but he didn't want the sheriff announcing anything about Mud Creek Flu.

Just as Alvin had just invented Mud Creek Flu, so he invented a scenario for Sheriff Jennings. The way Sheriff Jennings had been interested in his weights and said that sometimes some of the important things didn't pay much, Alvin couldn't help figuring that Sheriff Jennings had some secret hobby.

Then Alvin figured the sheriff had a basement where he conducted this hobby, though Alvin had no idea where he lived. And tonight the sheriff would be down working extra hard on his hobby. His wife would come down the wooden steps into the basement, the sheriff's workshop. She would say, "Come on up, honeybunch. You supper's gittin' cold. You have you a hard day out yonder?"

The sheriff would look up from what he was doing and would

say, "You wouldn't believe it, darlin'. I's dumb enough to arrest 'at Fuqua feller. You know the weight lifter one with the crazy sister? He shitted all in my patrol car. Got my two main trustees, they's cleanin on it all afternoon. Still stinks. I sprayed around with some Lysol, rubbed the dash down with Armorall. Best I could git it. Still smells like a French whore done took her a wet fart in there. Have to drive around with the winders down. Aw, honey, it was a mess. I missed Andy Griffith and everthang."

Alvin had been thrown off by the flashing blue light.

The Mussels seemed to be gripping him harder. He had to fight it. And he had to get all the glucose out. He'd do his ab work in the dry suit.

Then he thought about adding pressure. Alvin figured out he should go down deep, deep as Johnny Ray had done, to get rid of the Mussels, the glucose, the Dianabol, and everything that was trying to hang on to him.

The blue flashing light reflected off the storefronts and the courthouse as they came into town. He felt as though the blue were fire, scorching through his brain.

Sliding his hand across the car seat, he felt a mussel. It felt real. The story about Mud Creek Flu felt real, too.

He felt as if he were pulling the mussel out of the car seat and held it up when he noticed the sheriff looking at him in the rearview mirror.

Alvin wondered if the sheriff could see the mussel.

Forty-four

ALVIN SAT on Purple Commode, finishing what he had
started in the sheriff's car a couple of hours earlier. He had a little
bottle of Swim-EAR, and he held it up, tilting his head. But when
he squeezed the bottle, nothing came out. It was empty.

He threw it over at the waste can and said, "It don't shuck the
Mussels."

The little bottle bounced across the bathroom floor and finally
came to rest behind the commode. He held on to the towel rack with
his left hand. It felt as if he were holding on to the gunnel of his boat
and the boat was rocking.

He could hear the waves sloshing under the bow. Hearing the
sloshing again, he looked over into Purple Bathtub and saw a foot-
and-a-half-long alligator.

Alvin looked over at the gator again. He wasn't too sure it was
really there, but he was going to shave his legs in Purple Sink, just
in case.

It wasn't good to break the rule "Act like everything is real"
when he had the Mussels. He had broken it once today, and it almost
cost him a trip to the hospital.

After shaving his legs and upper body, he rinsed off with a washrag and then splashed rubbing alcohol all over. He put on a sweat suit and went to the kitchen.

Donna passed by him, carrying the coffee table from the living room. She said, "The carpenters are going to be here first thing in the morning. What should I do with that old paneling?"

"We need to build a fire. Get it warmer in here. We'll burn it."

Walking into the living room, he knelt at the heater and started putting little splinters of paneling in. Deward ran in from Freddy's bedroom, now his and Jenny's, and shouted, "Did you see 'im? Did you see 'im?"

"Who?" Alvin asked.

He had a box of Firechief kitchen matches that had been on top of the heater. He was trying to light the wood. Deward was straddling him and had his arms around Alvin's neck.

"Wally. Did you see Wally?" Deward asked.

Jenny came in and kicked some paneling out of the middle of the floor. She had a book in her hand. Getting the beanbag from the corner, she lugged it over to the place she had cleared on the floor. She lay across it on her stomach and opened the book.

Alvin looked over at her, and she looked back. Smiling, she said, "We found one."

Alvin didn't know what she meant. He struck another match and put his arm inside the heater to reach the wood.

Deward said, "Wally. Wally's an alligator. Didn't you see him in the bathtub?"

"Oh, yeah! I saw Wally. He's a fine gator, all right."

"Can we keep him, Alv? Can we keep him? Purty please, can we keep him?" Jenny begged.

"Ya'll take care of him," Alvin said, meaning, if ya'll take care of him.

"Oh, goody!" Jenny hollered.

Alvin struck another match, but he couldn't get the wood to light.

Deward said, "Let me do that, Alv. You need smaller pieces of wood. Daddy showed me how to build fires."

He crawled off Alvin's back, and Alvin backed away from the heater. Deward took the matches and got where Alvin had been.

Fires, motors, a lot of things. There were many things Alvin didn't know anything about, but there had always been somebody to fix them for him. "Thanks, Deward," he said. "I don't know fuck all."

The fire crackled. Deward ripped up bigger pieces of paneling to put on it. Alvin felt as if he were upside down and then right side up. He stared at Jenny. She looked up at him, but it wasn't Jenny's face. It was Johnny Ray's. It was foggy, but it got clearer and clearer. Then one of the eyes winked at him.

He knew it was some kind of sign. He grabbed the arms of his chair to keep from floating up, not knowing how to figure it all out.

"I don't understand all I know about this," he said. He had heard Cliff say that many times, and it seemed like the thing to say.

Alvin remembered Johnny Ray telling him, "You know where you grandpappy is right now, Alvin Lee? Out driftin' in the channels. Drinkin' wildcat. Lookin' for flyin' saucers. Waitin' for a sign. Out there sittin' and waitin' for some spaceship to take him off. He's old and crazy, Alvin Lee. There might be a time fer waitin'. But mostly waitin' ain't from shit."

He knew he just couldn't wait anymore. He stood up and said, "Deward, would you find me a flashlight?"

Too much shit was coming down he didn't know what to do about. Now he realized he couldn't hide any longer from the Johnny Ray test. He was going to have to hook up fifty more feet of air line to his old line.

Tonight he would take the flashlight down to the boat and put on the extra line. He was going to have to go on down and feel the pressure.

He went to his bedroom and looked at the map on the wall. His muscles were telling him they wanted pressure. They needed pressure to get every bit of the fat off. To cut up. To get the definition it would take to win Mr. America. It would be good for his muscles.

The map seemed to get bigger and bigger, and then it seemed to blow up as big as the Tennessee itself.

Then Johnny Ray started calling him. Johnny Ray was calling him to the channels.

Forty-five

ALVIN SAT on the front porch in his dry suit, sweating and sipping on some orange juice. He had just finished working his legs, and as soon as he finished the juice, he was going to go out in his boat to do his newly invented underwater abdominal routine.

There were a few carpenters' trucks parked out front, and banging and sawing noises came from inside. He didn't mind the hammer banging too much. But the electric Skil saw sent knife-cutting vibrations through his muscles when someone ripped a board.

Another car pulled up, and Alvin said to himself, I hope this son of a bitch don't run one of them ripsaws. I'm tired of listenin' to that shit.

But it was a plain-looking car, not a work truck. A man in dress slacks and collared shirt got out and walked up onto the front porch.

He said to Alvin, "Hello, I'm looking for Donna."

"She ain't out here. Just me and you out here," Alvin said. He always spoke when spoken to when he had the Mussels. But it didn't mean he couldn't entertain himself with it. It didn't mean he couldn't enjoy the spectating of it.

The man stared at him, trying to make out what it was Alvin

had on. Then he knocked on the door. The wooden door was open. A carpenter showed his head behind the screen door.

The man said, "I'm here to see Donna, please."

The carpenter walked away from the door and hollered, "Donna, there's a man here to see you," and then went back to hammering up the Sheetrock.

Donna came to the front door. She walked up close to the screen and said impatiently, "What do you want?"

"Did you change residence?" the man asked in a sweet tone that made Alvin almost puke in his orange juice.

"What is it to you?"

"Whose house is this?"

"Alvin Lee Fuqua. Mr. Alabama," Donna said with conviction.

"Alvin Lee Fuqua. Mr. Alabama," Alvin Lee Fuqua echoed.

The man looked over at Alvin. He looked him up and down again and asked, "Are you Mr. Alvin Fuqua?"

"That's right," Alvin said, looking at him. "But *you* can just call me Mr. Alabama."

The man looked back at Donna and said, "Well, I have some things I have to ask you. It's my job."

"Get another job," Donna said.

"Get another job," Alvin echoed.

"I'm here to help you. To work with you and your children. To help make sure you're all adjusted."

"We're not television sets," she said.

"Yeah. We're not television sets," Alvin said. "The television set took itself a shit."

Alvin heard Donna walk away from the screen door. From his angle, he couldn't see through the screen; it was opaque.

The man looked at Alvin with disgust.

Alvin snapped, "Man, don't look at me like that. I don't like to play. I quit school because they had recess." Alvin didn't give a shit. That man and Old Lady Higgins were of the same mold to Alvin Lee. They weren't from shit.

Suddenly the man jerked his head back around and looked into the screen. Then Alvin heard an explosion and saw the man fly off the porch backward onto the ground. He watched a spot of wine-colored blood, the size of a washboard mussel, appear at the man's gut.

The man lay on the ground on his back. The blood didn't seem to be flowing much.

Donna walked out onto the porch and fired another shot. Alvin saw dirt fly by the man's head.

Stepping off the porch, she stood above the man and pointed the revolver toward the spot right between his eyes.

She pulled the trigger, just as Ferris grabbed her from behind. Ferris took the revolver from her and let her go. All the other carpenters came rushing out.

"I told that shit-ass pipsqueak," Donna explained calmly, "he come fucking around with me and my kids again, I was gone shoot him with Johnny Ray's three-fifty-seven Magnum."

"She told that shit-ass pipsqueak, he come fucking around with her and her kids again, she was gone shoot him with Johnny Ray's three-fifty-seven Magnum," Alvin confirmed into thin air.

Alvin got up, walked down off the porch, and just stood over the man. He was just moaning and kind of wiggling his feet. Alvin didn't see any blood coming out of his head, just the big spot at his stomach.

Two of the carpenters were attending to him.

Looking at the washboard mussel-size blood spot at the man's abdomen reminded Alvin it was time for him to go work his abs. He was glad the carpenters were there, so he didn't have to fuck around with the man. Mussels or no Mussels, Alvin would have gotten pissed off if any of his training got interfered with.

Alvin told the carpenters, "When he quits bleedin', you need to wash down that blood. Even though it's coolish weather, it'll still draw flies. You know, like when you kill hogs."

Then Alvin walked on down to the dock and his mussel boat.

Forty-six

THE SHERIFF SAID, "Now look at 'is right here," and bent over to get something out of one of his drawers.

Alvin was sitting in a swivel chair at the edge of the sheriff's desk in the courthouse. He still had on his dry suit.

He had been trying to light some driftwood the kids had collected in the heater when the sheriff called and told him he had better come to the courthouse, that Donna had shot the welfare man. Alvin had said, "Yeah, I know. I seen her do it. It was in self-defense. She had tol' him she was goin' to shoot him if he didn't leave her alone. His making sexual advances on her, and such." The sheriff had acted as though he hadn't heard that.

Pulling out a short-barreled revolver, the sheriff held it in the palm of his big hand and offered it out to Alvin.

Alvin took it. It felt like a big washboard. He was trying to keep from spinning in the swivel chair.

The sheriff said, "Now 'at is a three-fifty-seven Magnum. It ain't the one 'at Donna used, but it's one jest like it."

"Uh-huh."

Sheriff Jennings handed him a bullet and said, "Now, put the shell in one 'em holes in the cylinder."

Alvin tried to swing the cylinder out but dropped the revolver on the desk. The sheriff picked it up, swung the cylinder out, and handed it back to him. He pushed the shell into one of the holes. Then he pulled it out. It felt as if he were pulling a mussel out of sand.

The sheriff said, "Now 'at was a thirty-eight special shell. A thirty-eight'll fit in a three-fifty-seven Magnum. Now Donna had a three-fifty-seven revolver, but it had thirty-eight shells in it."

Alvin held on to the desk. It was a desk like Roger's.

Alvin said, "I don't need them Dianabols. They deadly."

The sheriff said, "Wull, the man ain't dead. 'At's whut I's telling you about these different size shells for. It bein' thirty-eights in there kept him from bein' blowed in two. The shot in the stomach they gone be able to fix up purty good. Didn't hit the spinal column. 'At carpenter knowed first aid purty good. She just grazed his head with that other shot. It didn't hit him in the brain or nothing. Didn't git his spinal cord or his brain. That's purty good."

"Real good," Alvin agreed. He thought it was time he said a little something. "Best news I got all day."

"Yeah, it's a good thang Donna's a bad shot," the sheriff said, and smiled.

"Yeah. Can't hit the side of a barn. Needs her one them little sawed-off shotguns," Alvin said, but the sheriff didn't pay any attention to what he said; he might have just as well said he wished the welfare man the best—that's the way the sheriff took his statement.

"He'll live. Be just fine. Long as don't any complications set in."

"I better go get Donna and get on home. The kids and all, you know," Alvin said.

"Alvin, it can't be like that now. Can't you git it through your head she just shot a state man?" the sheriff said, and then stiffened up a bit, as if he let the last question just slip out. "Can't you get it through your head" might just be the words that made Fuquas cut people up for catfish bait.

But Alvin didn't even react, so the sheriff relaxed back the way he was.

For a second Alvin thought he was playing a part in a Burt Reynolds movie and he was sitting there talking to a detective. Alvin said, "That man tried to rape her."

"Alvin, there were five witnesses. The man was just out there doing an interview for the welfare department, the child care division, whatever they call it nowadays."

"Oh, not then I'm talking about. I think he must have tried to rape her back at the other house. When nobody was around. You know Donna, how peaceful and easygoing she is. Some man stabs Deward. Now this rapist guy. I think you should look into them."

"Aw right. Aw right. I don't think he done nothing, though," the sheriff said.

"Well, let me git outta here and go get Donna," Alvin said.

The sheriff lit a Swisher, took a puff, and blew out the match. "You don't understand, Alvin. First thang, she might near killed a state man. Bail ain't been set yet. Next thang. Wull, Alvin, I don't know. I don't know how to tell ye, Alvin, I really don't. I wisht I could tell you everthang's all right."

The sheriff stood up. He looked a foot taller to Alvin than he ever had.

"Donna ain't just right, Alvin. You just have to see for youself." He took a long suck off the cigar.

Alvin stood up and wondered if this was really happening or if he wasn't really in his bedroom. He wished Donna would come through the door. That would be more fun. He wanted to see Donna. But he knew to keep his Mussel rule. He had to act as though it were all really happening.

The sheriff went on, "I'm gone go down to the jail and then come back here to my office. You't to jest ride with me?"

"Yes sir. I'll just ride with you."

Alvin followed Sheriff Jennings down the hall.

Maybe the Mussels were with him to stay this time, he thought. Maybe he would spend the rest of his life with the Mussels.

The sheriff stopped and opened the door for Alvin to walk out into the darkness.

He said, "Shore does git dark quick with this slow time."

Alvin walked across the padded floor and squatted down in front of Donna. He put his hands down on the floor, feeling as if he were floating on top of the water, and he kept waiting to go under.

He said, "Hey, Donna."

She had on a white gown, and she was sitting with her back very straight, staring straight ahead with glassed-over eyes. "Did you sell the fish already?" she asked.

"Yeah." He stared at her, and she stared back.

"Well, I better be going, Donna."

"Are you going to cook whiskey tonight?"

"Naw. It's too damn cold. And there's not any money in whiskey anymore. Mussels is where the money's at."

"Are you going to take little Alvie with you?"

"Little Alvie's stuck in a back alley in Birmingham, trying to stuff the blood back up a bootlegger's son's nose."

"He's so sweet. Alma, too. Try to take extra time with them, Johnny Ray. You know. They don't have a mother. Such sweet children, and they don't have a mother. You know the wind flipped her boat over in that freezing storm. How strong she was to swim a mile in such freezing weather. Froze to death when she pulled herself out of the water. Froze there with her eyes open, holding on to the tree root. Froze like a statue."

" 'The Vulcan,' " Alvin said. He couldn't remember his mother dying. All he could remember of her was telling Alma the wind was going to blow her out across the river.

"I don't know why Alvin won't play with other children his own age. Why?"

"Alvin don't like to play. He might quit school if they have recess. Alvin don't like to play. He's got to train."

"Johnny Ray?"

"Johnny Ray's dead. Out riding around in his magic casket."

"What do you think little Alvie will grow up to be?" Donna said.

"Mr. America."

"Oh, that's it. Yes, he's going to be Mr. America."

Alvin stood up, wondering why they had Donna in a padded cell. She wasn't crazy; she had plenty of sense.

Alvin walked to the cell door, and the sheriff came up to let him out.

The sheriff said softly, "I'm sorry, Alvin."

"I got to get home. The kids'll be by themselves."

"Alvin, they was put in a temporary foster home."

"I'll go by and pick them up."

"You can't, Alvin. They have to stay where the state puts them. They'll be OK. Don't worry."

"They live with me, Sheriff."

"Yeah, Alvin. But it's not their permanent legal residence. You're not blood kin to them. You not they legal guardin. Look, Alvin, I'm give out. You look tired and upset. The kids gone be fine. Donna's gone be fine. She'll git her a good night's sleep. Why don't we all just git us a good night's sleep? Tomorry you come up the courthouse, me and you'll figure out what we kin do about all this."

"Naw, I won't worry," Alvin said, knowing he wouldn't because Jenny and Deward had enough sense to break loose and come home.

Alvin started walking down the hall. The dry suit was too big, making him look as if he were wearing a John Deere tractor inner tube. The metal-looking walls of the halls made echoing sounds that bounced back and forth in his head. Losing his balance, he rammed against a wall, then caught himself. The sheriff was right behind and reached out to steady him.

Alvin's muscles told him it was time to go on down deep.

The sheriff said, "You all right, Alvin? You sure you don't need to see a doctor?"

"Naw. I'm fine. The flu's gone. I'm tired. Been diving all day. I need to get back out to the house. It's this dry suit. So clumsy. You ought to try wearing one sometime."

"Naw, you ain't gone git me in one them thangs," the sheriff answered. "I reckon you been down on the bottom of the river, gittin' them mussels like pickin' cotton. What's it like? Crawlin' along pickin' cotton, puttin' it in a sack?"

"Just like pickin' cotton."

Forty-seven

ALVIN HIT the automatic starter that was supposed to crank his forty-horse Mercury outboard, but it just made a groaning noise and went dead. He stood up, fell over, and held on to the gunnel.

The Mussels were lying in heavy on him. He knew where he had to go and what he had to do. No need to think about that.

There was a moon rising, and it made the night not so dark as usual. Alvin stood up and looked around, as if there were something to see out in the darkness.

He turned around, knelt down, and wiggled around on the cables coming from the battery. He hit the starter again. Nothing. He started to wiggle around on the cables some more but gave up on it. He knew it wasn't going to start. The battery needed charging, and he didn't have the time to recharge it. Or even to change it out with another battery he had in his shed, and then maybe it not working either.

He opened the outboard motor clamps at the transom and then got on the dock. Leaning over, he pulled the Mercury off the boat. As he was lifting it to the dock, it dropped between the boat and the dock. He watched the splash and stared at the place where it had gone to the bottom of Mud Creek.

After watching the water calm, he walked over to Freddy's boat, which was swamped against the bank. He loosened the screw clamps on the old Johnson motor and dragged it out onto the dock. Then he got into his boat and wrestled the outboard over the stern, securing it on the transom.

His own fuel line wouldn't fit the other fitting, so he had to go get Freddy's half-full fuel tank.

He connected the fuel line to the outboard motor, squeezed the fuel bulb a couple of times, and then wrapped the rope around the magneto. On the first yank the motor tried to hit. He pulled out the choke, wrapped the rope again, and yanked. It started.

As the motor was idling and warming up, he filled his compressor engine tank with gasoline. Smoke came from the exhaust of the outboard and moved up Mud Creek like a fog, disappearing into the darkness of the swamp.

Alvin unmoored the boat, reached back, pushed in the choke, and put the motor in forward gear. The boat cruised down the creek.

The brightness of the moon made everything look so clear. He wondered if the Mussels were making it look that way or if it was just the time of year and the atmospheric conditions.

He stared back at his house to get his bearings. It looked unreal, as though it were a prop. He could remember its looking that way one other time, when he was five. He was going out with Johnny Ray to run trotlines, and he told him how it looked different. Johnny Ray had looked back at the house and then turned back around in the boat, with his left hand on the throttle and his right elbow on his right knee. All he had said was: "Don't believe nothin' you hear and half of whut you see."

Alvin turned around and leaned his right elbow on his right knee.

He came out of the backwaters. The water was whitecapping. The sky was clear, and Alvin was able to tell where he was going without the aid of a running light.

A large swell brought the bow of the flat-bottomed boat out of the water and then slammed it down on the next swell. The wind blew in his face, and the spray was wetting his hair, which had been uncut for several months.

He rounded Hatchett Island but didn't go toward the flat. Heading in the other direction, he opened the eighteen-horse Johnson and rode the swells at an angle.

Down the river, toward the channels, was where he headed. Toward the deep channels.

Once he got there, he stopped and let the boat drift. He knew exactly where he was going and was sure he was going to get there.

After strapping a knife to his calf, he cranked the compressor engine and threw the hundred feet of line overboard. With two weight belts strapped to his waist, he snapped the end of his air line to the clip at the back of one of them. He pushed the button to the regulator, listening to the rush of air.

Then he carefully knelt near the side of the boat. He hooked his armpits over the gunnel and splashed out his mask, spit in it, and rinsed it out.

Alvin went to the bow. Kneeling, he got on down and looked right over the edge of the boat. The Mussels seemed to sharpen his vision. It was almost as if he were looking through a cross-haired telescope. Straight ahead, a lighted buoy lined up with the western tip of Hatchett Island, and both lined up with Hatchett Point on the mainland and the cluster of trees that was Hatchett Cemetery.

At ninety degrees, the southern edge of the base, a power line tower in the river, lined up exactly with the northern edge of the train trestle that spanned the river.

Alvin knew this was the exact spot. About sixty feet down he would hit a sloping valley. It didn't matter which edge of the valley he hit. He only had to go on to the middle of that valley and follow it toward the deeper channels, toward the old channel of the riverbed, long before the TVA had dammed the river up.

As long as Alvin landed within a hundred yards of the spot, all angles downward would lead right to where he wanted to go.

All this was on a note in Johnny Ray's personal effects. All on a torn-apart paper bag he had scribbled on. Had folded up and stuffed in his billfold. Had died with it on him.

Alvin stood up, put the ladder over the starboard gunnel, pulled the hood of his dry suit onto his head, and checked it for proper fit. He put on his mask.

He vaulted overboard, never letting go of the gunnel. There seemed to be power in the dry suit gloves, as he pulled himself hand over hand to the bow. The gloves felt good on his hands. Maybe he should start wearing them to do his workouts, he thought.

The Mussels made him lose his orientation, but he held fast to the bow. With his left hand, he found his regulator, put it in his mouth, and took slow, deep rhythmic breaths.

Then he pulled the air line tight from where it came over the bow, holding with both hands now.

Alvin looked up and down the river at surface level. The light of the moon reflected off the surface. The boat was rocking slowly with the chop of the water. It was a sight he liked.

His legs dangled underneath him. Alvin let himself down about a foot under the water; it was pitch-dark.

He slowly lowered himself. It got colder and colder, but Alvin could feel his own warmth trapped between his skin and the dry suit.

Soon he could no longer hear even the faintest hum or vibration of the compressor in the boat directly above him.

He stopped several times to clear his ear canals, getting used to the added pressure. He pointed his toes downward. There seemed to be no bottom under him, though there had to be. But no amount of sane reasoning assured him that there would be an end to the descent.

After what seemed miles, Alvin touched the point on the air line where the two fifty-foot lines were coupled together. There seemed to be too much black, cold, silent unknown above, below, around, and all about him. There was a line bringing air down to him and a weight belt that gave him his only sense of direction.

Suddenly Alvin touched bottom.

It was hard and slick. He stepped around. There was no slope.

He couldn't tell about the pressure. Perhaps he had missed the spot, drifting as he descended. He could feel pressure on his body but couldn't tell if it was the depth or the Mussels.

"Now what the fuck am I supposed to do?" Alvin mumbled into his regulator. He didn't know if he should walk around or go back up and try to get better bearings. But the sighting he took seemed perfect. There was no way he could improve on that.

He wasn't just going to stand there until he got scared shitless. Even with the slopes, he thought there would have been a sign. He wouldn't at all have been surprised, was even expecting some big-ass neon sign like the one on Morris Avenue in Birmingham, just pointing the way. A mother-of-pearl sidewalk leading there.

He started taking cautious steps, then slipped and fell forward slowly until his chest hit something. He felt about. There was a board that went both ways as far as he could reach. He put his hands under his chest, making sure his shins were on the other side of the board, and he righted himself up with an explosive push-up.

He was on another board, so he got down and crawled to the end of it. Yet another board connected with it, going in the opposite direction. He stood up and followed it, bending over, not losing his grip on the board.

As he stepped to another board, Alvin realized he was on something really big. Something huge.

Forty-eight

ALVIN TOOK another step, slipped again, fell on his side, and started sliding down a slick forty-five-degree incline. He grabbed for the air hose, attached to the back of his weight belt, but couldn't catch it. He was going down too far, too fast.

He hit something flat and hard and stopped.

He lay there and got oriented as to which way was up. Then he raised himself up a bit, slipped again, fell through a hole, and dropped ten feet, crashing to another bottom.

Water entered his mask. He blew it out by pressing the mask to his face and exhaling through his nose. He lay there motionless, his heart pounding, making his whole body shake. He swallowed several times, pinching his nose with his fingers until his ears were equalized.

Reaching behind him, he found his air line and brought it around in front of him. Although he pulled it tight, it didn't lead upward but sideways.

It was time to get out.

Alvin was sure which way was up. It was the way his weight belt wasn't pulling him. He stood up and followed his air line. After several feet he found it wedged in the corner of some board. He felt around. There was a wall there.

A current was pressing him right up against the wall, almost spread-eagled. He felt like he was thousands of miles away from where he had been an hour ago. The house on Mud Creek seemed to be in another world entirely.

The current pulled him along the wall. He almost fell through an empty spot. It was about a three-foot-square opening. Thinking he could hear something through that opening, he looked in; there seemed to be some light in there.

The Mussels started to lay in heavily on Alvin, even at this depth. He couldn't really make anything out.

And then, damned if it didn't look like a misty facsimile of his own living room. It felt as though Johnny Ray were there. Alvin stepped through the opening, thinking: He has been trying to call me.

All of a sudden a ball of light floated in front of his face. In that ball of light was Old Lady Higgins's head.

It screamed, "Alvin Lee Fuqua. River trash! You don't deserve to live in America. You don't deserve to be loose in the world. Mr. Alabama! Huh!"

She spit phlegm.

Her face was soggy and rotted, and seaweedy-looking hair hung from her scalp. The left side of her face was gone, bone showing.

Alvin said, "You still look like you did in high school. You hadn't changed a bit."

"This is the perfect place for all you scummy river rats," she spit. She stuck out a lewd-looking tongue. Phlegm dripped from it.

"All kind of shit floating around in the bottom of the channels out here," Alvin said.

Old Lady Higgins cackled with laughter. "You come to find Old Hothead? Ha. I'll have all of you soon. Your sister will be right behind you."

He slid his right hand down to his calf, through the strap of the knife handle, grabbed the knife, jerked it from the sheath, and held it up in the Vulcan pose.

He screamed, "I am King of the Mussels!"

Alvin grabbed Old Lady Higgins's head by the sparse, stringy hair and jerked it to him. He quickly plucked her eyes out with the knife. Then, after pinning her head down to the floor, he started stabbing her skull.

He couldn't get her to die, so he stabbed harder and swifter. Her head began to get brighter and brighter. He felt it was going to consume him. After raising the knife high, he came down in a kill blow.

The knife sank into the skull, embedding half the blade. When the hilt hit bone, the head exploded into a brilliance of light and then dissipated.

He didn't even flinch. He just mumbled into his regulator, "You blew your top, you dip shit." But for the first time he felt pity for the old lady. "Ugly, fat, and stupid. Nobody loved her."

He stood up. Discovering his right hand was entangled, he tried to shake it loose but couldn't. He felt the tangle with his left hand. Stuck on his knife was a burlap bag with a neck loop on it, like his bag for collecting mussels. He couldn't remember having put one on when he entered the water; he must have done it automatically.

Lifting the bag, he could tell by the weight there must have been a good many big washboards in it. And he certainly couldn't remember having gotten up any mussels. Because the knife blade was entangled through the burlap material and the knife strap looped to his wrist, he was unable to get the bag open or off.

Just as he started to untwine it, some force hit him and shoved him. He yelled, "Johnny Ray! Johnny Ray!" into the mouthpiece. He jerked around, trying to see in the dense blackness, trying to grab for him.

He collided with the wall, slid, and was pushed back out the opening. He reached back for Johnny Ray, hollering his name. It had to have been Johnny Ray.

It was the same way Johnny Ray had pushed him into his car when Alvin was trying to chicken out from going to his first body-building meet. The way Johnny Ray had pushed him to the phone to ask out Veronica Belle Peoples to his first school dance.

The current was sliding him feetfirst along the slick floor, with his entangled right hand trailing. With his left hand Alvin reached behind him, got his air line, and pulled it in front of him again. He began reeling in the line, clasping it between the bundled burlap of his right hand and his chest after each pull, so as not to lose ground.

For a while Alvin was motionless, taking up the slack. Then he started moving along the floor, against the current. The line had been caught on something but now was set loose.

Alvin gasped, thinking the air line had been broken. He consciously tried not to hyperventilate in his excitement.

Sliding with the current again, he pulled in the loose line as quickly as possible. After several quick arm's lengths the line was again taut. But this time the line was going up, to freedom.

Forty-nine

ALVIN BEGAN his ascent, holding his right hand, which was wrapped around the air line, to his chest, using his legs to help climb. Ten feet up, he tried to drop his extra weight belt. He discovered it crisscrossed under the weight belt the air line was attached to. Instead of hanging there, trying to figure a more efficient way to ascend, he knew the way he was doing it was working. He continued climbing.

Twenty more feet up. He stopped to rest, clutching the air line tightly. He took a deep breath. The air was hard to pull in. The compressor must have gone off—out of gas, or a big swell had tossed the boat in such a way to flood and kill the engine. It had happened plenty of times before, but when he was only fifteen to twenty-five feet deep. There was enough pressure in the compressor tank, he knew, to give him a few more minutes of air if he was conservative with it.

He resumed his climb.

At the coupling where the two long hoses were joined, at the fifty-foot mark, Alvin abruptly realized he no longer had the Mussels. His orientation and his perceptions returned. He had no idea why they had disappeared, but since there seemed to be more pressing things to consider and do, he, for the moment, just heeded the advice of one of Johnny Ray's quotes: "Ask not how food is delivered into the mouths of babes." Alvin didn't know if it was from the Bible or from John Kennedy.

Halfway on up the last hose, he started getting tired. The air was getting very difficult to inhale. Even though it was pitch-black, it seemed a lighter blackness to him. He swallowed, equalizing his ears to the greatly reduced pressure.

Finally, when the water seemed as pressureless as air, the top of his head broke the surface. He reached up and held the gunnel at the bow, looking up and down the moonlit Tennessee River. It was smooth as glass.

Unable to pull much air from the regulator, Alvin tried to pull his mouth up out of the water. He couldn't get himself one inch higher and was glad he hadn't spit out his mouthpiece. It would be embarrassing, he thought, to go through all this and then drown two damn inches underwater.

Half the musseling sack was still entangled on his hand and wrist, yet the heavy contents dangled down about two feet. He grasped that weight between his feet, to relieve the pressure on his right shoulder. Though he was exhausted, he knew if his grip let go now, he would drop like an anchor back down to the channel floor, so he lugged his weighted right hand up to his shoulder, as if cleaning a dumbbell. With strain, he got several shallow breaths of air from the regulator. Even his lungs felt tired.

He hooked his wrist over the gunnel, the end of the mussel sack hanging down into the water. The constriction from the tightness and weight to his wrist made his hand numb.

Even pulling up with both arms, Alvin was still unable to get his mouth or nose above surface. Through the regulator he got only a minimum of air with maximum effort.

He pulled himself along the gunnel to the ladder and stood on the bottom step, giving relief to his arms and upper body. He hugged the ladder, inhaling to get a small breath of air, almost nothing.

After getting the musseling bag between his body and the ladder, he reached in with his right hand to entangle the bag more onto the knife blade. Grunting and screaming into the regulator, he lugged the bag over the gunnel and into the boat.

Quickly working his hand out of the bound handle of the knife and free of the burlap, he got a grip on the top of the ladder. Now, with both hands in place, he stepped up two rungs, positioning himself in a full squat, with his mouth still under the waterline.

He sucked in. There was no air left to inhale.

He gripped tightly. In a maniacal surge, pulling with his arms, pushing with his legs, he broke the surface. Spitting out the mouthpiece, he inhaled greatly as he was still rising, water falling off him. When his legs were fully extended, he shot his arms up into the sky.

"I made it!" Alvin screamed, and fell over into the boat. He lay breathing in and out strongly and slowly.

He giggled.

Fifty

AFTER HE HAD CAUGHT his breath, Alvin felt himself wanting to slip off into sleep. He had taken off his mask, hood, and weight belts. He lay in the bottom of the boat, still in his dry suit, now unzipped to his stomach.

He opened his eyes and looked up.

"God, I feel good," he announced to the starlit sky.

It was the first time he had been free of the Mussels in days. It was the first time he had been clearheaded since Johnny Ray died.

Knowing once he nodded out it would be hours before he awoke, Alvin made his way back to the stern. He wanted to get home. The thought of a long, restful sleep invigorated him.

He effortlessly cranked the outboard. The moonlight was enough for him to see his way back up the channel. Soon he was steering toward Hatchett Island. His flashlight was not on the seat, so he felt under his legs and found it lying there on top of his musseling bags.

He shone the flashlight beam out in front of the bow, expecting to find driftwood and logs this close to the backwaters. Then he aimed the beam at the place where he had found the flashlight.

He swallowed the lump that had suddenly formed in his throat. He picked up his only two musseling bags. They were burlap tow sacks he had gotten from the Robert's Crossroads grocery, with a small length of nylon rope for a neck strap surrounded by a one-foot length of garden hose to cushion his neck so the rope didn't burn as he dragged the sack.

He cut the engine. The boat glided on in the direction of Mud Creek. Getting up, he stepped to the mid-thwart of the boat and shone the light on the other side of the air compressor. There it lay, Johnny Ray's mussel bag.

Most of the divers used any old tow sack. Not Johnny Ray. He used empty coffee sacks he got from a small grocery store in Muscle Shoals that ground their own beans. The sacks were about twice as big, held about three times as many mussels, and lasted five times as long.

There was no question it was Johnny Ray's. It lay there, silt-coated, waterlogged, cut and gouged from Alvin's knife. But unmistakable.

Alvin knew that was what Johnny Ray had lost on his last dive. But in the next instant realized any mussels Johnny Ray put in that bag would have either worked themselves out or died and rotted by now, leaving only some light empty shells in there.

Alvin stepped over to the bag. He started to reach in but decided instead just to cut it open with his diver's knife. He did and then laid the burlap aside.

He hunkered over the small pile, picking up and examining what looked like an eroded hinge. He tossed it aside. Then a glass doorknob. They were obviously articles scavenged from the wreck Alvin had just been on top of.

Then he picked up what looked like a crudded-up diver's weight. As he began to inspect it closer, he noticed a coin. He dropped the weight and lifted the coin from the sack. It was the size of a silver dollar. After rubbing it with his fingers, he used his diver's knife to scrape it. He turned his flashlight onto the coin and knew it was gold. He was sure. It had to be.

He scrambled back to the stern and found the wire brush he used to clean his battery posts. He brushed the coin frantically, then picked up the flashlight to inspect it again.

"Confederate States of America," was minted there.

"They must have begun coining gold money," he said, out loud. He didn't think that was known history. If that was true, he was holding some very, very rare and desirable coins.

He grabbed the wire brush and jumped back over to the pile of objects. Taking one of the small weight-looking articles, he brushed it vigorously and then inspected it with the flashlight. It was the same material as the coin—gold.

Alvin tossed it back into the pile as if it were a mussel he had just opened up and inspected for a pearl with no luck. Over into the pile of fifty pounds of the gold bricks.

He wondered why Johnny Ray had left the bag down. Or maybe he had gotten back up to the boat with it but it had gotten away from him and fallen back to the bottom.

Johnny Ray had probably never seen what was in it, only felt it with his hands down on the riverboat, guessing what it was, in the pitch-dark channel depths. Never having brought it up to light, not even wanting to tell Alvin what he thought he might have found, not until he was sure.

"He gave me his gold," Alvin said into the darkness.

He headed back up into Mud Creek. He didn't care to think about it. Even though he was clearheaded, he was tired to the point of collapse. And now there was a crunching, piercing ache in his right elbow.

As he was pulling up to the dock, he tried to figure out whom he was to tell. He could get fancy underwater metal detectors, see if there was more. Johnny Ray had found it. Almost mystically given the knowledge of it to Alvin, though he knew part rightfully belonged to Donna and the kids.

But Alvin wouldn't have to worry about the gold anymore tonight.

He said, "Damn. The kids."

He cut the engine, stumbled to the bow, reached out to keep the boat from hitting a piling, and moored the boat to the dock.

He tossed his musseling sacks over the gold.

Fifty-one

ALVIN STEPPED slowly up onto the porch. He was very tired. The dry suit made him feel he was waddling around in armor. Dr. Dick lay on the porch, up against the wall. He started wagging his tail, then got up.

"Hey ya, Dr. Dick," Alvin said as he stepped up to the front of the door. Dick's tail made a thumping sound against the leg of his dry suit. He found the key where he had placed it over the doorframe ledge, undid the padlock, and walked in.

Going into the kitchen, he got a few Liv-A-Snaps. There was a pot of hot coffee on the Mr. Coffee. "Just what I need," Alvin said, and poured himself a cup. He went back into the living room and turned the light on.

Dick was jumping about. Alvin pitched him a Liv-A-Snap and then sat down in the La-Z-Boy. He looked up at the walls. The one behind the heater was all barnwood. The other three walls were barnwood three feet up, then wallpaper to the ceiling. He looked at the scene on the wallpaper.

"You like the new wall, Dr. Dick?"

The scene was of a wide river with a big clear blue sky. A huge live oak with Spanish moss hanging was in the foreground. In the background was a riverboat.

"I like it, don't you?" He tossed Dick another little cracker. "There's a lot of blue. I like blue."

Dick jumped up into his lap. Alvin gave him the last Liv-A-Snap. Dr. Dick jumped off onto the floor and trotted off to the little bedroom with it.

Alvin couldn't straighten out his right arm. It felt like the inside of the joint was lashed together with barbed wire. He took another sip of coffee. He knew it wasn't just fatigue. He remembered the doctor telling them the symptoms of the bends. There wasn't any use in waiting. As Johnny Ray had said, waiting wasn't from shit.

His leg was also stinging. He tried to scratch it through the dry suit and thermal underwear, but it didn't give much relief.

A card by the phone listed the emergency numbers. He picked up the receiver and punched off the sheriff's number.

When there was an answer, he said, "Sheriff Jennings, please. Alvin Lee Fuqua calling."

A few seconds later he heard, "Hey, Alvin."

"Sheriff. I got the bends. Call NASA in Huntsville. Have them fix me up a decompression chamber. Send a fast car to my house to take me there. Can you do that?" He knew Sheriff Jennings liked special problems.

"Consider it done, Alvin."

Alvin hung up the phone and sipped on his coffee. Everything seemed to happen at one time. It had always been that way on the swamp. Things would go along as if they had been that way forever and were always going to be. Then one day everything would change.

He remembered his daddy saying, "You grandpappy thanks it's the moon. Says the moon and planets makes everthang happen all at once't. But I don't think 'at's right. It's just when it rains, it pours."

Alvin knew things didn't look too bright for him. Even with the gold sitting in his boat and with a clear head to think, he knew all the more that certain things didn't look too bright.

The phone rang. He answered, "Yeah."

The sheriff said, "They don't have no decompression chamber at NASA in Huntsville. Used to, they said. Back when the space program was full blast. I don't know what outer space's got to do with diving. Anyhow now the closest one is four hundred miles away in Mobile."

Alvin remembered that ye can't depend on nobody but youself, even though he knew the sheriff had nothing to do with it.

"I'm sending a ambulance down there to git you, Alvin," Jennings said. "You just hold on."

"Thanks," Alvin said. They hung up.

He was dead tired. He didn't know what he could do about anything or anybody, even himself. Maybe Cliff could take care of Alma. But Cliff was in New York. Donna, that was a tough one—he couldn't come up with anything. The kids. Freddy. He had one little idea about Freddy.

After pulling the phone book into his lap and thumbing around, he picked the phone back up and punched off a number.

"Mrs. Jacobs? . . . Yes, Alvin Lee Fuqua . . . Yes, ma'am, *the* Alvin Lee Fuqua. . . . Wonder if you had Boots's number. . . . I got it wrote down now. . . . I'm glad he asks about me. . . . He's coming home this winter? . . . Great . . . Yes, ma'am."

One minute later Alvin had Boots in Cincinnati on the line. "Yeah. All right . . . Can you see what you can do with Freddy? . . . You need somebody to train with you during the winter here. . . . That would be good. . . . You don't take that ol' dope, do you? . . . I see how it could almost have wrecked you baseball career. . . . Naw, naw . . . Freddy don't take dope. . . . So you be in Alabama in a couple of weeks. . . . Take care, Boots."

When Alvin hung up the phone, he thought the receiver was still rattling on the hook but then he noticed it was the floor that was rattling. There was someone running on the front porch.

The door flung open, and Deward and Jenny hollered, "Alvin! Alvin!"

Deward screamed, "We busted out!"

Alvin remembered they had been put in a foster home. He felt sorry for them for a second and felt a good bit ashamed of himself that it had ever happened.

"Yeah?" he said in response to Deward.

Jenny said, "They's crazy enough to put us in this house down off the other side of Robert's Crossroads." It was only about five miles away.

"How'd you git here?"

"We come through the woods to Beaulah Town. Then we got Coins Collier to drive up here in a taxicab."

"I didn't hear a cab come up," Alvin commented, not suggesting that he disbelieved them, just he had not noticed a car drive up.

"That don't matter," Deward said. "We charged it to you."

Jenny was rubbing on Alvin's dry suit with her hand, feeling of it carefully. Alvin was wondering how to tell them about their mother when Deward said, "They throwed Mama in the jailhouse."

"She'll be here in seventy-two hours, though," Jenny said. "She don't have to stay in jail because she has money, and money talks."

"Money don't talk," Deward contested.

"Don't be stupid. You know what I mean."

"Mama has a million bucks," bragged Deward.

"Mama don't have no million bucks. She has like almost a million bucks. Like a hundred thousand dollars, or something like that," Jenny said, not really sure of her figures.

"What are you talking about?" Alvin asked. It was about time he said something to try to make some sense of what was going on.

"Alma has a part in a Burt Reynolds picture show!" Deward hollered abruptly.

"Yeah!" Jenny yelled, confirming it.

"What are ya'll talking about?" Alvin asked. He was trying to scratch his legs. "Where'd ya'll hear all this?"

"We tried to call you when we got to the Twilight Café," Jenny explained. "But nobody answered here. So we called up Freddy and Alma and Cliff. Damn near everbody."

"Yeah," Deward said. "I had everbody's phone number in my billfold." He patted his hip pocket. "Like you told me to."

Alvin said, "Wait a minute. You say you talked to Cliff? Cliff is in New York. He's not in Birmingham."

Deward answered, "He's not in New York. He's not in Birmingham. He's with Alma, and they on they way here."

"Naw, naw," Jenny cut in. She was tugging on Alvin's stiff, aching arm. "Listen, Alv. They got to Huntsville, see. That private detective and Cliff got to Huntsville, and Cliff told that detective to tell his ex-wife to go piss on herself. If she want to see him, she could come down here where he was. That this was where he belonged. That detective didn't mess with Cliff. Cliff knows that Jap fightin'. So he and Alma and Freddy are coming. See, Mama and Daddy knew this famous recording star from Muscle Shoals. He recorded in Muscle Shoals. I don't know where he was from. Probably Nashville or Texas or somewheres. I can't remember his name."

"But he was famous," Deward offered. "He was rich, too."

Alvin couldn't figure out what the kids were telling him.

"This recording star," Jenny went on, "he hooked Mama up with this man in Nashville. This man that would take people's money and put it in banks and stuff so they wouldn't lose it all. You know, piss it all away. He takes care of a bunch of recording stars like that."

"Mama got a whole lot of money," Deward said. "She has a million bucks. Daddy had insurance worth a million bucks. He had made a million bucks musseling. And he had a million bucks' worth of pearls he'd never cashed in!"

"Not a million," Jenny corrected. "Like hundreds and thousands."

"They gone let her out in seventy-two hours," Deward said.

"She tried to act like she was crazy. To git out," Jenny said, to Alvin's relief. "But it just made things worst. She figured if they thought she was crazy, they would let her go home, but they just locked her up more."

"Alma's gone be in a Burt Reynolds movie. Alma's gone be in a Burt Reynolds movie," Deward hollered. "Burt Reynolds and them come in to the Comet Café, and they want her to have a part in one of they movies. She'll probably make a million bucks."

"She won't make no million dollars. She might make a thousand dollars, or five hundred. Something like that," Jenny said.

Alvin was just sitting there, trying to soak it all up. What a hell of a time to have the bends.

"We got to get ready for the party!" Jenny shrilled, as if she had forgotten about something important. "Everbody's comin' out here for a party."

"I think I need to git me a workout first," Deward said. "You't to grab a workout, Alv?"

"I got the bends," Alvin announced.

Jenny and Deward stopped jumping about and stared at Alvin wide-eyed. They knew all too well what the bends were.

"I reckon we have to take ye back down," Deward said quietly.

"What?" Alvin asked. He was scratching his dry suit again.

Jenny ran off to the bedroom.

Deward said, "Take ye back out, decompress ya. Breath all 'at deepwater air out."

Jenny arrived back with a book.

"You mean I don't need a decompression chamber?"

"Nah, the Tennessee River'll do jest fine," Deward informed him.

Jenny shoved the book up in Alvin's face. It was opened to a chart of numbers. "We have to figure out how deep, how long you was down. 'At's all. After Daddy died, this Yankee that lived in Huntsville come out our house and explained it. Fixed up a little blackboard and everthang."

"Ya'll don't mind taking me out?"

"We going out in the boat! We going out in the boat!" they both hollered at the same time.

Jenny ran off to the kitchen to leave a note for Alma and them, telling where they were going.

Alvin looked seriously at Deward and said, "You don't mind? You don't mind puttin' you workout off a little while?"

"We got to decompress ye," Deward explained. Sensing Alvin wasn't satisfied, he said, "Look, Alv. It ain't no sweat off *my* balls."

Alvin explained to Deward where he had been down. That he had been down around ninety feet. He looked at his watch and estimated how long he had been down.

Deward disappeared out the front door.

Dr. Dick came back in, hopped up in Alvin's lap, and wedged himself between Alvin's left leg and the chair arm.

"Ain't life crazy, Dr. Dick? Here thangs are. Everthang 'bout to break loose. Donna's gittin' out of jail. Cliff didn't go to New York. I don't know what they talking about Alma. And goddammit, if there idn't who knows how much worth of gold sitting in the musseling boat. Damn knows what's down in that wreck. Possible even artifacts of historical value. And what am I doing, Dr. Dick? Sittin' here with nitrogen bubbles lodged up in my elbow. I want to say I'm gone live, but life being crazy the way it is, it would be just like things for me to drop dead about now. Ain't life crazy, Dr. Dick?"

The dog whined and put his head on Alvin's leg.

The phone rang, and Dr. Dick jumped off onto the floor, not because of the phone, but jumped up onto the sofa and put his head down on his paws and closed his eyes.

Alvin took a sip of coffee and reached over, picked up the receiver, and put it to his ear.

Alvin said, "Yeah?"

"Alvin?"

"Yeah."

"This is Ginger. I've got to talk to you."

Alvin wondered why Ginger always told him she needed to talk to him when she was talking to him.

"What?" he asked.

"Alvin. I don't know if this relationship with Eric is going to work or not. It's rough sometimes, Alvin."

"You call the wrong damn number. If you having trouble with Eric-poo, you need to be talking with him, not me."

"I've been thinking and longing for you, Alvin. All Eric is doing is reminding me how much I miss you."

"Longing? Shit," Alvin said, mostly thinking aloud.

"I want to come out and see you, Alvin."

"You come out here Donna'll shoot ya and Deward'll stab ye."

"Alvin, Alvin. Oh, Alvin. Is something wrong? Are you seeing another woman?"

"Not *another* woman. Donna's living out here. And if she wadn't livin' with me, I'd be chasing after this little ex-heroin shooter I know. So why don't you just go whine to Eric, all right?"

"Alvin, I thought you were up shit creek without a paddle."

"I'm up shit creek with twin rebuilt high-performance fifty-five-horse Mercs. But, Ginger, we don't have to stop seeing each other. Why don't you just go up to your shop and start waiting? Maybe I'll come by sometimes and we can 'catch lunch' together. I love you in a different way. Not the same way I love Donna, Jenny, and Deward. No. I love you the way I might love a seven-pound mussel."

Alvin hung up the phone and said, "All kind of shit gits caught up in these phone lines."

The kids started calling him.

Fifty-two

THEY WERE WALKING down to the dock. Jenny led the way, with the book under one arm, and Tarzan in the other. Deward was next, with a box of cookies in one hand and a flashlight in the other. Alvin walked in a straight line behind Deward. And Dr. Dick brought up the rear.

When they got to the dock, Deward announced, "That's Daddy's old Johnson," pointing to the outboard.

For some reason, Alvin had forgotten that Johnny Ray had had it on his fishing rig for ten years until he sold it to Freddy. It wasn't so much that fact he remembered as it was that Freddy and Johnny Ray had dickered all afternoon over the price, back when five dollars mattered.

They all got into the boat. Deward wrapped the rope around the magneto and cranked the outboard on the first yank. Jenny was in the bow with the flashlight, Tarzan in her lap. Alvin lay in the middle of the boat, next to the pile of artifacts. He was leaning back against the live well. Dr. Dick lay up next to him.

Suddenly Alvin remembered the compressor and said to Deward, "The compressor's out of gas."

"I done come down here and gassed everthang up while you's on the phone," Deward replied. He got the boat untied, put the engine in gear, and they slowly cruised down Mud Creek.

Alvin was looking over the starboard gunnel. When the creek came back into a bend to empty out into the backwaters, there was a short spot that he could look back and see his house. For some reason, he wanted to see it.

Just as they arrived at the spot, Jenny hollered for Deward to stop, and he threw the outboard into neutral.

"There's a log waterlogged right under the surface here," she said. She was standing up in the bow now, trying to push the log out of the way with a paddle.

"Hurry up!" Deward hollered.

"I am hurrying up! You don't be worrying about me. Shut up!" she hollered back.

Alvin looked to the house. He could see it well. The moon seemed to be sending down a spotlight on it. He imagined himself on the front porch posing, with the whole world as his audience.

He knew he could do it. He could pose the way he did in Birmingham. He wasn't posing for the judges. He was posing for the audience. They were his reason why.

An ambulance came barreling around the house, with red lights flashing, and parked. The attendants jumped out, knocked on the front door it appeared, and then rushed into the house.

Just as they went in, Freddy's blue Camaro came speeding around the house and fishtailed to a stop.

"There's gone be a party!" Alvin said. "I can just feel it forming. I bet Eddie, Bart, everybody somehow or another shows up."

Freddy jumped out of the driver's seat and ran into the house, as if he were chasing the attendants. Then Cliff crawled out of the back seat of the car on the driver's side and raced behind Freddy.

And there was Alma.

She stepped out of the back seat from the passenger's side. She was tall and beautiful. She was still very slim, but she was wearing a dress that showed her figure. It had been years since she had looked that good.

Deward yelled, "Am I gone have to come up there, push that log out of the way?"

"I'm doing my job. You just worry about yours."

"You doing it. But when you gone finish? We got an emergency here—"

"All right!" she hollered. "It's clear. Hurry up. Git moving."

"You don't worry about me. I got two speeds. If you don't like this one, I know damn sure and well you won't like the other one."

Deward paused a moment to show Jenny who the boss was and then engaged the outboard. The boat went forward slowly.

Alvin's body went tense. He grabbed the gunnel with all his might. Just as they pulled forward to where he couldn't see the house anymore, he could swear, he could have sworn, he saw Burt Reynolds get out of the front passenger seat of Freddy's Camaro.

He watched the shadowy trees clip by in the darkness, thinking about how many times he had come this way to go musseling, run trotlines, and haul wildcat whiskey. How many times his daddy and granddaddy had come this way to run trotlines and go make wildcat.

He looked back at Deward, watching him drive the boat. It looked like Johnny Ray sitting there.

Alvin let it slip out. "You look like Johnny Ray."

Deward looked Alvin in the eye and said, "Don't look at me like that. Even I can't be Johnny Ray *all* the time." Deward smiled and then made a giggling noise that did sound like Johnny Ray.

"That's what Daddy used to have to tell Mama, ever once in a while," Jenny explained, as Alvin looked from Deward to her. She smiled at him.

"Oh, God," Alvin said.

They came to the mouth of Mud Creek and into the backwaters, heading out toward the Tennessee River.

Jenny pointed down the river with the flashlight. She hollered over the roar of the motor at Deward, "Down back that way, towards the channels."

"I know where we going to," Deward hollered back.

"Me, too. Me, too," Alvin hollered.

Alvin lay back and looked up to the moon, enjoyed just the being out on the river. He didn't seem as tired as he had been, but he was aching.

Deward opened the eighteen-horse up and navigated the boat into the channel. He slowed the boat, turned on the depth finder.

Deward said, "Not but sixty feet deep here."

"Go on up toward the point," Jenny said.

Just as Alvin was thinking how the kids were operating the boat and equipment a little *too* expertly, he remembered how they had practically grown up in rigs like the one they were in. How they had helped Johnny Ray run trotlines since they were old enough to walk. How they had gone out with Johnny Ray musseling, tending the compressor for him. He remembered how dark and tan Jenny had gotten at the first of the summer. How when she had gone uptown with him, the people, some of them, would look at her as if she were a mulatto. It was only the whiskey making and whiskey running that Johnny Ray had kept them from.

Deward opened the throttle up again, traveling up the channel some several hundred yards, then slowed, checked the depth, then cut the engine.

He said, "All right, Alv, we got ninety feet here. Once we git ye down, I'm gone hold her in this area."

Alvin climbed up toward the bow. He started putting his hood up, got his mask. He found his joints to be stiff, almost locked.

Jenny started scrambling around. She got the weight belt with the regulator on it and laid it down at Alvin's feet. She found another weight belt. Then she started looking for another.

That's when she came upon the bag of gold. She reached in it and pulled out a bar.

She said, "These weights not got no slits to put 'em on a weight belt."

Alvin said, "Those aren't weights; those are gold."

She took the flashlight and shone the beam down on it. "You gone cut slits in 'em or something?"

Alvin, realizing she didn't get what he was talking about, said, "Naw. That's real gold."

Jenny looked at it again. Then started pulling the bars out of the sack. "You mean, this is real gold? You mean, *real* gold?!"

Deward scrambled over the live well to look at the gold. "Golly bum! Alvin! How much all this worth?"

"I don't know. There's fifty, sixty, seventy pounds of it. Sixteen ounces to a pound. Six or seven hundred dollars an ounce. You figure it out. Hundreds of thousands of dollars."

Jenny just stared down at it. "God a'mighty!"

Deward snapped out of it and scrambled up to Alvin. He began helping Alvin put on the weight belts. "Come on, we can't shit around. You got to git you down, Alv. You go all way down. I'll hold the boat over this spot. We gone give you three tugs, you come up ten feet, all right?"

"All right."

Deward said, "Now soon as you git down, everthang ought to be fine. You joints hurtin'?"

"Yeah."

"That'll stop soon as you git down. Soon as you git in the pressure, it'll go away." Deward turned around and hollered louder than he needed to to Jenny, "Crank up the compressor."

Deward grabbed at Alvin's wrist. "Give me you watch. We got to time this aginst the book."

Jenny started the compressor. Alvin climbed over the gunnel while Deward was throwing the air line over into the water. Alvin pulled himself around to the bow.

Holding on to the bow with his right hand, Alvin put his regulator in his mouth and tested it. He was already getting a good air supply, though the compressor had been running only minutes.

He tangled the air line coming right over the bow around his leg, so all the weight wouldn't be on his arm.

Deward lay down with his chest on the bow thwart, his face right above Alvin.

Deward asked, "Everthang all right? Weighted down good enough? Got plenty of air pressure?"

Alvin dropped the regulator from his mouth. "Everthang's just fine, Deward," Alvin said, and smiled, then gritted his teeth against an elbow pain. Alvin reached up to put his mask down over his face.

Deward spoke in a high pitch, trying to make sure he was heard over the rumble of the compressor engine. "Hey, Alv. I got one question for you."

Alvin froze and looked up at Deward.

Deward asked, "If we all so damn rich, why come we don't live in a castle or something? Down in Florida or France or somewhere?"

Alvin looked up at him intently. He really didn't have an answer, a real answer. But he said, "I don't know, Deward. That's a good one. I'll do some thinking on it." He put the regulator back in his mouth.

Deward gave him a thumbs-up.

After fixing the face mask snugly, Alvin let himself down another foot so that he was eye level with the surface of the water. He looked up the channel and down the channel, the way he liked to do before submerging.

The river was almost glass smooth, streaks of illumination from the beams of a full moon. He almost expected Johnny Ray to go skimming by in his hydroplane casket, but he knew it was only an entertainment of his own device.

As Alvin was about to submerge, Deward hollered to him, "We having fun, ain't we, Alv?"

Alvin nodded the answer, waved with his right hand, and then submerged into cold darkness.

Going down about three feet at a time, then pausing to clear his ears, Alvin was soon down to the fifty-foot coupling. Already it seemed as if the bends were easing up on him.

He was thinking it was going to be all right. Donna, she would get out of jail. Maybe Cliff and Alma would get together. Alma had her a part in a Burt Reynolds movie, and she didn't look as if she were going to starve herself to death. Freddy, he could train with Boots this winter; then he could do what he wanted to with that. Everthang wadn't as serious now.

Heading on down toward seventy-five feet, he was thinking how the Burt Reynolds thing was amusing. How he had always planned it out to win Mr. America and then make pictures with Burt Reynolds, and right now there seemed a strong possibility that he was in fact at his house. But he only found that amusing. Going on down, he realized they didn't give whiskey runner parts to whiskey runners. They gave whiskey runner parts to people like Alma who had spent fifteen years being trees and doorknobs, the way he had spent almost fifteen years trying to be Mr. America.

Then, as Alvin hit eighty feet, he got Mr. America on his mind. Fuck the judges. Even to hell with the title. He couldn't spend his life counting on some judges to decide one day they ought to give the title to him. From now on he was posing for the audience. He might even pose for other Mr. Americas. Naw, he might just be too good, the judges wouldn't even know what they were looking at.

Alvin touched bottom at about ninety feet. All the time he had spent up in a boat in the channels with the feeling that the channel was bottomless, here he was.

He knelt and then lay on his stomach, almost as if he were going to start musseling. He cleared his ears and lay motionless in the cold, black-dark channel bottom. The bottom was hard like a rock. His weights kept him motionless, but still he could feel a current passing by him, though if it were a bit stronger, he would scoot along the bottom.

Deward had been right. His symptoms of the bends had dissipated. He just lay there, enjoying the sensation of that dissipation. Feeling the pressure of the depth, the cold that was making his face, hands, and feet almost numb. The hard, cold, wet, lightless bed of the bottomless channel.

He knew sooner or later Deward and Jenny would tug at the line for him to come up a stage, but he just wanted to lie there. It

was like when he was little and had gone up the Elk River with
Johnny Ray to drop off a haul. It would be late at night, and they
would be coming home. Alvin would be sleeping in the bottom of
the boat, would wake up, look around drowsily and hope home was
still far away because he liked the humming of the Mercury outboard,
the darkness of the night, the comfort of having Johnny Ray near,
the vibration of the boat against the surface of the river.

What Alvin liked best about the riverbed was that there was
only one way to go and that was up.

And he knew which way that was.

ABOUT THE AUTHOR

PHILLIP QUINN MORRIS was born and raised in Limestone
County, Alabama. He has worked as a meat cutter, engine
rebuilder, house painter, and mussel diver. He currently lives
with his wife, Debbie, in Coral Gables, Florida.